I0701660

A TASTE OF BLISS

THE BORN AND MADE SERIES
BOOK ONE

SAOIRSE BREY

Copyright © 2025 by Saoirse Brey

All rights reserved.

The characters and events in this book are fictitious. Any similarity to real persons, living or dead, is coincidental and not intended by the author.

No part of this book may be reproduced in any form or by any electronic or mechanical means, including information storage and retrieval systems, without written permission from the author, except for the use of brief quotations in a book review.

Without in any way limiting the author's exclusive rights under copyright, any use of this publication to "train" generative artificial intelligence (AI) technologies to generate text is expressly prohibited. The author reserves all rights to license uses of this work for generative AI training and development of machine learning language models.

Edited by Lucy York

Cover artwork and design by Samantha Sanderson Marshall

For Elena

AUTHOR'S NOTE

Dear Reader,

This book may contain some content that could be triggering to some individuals. Please note that while I wouldn't consider this book particularly dark, it does deal with mature themes. There's blood, gore, violence, murder, and on-page/open-door spice.

In addition, this book contains:

- Domestic abuse with FMC's previous relationship (physical, verbal, and emotional)
- Suicidal ideation, mentions of suicide
- Mentions of self-harm
- Pain as a coping mechanism
- Depression and grief
- One spicy scene in which the FMC is unconscious at the start (though please note the scene itself is completely consensual on both ends)
- Magical cannibalism
- On-page car crash

I've tried to cover everything, but this list might not be exhaustive. If you think this book might trigger you, please don't continue. Your mental health is more important.

For those of you wanting to continue, especially those of you who saw "magical cannibalism" and thought "Hell yeah!" (no judgies), welcome to the *Born and Made* series!

TYPES OF FAE

Born Fae
(Include, but aren't limited to):
Vampires
Succubi
Incubi
Shifters
Elemental fae
Nymphs
Banshees

Made Fae
(Include, but aren't limited to):
Vampires
Shifters
Sirens
Warlocks
Mares
Hellhounds

<u>Other</u>
Kindreds
Wraiths

CHAPTER ONE

BLISS

says, an amused grin on her face. She pointedly watches me walk
out of the storage closet. I fix my skirt that, about two minutes ago,
had been pushed up around my waist as a very tall, very handsome
bartender made use of his very talented tongue. Something I wish I
could take more enjoyment from. "A succubus working here—well,
I was worried this venue would turn into a brothel honestly."

"And now?" I wince at being caught. Not that my boss cares. Fae
by nature aren't the prudish type—I'm the exception. I know once
the high of sex dissipates, shame will take its place. I reach behind
my head, feeling for my hair ribbon and giving it a slight tug back
in place.

Normally I would never hook up here. In fact, lately, I haven't
been hooking up at all. Two gym bros turned cowboys were about
to use our bar's chairs to fight each other, and I stepped in with my
remaining power to persuade them to take it outside.

So I needed a top off.

"Best idea I've ever had." She grins at me. "I don't think we've
had a single brawl since you started."

"I'm pretty sure the idea was mine," I say, matching her grin, despite myself. Or rather, because of the high I'm riding. "So you're welcome."

I follow her out of the back rooms and stand next to the bar, looking out at the open-floor space of The Wild Mare. A pop country band is finishing up their set, and patrons in cowboy boots are making use of the ample space to dance around a bit to the music.

"This band is great! Where did you find them?" Amber asks, speaking louder now that we're out by the music.

"Social media!" I match her volume. She nods appreciatively.

Being an event coordinator for a country bar is so not where I thought I would end up. It very much isn't my scene. But I've started to feel at home here anyways. I throw Amber one last smile as I go behind the bar. I pour myself a tequila shot and start helping the two bartenders—including Lowell, the one with the skilled tongue—with the last rush of the evening.

I fight down the blush that threatens to creep into my neck and cheeks. I'm a succubus, after all. I'd die without sex, and lately it's like I've been walking around with a cold that just won't go away. But the idea of hooking up with guys I have no feelings for? I can't bring myself to do it unless I absolutely have to.

As the band finishes up their set, the dance floor thins, some patrons vacating it in favor of grabbing another round and clustering around tables. A few of the livelier groups stay to dance, enjoying Amber's playlist of favorite country songs that's come on over the PA system.

Things continue to slow down steadily over the next few hours until it's just me, Lowell, and Devon—the other bartender—and a handful of regulars who normally stay right up until closing.

Amber's gone home for the night, so I take over her usual tasks, including shutting down the PA system. But we still have about twenty minutes before we have to kick out the remaining patrons. I pick up the microphone stand, setting it up over the keyboard we usually keep up here for open mic nights.

With the buzz I have going from the couple shots I had and the pretty great orgasm in the storage closet, I sit down at the piano, playing a few notes. I ignore an encouraging whistle from Lowell as the notes flow steadily out of me, singing one of my all-time favorite songs.

When I reach the final verse, the last notes echoing around in the mostly empty bar, a slow clap sounds from the entrance of the venue.

I think it's one of the regulars, but I look up and see a familiar face. My heart leaps up in my chest and falls into the pit of my stomach. My best friend steps out into the dim light. Dericia looks completely out of place here, the western-themed decor clashing with her black lipstick and head-to-toe black outfit that seems entirely too warm for the abnormally hot spring weather we've been having in Seattle.

"You know, I've always liked your version of that song better than the original," she says by way of greeting. "Nothing against Voracious Maw, but 'Darkest Impulses' should definitely be sung by a woman." She grins at me, which sets me more at ease.

It's not that it isn't nice to see her. I just can't really remember the last time we talked. A text here, a phone call there. A coffee chat every other month.

I shrug in response, getting up from the piano and busying myself with turning off the equipment left on stage. "What brings you here?"

Dericia's grin falls a bit. "Shouldn't the fact that my best friend works here be enough of a reason?"

"We're about to close."

"The bar still looks open to me," she responds, looking over at Devon. "Can I get a tequila shot?" He glances at me as if to ask for permission. I nod and he pours her a middle-shelf shot, not bothering to charge her.

Dericia goes to the bar, takes a seat, and shoots the tequila back with ease, not even grimacing.

"I'm surprised you know where this place is," I say, as she sets the shot glass back on the bar.

"I'll admit, it's my first time inside, but it's not too far from The Antler, so it was easy to find."

The Antler is a venue fairly similar in size to The Wild Mare, except it caters to the metal music scene. It is also down Starlight Avenue, which is solidly in one of the fae districts of Seattle, while The Wild Mare—though still fae owned—set up shop fully in the human domain.

Some of my favorite bands are ones I've seen play at The Antler. I've spent countless nights there with my sister and Dericia and the rest of their band. But that was ages ago. I'm not that same Bliss anymore.

"Get to the point, Reese," I tell her, using her nickname. I hop off the stage, coming to stand in front of her.

She raises her brow at me, and my gaze falls away from hers, resting on the tattoo inked on her warm brown skin, peeking out from her collar. I went with her to get that tattoo. My eyes slide down her arm to her wrist, where raised skin forms the kindred rune—a series of intertwining swirls that form a circle, which allows a human to move freely between the human domain and the fae districts, and provides a measure of protection against certain fae magic, like compulsion.

Memories of our friendship flitter through my mind as I wait for my friend to finally muster up enough courage to broach whatever topic she's come here to discuss. Dericia Ravenmore—Reese—has been my best friend since I can remember. Her fae parents, who lived next door to mine, adopted her just after she was born to humans. We grew up together. We went to school and university together. We've been joined at the hip most of our lives, until about three years ago.

"Look, I get things have been off ever since—" She waves her hand, trailing off at my warning glance. "Anyways, I think it's long past time for us all to patch things up. So you, me, and Amelia are going to have a girls' night."

I stifle a groan at the mention of my sister and a girls' night out. Dericia and Amelia's idea of a good time is getting dressed up and going to a bar to dance and find men to hook up with.

"I don't think that's a good idea."

Reese stands up from the barstool, towering over me in her black high-heeled boots. "Bliss, I need my best friend back. And you and Amelia need to get back to normal. Come hang out with us. Let Amelia know she's welcome to come to your bond activation ceremony."

My stomach plummets at the reminder of the ceremony later this week.

"I doubt she'd even want to go to that," I mutter.

"She does. She told me so." Reese takes my hands in hers, pulling me into a hug. "We'll go out to a club where we won't run into anyone we know and we'll have an amazing time, alright?"

"Yeah, okay."

She releases me, smiling gently, and takes a look around the place.

"Maybe Amelia and I will come to a show here sometime," she says with a grin. I let out a snort. Amelia hates country music.

"You're welcome anytime," I tell her. She nods and heads out the door.

I watch her leave, a large part of me wishing I could go with her.

There's a distinct change in the atmosphere when passing through the veil between the human domain and a fae district. The air seems to pulse around me as I turn onto Starlight Avenue, my interaction with Reese the day before on repeat in my head. The veil's magic caresses my skin as it slides over me, allowing me through. If I was a non-kindred human, I'd have emerged on the other side of the Starlight District without any inkling there existed something in between.

On this side of the veil there are noticeably fewer people. It's one of several fae districts in the Seattle area, and one of the only ones with a portal—though I don't often have occasion these days to use it.

But that will be changing soon.

Once my bond is activated, I'll take time off work from The Wild Mare to travel for my starmoon—a little vacation fae go on in hopes the stars will lead them to their mate. It's pretty customary for fae to do this, though results are mixed. The stars aren't to be rushed when they don't want to be.

And then there are fae like my sister, who wouldn't be caught dead doing something like that.

I, on the other hand, am hoping to do a bit of traveling around Europe.

Reese and I planned a while ago that she would come with me, though it's not something we've talked about recently, so I'll probably be going on my own.

You could still ask her. She'd probably love to go, a wiser part of my mind counters. Guilt settles into my stomach, almost like it's returning home.

Considering it's midday on a sunny afternoon in Seattle, I'm surprised to see so few fae and kindreds around. I would have thought it would be busier with people making use of the portal as they run errands and go to and from work.

Finally I arrive outside my aunt's shop, pausing long enough to take a deep breath to steady myself before entering. My eyes snag on The Antler just a block away, focusing in on the gothic font of the venue's welcome sign.

Stab My Heart is playing this weekend, and a wistfulness winds through me. That would be a fun show to see, but there's no way I'll be going.

I push the thought from my mind and push the doors open.

A bell chimes as I enter, and I hear Dericia call a greeting from the receptionist's desk. Her nose is in a metal music magazine, the cover showing off the keyboardist from the Phantoms.

"You got the one with the feature on Stormy?" I ask, letting the door fall shut behind me as I make my way over to the counter.

She lowers the magazine, grinning at me. "Bliss!" She stands, coming around the corner and enveloping me in a crushing bear hug. I squeeze her back. "I didn't think I'd see you till tomorrow." Tomorrow, when she'll be forcing me out of the house for dancing. I stifle a groan.

She leads me back behind the sales counter, bringing up another chair and handing me the magazine. "Let me guess, you got the one with Grim on the cover?" The magazine has done a special on the Phantoms, a pretty legendary metal band that we've been listening to for years now. They've done an issue for each of the members. Serious fans of the band will have collected all the issues.

I grin, shrugging nonchalantly. "He's just so hot. I can't help it. And the Stormy ones were all sold out."

"She's definitely the favorite," Reese responds, putting her feet back up on the counter and resting back in her chair. "So what's up? Are you here visiting me or Liz?" She arches her brow at me. "Or are you here to see Amelia?"

"I came by to see Liz. Amelia's here?" I ask, my brows raising as well.

"Yeah, she's giving blood. We're running low on our Essence of Succubus supply," Reese informs me. Essence of Succubus is a very rare, very expensive potion that my aunt sells. It requires blood from a succubus—obviously. And fae who drink it experience a very powerful, concentrated high after orgasm. It also helps males who can't rise to the occasion. My sister and I get forty percent each of the proceeds, leaving twenty percent for Liz, who mixes it and sells it.

But if Amelia is here giving blood, that means I should be too. And I realize my aunt didn't tell me she needed more blood because she probably suspected that my power is low. I try not to think too much on that, but it feels like yet another reminder of all my failures.

A sparkle of light catches my eye near the front desk, thankfully distracting me from my spiral. On a jewelry display hangs a thin gold chain necklace with a dainty pink crystal. "Is that bond quartz?" I ask.

"Hmm, I think so." Reese picks it up off the display and hands it to me. "Probably a good idea to get some with your bond ceremony so close." She grins at me, a hopeful look in her eyes.

"I don't think it actually works." I set the pendant back on the counter.

"They do! Do you remember Becky from freshman year? I heard that after her bond ceremony she bought a ring with bond quartz on it and she found her mate the very next day."

"I hadn't heard that," I respond, the disbelief in my tone clear.

"She's not the only one who's used it," Dericia continues. "You really should buy it."

I glance at the price. "It's sixty-five dollars." Too much, in my opinion, for something that probably doesn't work. And even if it does, I'm pretty sure I'm a lost cause.

"It's on me," my aunt calls from the hallway leading back to the spa rooms. "Hey, Bliss," Liz says, giving me a one-arm hug, a folder of papers tucked under her other arm. Her dark brown hair is pulled into an elegant bun at her nape, a few pieces left out to frame her light, oval-shaped face. Her eyes are the same piercing blue as Amelia's and my mother's. But unlike my mother, my sister, and I, Liz is a kitsune, a fox shifter. "Glad you could stop by."

"Who was on the phone earlier?" Reese asks. I glance over, wondering if someone had called just before I arrived.

"The fae council calling, *again*," Liz responds.

I arch my brows at my aunt. "Still trying to get you to go back to work for them, huh?"

Liz sighs. "I'll call them back later. There's this case my old boss is working that he wants my help on. Plus all that nonsense with the warlocks." That "nonsense with the warlocks" has been all over the fae news channels recently. It's all any of them are talking about. "What brings you by, Bliss?"

"Just making sure we're still on for dinner after my ceremony," I say, running my fingers over the bond quartz pendent and clutching it to my chest. I hold onto the necklace as tightly as I'm holding on to the hope of finding my mate.

And trying to push down the fears that he won't like me.

"Of course," Liz responds. "Reese, you're coming to dinner too, right?"

"Wouldn't miss it!" Dericia flashes her smile at me.

"Good." I smile back. I fish around for another topic to take attention away from my looming ceremony. "Should we be worried about these warlock attacks?"

Liz puts on a smile, but years of experience tell me it's a little bit forced. "No. It's been a very isolated couple of attacks. Some of the council are making it out to be a bigger threat, but just in case maybe stay clear of any."

"What's the point of attacking?" Reese asks, flipping back through her magazine. "What's their motive?"

Liz shrugs. "The council hasn't figured that out yet. But there have been three attacks so far, in different fae districts, and the council isn't even positive they're related. They've been violent and unprovoked, as far as they can tell."

The first attack was in Memphis. A warlock attacked a couple in a restaurant, and then ran off, hurting a few more people as he evaded the fae constabulary. Alone it might not have gathered much media attention. Made fae were volatile, their immortality the cause of callousness and apathy. Newer Made fae had little control over their powers, and while control came with age, their humanity diminished in kind.

But in recent weeks, two more attacks occurred and the media started labeling the warlocks as terrorists.

"Amelia knows you're here, by the way," Liz says, looking at me meaningfully, interrupting my thoughts. "You should go in and say hi."

"You too?" I ask, looking between her and my best friend. I let out a sigh. "Fine." I'm not at all surprised Amelia sensed me as soon as I walked in. She's one of the most powerful fae I've ever met. We're opposites in that way. She was born to be a succubus, whereas I'm pretty sure the stars made a mistake when I was born.

That's not where our differences stop, either.

I make my way down the hallway to the procedure room. When I open the door, I'm reminded of just how different we are. Where I have light brown hair, slightly wavy, she has long, straight almost black hair that she's never once dyed. She's tall and leggy where I'm shorter and curvy.

Most people never guess that we're related.

My sister is scrolling her phone, one hand gripping one of those squishy stress balls. A needle connected to a long plastic tube is taped to her arm, thick red liquid flowing into a machine that collects it. Her expression is unreadable as her eyes lift to mine.

"Thought I felt you walk in," she mutters, looking to the side. It's been a while since I've seen her—two months, maybe? Liz makes us have family dinners every so often, but they've been growing further and further apart.

"I was stopping by to see Liz," I say, tentatively taking a step inside the cozy but sterile room. "I'm glad I caught you, though."

She glances at me and back to the wall. "Yeah?"

"Yeah," I say, nodding, even though she's not looking at me. "My ceremony is in a couple days. I was hoping you'd be able to make it." I pull up a seat on a nearby stool. "I'm kind of freaking out about it," I add, hoping she'll take the bait and look at me.

It works. Her eyes meet mine and she frowns. "Why? Why are you nervous, I mean."

I let a smile pull at my lips. "What if I meet him and he doesn't like me? Or what if I don't like him? What if he's a douche?" My voice falls to a whisper on the last question. "What if I never find him?"

She jumps up out of her chair, carelessly ripping out the needle from her arm and tossing it aside. Standing in front of me, she places her hands firmly on my shoulders. Amelia pins me with her super serious blue eyes and gives me a little shake. "Literally none of that is going to happen."

I try to let her words comfort me. I want to believe her.

But somewhere in the depths of my mind there's a voice saying it's going to be so much worse than I fear.

CHAPTER TWO

PISCES

A SPLATTER OF RAIN FALLS ON MY CHEEK. I TUG MY HOOD DOWN OVER my forehead instead of stepping further back into the alcove my friends and I are waiting in.

"Any sign of him yet?" Shaun asks in his usual matter-of-fact way. Especially at times like this, he's all business.

"Nope," I say, popping the "p" and glancing over at him with a brow raised. Somehow, despite the dismal weather, not a single strand of his short golden blonde hair is out of place. "How long are we going to wait?"

It's already getting light out and we've waited for this vamp almost all night.

Evan shifts his position on the ground, switching which leg he has extended out in front of him. He flicks his lighter open, letting the little flame dance. As a fire elemental, he can still wield the other elements, but fire is his strongest and flame or heat is the only way he can recharge his magic. "You do have a busy day tomorrow, mate."

Shaun ignores him, glancing at his watch. "Marcus said there's been a turned vampire feeding in this alleyway for the past three nights. He'll show."

"Maybe he's gorged himself and is still sleeping it off," Benny supplies, running a hand casually through his dark brown waves. He sits on crates stacked along the back wall of the alcove. "That's what happened to me when I turned."

Evan and Shaun exchange a look. "We know," Evan responds with a small smirk. Benny huffs out a breath and returns to watching the alley in the direction behind me. I follow suit, trying to keep my mind off tomorrow—well, later today.

I slow my breathing, attempting to check in with my friends' emotions. Shaun and Evan are fairly unreadable, but that's normal. I think they've developed ways of shielding me out. But Benny is an open book. Thankfully, he's peaceful, with just a hint of anticipation. Very at odds with the adrenaline poised to run its course through my veins. My fingers twitch with the desire to move across piano keys in an effort to dispel the excess energy. But I have a job to do, so I clench them firmly at my sides.

"Incoming," I say, spotting two women attempting to walk down the cobblestone alley in high heels. They look hungover and tired from a night of partying. Perfect prey for a ravenous vampire.

The others follow my gaze. Evan snaps his lighter shut, getting to his feet and coming to stand next to me. He's an inch taller than me when we're both wearing shoes, since he always opts for boots with a bit of a platform. As if being six five isn't tall enough.

We barely have enough time to react when a large body jumps off the fire escape of the building across from us, slamming into one of the women, knocking the other over in the process. It's a mix of screams from the women and hungry shrieks from the vampire as he bites into the neck of the blonde one. Her friend gets to her feet, screaming her head off.

But then Shaun is there, ripping the vamp off the blonde and throwing him to the ground in front of Evan, who makes a disgusted face. "Stars, do you think he's high?"

My attention snags on the vampire's face. His eyes are bloodshot, and there's blood and gore caked all over him. He snarls up at Evan, crouching, readying to attack again.

I can't help but allow my siren teeth to slide out of my gums. It's a reaction to the blood and the violence. The urge to rip into someone is strong.

I push it down, though, even as the newly Made fae launches at Evan, who puts out his hands to wield his magic. The ground around the vampire rumbles and cracks, and his uneven footing sends him crashing back to the now destroyed cobblestones. Benny is able to restrain his arms from behind him, but the vamp struggles against Benny and gnashes his teeth at Evan, his gaze finding mine.

I stare him down, sparing a quick glance at Shaun. He has successfully gotten the two women a safe distance away. Sunlight starts to gleam down on us. "We need to use the tranq," Shaun orders. "Evan, heal them and get them out of here."

Benny takes the tranq needle out of his pocket, holding on to the vampire with only one hand. The vampire falls still for a moment. He turns, sinking his teeth into Benny. He lets out a groan —probably realizing that fae taste way better than humans—and pushes Benny to the ground, the rest of us forgotten.

Maybe it's the scent of my friend's blood—a scent that causes me to salivate—but suddenly I'm ripping into the vamp from behind. I think Benny is able to kick himself free of our tangled limbs, but I'm not sure because all I can focus on is taking another bite and another. I turn him around, straddling him as I rip into his neck, relishing in the taste of his blood and flesh as I swallow it.

"Pisces! Let him go!" someone shouts at me.

Strong hands pull me off the vampire, who's now gone slack and wide-eyed, staring at me like *I'm* the monster. Benny finishes his job of tranquilizing him as I sink into Evan's side, satiated. Awareness floods back into me as the vampire's scared expression fades into sleep.

I rip out of Evan's hold, pulling my hood up once again as I leave my friends behind in the alleyway.

We were there to catch a monster.

Fucking hypocrites.

Because I am a monster, much more so than any vampire.

"He's awake," Benny says softly from the door to my bedroom. I thought I'd closed it. Locked it, actually, but Benny's never met a lock he couldn't magically pick.

"Is he healed?" I ask, throat tight. Images of me ripping into the poor turned vampire flash through my mind. I can see myself attacking him, my hood falling back, blood splashing my light skin and dark hair. And then later, the blood rinsing down the drain in an almost unending stream.

"Good as new." Benny sits on my bed, but I don't look at him. I keep my gaze on the ceiling. "Sces?" he asks, shortening my name in a way that used to annoy me when we first met.

It's been about six years since I moved in with them, into an old church that Evan bought and slowly fixed up. It's become a haven for the four of us and anyone else that needs it. Currently about nine of us live here, a mix of Born and Made fae and kindreds who have nowhere else to go. And it hasn't just been a roof over my head.

I've found a slice of salvation—as much as a wraith-made fae like me can.

"That's the perk of feeding off other fae. It's really fucking hard to kill one of us that way," Benny reminds me, picking up my hand and threading his fingers through mine. I squeeze his fingers, closing my eyes against the tears that threaten to spill. At least I haven't fed off a human since the night I found out what I'd turned into.

But the memory of what I did that night lingers fresh in my mind, as if it happened yesterday.

"I lost control," I manage to say, even as tears leak out of my closed lids.

"That's normal," Benny soothes. "It takes time to get things under control. You have to learn how to forgive yourself."

"How did you forgive yourself?" I look at him, a sob wanting to escape me, but I take a deep breath instead. "You said you were like that vampire, that you went on a binge?"

He nods, looking out my window into the gray London sky. "I killed a lot people, Sces. I honestly don't even remember most of it. When vampires turn we go insane with bloodlust. I'm just grateful Evan and Shaun found me when they did. And that's why I stayed with them. It's why I help them out, *and*—" he looks at me pointedly, "—it's why I wanted to play music with you so badly."

"Why?"

"For the same reason you write it, I suppose," he says cryptically. I stare at him until he says more. He lets out a sigh and nudges me with his shoulder. "It's absolving."

Benny stands up, tugging me off the bed. "Come see the newbie vamp. He's completely healed, awake, and not unhinged by blood anymore." The corners of his mouth tick up. "You can apologize for trying to eat him."

I allow Benny to lead me to the basement, where we found it was necessary to install a few barred cells to restrain newer fae when we first find them. All but one cell is empty, the vamp sitting cross-legged on a cot in the corner.

Evan's arm snags out and stops me from entering the room. I glare at him, looking between his face and his arm. Some of his bleach blonde hair has escaped his bun. "Problem?" I grit out.

"You good?" he asks, green eyes fixed on me.

I flash my teeth at him. My normal ones. "Peachy. I ate not too long ago, if you recall."

I push past him, knocking his arm away from me, and follow Benny into the room, catching Benny's disapproving look to Evan. The vamp shifts on his cot once he notices me.

"Austin, this is Pisces."

"The one that tried to eat you," Evan supplies from behind me, as if anyone could forget me feeding off them.

I look over my shoulder at him. "Thanks," I deadpan.

He smirks at me. "Welcome."

"Would you two do this later?" Benny chides, stepping into the cell. I didn't even notice him unlock it. He leans against the bars, turning his attention to Austin. "Do you remember when or where you were turned? And by who?"

Austin looks between Evan and I for a second. He nods. "I don't remember when or where exactly. Time kinda stopped making any sense."

"That's fairly normal," Benny says, nodding as well.

"But I know who turned me. It was a vampire named Stretcher."

"Stretcher?" Evan asks. "What the fuck kinda name is Stretcher?"

Austin shrugs. "He's a friend of a friend. I don't think that's his real name, but he's in a band and they all have these weird stage names."

Benny looks out of the cell at Evan and I, grinning. "Fucking weird."

I can't help but smile back. All four of us have our own stage names.

Though none as bad as Stretcher.

"Why'd he turn you?" Shaun asks from the doorway. I shuffle over to make room for him to stand outside the cell with us, forcing Evan to also take a step back. He shoots a glare my way, half-heartedly elbowing me in the chest, hitting my right nipple piercing. I rub at the sensitive bud and I show him my canines again.

"Would you two stop fucking around?" Shaun barks, then pins Austin with his stormy blue eyes.

Austin seems to curl into himself on the cot. "We uhh—we hooked up a couple of times. Just after shows and stuff. It wasn't anything serious, well, at least I thought, but then he started showing up everywhere."

"Seems like his stage name should be Stalker," Evan huffs out.

"At one point he showed up where I work, and he was saying all this crazy stuff about wanting to be together forever." Austin breaks out into a sob. "Why did he do this to me?"

Benny lowers himself onto the cot beside Austin, comforting him. "It's not uncommon for vampires to get like that. Possessive. Obsessed."

"You seem normal," I say, trying to offer the newer vampire hope.

Benny nods. "Inner work is pretty helpful."

Austin leans into Benny, his sobs only getting louder. Benny exchanges a look with Shaun and the wolf shifter herds us out of the room. "I think only Benny being in there for now will be good. Austin needs to see what he can become if he puts in the work."

I nod, exhaling through my nose. "I wanted to apologize to him, but I guess it can wait."

"It's not like you were doing anything he wasn't doing," Shaun says, shrugging.

"It still wasn't right."

"No, it wasn't," Evan cuts in before Shaun can. "You lost control. If he'd been human, you would have killed him." Evan glares at me, and I know he's thinking I should have this handled by now. He turns away from me and heads back up the stairs, leaving Shaun and I standing there.

Shaun takes a few steps up the stairs and turns, looking down at me. "Pisces, you're doing good. Evan's never been through what you have. He doesn't understand what you're battling. I'll talk to him."

"Don't." I shake my head. "I need him to be hard on me."

"Are you calling Benny and I soft?" Shaun asks, a rare smile coming to his face.

I grin. "Yes, that's exactly how I'd describe you both," I say, a genuine laugh bubbling out of my throat. "Nah, Evan just gets under my skin sometimes."

"He'd say the same thing about you."

My grin grows. "Well, then I'm doing something right." We

continue up the stairs. "Probably time to get ready for your cere-mony, isn't it?"

CHAPTER THREE

BLISS

"WHEN WAS THE LAST TIME YOU HAD SEX?" MY SISTER ASKS, EYEBROW raised as she twirls a straw around her drink.

And here I thought our first girls' night after so long would be *awkward.*

The EDM music is thumping so loudly that my glance around the tables nearby ours is unwarranted. But even if no one did over-hear us, red creeps into my cheeks, and I roll my eyes at Amelia.

I met Reese and Amelia at my aunt's house—which I have only been back to a handful of times since moving out—to get ready for our girls' night. Amelia and I weren't *not* on speaking terms, but things haven't been right between us for quite some time. As we got ready together in her room, the chill slowly started to thaw and we fell back into old patterns; for example, Amelia constantly butting into my sex life—or lack thereof.

"This is what you want to talk about?"

"It's a valid question," Amelia continues, completely ignoring my humiliation. She looks to Dericia, and I shoot a warning glare at my best friend.

Dericia shrugs and smiles at me and Amelia. "I'm not getting involved in a sisterly fight, especially not a succubus sisterly fight."

"I'm not talking about this," I tell Amelia, wishing I had ordered a stronger drink.

Amelia picks the straw out of her glass and points it at me, droplets of her Sex on the Beach cocktail flying onto the tiny table we're seated at. "You look tired, and I want to make sure you're taking care of yourself."

I search around for anything to change the subject but come up empty. "You and I both know, taking care of ourselves doesn't power us up. If it did, I wouldn't be so tired all the time."

"Why doesn't that recharge you again?" Reese asks. "It's still sexual energy. It should count."

"It needs to be other people's energy," Amelia explains. "Just how a vampire can't feed off their own blood."

Reese makes a face like the stars should make an exception for me.

"So you've gotten no dick recently, then?" Amelia asks, returning to my oh-so-favorite topic.

Dericia snorts and I shake my head, letting loose a sigh that is quickly swallowed up by the music.

"No, I haven't." It's been a while, a long while. I've stuck to… uh… slightly less intimate options, and usually only in emergencies. Maybe my sister is right to be worried.

"We should find you a guy tonight, then," Dericia says, starting to scope out the club. I put my hand on her forearm to bring her attention back to the table.

"Please, no. I don't do one-night stands."

"Bliss, you're a succubus, a single one," Amelia explains, as if I don't know this already. "You have to be open to one-night stands. For your health. Plus, they're sexy as hell."

Dericia nods enthusiastically, swinging her long braids over her shoulder, as she goes back to looking for cute guys. "What about that one?" She points at a tall blonde jock type with lots of muscles who's hanging out with a group of friends.

"Definitely not her type, Reese," Amelia says, almost spluttering in concern. "My sister is not going home with someone who peaked in high school. We should have gone to a different club." She sighs.

"This club is great," Reese stresses, shooting a warning look at Amelia.

I look down at my drink, putting both my hands around it. We came to this club in particular because we all knew we wouldn't run into anyone from the metal scene—well, besides Amelia and Dericia. The crowd they hang with is pretty great, but ever since my breakup, I just haven't really found it in myself to hang around in that circle. It's *his* space, and I have to avoid it at all costs. Facing him again just isn't something I can do.

"You know, I actually love this song," Amelia says, downing the rest of her drink and hopping off her barstool. Her black minidress slips up further than is probably decent, but she doesn't rush to right it. My sister could be in this club completely naked and still walk around like she owns the place.

Dericia follows suit, reaching out her hand to me. "Come on, Bliss. We're gonna go dance and find you a sexy man to take home."

"I'll agree to the dancing," I reply, taking her hand and hurriedly finishing the last little bit of my drink. She hauls me out onto the dance floor alongside her. Amelia already has most eyes on her as she moves to the center of the dance floor. Her long, pale legs draw male attention quickly, and soon the three of us find ourselves surrounded by a few different groups of fae men.

Amelia, recently topped up on power, is a magnet. But even though I haven't fed in a while, I still possess some of that same allure, and Dericia, with her huge chocolate eyes, flawless warm sepia skin, and long braids that hit the slope of her ass, has her own captivating presence. So between the three of us it almost seems like every male in the club is making their way towards us. Dericia and Amelia smile at the attention, knowing it means more options for them and—they hope—for me.

All it does is make me want to shrink into the shadows of the room and disappear. Which unfortunately is not a power I'm blessed with.

"What's your name?" a sweaty voice asks right next to my ear. I recoil from the heat of it and swivel around to see an equally sweaty guy with slicked back greasy hair and a button-down shirt open almost to his navel ogling me.

"No thanks," Amelia says to him from behind me. She waves her hand dismissively at him. "We can definitely do better than that," she says to me.

"We're not doing better than anything," I remind her. "I'm just here to hang out with you and Reese." It has been ages since we've had a girls' night. We used to do stuff like this all the time, but now we lead such different lives and it feels like a huge distance has risen up between the three of us. Tonight was just supposed to be like old times. And maybe it already is, because since when did my sister *not* meddle in my life?

I look around for Reese, catching a guy with dark hair grinding with her, his arms around her waist, his lips murmuring something in her ear. She sees me looking and grins excitedly, obviously super into the guy. And he is hot, so I smile back at her. "I'm going to get another round of drinks," I tell them, as Amelia draws a guy towards her with just the simplest crook of her finger.

They shout their drink preferences at me as I try not to stumble all the way to the bar. Taking off these heels at the end of the night is the closest I'm coming to an orgasm today. A couple of the guys from the dance floor trail after me, so I let one of them buy the round of drinks, but I make sure to carry all three back to the dance floor so no one gets any ideas of slipping anything into them.

Amelia and Dericia reach out and take their drinks. Amelia exchanges numbers with the guy she was dancing with, winking at me as he heads back to his friends. "I'll circle back to him before we leave," she says, glancing down at her dress, which keeps riding up. She tugs it down with her free hand. "Anyone catch your eye?" she asks me hopefully.

"Nope, but Dericia definitely seems to have caught many eyes," I say, noticing a guy in a red shirt with his hair pulled up into a bun trying to pull her away from the guy she's been dancing with now for several songs. Her dance partner twirls them, so that Dericia is facing away from us, trying to put himself between her and the guy with the red shirt.

Amelia and I gasp as we catch a glimpse of the back of his neck. Thick ridges line the center of his back. It's not as apparent through his shirt, but above the collar we can see where his ridged spine pushes through his skin.

A warlock.

Before we can attempt to disentangle Dericia from the warlock, the red-shirted guy starts shouting at him, and a crowd starts to form as everyone tries to get a look at what's happening.

"Let her go, you Made fae piece of trash," the guy in the red shirt says, baring his fangs at the warlock.

The warlock tightens his arms around Dericia, who swivels in his grasp to find us, her eyes wide. "We were just dancing," the warlock says, fury lacing his words.

"I don't understand why this place even lets in your kind," the red-shirted vamp says, grabbing onto Dericia's arms and trying to pull her out of the warlock's grasp. "Don't worry, babe, I won't let him hurt you."

"I'm not going to hurt her," the warlock shouts.

Amelia and I exchange glances. More and more fae are starting to congregate around the scene these two are making, with Dericia smack-dab in the middle of it. We have to get her out of there before anyone starts using their powers. While her kindred rune protects her from some fae magic, like compulsion, it won't protect against direct hits, and she doesn't have magic of her own to defend herself if she gets caught in the magical crossfire.

Amelia sucks in a breath, raising her arms out around her, and a whooshing sensation rushes past me as she lets out a calming energy. I can tell immediately when it reaches the two guys. The Born fae vampire relaxes a bit, but he is still trying to pull Dericia out of the warlock's grip. "She's human, man. Just let her go."

"Just because I'm Made, doesn't mean I'll hurt her," the warlock replies, but the fury in his voice is gone.

I step between Dericia and the vampire. "Hey, Reese, we're gonna go home now, okay?" She nods at me, her eyes no longer wide and a lazy grin on her face as she feels the effects of Amelia's magic. I gently remove the warlock's arms from around her middle and he stares at me with an almost sleepy confusion. Once I've lead Dericia away from the fae and we're behind Amelia, she lets go of her magic and the two fae whip their eyes back towards one another.

"Fucking Made fae, thinking they can just steal humans away. You probably wanted to turn her, didn't you?" the vampire asks. He doesn't wait for a reply as he drunkenly swings a fist at the warlock.

The warlock tries to conjure some magic to defend himself, but the vampire hits him square in the jaw. The warlock gives up on magic entirely, launching himself at the vampire, knocking him to the ground. Others pounce on the Made fae, pulling him up off the vampire and throwing him back to the ground, where they start to beat on him.

Despite the news of the warlock attacks, I'm desperate to get the other fae to cool off. My power ebbs to the surface, reluctantly dusting itself off. I raise my hand, letting a dribble of power out. The small fae mob show no sign my magic has any effect. Not a single person stops what they're doing. None of the onlookers step in to help.

Amelia tugs on my arm. "Let's go."

I turn my pleading eyes on her and she shakes her head. But I see her look behind me at the fight. Her eyes widen and she sends another wave of her power blasting at the group. They all slow to a halt, dazed smiles appearing on their faces and laughter bubbling up their throats.

Amelia and Dericia tug at my arms as I stand there, frozen. We should still help the warlock, shouldn't we? Find his friends, maybe? "We gotta go, Bliss."

As they drag me out of the club, I can't help but shiver.

"Gross, I can't believe I was dancing with a warlock," Dericia says, shaking out her arms like she can somehow shake off any germs he might have left on her. "Ugh, what if he was like two hundred years old?"

"He seemed nice enough," I say, though the warning all Born fae have been given echoes in my head. We're taught not to interact with Made fae if we can help it. They don't have our morals and many kill without remorse and turn humans against their will.

"Bliss, did you not see the ridges on his neck?" Amelia asks, shuddering. She feigns gagging.

I shrug and let out a yawn. "I guess we should probably call it a night, huh?"

"We didn't find you anyone, though." Dericia drunkenly pouts.

"It's okay," I say, just as a second later Amelia says, "No, it's not."

She turns to me, towering almost a full foot over me. "Bliss, your bond activation ceremony is tomorrow. You need to power up."

"I'll be fine, *Mom*."

"Okay, fine, let's go home and get some sleep," Amelia says, throwing her arms around me and Reese.

"I still can't believe humans aren't allowed to attend the activation ceremony," Dericia complains as we start the walk home.

"Don't worry, I'll record the whole thing for you," Amelia says.

"You'll do no such thing," I shoot back, giving my sister the most threatening look I can muster.

"Oh yeah? Whatcha gonna do about it?"

"Don't push me, Amelia, unless you wanna be bald again."

Amelia lets out a shriek and pulls me under her arm, rubbing her hand over the top of my hair, stupendously messing it up.

"Why would you remind her of that?" Dericia snorts. "She didn't talk to you for months after the Great Fae Nair Shampoo Tragedy of sophomore year."

I grin, even though Amelia is still pushing my head down and can't see me.

"Karma's a real bitch," I tease.

Amelia releases me and I stand up, smoothing my hair back in place and allowing Dericia to retie my pink ribbon, which floated to the ground in our tussle.

"How many times do I have to tell you that Todd Andrews kissed *me*? Not the other way around."

"Because you were throwing your succubus charm around all day every day at school as soon as you got your period for the first time."

"I didn't know how to turn it off!" Amelia shouts at me, now pretending she's going to push me out into oncoming traffic.

I laugh, remembering how awkward going through puberty was for us. Fae children tend to mature later, usually in our teens. Thankfully, Reese had already gotten her period, so she was able to help us through that part of things.

My best friend laughs. "You two always find a way to make me so glad I don't have sisters."

Amelia and I stop our bickering and look at her. "Um, excuse me?" Amelia says with a laugh. She points her finger at Dericia and moves it in a circle, motioning to all of us. "We, the three of us, are sisters. You are included in this, whether you like it or not."

Dericia looks like she's about to start tearing up out of joy, but then she huffs out a laugh. "Just as long as Bliss stays away from my hair," she teases.

"Oh, I would never mess with your hair," I say with feigned incredulousness. "You'd look super weird bald," I add with a grin and a shrug.

"You take that back!" Dericia says, running towards me. I yelp and scramble backwards, laughing my ass off. "I'd look fucking amazing bald! I totally have the bone structure to pull it off!" She runs after me, swinging her clutch at me, trying to swat my ass with it. All three of us end up laughing so hard we run out of breath and end up falling to the sidewalk in heaps, trying to gulp down air.

"Fuck, don't make me run like that, ever," I manage to get out, throwing my arms around Dericia.

"We are never going to get home at this rate," Amelia sighs, tears leaking out of the corners of her eyes.

"Let's call Tay Tay," Dericia shouts excitedly. She fishes around in her purse for her phone.

Amelia eyes me, suddenly looking sober. "Is that okay, Bliss?"

"Yeah, Taser's cool," I say.

"I just figured it might be weird between you two since he started dating Stacey."

"Oh—" I pause. Taser and I had a bit of a friends with benefits things going for a while. I'd feed off him, and he'd feed off me, drinking a bit of my blood after we slept together. It was the most comfortable with a guy I've ever been. "I didn't even think of that. I thought you were asking because I don't hang out with you guys as much these days."

"You avoid everyone from that crowd like the plague. Including us," she points out.

"I'm not trying to avoid you," I say after a beat. "Things with Goddess' Trance just weren't the same, and I needed some space away from it all." Goddess' Trance is my sister's band. She's the lead singer, and Dericia is their bassist. They're incredible. I smile at Amelia as she nods in understanding. "It's not an issue, I just feel weird. It's not my world anymore, is all."

"It doesn't have to be that way," Amelia says, putting a hand on my arm.

Dericia pushes to her feet excitedly. "Tay Tay is on his way way!"

Amelia and I exchange a glance. "How many drinks did she have?" I ask.

Amelia grins and shrugs. We move past the previous topic, though I can't help but hear her words echoing in my mind.

"She's a fucking lightweight, our sister," she replies, her meaning twofold. Dericia is no doubt also still feeling the effects of Amelia's magic.

"Sisters!" Dericia yells out, the widest of grins plastered on her face.

We hang out for a bit before Taser pulls up in the band's van, and we all shuffle into it. Before I know it, I'm tucked into my bed in my old room, with Dericia snoring softly beside me, and I smile to myself for the first time in a long time, feeling ever so slightly content.

Maybe some things can go back to normal after all.

CHAPTER FOUR

BLISS

I HESITATE AT THE THRESHOLD OF THE DOORWAY THAT LEADS OUT into a circular amphitheater. All sorts of Born fae idle, glancing nervously around as if they might be able to spot their mate early. A shudder goes through me, and my mouth goes dry. The content feeling I went to sleep with was gone when I woke up. As soon as I remembered what today is, an uneasiness took up residence in my stomach and refused to leave.

"Here." Amelia shoves a water bottle into my hand. "Drink, and apply lip gloss, just in case."

"Lip gloss?" I ask absently after gulping down some water. *Shoot, what if I have to pee in the middle of the ceremony?*

"Well, yeah, what if you meet your mate down there and are overcome with lust and start making out? You wouldn't want to have dry lips during your first make out session with your soulmate."

I arch my brows at her, handing the bottle back and shaking my head. "It's pretty unlikely my mate is in this crowd. His bond could have already been activated, or he could be younger than me and I'll have to wait until he's twenty-eight. Or we could be the same age, but he could be on a totally separate continent."

"Well, hopefully there's not an entire ocean separating you two. But doesn't matter anyways. The bond will lead you to him soon enough."

"Yours hasn't."

My sister's two years older than me, and just like every Born fae, her bond was activated at twenty-eight. And yet at thirty, she's still casually dating.

She shrugs. "I'm always fashionably late anyways. No reason for this relationship to be any different. Besides, my career is way more important than some guy. It's a good thing if I don't meet him for another few years."

"Is it bad that I don't want to meet mine at all?"

Now it's her turn to raise her brows. "Why would you say that? You, out of everyone, *need* to have a soulmate. A succubus who doesn't like casual sex? This is why you're tired all the time, Bliss." It's almost exactly what she said to me last night at the club, but it's a speech she's given to me countless times, so I shouldn't be surprised.

"What if he doesn't like me?" I finally mumble.

"He's your bond. Your mate. How could he not?"

I let out a sigh, surveying the crowd again, wondering if he's one of them. "I should get out there," I tell Amelia, ignoring her question.

I know she means well. But the bonds between Born fae aren't always so straight forward.

And a part of me doesn't think it will be so easy.

To me, there's a very apparent possibility my mate won't like me.

I'm not even sure *I* like me.

"Liz and I will be waiting for you after, okay? And then dinner with Reese?" She rests a reassuring hand on my shoulder and squeezes gently. "The ceremony takes like ten seconds. And there are so many people down there, no one is going to be paying any attention to you. And your mate is, like you said, probably not even there. So just go and get it over with and then we can get out of here."

I nod, giving her what I hope is a reassuring smile. I don't like being the center of attention, but like she said, there are at least fifty fae down there already. I carefully walk down the stairs, managing to stumble a few times on the steep steps. I wedge myself in between two groups of female fae. *Must be nice to have friends here with you,* I think, wishing not for the first time that Amelia was my twin. It would have been so much easier growing up. I would have always had her by my side going through life. We would have started high school at the same time. Learned how to drive together. Maybe developed our powers at the same time.

We would have been standing here, about to activate our bonds together.

I would have been able to lean on her and borrow her fearless strength.

I fiddle with the hem of my blouse and look around as the group settles into silence. The fae leading the ceremony walks out into the very center of the stage, where a carved stone stand has been placed. She nods to a couple of male fae behind her, who together hoist a large opulent crystal onto the flat surface of the stand. It looks like it'll be right at waist height for most fae. I remember Amelia's ceremony. We're all expected to place our hands on that stone and that's what activates our side of our bonds.

Once the stone is in place, the crowd is asked to be seated. Silence ripples out from those of us on stage to those sitting around us witnessing the ceremony. I spot Amelia and Liz towards the front. They both grin encouragingly at me, but I just put my attention back on that stone.

The ceremony starts. The female fae—a water nymph from the fae council, if I'm not mistaken—reads from an ancient looking scroll in an old fae language that I never bothered to learn. But I know from years of anticipating my bond ceremony that it talks about our history. The story details past generations' efforts to rid the realm of the wraiths that created Made fae and cursed them with immortality and bloodlust. Then it covers how, because Born fae defeated most of the wraiths in a decades long war a thousand years ago or whatever, the stars blessed us with mates.

Once a fae touches that stone, they're on the lookout for another fae whose left eye has a rune only their soulmate can see. I see that rune on anyone's eye and that's it. Technically, the bond isn't complete until it's consummated, but the stars will just keep pushing us together over and over until that happens.

The fae switches to English, looking out at the participants. "We have been blessed by the stars with bonds no other creatures are given. Born fae are the only among fae and humans with these divine bonds. The stars have rewarded us, shown us how special we are through this gift. It allows Born fae to continue to be strong. The stars choose our mates for us to foster the strongest relationship, and to continue creating the strongest of fae. This auspicious day signals the beginning of your adult life. Your aging will slow, another gift from the stars. Your fertility will awaken from its slumber. And if you follow the stars' guidance, you will be led to your love."

The fae leading the ceremony stops and looks around at those of us on stage. "It is time to begin. May the stars belong to you."

"May the stars belong to you," repeats throughout the event hall, both from participants and those in attendance.

As if in response to the echoing statement, the stone flares to life, almost like a flame is inside it. The glow emanates outwards, beckoning us forward. But I don't move.

The ceremony has always been popcorn style. Whoever wants to, goes first, no order to it.

A tall dark-haired fae flashes a toothy grin to his friend next to him. "I'm about to find me my man," he says to her. They fist bump and he strides towards the stone. He puts his hand on it and nods to the crowd as cheers go up from a group—his family, probably—seated to my left, only a few rows from the front.

I watch as fae after fae look around, then take a step forward, some tentative, some more surefooted. After they touch the stone, they look around the group, towards the ones that have already gone, waiting to see if they see their partner's rune.

Nothing special seems to happen after anyone touches the stone. There's no noise. No shift in the energy. Amelia said the stone feels warm and there's an odd sensation that flows through you, but that's it.

I continue to watch as others offer themselves up to the stone, but even though I know I'm free to leave after I touch it, I can't seem to force my feet to take a step forward. A fae with red hair finally steps forward with encouragement from her friends.

She touches the stone and then, as she looks around at the other fae who have gone before her, she locks eyes with a blonde guy and he lets out a low gasp. Without any words, she runs forward and he wraps her up in his arms. He leans in and kisses her. Immediately the crowd starts cheering and clapping. The two break apart, smiling, and walk off into the sunset holding hands. Okay, so maybe they just walk off the stage and out into the lobby, but whatever.

I stand there completely frozen as the fae in charge ushers the next person to the stone. There's hope in her eyes that she too might meet her mate on this stage. I hope to the stars I don't. Because I wouldn't be able to handle the humiliation of him rejecting me in front of all these fae.

It takes me a while to realize that everyone is staring at me, because I'm the last one and I'm just standing there, making no move to approach the stone.

The water nymph in charge clears her throat. She looks around the amphitheater as if someone from the crowd will come and encourage me to touch it. I don't want to.

I cast a quick glance over at the rest of the fae who have already finished the ceremony. Some of them look worried, as if I might be their mate and they want to see the stone activate my bond so they can be sure I'm not.

The nymph glares at me and looks pointedly at the stone. I loose a sigh and ignore the urge to look for my sister. She can't help me. I finally force my feet to move.

"What is her problem?"

"Why is she just standing there?"

"Fucking weird."

I hear their whispers as I stumble towards the stone, slowly reaching out to touch it as if it might bite me.

The second my skin makes contact with the smooth glass-like surface, a zap goes through me and it feels like my skin is burning. The jolt sends me flying back and I land on my ass with a thud.

Burning pain rips through my arm, starting at my hand and radiating up to my elbow. I wince, but I don't take my eyes off the stone.

What the fuck just happened?

It's like the fucking stone itself rejected me. I finally glance down at my hand, seeing the reddened flesh and—Oh stars, is that what muscle looks like underneath skin?

I wince in pain, looking anywhere but at my hand. Even through blurry eyes, I see the fae running the ceremony just standing there, looking between me and the stone. Amelia and Liz force their way onto the stage.

"What just happened?" My aunt shoots the question at the water nymph. She's now speaking in hushed voices with a few other fae that also must be members of the council. Liz pushes her way into their circle.

I look again at my hand, even though the sight of it freaks me out and makes it hurt that much worse. But it saves me from looking up at the faces of everyone else. Everyone knows now that I'm unlovable. That I have no mate. That's what this has to mean, right? My mind spins, embarrassment warring with self-pity and a hollowness in my chest. Tears threaten to cascade down my cheeks.

"Are you okay?" Amelia asks, lifting my hand gently, forcing me to look up at her. She doesn't seem concerned about anything else other than my hand.

I search Amelia's face for answers, but she just takes the first aid kit someone offers her and wraps my hand. "You need to recharge your power."

"Who with?" I ask bitterly. "Not with my mate, seeing as they don't exist."

"What?" She finally looks me directly in the eyes.

"The stone *rejected* me. What else could that mean other than I'm mateless?"

"I don't think that's what it means. It's probably just broken."

I glance at the stone. It seems just fine to me, still ablaze with its internal fire.

But I don't voice that. Instead, I allow her to pull me up and lead me outside, trying not to feel the thousands of eyes that are trained on me. Because I know not a single one of them has a rune meant for me.

CHAPTER FIVE

BLISS

AMELIA WAKES ME UP THE NEXT MORNING WITH A FRESH HOT CUP OF coffee. I watch the steam rise off it, though I make no move towards it. I'm bundled up under the covers in my old bedroom, and if I could manage it I would pull them up over my head. But I don't.

Mostly because I can't. My limbs don't want to move and Amelia and I both know why that is. Succubi need sex.

And I haven't gotten any in months. My magic tried its best to heal my hand, which only resulted in a slightly less burned hand and power so low, my brain might shut off completely. And part of me really doesn't care. "I called Taser," Amelia tells me, nudging the mug of coffee closer to me. "Drink this, and get showered. He'll be here soon and you *will* use him to top off your reserves, okay?"

"No thanks."

"Bliss, this isn't a joke. You could seriously die. That stone injured you and you were already super low."

The ache in my chest that always comes with low power gnaws at me. It's ten times worse than being hungry.

"You've slept with him tons of times, what's the problem?"

"He has a girlfriend now."

She rips the covers off me. "I'd rather him cheat on her, than have you die."

"I'll find someone else."

"No, you won't, and even if you would, you don't have time."

"Get my phone. There's a guy from work—"

"He won't get here in time."

I know she's right, but part of me just doesn't care. If I could just fade slowly into sleep and then into death, I'd allow it. I'd slip beneath the covers and never emerge of my own accord. But dying due to power fading that low is an excruciating pain. In fact, death by power outage isn't a very successful suicide method for fae. We usually fall into a primal energy and end up seeking out what we need. It becomes no longer our choice, but the choice of our magic.

So when my bedroom door squeaks open and Taser pokes his head inside, I grumble and finally push myself out of bed. I practically chug the coffee and it scalds going down, but I don't mind it. I go into the bathroom and turn on the shower, pushing the knob over enough to make the water match the temperature of the coffee.

I can hear Taser follow me into the bathroom, no doubt being prodded by Amelia.

"Bliss?" he asks slowly, locking eyes with me through the glass door of the shower. The steam from the water has already fogged up the glass, but I can see his beautiful deep brown and completely rune-less eyes. My stomach drops a little at that. Taser would have been a safe mate. He wouldn't reject me and I think we could grow to love each other. But part of me knows we are only ever meant to be friends. Our friends with benefits arrangement never once blurred the lines into something more.

I look away from him, putting my hands out on the shower wall to steady myself.

"I don't want to be part of cheating," I tell him, a tear sliding down my cheek.

He pulls off his shirt, revealing a sculpted tan and tattooed torso. "I don't either." He begins to unbuckle his belt.

"Then leave," I reply, but lust has started to kick in, despite what my brain has to say about it. I can't take my eyes off him as he slides his jeans off and steps up to the shower door. He pulls it open and allows his gaze to rake down my body.

"We broke up." He takes my injured hand in his, pressing a gentle kiss to it.

"You did?" I ask, my head falling to the side to study him.

He pauses, then nods, his eyes darkening. "Well, she dumped me, anyway. Help me get over her?"

I know what he's doing. With us it's always been about helping each other. He knows I feel bad about using him, so he's trying to make sure I know we'll both get something out of it.

I finally nod, and he steps inside. I reach out, running my fingers over his chest. Then one hand winds around his neck, pulling his face closer to mine. My other hand trails down his stomach. Water already starts to dampen his light brown hair, streaming down his body.

He smiles, his mouth so very close to mine, as he closes the gap between us, kissing me hard. His tongue pushes into my mouth and I groan into him, allowing him to hoist me up so that my entrance is lined up with his cock.

My body is so desperate for this that I'm already wet. And Taser knows it. He doesn't hesitate. He backs me up to the shower wall and pushes inside me. He rolls his hips and I try to meet his thrusts, but mostly I just let him take me, my fingernails digging into his back. He pins me to the wall with his body, his fingers pressing into the flesh of my thighs. I can feel my orgasm building. When he puts his lips on my neck, sucking and kissing, I come undone around him, moaning out his name, my inner walls contracting and squeezing him. He follows me, a hoarse cry falling from his lips as he spills into me.

"Fuck, Bliss," Taser whispers. The high of succubus sex now flows through his veins. His pupils expand and a lopsided smile appears on his face. He lowers me to my feet and I glance at my hand, now completely healed. I'm still a little tired, but I feel better than I have in ages, physically at least.

Taser thoughtfully helps me wash, dries me with a towel, wraps me in a robe, and carries me out to my bed, where he tucks me back in. He settles down next to me, pulling me into a warm snuggle. We lay there for a bit and after a while a thought occurs to me.

"Taser?" I ask, wondering if he's fallen asleep.

"Yeah?" he mumbles, his mouth close to my ear.

"What was your bond activation ceremony like?"

He considers my question for a moment, and I can feel him shrug. "Normal, I guess?"

"So the stone was warm and you put your hand on it and nothing really happened? That's how Amelia described it."

"Yeah, I suppose it was like that," he replies.

"Where was your ceremony?" I ask. Taser is thirty-one now, so his ceremony would have been a few years ago, but I don't remember attending.

"I did it back in New York, so my family could go," Taser replies, reaching out and playing with a lock of my hair.

"And you were dating Stacey, even though she's human and you knew she wasn't your bondmate? Why?"

"Beats being alone." Taser sighs, and I can feel the bed shift as he sits up. "And I like her, well *liked* her, I guess. But, yeah, it's weird knowing that there's a type of connection out there bigger than that."

"Do you think you'll meet your mate soon?"

Taser leans over and gives me a quick kiss on the cheek. "I try not to think about it, actually."

"It's all I can think about," I murmur, the high of good sex making me sleepy.

Taser laughs and gets up, but I catch his arm, pulling him back to the bed.

"You didn't feed," I say, titling my head and offering him my neck.

He looks at me, a ravenous gleam in his eye. "You still need more healing," he says. "I shouldn't."

"Drink, and then come back tomorrow and fuck me again." Post sex, I really don't sound like myself.

I close my eyes, and for a few seconds I think he's left, but then I feel his fangs bite into me as gently as they can. He only takes a few sips of me and retracts, giving me another kiss, this time on the forehead. I hear the bed creak as he settles down next to me. His arms wrap around my middle as I drift off.

Pale morning light drifts in through the cracks in the blinds. It takes me a few moments to return to the present. I jolt upright in my old bed, looking around at all the familiar surroundings. I wasn't really in the right state of mind to take in everything about my old room yesterday. I was in too much pain and too low on power to even care where I was.

How many times have I woken up to the room looking exactly this way? The dust moats swirling in the air exactly as they are now? The hushed sounds of birds flitting in and out as they sing outside my window, as they always have? It feels so normal to wake up here, but at the same time, there's a sense that I no longer belong.

The Bliss that hung up all these old rock and metal band posters would have laughed if I'd told her I now work at a country bar.

I pull my old worn pastel pink comforter around my shoulders as I turn around and look up at the posters I'd hung above my bed. The one to my left is a Goddess' Trance poster. My sister stands in the middle clad all in black, with her long flowing dark hair and dark makeup. Dericia stands to her right, draping her arm over Amelia's shoulder, her braids collected together in a larger braid that falls over her shoulder. The two are surrounded by the rest of the band. I can make out Taser and Tubbs—the drummer—

standing further back to either side. But there is a rip down the poster, tearing it into two halves right where the fifth member should be between Amelia and Tubbs. Despite the tear, the poster has stayed up on the wall. It's been there so long it's practically glued to the paint.

The face missing from the poster haunts me more often than not, but I put that out of my mind by looking at the poster next to it. It features artwork from Voracious Maw's second album. Three years ago I caught Amelia hanging it up for me, wanting to replace the ripped poster with it. But I told her just to put it next to the damaged one. It didn't matter, because I was leaving. I wasn't going to make her choose between me and her band, so I moved out. Got a different job. Tried to move on with my life.

I stand up on my bed, facing the posters, my comforter falling from my shoulders with the movement. I reach out and let my fingers trail the red and black details of the poster on the right. This album got me through that period of my life. And for that reason, even though I love their music and they are probably my favorite band of all time, I never came back to retrieve the poster and hang it up at my apartment.

It just reminded me of where I was at around the time when the album released.

I let out a sigh and hop off my bed, picking up an empty water glass I drained before falling asleep.

As I make my way down the stairs to refill it in the kitchen, I hear voices. Taser and Amelia's muffled conversation barely reaches the top of the stairs. I must have woken up when Taser got up to leave my room. He didn't need to. I enjoy cuddling more than sex, honestly, and I always loved it when he stayed the night and was there in the morning. He knows that.

As I hit the last stair, the hushed tone of their conversation makes me stop short. Taser and Amelia stand in the open living space that sits next to the foyer. I can see them through two columns in the half wall that separate the stairs from the living room. I smile to myself as my eyes roam Taser's broad back, his shoulder blades biting through his shirt. He holds his shoes, obviously on his way out the door.

"How'd you get her to agree? I figured she would have put up more of a fight."

"I told her Stacey and I broke up," comes Taser's whispered reply. Hmm, that's a weird way to phrase it.

"You broke up?" Amelia asks, surprise in her voice.

He shakes his head.

"Oh."

The high from sex is doused immediately.

Tears well in my eyes and I race back up the stairs, throwing on some old clothes I never bothered taking with me. I climb out my window like I've done countless times before, needing to get the hell out of here.

CHAPTER SIX

PISCES

Bits of the wispy rift particles cling to my skin, hair, and clothes as we break through the portal but almost seem to scurry back into formation like ducklings to their mother. The rift has always seemed nurturing to me, passing through the foggy membrane an obvious metaphor for birth. The first time I went through a portal rift, I felt as if my very being was ripped apart and put together again. I puked up my earlier meal as Evan and Benny held me from completely crumbling to the ground.

Now it's just a gentle push through a thin purple film of a cloud-like substance. The four of us step through easily, careful not to touch the azkanite stone on either side. In gas form, the purple crystal is what powers the portals. In solid form, it's so powerful, the effects are unpredictable. A fae could end up in a totally different place in the world than they intended, sometimes with their torso separated from their legs—though that might have just been Evan trying to scare me.

There are legends too, of fae touching that stone and completely vanishing, never being found again.

Maybe these are just children's stories, told to make sure fae children don't let go of their parents' hands while traveling.

But I'm not going to test it out to confirm.

We come out of the portal along a path that leads up to Evan's family's estate. I've been here once before to announce myself to the fae council. The estate serves as the family home and is connected by portal to the headquarters for the fae council in Europe. All other councils in other countries answer to this one.

Evan and Benny brought me here, acting as my sponsors. It was a fairly quick and painless process to be registered, but it was clear from the looks of every Born fae that Benny and I were beneath them. I brace myself for that same veiled vitriol now as we head up the path.

I've been in a piss poor mood since Evan and Shaun left for Shaun's bond activation ceremony the day before. They came back in high spirits. I hid in my room almost all night. I couldn't help but think that if I was Born, my bond would have been activated two years ago. Benny and I—being Made fae—weren't allowed to attend the ceremony, let alone participate in it. Our blood is that of wraiths, apparently meaning we have no bonds to activate.

But even so, Shaun insisted that Benny and I come to the party Evan's parents are hosting for all recently activated fae from the most prestigious families. I'm not sure if this is their way of sticking it to their parents, showing up with a turned vampire and a siren, or if Shaun simply wants his friends around to celebrate with.

The grounds are decked in royal purple and gold. Lights hang on every tree and along every roofline and railing. We're not the only ones making our way to the grand front doors of the house.

Evan strides forward, Shaun matching his pace despite their height difference. Shaun's golden blonde hair is neatly styled like usual, Evan's in a high bun with unruly wisps escaping all over the place. They've always complemented each other like this. Shaun's strict nature smoothed by Evan's chaos. Evan's chaos tamed by Shaun's sense of responsibility.

Benny flanks me, hands in the pocket of his dress pants, as our group ascends the steps to the grand entrance. I'm struck again by disbelief that Evan grew up here. That he'd want to leave the comforts of this place.

Evan's family stands just inside the entrance, a portrait of stiffness and regality. His parents greet everyone with polite smiles and formal sentences. His two younger siblings stand perfectly still behind their parents, offering the same.

I'm not sure how it's possible, but at our arrival, Evan's father—Yves Lyra—stiffens even more. At his slight movement, his wife, Sonya, looks to us, pinning her son with a bit of a glare.

"Mother, how delightful to see you," Evan says, adding a flourishing bow. He steps forward and embraces her. She stiffly returns it, reaching out and smoothing down his hair.

"Evan, so glad you could make it." She lowers her voice. "Would it have killed you to get a haircut?"

"Or a brush?" His little sister snickers from behind their mother.

"Enough of that, Sonya, Erica," Evan's father chides. He shakes Evan's hand and promptly turns to Shaun. "Shaun, good to see you. Our guest of honor tonight."

Shaun dips his head in gratitude. "Thank you, sir."

"Maybe your mate will be here tonight, and we'll get to witness it!" Erica says, smiling at Shaun. Her twin brother, Eddie, rolls his eyes.

"Your bond hasn't been activated, so it's not like it'll be you," Eddie mutters. Erica gasps and elbows her twin in the stomach.

"I can't believe you just said that, in front of him!" she whisper yells, running off.

Sonya turns her wrathful gaze on Eddie. Without a word he dips his head and heads off after his sister.

Evan mutters goodbyes and something about holding up the other guests, and we part ways with his parents. I can feel the tension in my shoulders uncoiling. Neither of them even spared a glance at Benny and I. I'm not sure if I'm grateful for that or not. I wouldn't want their ire, but part of me wants to rage at the blatant Born fae superiority complex. How Evan turned out to be as open-minded as he is, is a fucking wonder.

Benny grabs two glasses of champagne off a tray as it passes by and hands one to me. "Drink," he orders, clinking his glass with mine and downing it in one go.

I do as instructed, knowing that tonight will be a lot more bearable with a bit of a buzz.

And it's not just the Born fae, but the jealousy that stirs deep within me that Shaun's mate might be here. Something that Evan doesn't want, even though his bond was activated three years ago. Something Benny and I don't ever get to have.

Benny and I are about five drinks in when Evan and Shaun find us down one of the halls of the grand estate, critiquing the art on the walls like we're professional art critics.

"I very much like the use of nudity in this one," I say in a serious tone to Benny, furrowing my brow, as we gaze up at a portrait of a very naked curvaceous woman and a man kneeling in front of her.

"It really evokes a powerful emotion," Benny says, nodding.

"Yes," I respond. "Lust."

"Very good," Benny agrees.

"For stars' sake," Shaun mutters from behind us. Benny and I glance over our shoulders at our Born counterparts.

"Can you blame us? This party is boring," Benny draws out the last word to really drive home his point.

Shaun shakes his head but hands us both glasses of champagne. "Drink up. We've got to mingle for a little bit longer."

Evan motions for us all to follow him, and I stop myself from groaning. I sling my arm around Benny and follow the others back out to the party where Shaun is stopped by an older-looking fae couple.

"Shaun! There you are," the woman says, patting his arm gently. "And your friends. Are you all here celebrating your new bonds?"

"Grandmother, you remember Evan." Shaun motions to the fire elemental. "He's had his bond activated for a few years now."

"Ah yes, now I remember." She inspects Evan closely. "And you still haven't met your mate?"

"Don't interrogate the poor boys, Maude," says her companion —Shaun's grandpa, I assume.

Evan smiles kindly at Shaun's grandparents. "I don't mind." He shakes Shaun's grandpa's hand. "It's good to see you again, Mr. Pyxus."

"Barton is fine, lad."

Evan inclines his head and steps to the side, motioning to Benny and me. "These are our friends, Benny and Pisces."

I nod my head in greeting, shifting a bit nervously on my feet. I've never met anyone from Shaun's family. I suspect he hasn't introduced Benny and I to them for a reason, so I'm not sure what to expect.

Maude peers closely at us. She leans in and whispers conspiratorially to Shaun. She must have noticed Benny's pointed canines. "A turned vampire? Your mother and father will blow a gasket," she says, though her words are accompanied by an approving nod. "And you, boy," she says to me. "What kind of Made fae are you?"

"A siren." I stand up straighter, as if this will make her approve of me.

Her face blanches and she looks over at Shaun, her smile turning wickedly gleeful. "I'd buy tickets to see your parents meet this one."

"Enough, Maude, they aren't spectacles to be gawked at," Barton admonishes.

She gives us an apologetic look. "Yes, I am sorry. How rude of me." She turns to Shaun. "You've got a good group here of good lads. Listen, you must come by for dinner sometime. It's been too long." She pinches her grandson's cheeks. "I'm proud of you, Shaun."

They excuse themselves then and Shaun grimaces. "They mean well, but they're still a bit stuck in the old way of thinking."

I let out a little laugh. "They're nicer than most Born fae I've dealt with."

Shaun grins. "Even Evan and me?"

I bark out a laugh. "Especially Evan and you."

Shaun leads us to another group, some of his old university buddies who also had their bonds activated during the ceremony yesterday.

"Gavin, this is Evan. I'm sure you remember him from uni? He was a few years ahead of us."

Gavin grins and reaches his hand out to Evan. "Good to see you again," Gavin says. His voice has a poshness to it that makes me almost instantly dislike him.

Evan shakes his hand but doesn't smile. "Been a while."

"We were just discussing the warlock attacks," the blonde fae standing next to Gavin explains, almost like he's doing us a favor by catching us up on their conversation.

I shift my weight to my other foot, practically buzzing with the need to get out of here. I look over to Benny, my face probably saying *we don't belong here*, but Benny just gives me a reassuring squeeze on my arm and grabs another two drinks off a passing tray. He hands one to me. I take a few sips, grateful to have something to hold, some job for my hands to do.

"I'm of course of the opinion that we should eradicate them," Gavin responds, proving my first impression dead on.

"You want to eradicate an entire species of fae?" Evan responds, a lethal note in his tone that Gavin doesn't pick up on.

"Well, yeah, a violent one that's starting to turn on us."

Another of the group speaks up. "Watch them try to bring wraiths back to this realm. We should have eradicated warlocks at the same time we banished all wraiths." I stop myself from rolling my eyes. This guy is an idiot to think the wraiths have all been banished. Some definitely still walk this realm. I'm proof of that.

"You make it sound like they're dogs that need to be put down," Shaun responds, his brow cocked in surprise. Though I don't know why he's surprised.

"Aren't they?" one of the group says and laughs, the others joining.

I can feel my siren teeth pushing at my gums, wanting to put these disgusting Born fae in the ground.

Where they belong.

"The same might be said of you," Benny says softly from beside me.

Gavin and his cronies look at Benny, their gazes narrowing. "What did you say?"

Benny shrugs, not repeating himself.

Gavin's blonde friend takes in a deep whiff through his nose and looks to Shaun. "Your vamp friend isn't Born, is he?" It's a guess. Scent wise there's no difference between turned vampires and Born vampires. Some fae can just tell, like Maude. Probably a combination of years of experience and a sixth sense. But this guy isn't one of them. The fae takes a threatening step closer to Benny.

I put myself in between them. "No, he's not."

"And what the hell are you?" He sniffs the air in front of me. As expected, a younger Born fae doesn't have enough experience or intuition to identify my species.

"Trust me," I say, my voice only deepening with hatred and violence. "You don't want to find out."

The group of male fae look between Evan and Shaun. "I'd heard rumors you'd really fallen down the social ladder. Didn't believe it till now," Gavin says. He closes a hand around his friend's arm, bringing him back into their group and closing their ranks. But not before throwing a vitriolic look my way.

Before I can do anything stupid, like rip into the guy here and now, Benny leads me down a vacated hallway, Evan and Shaun at our heels.

We stop near a credenza boasting a few expensive looking vases. I rein in the urge to smash them. Benny rubs a hand up my arm and back down, trying to soothe me. My eyes flash angrily between Shaun and Evan. "I can't believe you know those arseholes."

Shaun's lips press together. "Sorry about that. I just wanted to confirm some things I've been hearing."

"And did you?" Benny asks. If he's upset or confused as to why Shaun and Evan would stop to talk to that group, he doesn't show it or voice it.

Shaun nods, exchanging a look with Evan. "They're more bold about their views than they used to be," Evan says. "That's not a good sign."

I raise an eyebrow at them both. "We'll explain more," Shaun says, "once we get home. But I just wanted to check to see how radicalized Gavin and his friends had become."

"Why?" Benny asks.

"We need to keep an eye on them is all," Shaun responds.

"And if they become a problem?" I ask.

Evan laughs and claps me on the back. "Then you can eat them."

Tension eases out of me and I realize I've had my shoulders tensed up around my ears. They relax and I let out a soft laugh.

I'm about to make a joke that I could take care of that right now when my chest constricts painfully. Suddenly I can't breathe.

My mind flashes back to that night so many years ago.

Claws digging into my chest.

I fall to the ground, clutching at that spot, and my friends all crowd around me trying to figure out what's wrong.

CHAPTER SEVEN

BLISS

FOUR YEARS AGO

AMELIA ARCHES AN EYEBROW AT ME AS I STIFLE A YAWN. "HOW ARE you tired? Didn't you just *eat*?"

"Hell yeah, she did." Jordan smirks and runs his hand up my thigh. I squirm away from him in the booth with a little squeal, laughing as he grabs me, pulling me back towards him and nipping at my neck. "I'm gonna go grab a drink babe, be back."

Amelia watches him go, eyes rolling. She narrows them on me. "You can't keep faking orgasms with him."

"I don't," I mutter, watching as Jordan's head of dark hair disappears behind a group seated at the bar.

"Then why does he think he's some sort of sex god?"

I lift my shoulders and let them fall. "It's my fault. I never tell him that I'm not, you know…" I make a hand motion so I don't have to say it. Stars, that sounds ridiculous, and I brace myself for my sister to tell me exactly that. But after sex, Jordan and I snuggle and so, I dunno, I guess I've just never felt like bringing it up.

"It is absolutely not your fault," my sister says. "And succubi should never have bad sex."

"So I'm doing it wrong?"

"No, but obviously *he* is."

"I don't want to talk about this here," I tell her, heat creeping up my neck and into my cheeks and ears. My sister is a succubus through and through. Sex, as a topic, is always fair game with her, even if we are in public.

"Well, I'm not dropping the subject, Bliss. This is about your health *and* your happiness. I'm not just gonna ignore it."

"When we, you know—" I wave my hands, not able to bring myself to say the words out loud with other people potentially listening in, "—I still recharge my powers. It's fine."

"Barely," my sister counters immediately. "You barely charge them. It's like when you're starving and you only have a couple baby carrots as a snack. You're not nourishing yourself and you're certainly not *satisfying* yourself."

"Sometimes I..." I swallow and look around, seeing the rest of Amelia's band approaching. Our band, I correct myself. I am their manager, after all. I need to think like it.

"Sometimes you what?" Amelia prods.

I lean my elbow on the table, resting my cheek on my knuckles as I lower my voice. "Sometimes I satisfy myself afterwards, so it's fine," I rush to say before the others reach us.

"That doesn't recharge you, though," Amelia argues.

Taser takes a seat next to me in the booth and I shake my head at my sister, giving her a look that I hope sternly says we'll talk about this later

Taser bumps his shoulder into mine. "Oh, talking about recharging powers, are we? Please continue. I find the way succubi recharge *fascinating*," he says, grinning at Amelia and I.

Reese sits across from me, snorting out a laugh, and Tubbs, our drummer, gets into the booth from the other side, folding his lanky frame in next to Amelia and accidentally knocking the table with his knees.

He shakes his head at Taser, his short locs swinging slightly with the movement. I put my head in my hands with a groan and Taser laughs, slinging his arm around me. "Kidding, Bliss, kidding. We can talk about how I recharge instead." He picks up his Bloody Mary—with actual blood—and holds it out for us all to cheers.

"Let's *not* talk about that," Tubbs says, scrunching his face in disgust as he clinks his beer glass with Taser's. Some of his beer sloshes onto the sleeve of his dark blue henley. The color compliments his darker skin.

"I'll cheers to that," Reese says. I laugh and hold up my drink as well.

The Antler is packed tonight. We managed to snag a booth in the bar area upstairs. Progressive metal music streams from every speaker in the place and everyone looks like they're supposed to be here. No shortage of tattoos and black outfits. In fact, my eyes snag on any bit of color I do see. I glance down at my outfit, wishing, not for the first time, that I looked better in black. But I've never felt I could pull it off, so I always look a bit out of place with my sister's band, even though I've recently taken on the role of their band manger. Instead, I'm getting looks as the only one in the club wearing a pastel lavender top, jeans, and cute pink platforms. The white ribbon tying my hair into a high ponytail probably doesn't help.

"So Reese, how was that date you went on last weekend?" Amelia asks during a break in the conversation.

My best friend lets out a sigh. "Boring. I can't date non-kindreds anymore. It's so weird pretending fae and magic don't exist."

Taser grins at her. "Well, you know what they say, once you go fae..." He trails off with a shrug and winks, taking a sip of his beer.

Reese rolls her eyes. "Fae dicks are the same size as human dicks, just so we're clear."

Tubbs huffs out, like that couldn't possibly be the case, and Amelia, Reese, and I all exchange a knowing look.

"Dick size might be the same, but fae dicks have magical powers," Taser says, waggling his eyebrows.

"Bliss has always known that, that's why she's never felt the need to go anywhere else. Isn't that right, babe?" Jordan says, coming back with a beer in hand, a few of his friends trailing after him. "We're going to go grab a table over there. Come on, Bliss." He waits expectantly for me to get up and follow him.

"I'll be there in a minute. I wanna hang out with Reese."

Jordan lifts an eyebrow at me. He looks pointedly to Taser, who's sitting next to me, though not too close or anything. Jordan glares at him nonetheless.

"Come here, babe," he says to me again. I sigh and get up from the booth, trailing after him as he goes to sit with Jinx—his best friend, a kitsune with electric blue hair—and a few other guys. I avoid looking back Amelia's way, knowing she's giving me a look. Anger mixed with disappointment.

"Have you ever been to a Twisted Limbs show?" Jinx is asking one of the other guys.

Carter, a Born vampire who we went to college with, nods to me and Jordan as we sit down. "A couple times, actually. They're pretty good."

"They're average," Jordan responds. "Amelia keeps insisting we go to their shows because she's fucking their guitarist. I'm not sure what she sees in him." He nudges me as he laughs and I can see him stiffen when I don't laugh too.

"It's the blonde hair," I quickly joke, trying to keep things light. I add on a little laugh. He puts his arm around me and I lean into him, running my hand up over his other arm and smiling. I move in for a quick kiss.

He grins back at me and squeezes my shoulder. I wince a bit, but then his grip relaxes so I do as well. "Good thing you've got much better taste, huh, Bliss?" he teases, nipping at the spot on my neck that he bit into earlier. I had to use cover up to hide the bruises he left, since my power well isn't full enough to heal them on my own.

"Anyways, Twisted Limbs is a bit too old school for me. They're boring," Jinx says, glaring, though not at anyone in particular, I try to remind myself as his gaze meets mine. He breaks eye contact quickly, though, looking at Jordan, who's smirking in agreement.

"I dunno, I like that about them," Carter responds. "I'm excited to see them live."

I smile at Carter, who smiles back. "Me too. It's gonna be a good show."

I can feel Jordan's eyes on me, his grip tightening. But before our conversation can continue, Amelia's tall form appears to my left and I glance up at my sister. "We're gonna go backstage now and hang out a bit with the guys before the show starts. You coming?" She levels the question at me, completely ignoring Jordan, though I know she wants the whole band there to mingle and rub elbows with the other musicians. Her version of networking.

"Fine," Jordan mutters with a heavy sigh.

"We can hang out more with your friends if you want, babe," I say, throwing a pleading look at Amelia. She crosses her arms and waits expectantly with an eyebrow raised.

"It's fine." Jordan gets up out of the booth, pulling me along with him.

Amelia leads us backstage to a little area where Twisted Limbs and their crew are waiting before the opening band goes on in about thirty minutes.

Jordan takes my hand in his, but his eyes aren't on me. They're scoping out all the musicians around us.

Amelia spots Blake and flings herself around him, peppering him with kisses on his face. "Hey!" she says. "We wanted to wish you good luck. You better play my favorite song, or I'll never sleep with you ever again." She winks at him and Blake laughs.

"You heard her, boys. We better alter that set list or I'll be missing out for the rest of my life."

Amelia grins at him and he gives her a quick kiss on the cheek. They've never dated, but he's probably the closest thing Amelia's ever had to a relationship.

He smiles over at me. "Hey, Bliss, loving the pastels."

"Thanks," I say, looking down at my outfit, then smiling back at him. "Good luck up there. Not that you need it," I add. Jordan grips my hand hard. I wince and look up at him. "You're hurting me," I whisper to him. I wave apologetically to Blake and Amelia as I tug Jordan off to the side.

"Why does he always flirt with you?" Jordan mutters under his breath.

"What?" I look up at him in surprise. "He's not. He's just being nice."

"He wants to get in your tight slutty succubus pants." Jordan rolls his eyes and lets go of my hand. "I'm gonna go find Jinx."

He heads off in search of his friends, leaving me to stare after him, going over my interaction with Blake. He just complimented my outfit and I wished him good luck. Did I use a flirty tone? I don't think I did. I sigh and make a mental note to make sure next time I don't accidentally flirt with anyone.

I shoot one last lingering look at Jordan's back as he opens the door leading out of the backstage area. It slams shut and my shoulders droop, but I don't follow him. Best to let him cool off. I'll make sure to show him how much I care about him later. Turning back around, I spot Taser and I head towards him, standing awkwardly next to him as he exchanges banter with Blake.

I half listen in on the conversation, my mind wandering, bouncing between how to make things right with Jordan and how I don't really know what I'm doing back here. I'm not a musician, not really. I can play a few things on the piano but not super well. As Taser and Blake are discussing what guitar to upgrade to next, I'm reminded of how much I don't really fit in anywhere, despite being Goddess' Trance's manager. I rock a bit back and forth on my heels, my eyes roaming around the backstage area. Blake's band is scattered, some just talking, some checking over their equipment. Amelia is chatting with their drummer, Reese, and Tubbs.

I look over to the corner closer to stage left and see four guys standing a bit further away from everyone else. They're all masked and I wonder how I'm just now noticing them. Three of them wear black, structured masks, made out of dense embroidered fabric. There are no eye holes, giving the impression that the men can't see through them. A pair of golden, skeletal fingers wrap around the masks, like someone long dead is covering their eyes. Those same three wear all black, except for the tallest one. A rainbow scrunchie decorates his left wrist.

The fourth guy is wearing a lacy, black, hooded robe that's open to reveal his torso, which is painted in a blueish black grease paint. Something iridescent smatters his skin in patches. They shimmer in the light, like black scales. His face is covered by an intricate black metal mask. Skeletal fingers also cover his eyes, but instead of gold they look to be made out of mother-of-pearl. His hood casts the top of his mask in shadow. As I look closer, I see all the members have that same black grease paint on all exposed skin.

I try not to stare at them too much, but I can't really help it. They're whispering to each other, though the one with the more elaborate costume seems just to be standing there, only looking at the others every once in a while. He's angled slightly towards them, but he keeps his head down. I wonder if his mask is heavy.

I tug on Taser's sleeve, interrupting his conversation with Blake. Nodding towards them, I ask, "Who are they?"

Taser follows my gaze and leans in to be heard over the rest of the conversations around us. "That's Voracious Maw. Kind of up and coming. I think they're from the UK. Blake met them last year after some festival and asked them to open for a few shows here. They only use stage names. The one with the unique mask is Wrath. The taller guy is Eerie, their bassist. The shortest of them— that's Mist, the drummer. And the guitarist is Poison."

"What's with the costumes?" It wasn't unheard of in this genre, but something about theirs intrigues me.

"They're probably all really fucking ugly," Jordan says from behind me, making me jump. I didn't realize he'd come back. He runs his hand up the back of my neck. "Why else hide?"

I cringe at his touch, his words poking at an anger I don't usually have. "Maybe they're all really good-looking and don't want people to judge them solely on their looks." I try to sound indifferent, but my voice just comes out whiny and defensive.

"Yeah right, sure." Jordan takes my hand and tugs me towards him. "Let's go get a good spot to watch the freak show that's about to play." He steers me out of the backstage area before I can say goodbye to anyone. I glance back, hoping to catch Amelia or Reese's attention so they know where to find me, but instead my eyes snag on the guy in the hooded robe. He's looking my way, at least it feels like he is.

I can't see his eyes behind his mask, so there's no sure way to tell.

"Ladies and Gentlemen, Voracious Maw." My head turns to the stage as one of the venue staff walks away from the center microphone stand. Amelia and the rest of our band find me just as the lights dim and a hush goes through the crowd.

Taser slings his arm around Jinx, who's standing behind Jordan and me, thankfully shielding my short frame from any potential mosh pits that might start up behind us. We're close to the stage, so I can see just fine, which is nice. But I'm prepared to duck out if things get too crazy.

A few claps go around the crowd as some of the stage lights start up, but mostly everyone just kind of waits to see if the opening band is any good. I feel a shiver go up my arms as the hooded frontman makes his way to the center microphone, followed out by the rest of the guys. The one with the rainbow scrunchie goes to stage right and picks up his bass. He looks over to the guitarist, who nods and plays a single note. The lead begins singing.

His voice is softer than I would have expected, and he sings the first song in falsetto. The drums, guitar, bass, and piano are all very minimal. I look around the crowd. Everyone's pretty quiet, as if we're all collectively waiting for the music to get a bit heavier. The lyrics make me shiver, though, and Amelia looks over at me, nodding her head in approval. "This is a fucking sexy song!" she whisper yells at me.

And then just as the crowd is lulled into thinking this is a soft melodic song, the drums start to pick up, almost unnoticeable at first. The guitarist comes in with heavy strokes, adding a bit of a grungy feel to the song as the drums get even heavier and faster. The lead paces up and down the stage as he waits for his next verse. And as the drums and guitar quiet back down, he returns to the microphone, continuing to serenade the crowd.

"How is he singing that well with that fucking mask, bro?" Taser asks Tubbs. We all smile at each other, because literally how is he doing that? Dericia holds out her arm to me, her sleeve pushed up to reveal chills going up her arm. We beam at each other.

As the first song wraps up with some heavy guitar riffs and the full-bodied drums, the crowd is hooked, but I can tell by their body language, the band doesn't realize it yet. They almost seem nervous as the first song ends and they look around at each other a bit before beginning the next one.

The drummer starts the song off and the lead sings, his full baritone coming out in this song. It's more fast-paced than the previous one, the depth and body of the drums being fully showcased. The crowd is definitely more engaged now, really getting into the show as the guitarist starts in on a new riff. People are starting to throw up horns. I might be one of them.

It's the fifth song that sends shivers and goose bumps up my arms, and if anyone in the crowd wasn't impressed by this new band, they are now.

The lead takes a quick drink of water as the song starts and drops the plastic bottle on the stage floor. His movements are awkward and jerky, and even though their performance has been amazing, part of me wonders if he's drunk.

This song is more violent, the lyrics about being pierced through the chest, clawed into by something or someone. But also how he wants to find his way back to someone. The song is full of rage and yet somehow sensual, and I can't wrench my eyes away.

The lead wraps the cord of the microphone around the guitarist's neck, pulling it tight, and I can hear a slight wisp of a chuckle in his singing. The guitarist falls to his knees, still playing, and the cord falls away. The crowd eats it up, cheering.

There's a break in the lyrics and the lead begins pacing up and down the stage again, and as the guitar solo gets even heavier, he starts jumping and thrashing around as if he's in a solo mosh pit. His hands keep going to his mask, maybe to check that it hasn't budged, or maybe because he can feel it moving around. It looks heavy enough that it weighs on him and he doesn't have full range of motion with it on.

"That was definitely the best song they played all night," Jordan whispers into my ear, rubbing up against me from behind. I can feel he's hard as a rock. "Maybe we should find our way to a bathroom."

He wraps his arms around me, his hand drifting down to my pelvic region. I swat his hand away.

"What the hell is the matter with you, Bliss?" he asks, gripping my waist hard.

"We're in public," I say back, trying to be heard over the music.

"You're a succubus, Bliss. Maybe you should start acting like one."

My whole body goes rigid. What the fuck is that supposed to mean?

Despite loving the music of the opening band, by the time the main act goes up on stage, I'm getting tired of keeping a content fake smile on my face and wanting to go home so badly I'm about to call a ride for myself and leave Jordan here. But somehow I make it through the rest of the show, doing my best not to let anyone know that all I want to do right now is cry.

CHAPTER EIGHT

BLISS

My phone buzzes with a text from Amelia assuring me that this meeting is going to go well. They're going to tell me exactly what she has been telling me since yesterday, which is that I have nothing to worry about. My bond *was* activated and the stone just had a bit too much excess energy.

I don't reply, sliding my phone back into the pocket of my jeans.

I don't believe her words, and even though I've seen her twice since the night Taser healed me, she hasn't said a single thing about him cheating. I can't believe she's trying to keep this a secret, but I push that out of my mind for now. I have much bigger issues.

Liz stands next to me as we face the committee head. She's the same water nymph from the ceremony, long blonde hair styled perfectly in a low, neat bun. A sea salt scent, combined elegantly with a floral perfume, wafts from her.

"I'm so glad you were able to meet with us today, Ms. Rassard," the nymph says, looking me over. She motions for Liz and I to take seats across from her in the formal ornate sitting room. My aunt and I sit in matching antique upholstered chairs, a side table between us boasting a huge bouquet of expensive looking flowers.

"My name is Tessa Bridgely," she explains to me. "I'm the head of the Bond Committee, and I want to assure you both—" she glances at my aunt, "—that we're looking into the unfortunate accident with the activation stone very seriously."

I hide a smile behind my hand, flashing a look at Liz. Does the committee think we're going to sue them? Or is Liz's badass reputation just that widespread in the committee? I wonder if Liz and Bridgely have ever crossed paths before, when Liz used to work here.

"The stone does appear to be in working order, though," Tessa continues, a frown forming on her face.

"What does that mean?" Liz asks.

I look around the room, allowing my aunt to take the lead. The windows in here are closed and look like they don't actually open, which really sucks because the air is becoming hotter and more stifling, though maybe it's just me. I already know what all this means, and I can tell by the expression on Tessa's face that if it's not the stone's fault, then it's mine.

I focus on the window that overlooks the fae district located just west of the Kensington Gardens in London. Liz and I got up at an un-starly hour to travel via portal to arrive here just before noon. I stifle a yawn as I force my eyes from the park beyond the fae council's estate and refocus on the conversation.

"Well, we're unsure," Bridgely says diplomatically, clearly not wanting to come right out and blame me. I fight back a harsh laugh. "We'd like to have Bliss try again."

My eyes snap to hers. "Why? So it can burn me again?"

"Well, as far as we can tell, even despite the mishap, your bond should still be active."

"So touching it again would prove what? That it worked the first time?"

"Yes. If there's no reaction, then it's very likely the bond has already been activated, and whatever reaction the stone had to you, or you had to it, is something else. To those of us with our bonds already in place, the stone feels cold."

"And if it happens again?" Liz asks, glancing at my healed hand.

"Then the committee shall continue our investigation to see if there is something specific interfering with the magic, or if there is something unique about Bliss that is preventing her bond from activating."

"Something could be interfering?" A small hope starts to blossom that perhaps it's not something wrong with me after all.

"I've seen a few hexes placed on fae over the years to prevent them from finding their mates, though never a successful one, mind you. They usually backfire on the fae casting them, but it's possible someone tampered with you. Have you any idea of someone who would want to prevent you from finding your mate? A jealous boyfriend, or ex, perhaps?"

I exchange glances with Liz but shake my head. "No, nothing like that," I lie.

Jordan. I guess I wouldn't put something like that past him. But I haven't seen him in years, so it doesn't make a ton of sense. Though he always used to say that if we weren't bonded, that he'd kill my mate so he could keep me to himself. At the time, I hadn't thought he would *actually* do that. It was just something he was saying because he loved me so much. It had sounded romantic. Now I see it clearly for what it was.

"Could the stone have been tampered with?" Liz proposes instead, but she throws me an odd look, like she's not sure why I would have lied. She knows my history with him and I have a feeling she's thinking just how stupid it is not to mention him. But my aunt isn't like Amelia. She'll only bring it up if she knows I'm comfortable with it.

But I'm not. The thought of any sort of investigation reeling him back into my life makes my body physically freeze up.

Tessa gives a small shake of her head. "Absolutely not. It's kept under tight lock and key. Only I and a few other fae have access to it. It's only taken out during ceremonies and it's under guard while out."

I nod. "Okay, well, let's get this over with, I guess."

Tessa ushers us out into the hallway, where we follow her to a small but equally ornate viewing room. Two fae guard the stone, which sits atop a pillar like the one from the ceremony. It looks like it did before, a soft glow coming from within it, and the flames from the sconces along the wall flicker in the reflection.

"The enchantment that readies the stone has already been cast. You may reach out and place your palm on the stone."

Like I'm ripping off a Band-Aid, this time I don't hesitate, reaching out my palm to the surface of the stone. My eyes squeeze shut as I brace myself to be thrown backwards.

But all I feel is a cold glass surface underneath my palm. I open one eye and then the other and look around from my aunt to the other fae in the room. "Well?" I ask, keeping my hand where it is.

"Does it feel cold?" Liz asks, and I nod in reply.

Tessa makes a non-committal noise in her throat and looks to the fae standing beside her. He shrugs. "Well, it appears that your bond must have been activated. We will continue digging into what caused the excess energy discharge."

I take my hand off the stone and brace myself again to ask the question that's been slowly eating away at me. "Aren't you ignoring a possible explanation?" I ask.

"Such as?"

"That I have no bond?"

The fae in the room, including my aunt, all exchange shocked glances, like I've just uttered a gross expletive.

"Bliss, that's not possible," my aunt says, coming to place her hand on my shoulder. "Not all fae find their bond in their lifetime, it's true, but every fae has a bond."

"Not Made fae." It comes out before I can stop myself. I know I'm not a Made fae, but what if there are also some Born fae that don't have bonds? "What I mean is, isn't it possible that some Born fae don't bond either?"

"Impossible," the fae standing behind Tessa mutters. The sharp canines give him away as a vampire.

"There is no record of a Born fae not having a bond," Tessa says firmly. "Yours has been activated. There is some other explanation as to why the stone behaved the way it did." She speaks matter-of-factly, and it seems like it's the end of discussion.

But I don't budge, even as Tessa indicates we should follow her out of the room. "How can you be sure it's activated?"

Tessa pauses, looking thoughtfully at me for a moment. "There are a few more tests we could do. One of them would be a spell that will essentially tug on your bond. If we tug and it gives too easily, then it could be that your bond isn't attached to anything, and that would point to it being un-activated, but if we can pull it taut, then there's someone on the other side of it."

"Well, let's do that," I say, the words spilling out of me. I *need* to know. I want the false hope that I have a mate squashed before my mind can carry my heart away into a fake future of joy and happiness only for it to shatter. I don't think my heart can take that.

"It's not quite that simple," Tessa hedges. She clears her throat. "The spell can be quite painful. Not for you—for your mate."

"Oh," I say, my shoulders slumping. I don't want to cause anyone harm, least of all my maybe not real mate.

"It's not something that he won't recover from," Tessa explains. "We should still try it. I just want you to understand that it's a possibility."

Liz puts an arm around me. "It's alright, Bliss. You'll be able to apologize for it as soon as you meet him."

"Doesn't sound like a great way to start off our relationship," I mumble. "But he might not even exist so, yeah." I wave my hand in the air, indicating we should get on with the spell.

Tessa nods to the vampire behind her, who leaves the room, presumably to gather whatever materials the spell requires.

About ten minutes later, the vampire returns and he and Tessa get to work erecting a circle around me. I sit on the cold marble floor, inside a ring of crushed up rose quartz, candles spaced evenly around the circle. A book lays open in Tessa's hands. The vampire places a black tourmaline stone right in front of me and steps gently outside the round of crushed stone, careful not to mar the shape of it.

"Place your hands like this," Tessa instructs, holding out the book to me with an illustration of a fae placing both hands flat on the center of their chest. I mimic the position and Tessa nods. "Let's begin."

She speaks in the same old fae language that the ceremony was in, reciting whatever incantation is in the book she holds. Her words wash over me and I feel a sensation crawl up from the floor around me, slithering to my heart and then somehow going into me, but also beyond me as it searches for my bond. I imagine some sort of spiritual snake made of ether traveling along my bond, searching for the perfect place to tug.

It doesn't take long for the snake to find it.

I breathe in harshly, gulping down air as it feels like my breath has been snatched away from me completely. I don't feel pain, but I feel where the snake has pierced its fangs into my bond, slithering with all its might backwards towards me.

But instead of the bond coming flying backwards as if it's not attached to anything at all, the snake's fangs are ripped out almost immediately, the bond completely taut, absolutely no give in it whatsoever.

I can hear Tessa draw in a sharp inhale.

I open my eyes as soon as I feel the snake hastily slither back from wherever it was called from.

"What just happened?" I glance from Liz to Tessa to the vampire, who looks on at us stoically.

"The bond—it was as if it was made of concrete, immovable," Tessa says, her confusion making me apprehensive.

"And that's a good thing, right?" Liz asks. "That means it's attached to something."

Tessa doesn't answer her right away, looking between us.

"Do I have a bondmate or not?" My voice comes out harsher than I intend it.

Tessa takes a deep breath, and I feel bad, realizing that spell must have used up a significant amount of her power.

"I'm sorry, but the spell is inconclusive. I've never felt a bond like that."

Tears threaten to spill down my cheeks, but I clamp down on the despair that's trying to spread through my body. I can cry when I'm home, alone in my bed. I just need to make it there first.

"Thank you for trying," I manage to get out. I run from the room, the tears forcing their way out despite my best efforts.

I hear Liz running behind me, calling my name.

Somehow, despite my blurred vision, I make it to the wide front steps of the fae council building. Hurrying off to the side so at least I'm less noticeable to anyone coming and going, I let the tears stream steadily down my face, no sign of letting up anytime soon.

Liz holds me as I cry.

"It's so stupid," I finally say, not sure I'm even talking to Liz, or if I'm addressing the stars that are hiding behind the bright blue afternoon sky like the cowards they are. "Before the activation ceremony I didn't want to meet my mate. I was worried he wouldn't like me. And now, I don't even know if I have one. What if because I didn't want to meet him, the stars took my bond away?" I sob harder as that idea takes root in my mind. What if this isn't something that was done to me, but something I did?

"Bliss," Liz says softly. "You don't know any of that is true. Just because Tessa Bridgely hasn't seen a bond like yours doesn't make it a *bad thing*. Maybe yours is just special and unique."

A half-laugh, half-sob escapes me. "How can you be so optimistic?"

She squeezes me tight and smooths a hand down my hair, careful not to mess up my ribbon that's pulling the top half of my hair out of my face. She gives it a gentle little tug, though.

"Your mother started putting ribbons in your hair the day you were born, did you know that?"

I wipe the tears from my cheeks, though new ones are still forming rapidly to take their place. I look up at my aunt. "Really?"

She nods, a smile lighting up her face. "You were born with a full head of hair. And your mother couldn't help but play with it.

Amelia and your dad had gone out to get your mother a gift. She'd been in labor for hours and hours and they wanted to get her something nice. And there was a beautiful pink ribbon on the gift wrapping. Before Charlotte finished opening her gift, she took the ribbon and tied your hair up in it. We still have the pictures somewhere. I'll find them for you when we get home, okay?"

I nod, a smile tugging at my lips. I don't remember my mother well—or my father. They died when I was five. And Liz—at only eighteen—has raised Amelia and I since. But one of the few memories I do have of my mom is her putting ribbons in my hair each day.

When I started high school, I was made fun of a lot. Not for any specific reason, just that kids were mean. I started wearing ribbons again to remind myself that I had been loved, that I had been cherished, even if most days it didn't feel that way.

Sure, it gave the other kids another thing to tease me about, but it also gave me the strength to endure it better.

Liz runs her fingers over the end of my ribbon and looks up at the sky. "This is how I can be so optimistic. Because I know your mother is up there with the stars, and she'd be giving them hell if they ever dared mess with you like that."

My smile widens at the thought. I breathe out a sigh, the tears finally coming to an end. "So what now? I'm just supposed to wait around?" I ask after a few moments of us sitting there, Liz's arms still locked around me in a tight hug.

"No," Liz says, her eyes going a bit misty. I squeeze her back, knowing her thoughts are going to when she met her mate. They were perfect together. One of those love stories I always heard about growing up, where two fae who were already dating get their bonds activated only to find out they're mates, like the stars just couldn't wait any longer to push them together. I grew up hoping to find what they had. "You don't wait around, Bliss. You live. You follow your joy and that joy is what leads you to him and he to you. It's like a beacon."

"I don't know what my joy is, though, which I suppose is ironic,"

I say, laughing a bit. There's also a twinge of guilt. My uncle died only a year after they bonded. Liz has way more reason to curse the stars than I do, and yet here she is, one of the most positive and happiest people in my life.

"Bliss, your name is perfect for you. Just let it be a reminder, okay?"

I can only nod, and we sit there as finally my tears dry up. My mate is out there, supposedly, and all I have to do is be happy.

Why does that sound so hard?

I duck into the restroom just inside the lobby of the council building to freshen up and try to make it look like I haven't just been bawling my eyes out.

My red and puffy face looks back at me in the mirror and I sigh. There's not much I can do about that, but at least Liz and I are going to head straight home. I roll my shoulders and with one last look at myself, I head out, finding Liz in conversation about hexes with a middle-aged fae.

"I've never seen anything like it. The materials aren't typical and the magical signature isn't something we've encountered before."

The man bears a quizzical expression that's almost comical. Liz reaches out and pats his arm, giving me an apologetic look. "I suppose I can take a quick look." She turns to me. "Bliss, this is Randy Urvine, my old boss. There's something he'd like my opinion on."

Randy turns his pleading eyes to me. "You wouldn't mind, would you? It'll be quick."

I smile at him. "Sure, no problem."

"Wonderful, that's wonderful!" he says, brightening up significantly. "If you head down that hallway, it connects to the Lyra Estate. The portal is open and there's a party for recently activated fae just like yourself. They're having food and drinks. You are most welcome to wait there for your aunt."

I nod at his rambling. Liz promises she won't be long and she'll come find me.

I head down the hall, seeing the familiar purple glow of a portal at the end. Through the portal I can see bits of another hallway that almost seem identical to this one. I step through, mindful of a rather large piece of azkanite jutting out from the right angle of the door, purple particles evaporating off it. On the other side, I find myself in much the same style of building, though the decor here is more ornate.

Ostentatious, really.

Classical music wafts its way to my ears and I follow it and the scent of warm, freshly cooked food. As I pass through another of the many hallways, I try to note certain things about it so I can find my way back to the portal if need be. In case Liz gets too caught up in her old work.

I pass an opening that leads down another shorter hallway and take a quick peek. I realize I should definitely keep going straight. Three males are all standing around a fae who's propped up against the wall. Probably had too much to drink.

Fae make their drinks *strong*.

I continue straight, the hallway opening up to a large banquet room. The tables set up are fancier than necessary. Gold-lined china plates and crystal stemware decorate the tables, and each centerpiece is a flower arrangement bigger than my head with lots of lavender and purple flowers of all kinds.

The buffet table is equally as fancy, with golden serving tongs and the most exquisite smelling food. My stomach growls as I approach it, picking up one of the nice plates and reminding myself over and over again not to even think about dropping one of these plates. It probably costs more than a week's pay at my job.

Not that money is too much of an issue for me. But I still wouldn't want to destroy such a nice thing.

I pick a few things off the buffet table, placing them gently on the plate, and turn around to scan for a place to sit quietly and eat.

"I'd steer clear of that mini quiche, if I were you," someone to my right says. I look up and see a tall, dark-haired fae with an almost eerie set of blue eyes, with a hint of violet.

Runeless eyes.

Again.

"You've got your bond activated, then?" the stranger asks.

"What?"

"You've got the look all recently activated fae get. The prolonged eye contact as you search for runes gives you away."

A blush ripples underneath my skin, and I look away. "Sorry," I mutter.

"It's hardly your fault. You're all so eager to find your mates. I think it's nice."

I glance back at him. He's smiling kindly and I feel a bit of easiness creep back into me. I let out a little laugh. "It's a bit pathetic, though, isn't it?"

"Maybe a little. But aren't we all?"

My smile widens. "So no mini quiches?"

"No, they're burnt on the inside, if you can imagine."

I pick mine up and examine it, pulling it apart, and sure enough, the inside is somehow blackened. "Some sort of English fae delicacy?" I ask.

The stranger winks at me. He nods over to an empty spot on the wall where we can chat out of the way of the buffet table.

"I'm Bliss," I say, extending my hand. He takes it and instead of shaking it, places a kiss on top of it.

"Dylan," he replies, letting my hand drop.

"Have you found your bondmate?" I ask, my eyes going to his again. Fae can't see the runes of another bonded pair, but I still look intently as if I could.

"No, I'm unfortunately not so lucky."

I nod in agreement, but I don't say anything about my weird bond. I don't think I could take the pity he'd likely offer.

I'm about to ask what brought him to this party when a familiar howl of laughter pierces into me. My back goes ramrod straight, and the plate falls out of my hands, smashing to the ground. My fingers and toes have gone almost numb. Everyone's eyes fall to me and Dylan as a cater waiter rushes forward and cleans it up.

"Very sorry, friend, she just took a bite of the mini quiche," Dylan says to the waiter, who nods, despite wearing a baffled expression.

Dylan steers me out of the room and down a hallway as I search for Jordan. I know that laugh. He's here, somewhere. "I need to go." I pull Dylan to a stop. "Sorry, I need to get out of here."

"He's not your mate," Dylan says lowly. His voice has changed, but I can't quite put my finger on the difference.

I turn around, catching that his expression has shifted from friendly to… bored? No. That's not it. The hair on the back of my neck prickles. "What?" I take a small step backwards.

"Your ex, he's not your mate." My eyes narrow as I place the shift in tone. The earlier ease and kindness have disappeared from his voice.

"How do you know who my ex is?" I take another step back, watching him warily.

Dylan doesn't move, just cocks his head at me. "Tell me, Bliss. Do you enjoy being a succubus?"

My shoulders tense. It's not entirely crazy that he'd clock my species. Succubi don't have distinguishing markers like warlocks and vampires, but sometimes our scent gives us away to an experienced fae. Other succubi have always smelled rich and warm to me, but in slightly different ways. How the hell does this guy know about Jordan, though?

"Are you a friend of his?"

Dylan looks off the way we came, where Jordan no doubt is enjoying the party. I should have assumed he'd be here. His family has amazing connections within the fae council and this is a party held for all fae in this prestigious circle. "I am offended you would think such a thing. No, I am not."

My brows raise. "How do you know he's my ex?"

Dylan leans against the wall, glancing further down the hallway. "Unimportant. Now, answer my question, if you would be so kind." His almost violet eyes narrow on me.

"Why do you care?" My feet shuffle backwards and I look over my shoulder, readying to bolt out of this hallway.

"I wouldn't."

I freeze in my tracks, but not of my own accord. It's like something is physically wrapped around my feet, but there's nothing there.

"Fine," he continues, "I won't waste either of our time. I think I have something you might like. And I'm willing to offer it to you for a very simple exchange."

"And what is that?" I ask. "What do you think I want?"

He smiles, but it doesn't reach his eyes. "Your mate." He lifts off the wall, coming to stand in front of me. "And I think when you are alone and can be completely honest with yourself…" He trails off as he leans down to be somewhat eye level with me. "I think you wish you could be anything other than a succubus."

I stay silent. Of course I want my mate. But how does this guy know I've fantasized about being anything *but* a succubus?

I've thought countless times about what it would be like to be a wolf shifter, or an elemental fae. A water nymph has always sounded appealing. But succubi are constantly treated less than, as sexual objects, or as sluts by other fae. So was it really a leap that a stranger might clue into that?

"So you're good at reading people," I fire back defensively. "It's not like you have any control over those things." I want to run. I want to leave this hallway, but my feet won't budge. What type of magic is he using on me? He hasn't muttered any incantation, nor used any potion that I can see. If he was an incubus, or a wolf shifter using his command, I would have felt his magic influencing me. And fae compulsion only works on non-kindred humans.

His smile grows until I can see his sharp canines. "Oh but I do,

Bliss. Your bond is encased in strong magic that cannot be broken through. Without my help you will not find your mate."

How could he possibly know that? "Did Bridgely tell you that?"

He cocks his head again, his brow arching in confusion. But something tells me it's forced, that his face isn't used to making any expressions at all. "Bridgely?"

"So what? You were listening in?" An image of this dark-haired tall fae standing outside the room Bridgely performed the ritual in, with his ear pressed against the door, pops into my head, but it's all wrong. He doesn't seem like the type to need to do that somehow.

"I can *see* it." He places a hand on my shoulder. The sensation is odd, like I can only feel the ghost of his touch. "Bliss, can you tell me what type of fae I am?"

I look him up and down and pull in a deep breath through my nose, trying to find a hint of something that'll give it away. "No."

"Because I'm not one." He blinks and in a second his almost violet eyes are deep red.

I shrug his hand off and try to scramble back, but I still can't move. I open my mouth to shout, but he wags a finger at me and suddenly I can't make a sound.

"We still have much to discuss, Bliss." He steps back, and with a wave of his hand a plush upholstered bench appears. Without willing to, I take a seat and he sits beside me. "I can help you. I can break apart the magic so you can find your mate. *And*, I can transform you into any type of fae you wish."

He waves his hand again and suddenly I have my voice back. "And what? I just have to sell you my soul?"

"Wraiths don't deal in souls that way, Bliss," he says with a slight frown, as if he's disappointed I don't know that. "All I need is for you to collect something for me."

I raise my brows at him. "Oh, is that all? And this something, would it be, oh say, I don't know… illegal?" I try to get my legs to stand up, but they won't. I sit back, crossing my arms and scowling at the wraith, attempting to act as if my heart isn't hammering in my chest. A wraith? I've heard rumors that fae sometimes still summon them. That even after the fae council banished them, they found ways back into this realm. I never knew if I believed that or not, but I guess now I have proof. And if everything I know about wraiths is true, I need to get the hell out of here.

He seems to know where my thoughts have gone. "No harm shall come to you at my hands, Bliss." He unbuttons the middle button on his shirt jacket and relaxes back into the bench more. "If you agree, you can have everything you've ever wanted. Being a water nymph would suit you. You and your bond can retire to some coastal town together and you'd never need to be powerless a day in your life."

Since I'm stuck here, I allow my curiosity to run away from me, distracting me from my fear and helping me bide my time until he releases me. "And what would I need to collect?"

He holds up a finger. "That I cannot tell you just yet. But I can tell you who you'd need to collect it from."

"It sounds an awful lot like I'd need to steal something illegal from someone."

A grin teases his lips again. "Not illegal. Something powerful. Something he will willingly part from, I think."

"He?"

His grin widens. "Wrath."

"Wrath?" *Wrath*? He doesn't mean— "You mean Wrath from Voracious Maw?"

Dylan—if that's even his name—nods. "The one and only."

"Why?"

"He has something I need. And I think you're the perfect person to get it." What does that mean?

I shake my head. If I say no, am I even walking out of this hallway? "Why don't you steal it?" Yeah, why doesn't he? A wraith this powerful, it shouldn't be a problem.

"All will be revealed in time, Bliss."

"The fuck it will. I'm not doing it. Besides, you want me to steal something from a guy in an anonymous band? Unless you know his identity, how would I even get close enough?"

Dylan's small grin grows wider and he leans in as if he's sharing a secret. "This is exactly why you're perfect for it. Voracious Maw will be at the Alchemy Festival. It's the perfect place to rub elbows with other bands. And I know of just the band. Goddess' Trance. You can resume your position as their manager. It'll give you all the access you need to meet Wrath and get close enough to him to get what I need."

I notice the wraith has loosened up his magic on my legs, so I stand up. "Well, sorry to let you down, but I'm not on speaking terms with my sister. Too bad. You'll have to find someone else." It's not totally a lie. I'm mad at her and ignoring her texts, at least for the day.

"Hmm," the wraith mutters, standing with me. "No, that is not ideal. I'd suggest you get back on speaking terms, then."

"I haven't agreed to this, remember? Besides, my sister's band isn't even going to that festival."

"Don't worry about that part," Dylan says with a wave of his hand. "Take a day, think it over." The bench we sat on disappears and the wraith walks down the hall, opposite to the way the festivities are being held. "But Bliss, if you think the fae council will be able to fix your bond, you're sorely mistaken. They do not care about your bond. And even if they did, the magic affixed to your bond is stronger than they know how to deal with."

"How do I know you're not the one interfering?"

He shrugs. "I am not. But if I was, then maybe it would be wise to accept my bargain."

With that he vanishes from sight, leaving the hallway empty aside from me. Oddly, every picture, every vase, every piece of overly expensive ornamentation that decorated the hallway is also gone. Has he taken it all with him?

"Bliss?" Liz's voice calls from the other direction. I spin around, seeing my aunt and a man with graying hair walk into the now empty hallway. It's almost as if the wraith knew they'd be approaching.

Liz and I meet in the middle. "You ready to go home?" she asks me. I nod, not trusting myself to speak just yet. The man turns this way and that as his eyes take in everything missing from the space.

"What the bloody hell?" the man splutters, looking at me. "Where did all the furniture and decor go?"

Liz throws him a glare. "What do you mean?"

"There were paintings and side tables. Vases." He spins around and walks a few steps down the hall, as if he could view the hallway from a different angle and all would be back in its place.

I shrug. "I don't know. I was just looking for my aunt."

He looks to Liz. "This is Charlotte's daughter, then?"

"Her youngest," Liz replies with a nod.

He huffs and nods. "Very well," he says with a cursory glance at me. With unfortunate timing, a waiter picks that moment to walk down the hallway. The gray-haired male reaches out, snagging the waiter by the collar, his tray going flying and the food crashing to the floor. He spins the waiter around, his hand now on the back of his neck. "Notice anything unusual?" he asks, his voice laced with seething anger.

"Yves," Liz warns, putting herself between me and the male. So this is Yves Lyra, the head of the council. "Do you really think a waiter has had the time or the ability to rob a hallway while they've been shuttling food back and forth?"

Lyra turns his face back towards us. "He must have seen something. Well, boy? Did you see who was taking my property?"

The waiter, looking like he's about to pee himself, shakes his head. "Everything was just here the last time I came this way. I swear."

Lyra releases his grip on the waiter, who takes a shaky step backwards. "Go find me your manager, and clean this shit up." The waiter nods and runs out of the hallway. Lyra stalks off without so much as a goodbye, shouting for someone else about the missing decor.

Liz takes my hand and leads me out of the hallway, shaking her head. "What the hell was that?" I ask.

"Yves Lyra," she replies, as if that explains everything. We walk back towards the portal that leads to the fae council building. "Best to stay off his radar. He's a purist and not a big fan of succubi."

"Why?"

"Well, the purist part—because he's an ass and was raised by asses. The succubi part—rumor has it when he was younger, he asked your mother out and she rejected him."

"Sounds like a fucking prick," I mutter. I can't help but wonder how my mother ever crossed paths with him.

"He really is," Liz says with a sigh. We reach the hallway portal and she motions for me to go through first. We find our way back to the first portal we used to get here. When we come out on the other side, we're back in the Starlight District and the bright afternoon sun has been replaced by early morning darkness.

CHAPTER NINE

BLISS

THE TINKLE OF THE BELL ON LIZ'S SHOP'S DOOR SOUNDS AS I PUSH the door open, letting it swing shut behind me. I'm instantly lured into a sense of calm at the earthy musk of incense burning and the relaxing meditation music being played. Dericia glances up at me from the front counter, a grin coming to her face quickly.

"To what do I owe this pleasure? Twice in one week?" Reese asks, as she comes around the counter and hugs me. She holds me extra tight and I relish in the comforting feel.

"Liz said she restocked the Hair B Gone, so I stopped by to grab some."

Reese laughs, eyeing my hair that's braided into two plaits, both with white ribbons at the end. "Not for your scalp, correct?"

I match her laugh. "I'm not feeling quite that adventurous right now. Can I get the one with the built-in color guard?"

Dericia rummages through the shelves behind the counter, grabbing a pink lotion bottle and handing it to me. It's a spelled lotion that once applied, starts working to remove unwanted hair. It's super quick and the hair takes a while to grow back, so it's better than waxing, shaving, or laser.

Liz had been making this lotion for years before she ever

opened her shop. I *may* have been the reason she's added a bright orange color guard. It's now super obvious where it's been applied, and if washed off quickly enough, it won't take any hair with it.

"Anything else?" Reese asks in an over-the-top sweet customer service voice.

I laugh and take the bag Reese hands me with the lotion in it. "I also wanted to see if you were gonna be closing up shop soon?" I ask tentatively. After our night out, I really realized just how much I hated not seeing her and Amelia regularly, but since I'm still pissed at Amelia, I think a one-on-one hangout with my best friend is just what I need.

Not to mention I very much need to take my mind off the wraith's offer and my abnormal bond.

Of course I'm not going to go through with the deal.

Even if I can't stop thinking about what it would be like to have what the wraith is offering.

"I was just about to," Reese replies. "But then I'm gonna walk up the block to that craft store. I want to bedazzle my bass. Come with?"

"Sure." I nod, grinning as I imagine Reese holding her black bass covered in pink and purple rhinestones. I quirk my brows at her. "That doesn't sound like it'd be your taste, though."

"Black rhinestones," Reese says, as if reading my mind. "I just want a bit of glitter and glitz, ya know?"

I nod. "Okay, that I can see."

Dericia grabs her bag and turns over the open sign to closed, locking the door. We head up the block to the craft store, grabbing her a magical bedazzler that is also apparently enchanted to be skin safe, the glue lasting up to a week. We promise to try that out later and then wind up walking around until we're hungry enough to dive into a cute little restaurant for drinks and dinner.

Afterwards, I walk her back to my aunt's house, where Dericia is only a couple minutes late to band practice.

"Come inside with me," she says, holding out her hand as she pauses at the side door of the garage.

I can already hear Tubbs warming up on his drum kit. "That's okay," I say, taking a step towards the house. "I should probably…" I trail off, my traitorous brain not coming up with any plausible excuse. I don't have to be at The Wild Mare today, and it's not like I have any other social events.

Dericia grins almost wolfishly at me. "Get inside, Bliss."

It's not that I don't like my sister's bandmates. I love every single one of them.

But the distance that's grown between us all is too much for me.

And Taser just fucked me in my shower two days ago and lied about breaking up with his girlfriend.

I don't really want to see him.

And I still don't really want to see Amelia.

I'd suggest you get back on speaking terms, then.

The wraith's deal hangs before me. If I was going to take him up on it—which I'm not—I'd need to get Amelia to agree to bring me back as band manager. And that would require hanging out with everyone again.

But more importantly, I miss Dericia. The past couple of days have been odd in that I've actually seen her multiple times. Even though she's my best friend, our paths just haven't been crossing lately. Or maybe it's that I made sure they didn't cross. Because this isn't my world anymore.

It doesn't have to be like that, Amelia's voice sounds in my head.

And there it is, clear as day.

Two paths and a choice that is mine alone.

Dericia, Taser, Amelia—they weren't the ones that had pulled away. That's all on me.

I could walk back the way we came and head back home alone to my apartment.

Or I could go with Dericia into the garage and maybe reconnect with my friends.

Stars, I could even fight with Taser and Amelia, and maybe that would be better than just sitting around waiting. My conversation with Liz floats back into my mind as well.

With so many people's voices in my head, I'm starting to wonder what I even want.

But one thing stands out very clearly to me. My best friend, standing in front of me, holding the door open like an olive branch.

I can tell she's about to give up on me and head in, so I take a deep breath, step towards her, and put my hand in hers. She beams at me, pulling me into a tight hug, and ushers me inside the garage.

"Reese, you're late!" Amelia says from where she's putting her microphone back on its stand and adjusting the height.

"Yeah, but it was totally worth it! Tada!" Dericia spreads her hands out towards me like she's unveiling something exciting as I step through the door.

"Bliss!" My sister abandons the mic stand and rushes forward, hugging me like she hasn't seen me in months.

I remain a bit stiff in her embrace because I'm still mad at her, but I wrap my arms around her anyways.

"To what do we owe this honor?" Tubbs asks, seated at his drum kit.

"I literally had nothing better to do," I respond with a shrug and grin.

"That's her same reasoning for sleeping with Tay," Blake says, his grin matching mine, only much more wicked as he looks over at Taser.

"Ouch." Taser holds his hand over his heart. "What did I do to deserve all this hate?"

Well, you lied about something huge, for starters, I think, but I don't voice it out loud. He smiles at me, but I drop my eyes from him and flop down on one of the couches that's been pushed up to the wall facing the band's setup.

I look around the garage. I'm pretty sure the last time I was here, I was dating Jordan. I don't think I've stepped back into this space since. Too many memories. I run my hands up and down the couch cushion, feeling the slight scratchy fabric, my fingers finding a loose thread on one of the seams. I pick at it as memories flood to me.

Jordan and I making out on this couch for the first time.

The way I had butterflies and overthought every single thing I did.

The way I thought he was a gentlemen when he started to push for more and I told him I wasn't ready, and he said it was cool, we could just keep making out.

The bar was so low back then.

I think our first ever fight was right over there, where Blake's guitar rack now stands. It should have been our last fight as well, but only hindsight is twenty-twenty.

I push the thoughts from my mind, feeling the couch dip as Amelia sits next to me. "I'm so glad you're here. I want to play a new song for you and you have to give me your totally honest thoughts on it, okay?"

"What's it called?" I ask, a smile lifting my lips despite my anger at her. My sister has always been a bit self-conscious about her music writing. She's a perfectionist in that way. Earlier, while Dericia and I were shopping, Reese mentioned she's been having trouble writing lately. I'm glad to hear Amelia has finally broken through her writer's block.

"Ribbons," she says sheepishly. She reaches over and gives my ribbon a tug. "Um, I actually wrote it for you."

"For me?" My eyebrows shoot up to my hairline.

Amelia nods. "It's kinda about, like, how much I love you and yeah…" She trails off.

I mimic gagging, but despite myself I laugh and throw my arms around my sister, my anger dwindling a bit. I pull out of her embrace and motion at her to get up. "Get on with it already and play it for me."

Amelia has written many songs about many things. Old flings.

Grief over losing both our parents. Sex. What it's like to be a woman.

She has never written a song about me. I'm both nervous and touched. And weirdly, a little mad. I don't need anyone writing songs about me. I want actions over empty words. But Amelia isn't always the best at direct communication.

So I scoot forward in my seat, ready to listen. Amelia nods at Tubbs and he counts down before starting a slow cymbal swell. The sound crests into soft snare drum hits. Amelia's voice joins in, starting out soft and husky. *"Maybe I'm over protective, but sometimes ribbons fray, sometimes they float away."*

I smile widely at the lyrics despite myself.

"Please don't cut me off, please don't untie these bonds, am I not enough, to keep things all together?"

Even the guitar and bass seem to mix a grungy feel with something graceful, flowing easily from verse to chorus. Lyrically, it feels like an apology, from her to me. Sonically, it feels like a representation of how I wish I was, how I wish I could see myself.

The song finishes and Amelia looks at me hesitantly. "Do you like it?"

I get up and cross the room over to her, hugging her tightly. "I love it. It's perfect."

"Are you sure? Anything you'd change?"

I shake my head. "Nothing. The lyrics are beautiful." I look over at Tubbs. "I also love the softer drums."

"That was Tay Tay's idea," Dericia cuts in.

I look over at Taser. He's watching me, and when his eyes meet mine, he shrugs. "It fit better. When I think of you, I don't think of heavy drumming. I think of something a little bit softer." He fixes me with a meaningful stare. "But still metal," he clarifies, pointing his pick at me.

"Oh yes," Reese agrees. "Like a pink metal Barbie."

"Pink Metal," Blake muses. "Kind of sounds like a fun girly pop metal fusion genre."

We all chuckle, trying to picture how that might sound. "I don't hate it," Amelia says with a shrug. "Maybe we should experiment."

"Experiment later. We still have an hour or so before the neighbors complain about noise," Taser says, checking his phone for the time. He's kind of unofficially the parent of the group. Making sure band practice doesn't get derailed with everyone's crazy antics.

I settle back into the couch, tucking my feet up under me and wrapping a blanket around my shoulders to ward off the chilliness of the garage.

By the end of their practice set, I'm beaming. I haven't heard them play in quite a while, I realize, and they have really improved. It's saying a lot, considering I've always known how talented all of them are as musicians and artists. But it's like now they've really grown together as a *band*. And Blake seems like he's been with the band from the very beginning.

As everyone is putting away their gear, Taser comes over and sits next to me on the couch.

"Bliss," he starts but pauses as I avert my gaze from him, giving him the cold shoulder. "Is something wrong?"

Yes.

But I can't get myself to confront him. He's made me into a cheater. I roll my shoulders, hoping to ease out some of the tension coiled in my body. Then I force myself to meet his eyes. "Sorry, I'm just tired. And cold. This garage is always so fucking cold."

"It's nice in the summer, though," he replies, though I know he doesn't buy that everything's okay. "Are you sure you're alright? Do you need to top off again?"

"No," I reply quickly. I'm saved any further explanation when Amelia's phone rings. She inhales sharply.

"Fuck," she says, waving the phone around excitedly. "It's Bill from Moon Blood."

My brows raise as Dericia starts dancing in celebration. Moon Blood is an indie metal label and most of the bands they sign go on to even bigger record deals later in their careers. "Bill's been interacting with us a ton on social media!" Reese comes over, taking my hands in hers. "This is huge, Bliss."

We all wait with bated breath as Amelia answers the phone and puts Bill on speaker. "Hey, Bill, it's Amelia."

"Amelia, how are you?"

"Pretty good. And yourself?"

"Well, I'm in a little bit of a pickle. But I'm hoping Goddess' Trance can help me out. I had a band pull out of the Alchemy Festival."

The Alchemy Festival. The biggest metal rock festival in the entire world. The one the wraith wants me at in order to get close enough to the anonymous frontman of Voracious Maw in order to steal something from him.

Well, he did say he'd take care of that part. The demon works fast.

"Oh no, what happened?" Amelia asks.

"Well, you know Death and Devils, right? Their lead was in a car accident. He's gonna be fine, but he broke his leg and so they can't perform. Too bad he's not kindred, or it would have been no biggie to heal that leg right up."

"That's terrible," Amelia starts to say, but Bill interjects.

"Yeah, yeah, terrible. Anyways, Amy—" she bristles at her most hated nickname, "—I need a band. And I've been digging the videos you've been putting out on social media. It's just a small slot. Two shows, and you'd be the opener for the opener of the main headline for two nights, but this would be huge for you guys."

Amelia nods, almost forgetting to speak. "Yes, absolutely, we're in."

"Great. My assistant will send over all the details to you and help get your lodging sorted."

"Thank you so much, Bill!"

"Yeah, thanks." It sounds like someone else has taken away his attention. He hangs up. Amelia's phone screen fades to black. She looks up around the room, surprise and excitement lighting up her face.

"Can you fucking believe this?" she asks as her eyes fall to mine. I beam at her. In my excitement I've stood up from the couch and am ready to run to her, but everyone else surrounds her, all in one big group hug.

"Congrats," I say to my sister, and then I look to the side door of the garage, wondering if I should go ahead and leave the band to their inevitable night of celebration.

"Bliss!" my sister yells, as I take a step towards the door. "Get in here right now!"

The band opens up and Dericia all but drags me into the center of it, my sister's arms enclosing me and everyone else surrounding us.

But as much as I wish everything could just go back to normal, it can't.

I disentangle myself from the group, plastering on a smile. "I bet Liz has some champagne somewhere. I'll go grab a bottle?"

"Hell yeah!" Blake says, clapping me on the back. "We're celebrating tonight!"

I've made it out of the garage and have just started climbing the slightly mossy flagstone steps that lead up from the detached garage to the house when Amelia catches up to me, her black platform boots clomping on the ground. She links her arm through mine. "I'll help you search."

We enter the kitchen through the back door of the house and begin rummaging around, not only pulling out a bottle of champagne but also snacks.

"How are things at The Wild Mare?" Amelia asks, looking over her shoulder from where she's pulling out some red solo cups. Liz has forbidden us from getting into her nice glassware after Taser shattered not just one wine glass, but two, in the same night.

"Pretty good," I reply automatically.

"But you were still gonna take some time to travel, right? For your starmoon?"

I take in a breath. "I'm not so sure anymore. Not with the way the stone reacted."

"Liz filled me in on what that fae councilwoman said."

I nod. I figured she would. "It just seems a bit pointless now is all."

"Well, what if you came to the festival with us?"

I look up from where I'm pouring a bag of chips into a large bowl. "Why?" I think of the wraith's offer.

"You could take back your position as band manager. We could use you. You're perfect for it, Bliss. You know us, and our music. You've always kept us in line and made sure we never turned into one of those cliche bands that drinks too much and is always late to shows."

"Well, I think you could manage that yourself, you know, by not drinking too much and not being late to your shows."

She waves a hand dismissively as if that's not true. "Look, I know things didn't work out well last time. But Jordan's not around anymore, and we're maturer and wiser."

"Are we?" I ask, my tone all of a sudden having a bit of a bite to it. I look over to where I saw Amelia and Taser talking at the front door two days ago.

Could it really be this easy? I take up my old position, go to the festival, steal whatever from a sexy anonymous musician, get turned into a water nymph, *and* get my mate? Live happily ever after?

Amelia follows my gaze, her own narrowing. "What's that supposed to mean?"

"I heard you two talking." I force myself to look at my sister, even though I want to look anywhere but.

She takes in a deep breath. "Bliss," she starts, but I hold up a hand, stopping her.

"You both lied to me."

Her voice pitches higher. "I didn't know!"

"You might not have known beforehand, but you knew after." I throw the empty chip bag in the trash, opening another and grabbing another bowl. "And you didn't tell me."

"What would have been the point, Bliss?" Amelia rips the cork off the champagne bottle, the carbonated contents erupting and spilling onto the floor, until Amelia redirects it into her cup. She sets the bottle on the counter and drains her cup in one go. "What's done is done, and all you finding out about it would have done is made you feel like shit."

"Are you okay with what he did?"

"You know what, Bliss? I am. I am okay with it. Because you needed help. I was scared. And I get why he lied to you. He cares about you too, almost as much as I do."

"That doesn't make it okay."

"I don't fucking care! You're healed now and that's what matters."

I look away from her and take a deep breath. "This, this right here is why I can't be your band manager."

"What does that have to do with anything?"

"I don't forgive him and I don't forgive you. Being your band manager would just make it worse. It'd be like last time all over again."

Amelia looks like I slapped her in the face. "Is it that you don't forgive me for not telling you about Taser, or that you don't forgive me for how things were handled with Jordan?"

I throw my hands up. "Maybe both? I don't know! I just know I'm tired of being lied to. I'm tired of people telling me how to live my life." Between Amelia constantly criticizing how I live, to the stars not blessing me with a normal bond, I am so over not being in control of my own life. The wraith's deal almost feels like the first real decision I've been given in years.

I take a few steps towards the front door, turning back before I open it. "I really am excited for you, that you're going to the festival. It's huge and I know you'll be amazing." My hand is on the knob when I hear Amelia let out a huge sob.

I turn around and see her standing in the kitchen, her hand shaking around the empty cup, shoulders hunched forward, long dark strands of hair in her face. Amelia never cries.

I can count on one set of fingers how many times I've seen her cry.

"Bliss." She hiccups softly in between sobs. "I'm so sorry. I want — I want—" She can't manage to get the words out.

I roll my eyes at the ceiling and let go of the door handle, coming over and stopping in front of my sister. I gently take the cup out of her hand, setting it on the counter.

"What do you want?" I ask, trying to add some gentleness to my voice, but I don't think I succeed. She still can't seem to look at me.

"I want things to go back to how they used to be," she responds in a whisper, like she knows that can't ever happen. More tears flow and she wipes at her eyes, anger starting to creep back into her. My sister never stays sad for long. It always transmutes into a different emotion that she's more comfortable with: anger, lust, aggression. "I want you to move back in and I want you to be a part of the band again. I want you with me, and maybe that's selfish, but it feels safer when you're around! And I want to take one of Jordan's super expensive guitars and I want to fucking bash his head in for what he did to you. I don't want you to work at some stupid country bar and I JUST WANT TO HAVE MY SISTER BACK!" She lets out a cry of frustration and slumps to the floor, hair tangling around her and black eyeliner, shadow, and mascara streaking down her cheeks.

I take a seat on the floor with her, pushing some of her hair from her face.

"You were the very first person who ever encouraged me with music," she adds after a long silence.

"You don't need me anymore," I tell her. Though why I don't know. Something about this day has made me unable to continue denying the truth. I want what the wraith is offering me and this would literally be step one to getting it.

"I don't need you, I know that. I'm okay on my own. The band will be okay without you, but that's the thing, Bliss. We want you. I want you."

Something softens in me. Maybe it's that my older sister is such a mess right now. Maybe it's that I've just been needing to hear that I have a place somewhere in the world. I want that feeling of belonging and I want it with my mate. So maybe I have to steal something. And maybe I have to lie to my sister about my reason for accepting her offer of being band manager. But so be it. She'll understand eventually.

"Okay," I say simply, stroking a hand over her head, smoothing down her hair.

"Okay?" She looks up at me with huge raccoon eyes—literally she looks like a baby raccoon right now. "Okay what?"

"Okay, I'll be your manager again."

Amelia lets out a squeal and throws her arms around me, tugging me close. "Bliss, you are the best sister and best friend I could have ever asked for. I love you so much."

"I love you too."

She sighs contentedly and lets me go, rubbing a hand over her face. "Look, I know I should have told you about Taser. I thought I was protecting you. I didn't want you to feel bad over something you had no control over."

"And yet, I do."

"I know. I'm sorry. But Bliss, I would do it again. You didn't see how much you were fading and how fast. I really thought I was going to lose you."

"Okay fine, I forgive you, but you need to start staying out of my sex life from now on."

"I will," she hedges. "If you promise to power yourself up regularly. No more waiting until it's almost too late."

I think about it for a few moments. "Fine." I stick out my pinkie finger. She locks it in hers and we pinkie swear. As good as a blood oath in our opinion.

"Besides, this festival is like one huge party for fae. So you'll have so many people to pick from, you won't need to use Taser again."

I roll my eyes at her.

"You know, I'm really, really excited to perform, but part of me, the succubus part of me, is even more excited for all the fae dick we're gonna get."

"Hell yeah!" Dericia says. The back door swings closed. I hadn't even heard it open. "Sorry, I was so eavesdropping, but I needed to make sure my sisters were okay. So this music festival is really just one big huge opportunity to get laid a ton?"

"According to *Amy*, yes."

Amelia swings her arm around my neck and pulls me down so I'm in a headlock. "Dericia, did you overhear the part where I convinced Bliss to be our band manager again?"

"I did!"

"Well, I'm now thinking maybe she can be our *bald* band manager," she says wickedly. I can *hear* her grinning.

"You wouldn't dare!" I shriek at her. "Where would I wear my ribbons?"

Dericia lets out a chuckle. "You can always use my new bedazzler to glue them to your tits."

"It can do that?" Amelia asks, letting me go, eyes wide at the possibilities.

"Oh yes," Dericia responds, grinning.

I point my finger at both my sisters. "You stay away from my hair *and* my tits, got it?"

CHAPTER TEN

PISCES

"Are you sure you know what you're doing?" I ask Evan, eyeing him over the top edge of the book I'm flipping through. I came into the library seeking somewhere peaceful to try to write other than my room but found Evan in here, next to a pile of books on potions and earth magic. Neither of which he is particularly skilled at.

"I didn't ask you to help, you know," he mumbles as he skims a page of whatever he's reading. He's seated at a large table near the fire. The crackle of the flames and pages turning every few moments have been the only sounds for the last several minutes. "Why are you in here anyways?"

I toss the book I'd grabbed off the table to the ground, next to a few others I've already flipped through. None contained any mention of a temporary invisibility potion. I swing my legs up over the arm of the comfy loveseat I'm occupying and lean my head back on the other armrest, careful not to rest the back of my neck directly on it. I've gotten a few additions to my existing tattoo that spans from behind my right ear, across my neck, and wraps around to my left collarbone. Evan offered to heal it right after, but part of me wanted to feel human, even if just for a little bit.

"I have this chord progression I can't get out of my head, but I can't seem to find the words to go along with it. I thought a change of scenery would help."

I hear Evan close a book and open another one. "I'd offer to listen to it and help out, but I know how you are."

I huff out a laugh, closing my eyes. My bandmates know exactly how personal my writing process is. I never share anything with them until it's time for Shaun to add the drums. Then we make tweaks from there. I've always been like that. When I write, I pour my heart onto the page, so I can't just let someone hear the music before it's complete.

"About earlier," Evan starts to say, then trails off. I can feel his uncanny green eyes on me.

"Which part? Me attacking Austin, or the party?"

I open my eyes, meeting his gaze. He looks at me with concern, which is pretty rare for Evan. He's not usually an emotional guy.

"I was maybe a bit harsh to you, about Austin," he clarifies. "He attacked Benny and you reacted. I shouldn't have said anything."

I shrug, getting up and taking a seat next to him, pulling another book off the pile. "Don't worry about it. I wish I could say I attacked him because he was hurting my friend, but honestly it was Benny's blood that caused my siren to come out so fervently."

Evan claps me on the shoulder. "He's that tasty?"

I grin. "Oh definitely," I respond, winking at Evan. He just shakes his head.

He glances sideways at me. "Do we need to talk about the party?"

My grin falls, and I replace it with a fixed smile. "Nah, we don't need to go there."

"I guess I'm probably not the person to talk to about it. I'll never know what it's like for you and Benny."

I open the book in front of me, absently turning the pages, though I'm not really reading them. It's hard knowing my friends will find soulmates and get to grow old with them, while my aging has already started to slow. I'll look thirty for the rest of my years, but I'd trade that in a heartbeat for a mate. "I don't even know if I can blame Born fae for being so prejudiced. The stars bless you all with mates, and now with what's happening with the warlocks… I mean, I get it."

"What's going on with warlocks?" a familiar voice says from the doorway to the library. I jump out of my seat, striding forward and wrapping my cousin up in a huge hug. Simon squeezes me back and pokes his head around me to look at Evan. "You two getting overly gushy again?"

Evan huffs, ignoring Simon and going back to his reading.

I follow Simon back to the table, grinning. I take in his familiar features, the thick mop of wavy black hair, his wide boyish brown eyes and easy smile. He gets his coloring from his mother's side of his family, but he and I share the same nose. He's been gone visiting his grandmother in Seoul for a couple weeks and then stopped by to visit his dad's side—my side—of the family on the way home. I've missed him.

"So warlocks?" Simon prompts. I fill him in on the details, how the fae council have put out an advisory about warlocks in particular. Witnesses report multiple instances of warlocks seemingly going crazy and attacking other fae and humans, kindreds especially. "You need to be careful, and don't go wandering off by yourself too long during the festival," I tell him seriously. My cousin recently got his kindred rune, but I don't think I'll ever stop being overprotective of him. I brought him into the whole mess; the least I can do is keep him safe.

"Well, as my sponsor, I guess Evan will have to keep me company," Simon responds, grinning.

Evan groans. "You'd be much better off with Shaun in the event of a warlock attack."

"Fine by me." Simon's grin grows even wider.

I quirk a brow at him. I'm pretty sure my cousin has a small thing for Shaun, but other times I'm not sure if he's just joking to annoy the wolf shifter. Maybe it's both.

I notice Evan grin out of the corner of my eye.

"Okay, so stay away from warlocks. Got it. What is all this?" Simon asks, picking up a few books and reading the titles.

"Evan's going to attempt to make the potion for the sardines game," I tease.

"Why do I remember something about that not going so well last time?" Simon muses.

Evan bares his teeth, a growl emanating from deep in his throat. "It didn't go that badly."

"You set the kitchen on fire," I remind him.

"Hardly. Besides, this is a much easier potion." He flips the page of his book over so quickly I expect it to tear right out of the book. "Oh!"

Simon and I crane our necks to look at what he's reading.

"I think this is it. It's got a lot of ingredients, though. And—" he groans, "—it then needs to be amplified by earth magic."

"Well, you can do that, can't you?" Simon asks.

"Yeah, but I'm pretty shit at the other elements," Evan says. "I've gotten down the skill to clean blood and dirt out of things pretty easily, and I finally used my earth magic offensively when we caught Austin, but this earth spell isn't something I'm familiar with."

"Know any earth elementals or earth nymphs?" I ask.

"Some," he responds, but it's pretty clear his thoughts are focused on the potion and spell.

I nod towards the hallway and Simon follows me out. "Figure he needs to concentrate," I tell him, and Simon hums in agreement.

We walk along the hallway and find ourselves inside the nave, the part of the church mass would be held in, if this were still an actual Catholic church. I walk down one of the aisles, along a pew, and take a seat. Simon slides along it and lies down flat on his back, head near me, eyes looking up at me.

"The family really misses you," he says softly, watching my reaction closely.

I look down at him and then up towards the altar, at the cross still hanging on the wall, in the center. I swallow thickly. My gaze travels up to the ceiling, as if I can see the stars through it.

"It's better this way," is all I say.

Simon doesn't respond. I think he disagrees with me, but I know my decision to stay away keeps them all safer. And not just because of my siren teeth. I'm walking a thin line, and I can't allow anyone else I love to get involved. It's already bad enough Simon was pulled into this, but no matter how many times I urged him to stay away, he didn't. And part of me is so grateful for that, because I don't know what I'd do without him. The other part of me recognizes what a selfish prick I am.

He sits upright, resting his elbows on his knees. "I also got some bad news on the way back here," he says after the silence has stretched on for quite a while.

I glance at him, startled. "Is it—?"

"Nothing about our family, no," he rushes to assure me. "Presley —he got injured, falling off a ladder."

"What? Is he okay?" I pull out my phone, not finding any messages or calls from our band manager.

"He'll be okay. I told him I'd take care of letting you all know. But he's gonna be out of commission for a while. Broke *a lot* of bones. He's gonna have to skip the Alchemy Festival."

I raise my head again towards the sky, wondering what the fuck the stars are playing at. "Fuck," I breathe out. This definitely is not ideal, but mostly I just feel bad for Presley. While Simon is kindred and we can heal him with magic easily—well, Evan can anyways— Presley isn't. It'd be illegal for us to interfere. More bullshit Born fae laws to supposedly make sure fae continue to fly under the radar. "It's gonna be weird without him there."

Simon nods, clasping his hands together. "I know I don't have much experience," Simon says slowly. "But I think I can take over for him, at least until he's feeling better."

I bump my shoulder into his. "We'd be lucky to have you. Though I'm not sure we can get another drum tech this quickly. Think you can handle both roles?"

Simon grins, nodding. "At least in the meantime, yeah."

"Well, I'm sure you'll do great," I say, clapping him on the back.

He smiles softly at me, and then both our heads turn towards the doorway behind us as Marcus, our front-of-house engineer, and a few other of our crew including Niamh, my backup vocalist, enter. "Simon! You're back," Lily, one of our lighting techs, says, coming over and giving him a quick peck on the cheek.

"Hey guys," Simon greets. Marcus, Gwen—our stage manager—and Niamh all find seats in the surrounding pews, handing around a bottle of something.

"Want any?" Marcus asks, holding out the bottle.

I shake my head, getting to my feet. "I'm good. I think I'm actually gonna head out for a walk, get some fresh air."

They nod, saying their goodbyes, as Simon follows me.

"Need company?" he asks, standing in the hallway. Behind me it goes out to the front doors of the church. The opposite way leads back into the area Evan's renovated into a pretty luxurious and large house that we all live in.

"I think I need some alone time. I keep getting writer's block," I admit.

He nods knowingly. "Alright, mate. I'll see you later, then."

With that we part ways.

I can feel a bit of tension leave now that he's home, even with the bad news he brought.

I step out of the main entrance of the church, the grand doors swinging shut behind me.

It doesn't take me very long to get to the park that's my usual destination on my night walks. This area of town isn't as populated so no one is really around as I make my way across the street. I hop the fence since it's closed after dark and wander a path surrounded by trees until I find my way to a still, lifeless pond.

I sing the same song I sung for him all those nights ago. No idea if it will work.

But yesterday I had a pain in my chest that wouldn't go away. It brought me to my knees and then to the floor and subsided eventually into a low ache.

Right where his claws had pierced my skin, right where my heart is.

The song wraith must be back. I'm not sure what happened to him, or where he went, but we struck a deal and he hasn't yet delivered on his end.

"My favorite song," a voice says from behind me. I turn, seeing the song wraith sitting on a wooden bench a few paces behind where I face the pond.

"I figured it would get your attention."

"And pray tell, why do you need it?" he asks, that same bored look in his eyes.

"I've delivered on our bargain, and you've been nowhere to be seen. I want what you promised me."

He stands up, taking a few steps towards me. I look down at him, though only by a few inches.

He curls his lip at me. "You've delivered? Delivered what?"

"Voracious Maw has an audience. That's what you asked for."

The song wraith sneers at me. "That isn't nearly enough of an offering for me. What you're asking me to do is no simple feat, boy."

"How much is enough?"

The song wraith's form is starting to shimmer, as if he's somehow stepped through the veil into another realm but still has one foot here. "I will let you know when I have what I need." And then he's gone.

"Come back, you sick fuck!" I yell, willing my voice to travel after him. When he doesn't reappear, I grab a rock lying close by and throw it into the pond with all my might. The sounds of water crashing and sloshing sends me to my knees, air rushing out of me, and it takes a few moments for me to get my breathing back under control.

Haven't I given him enough? He's taken my entire life—my humanity—and is still requesting more? I let out another agonizing scream, my vocal cords constricting around all the pent up anger coiled in my body.

Her face bleeds into my vision as I close my eyes against the tears that leak lazily out of my eyes, at odds with the fervor of my wish that I could forget it all. That for once I could wake up in the morning not noticing the absence on the other side of the bed. That I could forget the hollow, harsh sound of her voice after a night of screaming words she supposedly didn't mean. That I could forget we ever met, ever crossed paths.

I look down at my arms.

The evidence of everything she ever made me feel.

I pull my sleeves down over my hands, hiding even my fingers within them, and I walk home, going in through a side door so as not to stumble into anyone else's sight. I want to sit in the dark. I want to feel pain.

My teeth slide out of my gums, elongating.

I consider what my teeth could do to my flesh. I consider how it would look if I ripped open my own arm and peered inside, seeing what the skin hides.

"Sces?" Evan calls from down the hall. His shadowy form emerges into more detail as he comes under the glow of sconces along the wall. "Is something wrong?"

My teeth are still out. I numbly shake my head, while trying to keep my mouth closed.

Evan's in his pajamas, holding a plate of nachos. He offers one to me, but I shake my head again, focusing on the blue plaid print of his pants. He offers me his arm, but again I shake my head.

"If you're hungry, you should eat."

"I'm not hungry," I manage to grunt out as finally my teeth slide back into my gums. "I'm angry. I want to rip into something so bad I—" I fall short. I take a few deep breaths.

"Eat some nachos," Evan says, holding the plate towards me again. "Do it. Trust me."

I glare at him but do as he says, biting into the chip loaded with melted cheese and a jalapeño. The slight spice bites into my taste buds and suddenly that's what I'm focused on.

I grab another with more jalapeños on it and as I swallow the spice soothes me. I luxuriate in it.

Evan nods with satisfaction and holds the plate up above his head, even though I could still reach it. He leads me to our gamer den, like a human leading a dog using a smelly treat. But I follow, suddenly hungry in the normal way.

We sit our asses down in the bean bag chairs on the floor. Evan puts the plate between us and turns on our latest gaming obsession. Within minutes the plate is empty and my emotions are in check. My anger is quelled and my sadness forgotten, at least for the moment.

CHAPTER ELEVEN

PISCES

BENNY CLAPS ME ON THE BACK AS WE COME TO A HALT JUST INSIDE the backstage area of the legendary Bell Theater in Seattle. It's an older venue with an almost church-like feel. "Definitely bigger than last time, huh?" he asks as we look out at the stage.

The venue hasn't opened up yet and we're early. Our masks and outfits are packed away still and we have a couple hours to get ready and do our final sound check.

A year ago we were in Seattle as openers for another band. This time we have a couple of small shows lined up along the west coast before heading back home. I nod at the guitarist for our opener, a local band we found last minute to fill in for our scheduled opener, who all came down with food poisoning last night.

"Hey man, are you Wrath?" the guitarist asks, holding out his hand and using my stage name.

I nod, taking his hand and shaking it.

"I'm Taser. That's Amelia, our lead singer, over there." He points to a tall woman with lots of tattoos and long black hair that shifts blue in the lights. She's chatting with a tall, lean guy with drumsticks sticking out his back pocket—their drummer, presumably—and another woman with long brown braids, also wearing loads of black.

"Thanks for bringing us on tonight." Taser shakes Benny's hand next. But Benny's eyes are on Amelia. He lets out a soft whistle.

"Of course," I reply, looking around for the rest of my band so I can introduce them. I find Shaun on the steps leading up to the stage, chatting with some of the venue staff. I don't see Evan.

I look back to the group of Goddess' Trance musicians and see Amelia heading back to one of the dressing rooms.

Benny follows with his eyes and glances at Taser.

"She's really something, huh?" he asks.

Taser grins. "Trust me, you're biting off more than you can chew with that one."

Benny looks over to me. "A succubus," he explains with an approving nod.

Taser eyes me and lowers his voice. "I've never met a group like you, with both Made and Born fae."

I stifle a groan. I know Goddess' Trance is made up of all Born fae—one of the reasons we picked them. It's better than a bunch of humans hanging out too closely with us—but I forgot how often Born fae can tell I'm not one of them.

"We don't discriminate," Benny says with a shrug, and I brace myself for the incoming vitriol of a Born vampire.

But Taser nods in understanding. "I wish the whole of fae society was like that." He looks at me and smiles. "I've never actually met a siren."

"I take it we're a bit rare?" I reply, looking at Benny questioningly.

"Oh, so you're new then too?" Taser guesses.

I chuckle softly. "It's that obvious?"

Taser grins in response. "I won't tell," he says, winking and clapping me on the back. "Listen, I've got sound check, but let's grab beers after the show, yeah?"

Benny and I nod and head off to track down Evan. Wherever you need him to be, is usually where he isn't.

I turn and bump into a woman who sticks out in the venue worse than a sore thumb.

She's petite and curvy, wearing light jeans, a pastel pink top, and a white ribbon in her brunette hair that's tied half up in a bun, the lower half cascading down her back in curls. My eyes fixate on the white ribbon; it's starting to come loose. And I've seen her before, last time we were in town.

"Sorry," she says, reaching out her hand and lightly resting it on my forearm. "Are you okay?"

As if her five-foot frame could have hurt me. She looks seriously at me and I suddenly find I can't speak straight.

"Ye— Erm, er— Good. I'm good," I finally manage to get out, and I wish so badly I'd already put my mask on because I can feel my ears turning pink.

"Good," she says with a smile. Her lips part as if she's going to say something else, but her hair falls into loose waves around her face. Behind her, the white ribbon floats to the ground. "Oh!" she exclaims.

I maneuver around her, bending over and picking it up. It's smooth and satiny and I can't help but liken it to her skin. I offer it to her, hand outstretched, palm open.

She breaks out into a grin. "Thanks." She takes the ribbon from me and ties her hair up again, pulling a couple strands loose to frame her face. "Does it look okay?" she asks. "Do I have any of those weird hair bumps?" She points at the top of her hair.

My gaze glosses over her hair and sticks on her eyes, looking from one to the other. She cocks her head to the side when I don't immediately answer. Heat races up my neck again. Words stick in my throat. "No, it looks good." The words come out thick and quiet. I run my fingers through my hair, trying to think of something else to say. I've never been good at talking much, but there's something so bubbly about her. Her energy is soft, welcoming, inviting, and I find I want to be around it.

She smiles softly at me. "Thanks. I'm Bliss. What's your name?"

Before I can answer, a man calls out to her, his voice sounding annoyed. "Bliss! Get over here!"

She rolls her eyes, even though he can't see it since her back is turned to him. "Sorry, that's my boyfriend. It was nice to meet you," she says with another smile, then heads his way.

"Bliss, that guy's a Made fae. Why were you talking to him?"

She turns over her shoulder and looks at me, her eyes going a bit wide. I can't tell if it's from confusion or revulsion, and I can't hear what she says back to him.

The heat from my earlier embarrassment evaporates, leaving me feeling a bit deflated. I wish I could have spoken to her more.

Evan slings an arm around my shoulder. I didn't hear him approach, but I could smell the air around me getting slightly more smoky, replacing Benny's more earthy scent. "That girl looks lost."

I look over at him, brow raised.

"She would look so much better in black, don't you think?" he continues. "Also, Benny mentioned you haven't eaten in a while."

I swallow and look away from him. "Benny and I have arrangements for tonight. I'll be fine."

My eyes follow the girl with the white ribbon as her boyfriend swings his arm around her waist, resting his hand in her back pocket. Her back is to me, but he looks over her at me, smirking, and whispers something into her ear. She pushes away from him, but he just grabs her more firmly, resting his other hand on her ass and giving it a squeeze. She looks around as if checking to see if anyone is looking and steps up on her tiptoes, brushing a kiss against his lips. She tries to pull away quickly, but he grabs her and forces his tongue down her throat. I almost take a step forward— but to do what?

They're obviously together. She pushes away from him again and this time he releases her. She laughs lightly but something tells me it's forced. A few more of their friends turn up and I force myself to look away.

The irony of it doesn't evade me. Being around Benny, I know a vampire when I see one. So while her boyfriend might be dangerous in a way, I am much deadlier. And who am I to save her when I've never been successful in the past?

Evan gives me a quizzical look and angles his head towards the dressing rooms. "We should start getting into character, mate."

I nod and follow him into the room, where Shaun and Benny are already dressed and applying black paint to their hands and necks, the only part of their skin that'll be exposed.

I pick up my mask from inside my bag and run my fingers along the cool hard metal, tracing the mother-of-pearl skeleton fingers. Benny spent months on this mask, and with a little help from Evan's elemental abilities, they crafted it to mold to my face perfectly.

I change into black pants and black boots, and take out my nipple piercings. I can't have a single identifiable marking. Benny helps me paint my torso and the lower half of my face that the mask doesn't cover. He takes a brush, spreading a potion across parts of my skin, concentrating it towards my lower torso and fading it upwards. Where the potion meets skin, shiny black scales erupt, magically glued onto my skin. They're thick and hard, each one about the size of my thumbnail.

For the second to last final touch, I add the cologne Evan made for us. It masks our scents enough that fae with superior senses of smell can't figure out what type of fae we are. It helps us keep our identities a secret, even if Evan forgets to use his all the damn time.

I slip my mask on, followed by my black lace shroud.

I pull the hood up over my head and settle it low on my forehead, putting some of my mask in shadow, and step out of the room.

By the second to last song of our set, I know I'm fading. I push through the slight strain I can feel in my throat. To an untrained ear I sound fine, but any vocalist or musician worth their salt would hear the slight raggedness, the pull of lyrics being dragged out. I'm physically exhausted as well. I stumble as I pace around the stage during the instrumental parts, but it just looks like it's part of the act.

I hold out until the very end of the last song, where my power has run so low during the show that I can't breathe anymore. My knees buckle and I gasp out the last verse, my body falling to the stage floor and the mic rolling out of my hand. As Evan and Shaun finish off the song, cheers go around the crowd. Thankfully, our theatrics are well known enough that everyone just thinks this is part of the show.

I'm able to gasp in a lungful of air and I push myself to my knees, bowing to the crowd, the wave of exhaustion and dizziness holding off long enough for me to amble off the stage. Once I'm shielded from the crowd, hidden away in a little nook, I can't help but allow tears to fall down my face, my weariness too high to continue fighting.

It's like this sometimes after a show. All the emotions of myself and the crowd mixing together sometimes leave me feeling entirely too much that I can't process. The only way to gain back my energy is to feed.

Benny finds me, pulling me up, and I drape myself around him, my height enveloping his smaller frame, but he steadies me with his supernatural strength and speeds off with me, getting us quickly into the tour bus, with no witnesses. It's how we evade fans so easily, even the ones who try to position themselves so that they can catch a glimpse of us coming out of the venue.

I push myself out of his arms onto the large bed at the back of the bus. He sits on the edge of the bed, looking at me, his eyes always full of kindness and compassion that I don't deserve. I sob into the mattress for what feels like hours as he waits, his hand on my ankle, holding firmly, grounding me.

Evan and Shaun poke their heads in to check on us but leave Benny to handle me.

My emotions always tend to get the better of me. When I'm angry, it's Evan who allows me to let it out the best. When I'm introspective, Shaun is the one that can read my mind and help me make sense of what I'm experiencing. But when I'm in anguish, Benny is the one that grounds me. I would be dead without them.

Eventually Benny pulls me up into a sitting position. He pushes my hair out of my face and I wipe at the dried tears on my cheeks.

"It's time," Benny says gently to me, tugging off his shirt. He offers me up his arm.

I want to ignore the burning, suffocating feeling of fae hunger in my chest, but I can't. Instead, my siren teeth—filing into points—descend from my gums around my human teeth, my jaw stretching wide as I lower myself to bite into the flesh of his upper arm. I tear into it, careful not to go too deep. I move up his shoulder and down his torso, gnawing at his body until I'm fully satiated.

He lets out a low whimper as I fall away from him down onto the mattress beside him. My teeth and jaw return to normal and I turn to the side, tears falling once again as I take in the damage. "Are you okay?" I whisper, tugging at his good arm.

"It hurts, but I'm okay."

His skin begins to knit itself back together, turning pink and then fading to his normal skin tone within a few minutes. He looks at me with a grin.

"A kiss would make it feel even better," he teases me, and I let out a low chuckle. But I do prop myself up on my elbows, maneuvering myself in between his legs and lowering myself down to his torso, pressing kisses onto his skin. I quickly graze my lips against his.

"Thank you," I whisper. I push off from the bed and toss his shirt to him.

"Anytime," he replies, stretching out his arms.

Evan pokes his head in again. "All done with your chew toy?" he asks, looking at all the blood staining the sheets. We nod to him and he comes in, waving his hand around, and suddenly the sheets are fresh, not a single speck of blood to be seen.

CHAPTER TWELVE

BLISS

THREE YEARS AGO

As we watch Voracious Maw wrap up their set and the
frontman Wrath collapses on stage, I look around to see if anyone
is going to help him. He's obviously in pain, but everyone is acting
like it's part of their show. I turn to Jordan.

"Someone needs to help him," I say, tugging on his sleeve.

"It's just part of their gimmick, Bliss. Don't be fucking dumb."

I let my hand fall away from his arm. "Don't call me that," I tell
him, my voice too quiet.

"I won't call you dumb, if you stop being dumb."

I turn and start pushing my way through the crowd. Jordan
sighs and follows me out, reaching out and grabbing my arm.
"Babe, look—he's fine."

He points up to the stage and I see Wrath thanking the audience
and walking off stage without saying anything or interacting with
the crowd. I think that's normal, but part of me wonders if he's also
just in too much pain.

"Bliss, I'm sorry. But they're just a lame band with a bunch of gimmicky performances. I just hate to see your compassion wasted on a skinny ugly freak show in a mask."

"Why are you so hateful towards them? Why do you care so much that they wear masks?" I want to hurl the words at him, wound him like he does me, but my voice once again barely carries. I know with his fae hearing that he heard me anyways.

"Because, it's not about the music with these fucking gimmicks. Everyone fawns all over them, while bands like ours don't get noticed because we're considered average. But if they didn't wear masks and all these fan girls could see how nerdy and unattractive those guys actually are, no one would be at this show."

"You don't know what they look like!"

"I saw them before the show and trust me, Bliss, they're just a group of skinny gamer types. And if you were wanting them to fuck you, you'll be seriously disappointed. Not one of them would be able to lift you up. You're too heavy for them. You'd just have to lie there underneath them while their tiny dicks barely fill you up."

His words hit a deep insecurity within me. He's remarked on my eating habits a few times over the past year, like he's worried I'm putting on weight. I usually like my body, my curves, but some-times I can't help but compare myself to Amelia and Reese. They are leaner, taller. My hand involuntarily moves to my stomach.

"Babe, you know I love your body. But it's why I lift such heavy weights, so I can have fun with you, throw you around a bit while I make you come."

My shoulders sag at that. I can count the number of orgasms he's given me during our whole relationship on one hand. And they all came after I'd been reading some really filthy smutty books.

"I want to go home," I whisper to him.

"We're going to the bar."

"I don't want to. I want to go home."

"Stop being a fucking bitch, Bliss. Why are you ruining tonight for me? I have work all next week. I just want to hang out after my show with my girl and my friends and you start a fucking fight with me."

I turn and walk out. If he doesn't want to fight with me, then fine. I won't fight. I'm going home.

"What are you going to do, just walk home?"

"I'm calling a ride."

"The fuck you are. You'll probably end up fucking the driver in his car."

I whip around. "What? Why do you do that? Why do you slut shame me just because of what I am? I have never, ever slept around on you."

"Well, maybe you should start, because Bliss, I hate to break it to you, but you're kind of boring in bed. Maybe you could use the experience."

"Give me your keys," I say, holding out my hand. "I'll drive myself home, and you can get a ride with Jinx."

"Fuck that shit. We're going out to the bar, Bliss."

"No."

"You're such a fucking bitch!" he yells at me as I stalk towards his car in the parking lot. I tug on the handle.

"Unlock the door and either let me drive myself home or you drive."

He comes around to my side of the car, his face livid. He unlocks the car and all but pushes me inside the passenger seat, slamming the car door shut repeatedly, over and over again. I scream at him to stop, but he doesn't, not for a while. I tuck myself inside the car so that I don't get caught in the door. My limbs lock up with fear and I stay frozen as he gets into the driver's seat.

Move, my mind whispers to me. *Get out.* But I can't move, can barely think.

Jordan starts the car and peels off, going way, way too fast. I'm too scared to tell him to slow down, worried it'll make him go even faster.

My magic floats to the surface in a thin fog, wanting to ease his anger, subdue him into a pleasant calm energy. But I don't unleash it. My powers aren't strong enough to overpower him. They rarely have been.

The one time I was able to seduce him, it brought out this really gentle side of him. We had sex and it was one of my most favorite times together. But after he was angry, feeling like I'd somehow duped him.

And I was punished for it. He gave me the cold shoulder. Ignored me for a week and then made me feel crazy, like I'd manipulated him.

So I push down my magic. I know it'll only make it worse.

I take deep breaths, trying to calm myself as we approach a bridge.

It's been raining all week on and off and the roads are slick. I grip the door handle with my right hand and the edge of the seat with my left hand.

He sees it out of the corner of his eye and pushes down further on the gas pedal, muttering something to himself.

I don't look at the speedometer, but I guess we're going about seventy miles per hour.

On a residential street.

We're almost to the bridge, and Jordan swerves around a sedan going the speed limit.

I shut my eyes. Moments later I open them. Mercifully, we've crossed to the other side of the bridge.

"Jordan," I whisper. "Please, please slow down."

It's a mistake.

He lifts his foot off the gas and at first I think I've gotten through to him. Then he guns it again.

I let out a scream as we hit a wide puddle of water. The feeling of the tires no longer making contact with the pavement throw my stomach into chaos.

We hydroplane over the puddle that's closer to the size of a small pond, and I feel the moment Jordan loses control of the car.

The back of the car starts swinging around, turning us.

I scream as in seconds the car spins around. A concrete wall comes out of nowhere, crashing into my side of the car.

I don't feel the impact.

I wake up with a pounding in my head, my bedroom coming into focus. Something pricks my neck and a weight shifts on top of me.

I groan, trying to push the thing off me.

How did I get here? What happened last night?

I catch sight of the window and my confusion increases. It's pitch black outside. Still night time.

Finally my brain starts working enough to register Jordan is on me, feeding off my neck.

"Get off me," I mumble, pushing at him. My vision is going blurry.

My body feels like I was run over by a car.

Car…

Jordan's car spinning out of control flashes through my mind in pictures. Just individual frames of the crash.

I wasn't run over but… Ouch.

"Get *off* me," I say, more forcefully. I wrench my neck free, which sends yet another dizzying wave of pain through my body.

"I just need a little more, then I can heal you," Jordan says, reaching for me.

"Don't touch me."

"Bliss, you need to feed. You're injured."

"Get out. We're done," I mutter to him.

His eyes go blank. I've never understood how he can do that. One minute he's looking at me like I'm his world. And the next, it's like all the shine has dried up and two dark, soulless eyes stare back at me. But none of those times are quite as frightening as right now, though I can't put my finger on why.

"Fine, die for all I care." He's up off my bed, one foot out the door, waiting for me to take it back.

"I mean it, Jordan. I'm breaking up with you. We're done."

He slams my door shut.

I fish out my phone from my purse before I can pass out. I'm dizzy from my injuries and now the blood loss. I rack my brain for who to call. My eyes land on a text from Taser. It's a video he sent me with an adorable puppy because he'd heard I'd had a bad day at work.

I call him.

"Taser?" I ask when he answers.

"Hey Bliss, what's up? Do you need Amelia? She's kinda busy flirting away with some guys she met at the bar. Oh and you won't believe what happened after the show—"

"Taser."

"Alright, alright, I'll go get Amelia."

"No, no, don't tell her I called, please. I, um, I need some help actually."

"With what?"

I leave out a lot of the details but explain the crash. "I need someone to, um, well, you know…" I leave it hanging there, hoping he's catching on to what I'm asking.

"I'll be right there, Bliss."

Twenty minutes later Taser slips into my bedroom. "You didn't tell Amelia, right?"

He shakes his head. "Nope." He pauses at the foot of my bed. "So where is Jordan?"

"We broke up."

He nods solemnly. "I thought that might have been the case."

I don't know how to start casual sex. I don't know what to do with myself. Taser sits next to me on the bed, and we decide to put on a movie so it's a bit less weird. Finally, he turns to me and leans in, kissing me. It's weird at first because I'm so used to Jordan, but I quickly find that I like kissing Taser so much more. It's still not mind-blowing or anything, but it's pleasant and I realize in that moment that kissing Jordan has always felt *wrong*.

Where Jordan was demanding and demeaning, Taser is gentle and soft, slow. We take our time adjusting to one another and he pays special attention to my needs, guiding me to a steady climax.

As I finish, I can feel my body healing itself, finally feeling that fullness that comes with topped off power reserves.

I'm buzzing so much with magic that my inner succubus demands more. We end up going for another round. When we're both done again, chests heaving, Taser looks at me and smiles and I find myself smiling back. "Bliss, can I ask a favor?" he asks, a bit timidly.

"Sure, anything."

"Would it be alright if I feed from you?" He looks shy about it. "I don't usually feed from strangers or humans. It's uncomfortable for me."

Tears erupt from my eyes, and Taser holds me close to him. "Bliss, I'm so sorry, forget I asked."

"No, it's not that. Jordan never asked, he just bit."

Taser continues to hold me as I cry. Finally the tears subside and I angle my neck out for him. "Go for it," I say encouragingly. For the first time in a long time, I'm overflowing with my magic, so I have some to spare.

He's tentative at first, but finally he lowers his teeth to my neck and bites gently. Jordan was never, ever gentle about it. He seemed to relish in the pain it caused me, but Taser's bite almost doesn't even hurt. He takes a few drinks, careful not to undo all the work he put into recharging me.

We hang out for a bit afterwards until Taser starts to fall asleep. I nudge him gently and he decides that's a sign to leave. He kisses me on the forehead. "Call me whenever you need, alright Bliss? We can take turns feeding. Friends with dinner benefits," he adds, chuckling to himself.

He leaves, and despite knowing that everything that just happened was a good thing, I curl into a ball and cry my eyes out until there are no more tears left. I sit there waiting for sleep, but it's taking its damn time.

Amelia slowly creaks my bedroom door open and maneuvers her way to my bed in the dark. She lets out a curse as she stubs her toe on the foot of my bed frame. As she steadies herself, she knocks over a pile of books I'd stacked on the floor ages ago. "Fuck!" she whisper yells. I reach over and turn on the bedside lamp. I arch my brows at her.

"I'm not asleep. You could have just turned the light on."

"Well, I can see that *now*," she mutters back. "Why aren't you asleep?" She holds up her hand to tell me not to answer that question. "Better yet, if you're not sleeping, why didn't you come out for drinks with us?"

"Jordan and I got into a fight."

Amelia rolls her eyes. "Bliss, you need to kick him to the curb already. I'm serious."

I throw the covers off my bed and get up. "I'm not going to talk to you about it. The answer isn't always to run when things get tough." I don't know why I say this, instead of letting her know what happened just hours prior. But I guess I just can't get myself to share when she's being so judgy and bossy.

Amelia stares up at me. "Is that what you think I do?"

I start pacing back and forth, the carpet showing a path I've already taken many times before. "You run from anyone good. Once something gets serious with a guy, you bolt!"

"Well, at least I don't run straight to the worst guy on the fucking planet!" she yells at me, getting off my bed. "I'm trying to help you, Bliss. You're fucking miserable, and you won't do anything to change it. You deserve the world, and you're settling for fucking scraps."

She storms out of my room, slamming my door shut, and I cringe at the noise, going completely still. My terror and anxiety from earlier in the night flood into me.

The car door slamming after we left the show. Repeatedly slamming. My legs begin to shake like they did the whole car ride.

CHAPTER THIRTEEN

BLISS

We only have two weeks to prepare for the festival.

Travel will be easy peasy. There's a fae district with a portal just outside of the festival grounds, meaning we'll be there in a matter of minutes, not hours, even dragging all our gear with us.

Lodging is taken care of by the event. We'll be staying in one of several townhomes used to house bands playing during the festival.

I've already signed us up to help out at a scavenger hunt for festival goers to win free stuff. I RSVP'd to the opening masquerade party and a band-and-crew-only day of games and activities. This festival is going to be a lot of work but also a ton of fun.

But unfortunately for me, Goddess' Trance's newly reinstated band manager, the merch situation is not ideal *and* Amelia and Tubbs keep fighting over the set list.

As I go through boxes of band tees and CDs, making an inventory of everything we have, Tubbs taps his drumstick repeatedly against the rim of his snare. "We can't fit all these songs in our one-hour set."

"That's why we're taking 'Glaze' off the set list," Amelia shoots back.

"That's one of our best songs, and not to mention has my drum solo. We gotta keep it. It's our heaviest song and this is a metal festival."

"Well, we're not taking 'You Can Always Reach Me' off the set list. That's not going to happen."

"Fine, then we'll take off 'Fractures,'" Tubbs says, whirling his drumstick around his fingers.

Taser picks up one of Tubbs' wire brush drumsticks and points it at him. "Hell no, that's *my* song."

"Your song?" Amelia arches her eyebrow. "Just so we're clear here, all the songs are mine. I wrote them."

"Parts of them," Tubbs says, rolling his eyes. He's not wrong. He wrote all the drumming music to the songs and Jordan has some song credits as well from their earlier years playing together.

"We aren't getting rid of my solo, okay?" Taser says, crossing his arms.

Dericia rolls her eyes and gets up off the couch. "Bliss, give me a call when they've all got their egos back in check, okay?" She heads out of the garage and I let loose a sigh as I repack a box of vinyl EPs.

"I hope you weren't counting on selling a lot of merch, guys, because we don't really have any," I say, motioning to the four boxes in front of me. One box of T-shirts. One box of vinyl. Two boxes of CDs that really don't sell anymore, which is why there are two. "And we don't have time to order more."

Amelia shrugs. "You know this isn't about money."

Taser laughs, but it's hollow. "Maybe not for you, Miss Succubus Blood, but it would be nice for the rest of us."

"The money will come in," I say, trying to ease the tension this festival is bringing to the surface. I can feel my magic rising, ready to try to influence everyone back into a calmer, more agreeable state, but I don't unleash it. If I did, I would have to feed that much sooner, and despite my promise to Amelia, I really don't want to. "All those songs stay on the set list, okay?" I tell them, looking over at Blake, who gives me a shrug as if to say I'm on my own here.

"Take off 'Butterflies.' It's a longer song with lots of atmospheric pauses and I think it's better for whenever you end up doing an acoustic set some day." I stare my sister down, trying my best to look as in charge as possible.

Amelia sighs, flinging herself down next to Blake on the couch and draping her long legs over his lap, pouting. "But I love that song."

"Amelia," I say in exasperation.

"Fine, fine, we'll do away with 'Butterflies.'" She waves a hand dismissively.

I look to Taser and Tubbs. "Everyone good with that?"

"Yes ma'am." Tubbs grins, flashing white teeth at me. "Look at you being all manager-y."

I snort out a laugh. Taser comes over and slings an arm around my shoulders. "Your first ever Goddess' Trance conflict back on the job and you resolved it in less than two minutes. I think we should keep her," he says, smiling at me. I give him a tentative smile back and make an excuse to shuffle out from under his arm.

I check my email on my phone as I move to start inventorying our gear. I need to tell the festival if we'll be bringing our own or if we'll need to use in-house stuff. We definitely need their front-of-house sound engineers, and we probably need some more tech guys to help set up and break down our set, but I think we've got enough mics for all the stage inputs we need.

Though none of this I actually know for sure. I'm going off videos I watched about sound engineering, and since this is literally something one can get a degree in, I'm not sure if I'm making the right calls. Once the band can afford to pay someone, we need a sound engineer for sure, not to mention technicians and a monitor engineer. The list is long.

"Oh my stars." I almost drop my phone as I reread the email, hardly believing my own eyes.

"What?" Amelia jumps up from the couch, followed by the guys, and they all crowd around me. "What's wrong?"

"Nothing!" I show her my phone so she can read the email. "We're opening for Voracious Maw."

I look over at Taser instinctively. He knows my slight obsession with their music. Though he doesn't know that this aligns perfectly with the task I've been given. If we're opening for them, that could be my way of getting close enough to Wrath to steal whatever I'm supposed to steal. Maybe the wraith also pulled these strings.

"Awww," Taser says sweetly. "Your boyfriend will be there, with his sexy mask."

I punch him lightly on the arm but laugh, forgetting I'm mad at him. "He's not my boyfriend. I just really love his voice."

"He does have a sexy voice." Taser shrugs.

Amelia's eyes find mine over the phone. She doesn't look pleased. "Bliss…"

"Yeah?"

"There was an attachment on this email, with the flyer for the event. It has all the bands listed that'll be playing."

She hands me back my phone and I look over the flyer, zooming in on it slightly. "What exactly am I looking at?"

"Third row from the bottom, towards the left."

My eyes snag over a third name in between Umber Doves and Mourning Coffins. I stare at it, a numbness worming its way into my body as I read the name over and over again.

Dead Hearts.

It's Jordan's band.

The one he started after Amelia kicked him out of Goddess' Trance.

I lock eyes with Amelia and simply shake my head. She's going to be so mad at me for backing out, but there's no way I can go to this festival now.

"Sorry." I pocket my phone. My feet begin to carry me to the main house, and before I know it I'm shutting the door to my old bedroom and sliding down it to the ground, where I try to just focus on taking deep breaths.

"Bliss," Amelia says through the door, softly tapping on it. "Open up."

"No," is all I can manage to get out.

She opens the door anyways, but it pushes against my back. "Bliss, get out of the way," she huffs out in a way only an exasperated sister can. "Let me in."

I crawl away from the door and it swings open. Amelia looks down at me, a softness to her expression that takes me a bit by surprise. When it comes to Jordan she is always so harsh, telling me exactly what I need to do. Trying to protect me in the only way she knows how.

"Are you alright?" she asks as she sits on the floor beside me. I let my head fall to her shoulder, inviting her energy to protect me. Her arm wraps me up in her protective and fierce fire, shielding me.

"I can't see him," I tell her.

"Can't? Or don't want to?"

"Does it matter?"

"Yes," Amelia says simply, pausing for a minute to allow the silence in the room to wash over us.

Finally she speaks again. "Bliss, 'can't' means it's out of your control. And if that's true, that's fine, we can work with that. But if you *can* and you just don't want to, that's different. There's power in admitting that. It becomes your choice then. I'm just worried you'll miss out on the festival because you think you *can't* when really you can and just don't want to." When the fuck did she get so wise?

"And if I just don't want to?"

"Then you decide for yourself if you're going to miss out on something this exciting and fun just because your dickhead of an ex will be there."

"Who are you?" I ask, looking up at her.

"I've grown a lot in the last year," she says haughtily, throwing her hair over her shoulder. A soft giggle escapes me, despite tears pooling in my eyes. She slaps my arm. "Bitch."

I smile, but then it falls. "It's not just that he was an ass, though."

"I know."

I lift my head up off my sister's shoulders and roll my own, as if that movement can somehow imbue me with the strength I feel I so desperately lack. "Fine. I don't *want* to see him."

Amelia nods and gives me a soft smile. She helps me to my feet. "How do you feel about going to the festival and we'll just avoid him? There are so many bands going, plus the crowds, the vendors —you might not even run into him."

I nod in agreement. A tear crests over my lower lid, sliding its way down my cheek. "Okay," is all I can manage to say. I swipe at the tear and the trail it leaves.

There's a knock at the door and Dericia pokes her head in. "Bliss?"

I motion for her to come inside and she tiptoes forward, pulling me into a crushing hug. "Tay Tay texted me and told me what you guys just found out. I'm so sorry. What's our plan?"

I can tell Amelia and Reese are looking at each other over my head.

"We're gonna pretend like he's just not even there," Amelia informs her, and I can hear Reese hum in approval.

"Good plan," she says.

I go to my mirror and start wiping my eyes and fixing my hair, which has gotten mussed with all the hugging. Dericia sits down on the edge of my bed, crossing her legs.

"At least you know that fucking douche isn't your mate," Reese says, gathering her braids over one shoulder and tying them into a ponytail to keep them out of the way.

Amelia's mouth hangs open. "I didn't even think about that."

"What?" Reese asks, confused.

"We don't know that, Reese," Amelia breathes out.

"But the stars wouldn't do that."

"Every Born fae has a mate, even dickheads who don't deserve them," Amelia explains. She comes and stands in front me. "It's statistically unlikely, Bliss. But we'll just have to make sure."

I take care not to nod too quickly. The wraith told me Jordan isn't my mate, and the way he said it, I believe him. But I can't explain that to my sisters. They would freak out if they knew I even talked to a wraith.

"How so? Making sure would mean I have to get close enough to him to see if there's a rune in his eye," I say after a few moments. I guess it would be good to double check. Maybe I was a complete fool to believe the wraith about any of this.

"Maybe not!" Reese says. She whips out her phone. "Maybe he found his mate already. Let me check his socials."

Amelia and I wait with bated breath as she scrolls on her phone. She looks up at us after a few moments, defeated. "Doesn't look like he's been mated yet. When was his bond activated?"

"It would have been last year," Amelia replies.

"Okay, so we'll just have to get Bliss near enough to him without him seeing her so she doesn't have to deal with him," Reese says matter-of-factly, as if that'll be easy. Jordan's a vampire, which means his superior senses might give me away. "You can borrow my perfume to mask your scent," Reese tells me, reading my mind somehow.

"That might just work," Amelia adds, as I sit down next to Reese and wrap my arm around her waist, leaning my head on her shoulder. Amelia sits down next to us and my two sisters encircle me, and for a little bit, I think I might just be able to take on Jordan if he does end up seeing me.

CHAPTER FOURTEEN

BLISS

AMELIA STOPS SHORT OF THE PRISTINE, WHITE FRONT DOOR, THE KEY hovering an inch from the deadbolt lock. She turns around, looking down at the rest of us scattered along the steps on the porch of the townhome that'll be ours for the next week.

"We need to take a minute," she instructs, shutting her eyes.

"A minute for…?" Tubbs asks.

She opens one eye to look at him and then opens both eyes when she realizes the rest of us are just staring at her. "To take it all in. This is huge, you guys!" She motions to the house behind her and then out to the street. Across the way we can see a few other bands also getting settled. I pull my hood up over my hair to hide my ribbon, just in case Jordan's band is also staying in one of these houses.

"We've made it. We're gonna play this festival, and—" She pauses for dramatic effect, grinning down at the rest of us. "We're walking out of here with a fucking record deal. Mark my words," she says the last part to the stars.

"Fuck yes!" Dericia yells, pumping her fist in the air.

Blake lets out a whoop and sweeps Amelia off her feet, spinning her around in a circle on the top step. She flips the key to Taser, who with a flourish slips it into the lock and opens the door.

Blake carries Amelia across the threshold like she's some gothic bride, clad in all black, and the rest of us follow. The boys take off running through the townhome, hollering out to one another, while us girls take our time looking through each room.

The townhome is spacious, with a living room opening out to the dining room and the kitchen beyond that.

Upstairs is a set of three bedrooms, and then on the top floor two more bedrooms (one a primary suite that Amelia claims immediately), and also a little nook to look out from the front of the house. It's all beautifully decorated, with light pastel colors. It's a bit of a contrast with everyone else's black outfits, but I personally love it.

Dericia takes the room next to Amelia's, leaving the boys to take the bedrooms on the second floor. I drop my things in the primary with Amelia, knowing even if I took a different room she'd probably end up sleeping in there with me at some point anyways.

"If you hook up with Blake while we're here, you do it in his bed," I warn her.

"Okay, as long as you hook up with Taser in his bed," she shoots back.

I raise my brows at her. "That's not gonna happen."

"You're still mad at him?"

"Of course I am. I haven't completely forgiven you either," I say, giving her a pointed look.

"Fine, you're in need of some new dick anyways." She throws one of the pillows at me, grinning.

I catch it before it can hit the wall behind me. "Your aim really sucks."

She shrugs. "I was never much for sports."

Again my brows raise.

Her grin grows even wider. "Sports, I said. I do love a good athletic man."

"Gross." I groan and head back downstairs, Amelia following one step behind me.

"What? You don't like a man with good muscles?"

"I know I sure do," Dericia says. She's standing at the bottom of the stairs with the rest of the guys, everyone ready to go out in search of food.

Amelia puts her finger to her lips in thought. "I guess now that I think about it, I don't think I've ever seen Bliss be into any super muscular guys. You like the skinny ones."

"I don't really have a preference."

"You definitely do," Taser says, and I can feel my jaw clench. "What about Wrath? He's a tall, super lanky guy. Pretty sure that's your type."

"Can everyone stop talking about my taste in men, so we can all go taste some food?" I sigh. "I'm hungry." I hold up a hand to Amelia to stop her from saying anything about me needing to "eat" in any other context than real food. "Hungry for dinner, so let's go!" I usher everyone out of the house, suddenly feeling a bit like a parent trying to herd teenagers.

"You know, Taser, you're a bit lanky too," Dericia says. She looks over to Tubbs. "So is Tubbs. Which is a little misleading."

Taser slings an arm around Tubbs. "You know that's not why we call him that," he says with a laugh.

"I know, but still—it seems like false advertising," Dericia responds.

Tubbs is his mother's maiden name. Nymphs used to stick mainly to themselves in matriarchal groups centuries ago, and a holdover from that time is the tradition of female nymphs keeping their last names. If their partner is male, the male fae generally changes his last name and any kids they have also take the female nymph's last name.

We've all met Tubbs' father, though. He is about as misogynistic as they come, and he insisted Tubbs' mom take his name instead. So in middle school, at first to piss off his dad, and later to honor his mother, he started having people call him Tubbs. It helped that he'd once played drums on huge empty tubs of ice cream leftover from the school cafeteria as part of an impromptu concert. Amelia and Reese had joined in before the teachers put a stop to it.

"So what about you, Reese?" Taser asks. "Do any of us lanky lads suit your preferences?"

She swats him. "Sorry, but unlike my sisters, I definitely will not be sampling from the Goddess' Trance pool."

"Is it sampling if I've only ever slept with one?" Amelia asks genuinely.

Tubbs turns his wicked grin to Amelia. "It's not, and I'm definitely in favor of you sampling."

She gives him a sultry smile. "Of course you are."

"As band manager," I say, stopping in front of the group and looking back at them, "I would definitely recommend any 'sampling'—as you're so charmingly putting it—should stop."

Amelia arches a single brow at me. "You're seriously no fun sometimes, Bliss."

"Need I remind you of any of the countless bands that have broken up because everyone was sleeping around?"

Blake and Amelia both let out a sigh. "No," she responds, coming and walking next to me instead of Blake. "I guess I should really take my sampling elsewhere during the festival anyways. It'd be a shame not to see what's out there being offered."

"Can we stop with the sampling analogy?" I groan.

"It's fun," Dericia says. "I like it." She comes alongside Amelia and I. "And I too am excited to see what's being offered this week." She nudges me with her shoulder and smiles. I roll my eyes but can't help matching her smile.

CHAPTER FIFTEEN

PISCES

"Do you have any more of that jet lag tonic?" I ask Benny, looking at him hopefully. I'm still a bit tired. We left London at ten pm, and even though we traveled through a fae portal to get here, the eight-hour time difference is still killer.

I'm laid on the couch in the living room of our townhome rental, gazing up at the crystalline light fixture. The rest of my band —including Simon—are all in the room. Most of the crew we traveled with, though, have gone out in search of food and to meet up with friends from other bands.

"Give it another few minutes to kick in, mate. That's definitely not something you want to overdose on," Benny says with a grin. He and Evan exchange looks.

Shaun clucks his tongue at all of us. "I'm not dealing with any of you if you get high on that shit."

I sit up straight. "You can get high from it?" Not going to lie, it sounds kind of fun.

"It's a trip," Evan responds. "Take too much and time becomes completely meaningless to you. I felt like a I was just a floating ball of nothing. It was amazing."

"Yeah, and then you vomited your guts out for hours after you came down," Shaun reminds him.

"Bet time wasn't so meaningless then, was it?" Benny claps Evan on the shoulder.

I let out a chuckle as Evan glares at the other two. He shrugs. "Worth it."

Benny brings out the tonic from the kitchen. "So Sces, what'll it be? You want another dose, mate?"

"I think I'll pass," I deadpan with a glance at Evan.

Besides, I need to be at my best for this festival. We've been riding a boost in our streaming numbers ever since going viral on social media. I want these performances at the festival to be amazing. In fact, I need them to be.

"Shall we go find a pub and get some beers instead?" Evan suggests, bouncing a leg up and down as he sits on the couch. "We can see if anyone else has arrived yet."

"Like who?" I reluctantly push myself off the very comfortable couch, standing up and stretching my arms up over my head.

"The Phantoms are here, and Locust—what's their lead's name? Francis? We could see what they're up to."

"Did you see the recent addition to the line-up?" Benny asks, handing me a flyer that was included with a little gift basket from the festival organizers.

My eyes gloss over the names, my irritation pricking as I see Dead Hearts towards the bottom. I look back up at Benny. "What am I supposed to be looking at?"

"They changed our opener, mate." Evan leans over, tapping the flyer just underneath our band name. And there it is, so obvious I'm surprised I didn't see it before.

Goddess' Trance.

"That's pretty cool," I say. They're a solid band with lots of talent and seem like pretty decent fae, even if they are all Born fae—well, except their bassist, if I recall correctly. She's kindred.

Simon hangs over the back of the couch, trying to get a glimpse of the piece of paper. "What are we looking at?"

I hand him the flyer. "Goddess' Trance. They filled in for our opener the last time we played in Seattle." We didn't have the funds at that point to hire any crew members, not even Simon. "I think I played you some of their music a couple months ago, actually." I think back to when I saw they'd dropped a new EP. It was amazing, and I had noticed a huge improvement in the guitar since they'd replaced Jordan Yarrow.

"I hope to the stars we don't run into Dead Hearts," I mutter. The last time we were at a festival with them it didn't go well.

"They know not to mess with us now," Evan says darkly.

"Something tells me they're dumb enough to not know that," Shaun replies.

Simon leaves the living room and goes over to the kitchen table, where the jet lag tonic is sitting. He unscrews the lid, giving it a sniff and pouring some into a glass. He brings it to his lips.

"Stop!" Shaun yells, the word so forceful in my mind that I still for a second.

Simon, however, is frozen, the glass looking almost stuck to his lips. He doesn't move a muscle but his eyes are wide, and they dart from Shaun to me and back.

Shaun rushes forward, plucking the glass out of Simon's hands. "Sorry, um, you can move again."

Simon all of a sudden stumbles forward, as if some invisible force was holding him upright. "Fuck, what was that?"

I think this is the first time I've ever seen Shaun's command in action. Wolf shifters can sometimes command other fae, but usually only for small periods of time. Shaun told me his only works when he's feeling intense emotions—fear, for example. According to Simon's bewildered look, he's never seen it in action either.

Shaun glances over his shoulder at Evan, an exasperated look on his face. "Have you not explained to Simon the difference between fae doses and human doses? If he had drunk that, he would have been higher than a fucking kite."

Evan is on his feet in less than a second. "Me?" he asks, genuinely confused. "What are you on about?"

"You're his sponsor, or did you forget? You haven't taught him about these types of potions?"

I make my way over to Simon, reaching out for the tonic, inspecting the label. "Is it not safe for humans?" I would never have guessed, though that's probably pretty stupid of me to assume humans wouldn't react differently to fae potions.

"I didn't realize he was even drinking it. I'm not his fucking babysitter," Evan says to Shaun, his voice getting a little louder and more irritated with each word.

"But you *are* his sponsor," Shaun replies. "This is exactly the type of thing you're supposed to be teaching him."

Evan rolls his eyes. "Maybe this is my teaching style—you know, learning by making mistakes."

Shaun shakes his head, muttering something, before saying, "You need to be more careful."

Evan shrugs. "Fine." He turns to Simon. "Don't drink tonics without looking up what the human dosage is, mate."

"Great, thanks." Simon rolls his eyes, but a soft twitch at the corners of his mouth shows he's not really all that mad.

I might be, though. Waves of anger have started undulating through me at how cavalier Evan is being about Simon's sponsorship. Simon's safety is, as far as I'm concerned, all of our responsibilities. If Evan isn't going to take this seriously, then I'll see if Shaun will mentor Simon.

But I'll bring it up later.

With the mention of Dead Hearts earlier and Evan shirking his responsibilities, I need to cool off. I need to get out, stretch my legs, and take my mind off things, hopefully with some really good food. "Let's go find something to eat."

"And a pint or two," Benny adds.

CHAPTER SIXTEEN

PISCES

SIMON KEEPS LOOKING AT ME WITH SUCH CONCERN IN HIS EYES IT makes me want to break down. It's been two months, and this is the first time I've really gone out to do anything. Simon wouldn't take no for an answer anymore. I understand his reasoning. Sometimes focusing on doing normal things is what one needs to let time heal everything.

But I'm too broken at this point. I can't help but think I could have all the time in the world and it wouldn't be enough to mend these wounds.

My cousin is probably the only person I could be around right now. Anyone else either blames me or pities me, and I can't handle that.

So we went to the cinema, which sucked, but at least it gave me something to focus on, other than replaying the memory of the crash over and over again.

Now we sit at a cafe, waiting for our food, food I'm probably not going to eat.

My appetite is non-existent these days. She's never going to eat again, so it feels like I shouldn't enjoy food either.

Simon gives me a soft smile as we sip on our drinks. "Pisces, I know it doesn't feel like it, but life will get better."

My eyes snap to his and I can see him flinch a little. He's been walking on eggshells around me all day. Guilt washes over me and my shoulders slump. "I don't see how. I don't see a way forward. And even if I did, I don't think I deserve one."

Simon shakes his head. "You don't deserve any of the blame you're getting, even the blame you're putting on yourself."

I hang my head in silence and shame. "I was driving."

"That's not the whole story."

"But it's what everyone knows. And even if I didn't cause it, I am still responsible for what happened."

"She made a choice, Pisces. One that hurt you too, might I remind you."

Silence hangs over us for a few moments and lengthens when the server brings the appetizers Simon ordered. He puts a few things on my plate, sliding it over to me.

"Do you know how many times I thought to myself, I should get her some help? I should tell someone—anyone—about what she was doing to herself?"

Simon shakes his head.

"Almost every single day." I let out a harsh laugh. "But I didn't. I didn't tell anyone." I rub the underside of my right arm, feeling the scarred skin, the constant reminder of my failings.

"It still isn't your fault. If she didn't want help, it's possible there was nothing you could have ever done."

"Maybe that's true. But maybe not. Maybe I'm the reason. She was happier before she met me. I ruin things, Simon."

He gives me a questioning look in response and breathes out a sigh, no doubt thinking through his next words carefully. "I'm not saying you don't have some things to learn about being in a relationship. We all probably do. But you can't completely blame yourself. It sounds like you two were just not a good match. You were toxic together. I wasn't around you two much, but I heard things. Maybe things could have been better, but you have no idea if that would have changed anything."

I nod. I understand what he's saying, but it doesn't ease any of the guilt I feel. It's still my fault what happened. I should have let her go, but I was so desperate to fix things, to keep her.

The image of her grabbing the wheel and yanking it to the left, the car spinning out of control and crashing through the railing, plays through my mind over and over. I take a few quick gasps, drawing a bit of attention to our table. Simon reaches out and takes my hand and I let a few tears fall, because I don't deserve this kindness. I don't deserve anything good.

"It's going to be okay," Simon says, giving my hand a little pat. "Eventually it's going to be okay."

I nod, even if I don't believe him. But it helps me stop the tears before they can become a steady stream. The rest of our food arrives and we wait in silence as the plates are set down. Once the waiter leaves, Simon picks up his fork and dives in. I don't touch mine.

"What about music? Have you been writing any new songs?" Simon asks between mouthfuls.

I pick up my fork and start pushing the food around on my plate. "No," I say hesitantly, like I'm admitting a fault. "I haven't been able to bring myself to even play piano," I admit. Why do I feel a prick of shame?

Simon's concern arrives back in his furrowed brow. "I'm no therapist, but wouldn't music help you? Catharsis and all that, right?"

The corner of my mouth hooks up gently. "I think that's what I'm afraid of."

"What do you mean?"

"If I process these emotions, then they're gone. I could heal and move on. And I don't deserve that."

"How enlightened of you," Simon responds, and I can tell he's fighting a grin, which only makes me break out into a smile of my own. I chuckle for the first time since the crash. Simon laughs a bit with me. In the break in conversation I take a bite of food.

After a few moments, Simon grows thoughtful. "Maybe you could reframe it."

"Hmm?"

"Maybe it helps you move on, but what if your music helps others move on? Helps others heal? Use your pain to help others and become worthy of healing yourself. Don't get me wrong. You're already worthy, but maybe this will help you *feel* worthy."

"That sounds selfish, like I'm doing it for the wrong reasons."

Simon shrugs. "Does it matter, if the end result is you and a load of other people are healed?"

I pause. I don't have an answer to that. Maybe it doesn't. But then another thought pops into my head. "But if I share my music and it helps people, then I'd have their admiration. I don't deserve that either."

Simon quirks his lips into a rueful smile. "Now you're just trying to find reasons not to."

"Maybe," I respond with a grin. But it is an actual issue. Every time I've performed in front of an audience, I've felt like a fraud. I was so concerned with how they'd perceive me and what they'd think, that I could tell I wasn't allowing myself to be real. And I'd always felt so underserving of their time and attention.

"Find a way to make it about more than just yourself, then."

He says it like it's so simple. I nod, but my brain searches for a way to do that and comes up completely blank.

We move on to other topics, but what he was saying lingers with me even after we leave the restaurant and even after I've walked Simon to his bus stop before heading home myself.

I take a shortcut through a dimly lit alleyway, unable to stop replaying Simon's words. Night is setting in earlier these winter days and I pull my hands into my sleeves to ward off the cold, even as lyrics pop out of nowhere into my head.

Maybe it's because I'm too busy hastily typing the lyrics into my phone that I don't see him until he steps out into the dim street light filtering down. "Hey there, mate," the stranger says. His voice has a slight hiss to it.

"Sorry, mate. I'm in a hurry," I tell him, barely glancing up. This part of town isn't terrible, but it's not great. Usually people leave each other alone here.

"Don't you want my help, though?"

I roll my eyes. The guy is probably on drugs. I don't respond and keep walking.

"She's in hell, mate. But I can help. She didn't deserve what you put her through and even now she's yelling out at you to help her. 'Pisces! Pisces!'" My name spills from his lips, but instead of his voice, I hear hers—Leighton's. It's like someone punched me in the stomach. I whirl around and glare at the stranger.

"What the fuck is going on?" I ask him. "How did you do that?" How did he sound like her?

He waves a hand and the air seems to sizzle and part right in front of me. A vision of Leighton in what has to be hell itself appears in front of me. "Pisces! Help me!" she screams out. I lunge forward, trying to get to her, but the air ripples and the vision fades, her screams echoing around the alley.

"What the hell is happening?" I ask, looking back to the man, my eyes as wide as saucers. He stands there looking solemn.

"She went to hell, Pisces. You know why. But you know she didn't mean it. She wasn't in her right mind. But you can help her."

"How?" I ask. My mind is spinning. I've always been open to hell as a concept. I went to a Catholic school, so it's familiar to me, but I've never truly believed it exists. And here is this stranger showing me visions of it. But how? Magic isn't real. Hell and heaven aren't real, are they?

"I can get her out. I just need your help."

Something tells me to be wary of this man. But what I saw felt so real. I have to help her.

"You'll be able to see her whenever you want and she'll be safe. I just need something from you."

"What?" I ask. I'll give anything. I don't have much, but I'll give it. I'll give him everything.

"Sing for me, and it'll fuel the magic I need to work to save her."

"Sing?" That's hardly a steep price. Though I haven't sung since I woke up in the hospital.

"Song is a very powerful magic." The man steps closer to me and I look around the deserted alleyway.

"All I have to do is sing?"

"And I'll do the rest," he says, giving me a small smile. "Go ahead, sing anything."

So I do. I sing a version of "Hallelujah" by Leonard Cohen. My voice starts off a bit rocky since I haven't sung in so long, but I quickly find the right pitch and I sing, the sound echoing off the brick walls around us. The man steps closer to me and before I know it, his hands turn to claws and he sinks them into my chest. Agony radiates out from where his claws have pierced me. I falter, gasping at the pain, but he shakes his head. "Don't stop," he says, and so I don't. I sing through the pain, even as blood pours from my chest. The song ends and I open my eyes, tears flowing freely down my face.

The man is still before me, but now I'm sure he isn't a man. A demon, maybe. His irises have turned red, almost the color of my blood that's splattering the stone at my feet.

"Thank you," he says, almost kindly. "You have a beautiful voice." He leans down, licking my cheek, and I fall to my knees, exhausted. "Such a pity for this world to lose you before you could truly become something. But you were such an easy snack, and a delicious one." The demon licks his fingers and vanishes, but I barely register it. I'm dying. Whatever he did, it's killing me.

As my eyes close of their own volition, I'm graced with a vision of her. It's just a memory, but one of the few good ones I have. I can even smell her, and I let her scent wash over me as I die.

I wake up in my own bed the next morning, no idea how I got here. My clothes are the ones I was wearing yesterday when I met with Simon, but they're caked in dirt and grime from the alleyway.

The alleyway…

I jump up from my bed, hurrying to the small rectangular mirror hanging over my dresser. I stumble into it, and it sways a bit under my weight as I grip the edges and look at my reflection.

My shirt has holes in it exactly where the demon pierced my skin.

Well, I guess that answers that. I didn't imagine or dream it. But I'm somehow alive. I ease my shirt off my torso and examine my wounds in the mirror. Except there aren't any. Just five little scars that are so faded, it seems impossible they could have come from last night.

But I didn't have them yesterday.

My reflection gazes solemnly back at me. Just more scars to add to all my others. I glance down at my forearms. They're covered in scars. The worst are from going over the bridge. The others are self-inflicted and quite old.

My jaw aches too for some reason, as if the singing yesterday was too much. I shake my head at my reflection. I'm the biggest idiot in the entire world.

Magic, demons—apparently real.

And I was tricked into feeding that demon?

The vision he showed me must have been fake. He showed me what he needed to, to take what he wanted.

Days later and I'm going hungry. I've eaten everything I can get my hands on and I'm still hungry.

I've never been one for casual sex. It's always felt weird to me, being touched by someone I don't know well. But there's this ache in my body, a thirst so awful I can't figure out how to assuage it. So I find myself here, in the backroom of the bar Simon and some other friends have pulled me out to, with a girl whose name I don't know. She's kissing my neck. Having gone so long without even my hand for company, I'm torturously hard. I grind myself into her and she lets out a soft moan. I want to taste her, want to be inside her. *I'm so hungry for her.*

I lift her onto a few sturdy boxes and push her dress up her thighs, revealing creamy white flesh that I want to lick. That I want to *taste.* She widens her legs for me and I get on my knees, ready to worship this woman I've barely exchanged a few words with.

I trail kisses up her left thigh, holding her apart with my hands as she runs her fingers through my hair. I practically purr at the feel of her tugging my head towards her. I use my right hand to guide her thong aside as I begin to taste her center, slowly licking my way until my tongue slides into her folds.

I groan at the taste.

I've always loved giving head. I pride myself on my skill, actually. The taste has always been nice, welcomed, but this woman, or maybe it's the thought that anyone could walk in and see us— something is making this taste particularly alluring.

I'm almost salivating at it.

And I'm so fucking hungry and thirsty all at the same time.

I give her a playful nip along the inside of her thigh. Teasing her.

She moans and urges me on with her fingers in my hair.

The smooth expanse of her thigh calls to me. She's thicker here, her thighs pushing together earlier when she was walking, rubbing together, begging for someone to be between them. I have an over- whelming urge to nibble her there again and so I do. I can feel myself salivating more, and an ache has settled around my teeth. Something feels like it's shifting in my mouth, but I'm too focused on that pale skin, fixated on it.

I go to nibble her again, but as soon as my teeth touch her flesh, they break it, puncturing in multiple places, and blood floods my mouth. Even though a voice at the back of my mind tells me something is wrong, it feels so good. So I bite harder.

I'm dimly aware that the woman is screaming, trying to push me off, but she tastes so fucking good. I bite into her over and over, moving up her thigh towards her center. She struggles to get away from me, but I crave her too much to let go. My fingers sink into her legs, holding her steady, and I keep taking bites, swallowing her flesh and her blood and reveling in it.

Flesh.

I'm literally eating human flesh.

What the fuck?

I force myself to push away from her, stumbling to the ground as she's screaming.

Oh God. What have I done?

But the hunger is pushing me towards her again, as I watch blood dripping from her thighs. I have to get out of here, but I don't want to just leave. The woman is looking at me like I'm a monster —which I am. I can hear people coming, her screams having finally been heard over the loud bar noises and music.

"God, I'm so sorry," I whisper, but she can't hear me. I don't know what to do, but I know if I stay here any longer I'm going to attack her again.

I'm starting to zone in on her throat now, her pulsing neck. I curse, pushing myself to my feet and forcing myself to the door that leads out back. I push it open, letting the cool air hit my skin. I realize the front of my shirt is covered in blood, and so is my face. I probably look like a lunatic.

My pulse is hammering in my veins. I need to get the fuck out of here before I hurt anyone else.

"Get the hell away from me!" I hear a woman shout. I look to my left down the alley and see two figures, one hovering over the other.

"Stop fighting me," the man tells her sternly, as if she's a misbehaving kid.

I take a few steps over, my hunger mixing with my anger at this man.

"Leave me alone!" the woman screams.

I stumble towards them, kicking a beer bottle by accident. It goes skittering across the cobblestones. The man turns around. "Nothing here to concern yourself with, mate. I'm just having a fight with my girlfriend."

"Please help!" she yells to me. "I'm not his girlfriend!"

"Shut the fuck up." He turns to me. "Seriously, don't concern yourself, mate. She's being dramatic."

I'm still in the shadows, otherwise they both would have taken off running at the sight of me covered in blood. I can smell the woman's fear and the man's arousal. It's odd, the two scents conflicting with each other. I don't like it.

I reach out and rip the man away from her.

"Thank you!" she says. "Thank you!"

"Run," I tell her, my face finally coming into the glow of the streetlamp. She lets out another scream and she runs. I turn to the man and he screams too.

He tries to take off in the opposite direction, but I still have hold of his shoulder.

My hunger is practically purring, my jaw aching so desperately that I don't hesitate. I bite into his neck, ripping chunks out with my teeth. My teeth that seem longer and sharper. I rip at the man's clothes, exposing his torso. He's dead now already. I tore his throat out.

But I continue to feast.

He falls limply to the ground and I descend upon his chest, taking more bites.

And then I'm literally ripped off him and thrown through the air into the brick wall behind me. I crash hard into the ground, too stunned to do much other than fall into a heap. From the corner of my eye I see another man crouch over the dead guy, checking for a pulse, even though he lies in a pool of his own blood.

Horror works its way through me. I attacked him.

I attacked the girl in the bar.

What the hell? I literally bit into them both and *ate* pieces of their flesh. I feel like I should vomit, but the hunger, the thirst isn't there anymore. I feel full. Content.

And horrified.

Another man, the one that threw me into the wall, I think, crouches before me. He's probably around five-ten, but he's obviously strong. I can see large biceps as he tilts my head to face him. His dirty blonde hair is cropped close to his head, parted neatly to the side, and his narrowed ice-blue eyes glower down at me angrily. "Are you stupid?" he asks. "Feeding in public like this? And you just left the girl to bleed out back there."

"Feeding?" I whisper, not able to make my voice work. "I didn't. I didn't mean to—" Didn't mean to what? *Eat them?*

"Have you ever done this before?" he asks me, his tone a little softer this time.

"No, of course not. I don't understand. We were just—I was just eating her out. I didn't mean to…" I watch, panicked, as the other man pulls the dead man's body over to the side of the alleyway, taking the man's wallet and keys out of his pockets and shaking some foul-smelling powder on his body.

The body begins to smoke and then it burns to ash, as if the man never existed at all.

The door swings open and the girl that I bit first stumbles out laughing with her friends. She sees me and she smiles and waves shyly, heading the other way with her friends. She looks to be completely unharmed, not a single drop of blood on her.

I stare after her, my mouth hanging open in shock. "But how?" I ask the men, pointing at her. "How did she? I mean, there was so much blood. I hurt her…"

The man squatting in front of me shrugs and hooks a thumb over his shoulder at his friend. "He healed her and compelled her to forget what really happened. Pretty sure he made her believe you were the best sex of her life and to go home with her friends and sleep it off. Compulsion is a handy trick. One you should really know, but you're brand new, aren't you?"

"Brand new? New to what?"

The other guy, the taller one, comes and stands behind his friend. "Hate to break it to you, kid, but you're fae now. A siren, by the looks of it."

"A what?" I try to push my way to standing, but the guy shakes his head at me. His long platinum blonde hair is tied up in a bun at the back of his head and it shakes with him.

"You're in shock. Best to stay seated, mate."

The one still sitting in front of me looks up at his friend. "What do you think?"

"We're not taking in another lost puppy, Shaun."

"If we don't, he could lose control again. He's already killed."

The other one shakes his head and shrugs. "He killed a rapist by the looks of it. Not like the world really lost anything special there."

"I would have killed the girl," I whisper to them. I was able to get myself outside, but just barely. Shaun leans back on his heels, regarding me. He's covered in tattoos and wearing all black. I try to focus on one of the tattoos to calm my breathing. I *ate* someone. I *killed* someone.

"Well, you were literally starving to death. You can't really blame yourself."

"I ate pieces of her, and then I ate him," I say, voice flat. I stare into his blue eyes. "I *ate pieces of human flesh.*"

"Yeah, we saw," the other guy says. Even sitting down I can tell he's at least as tall as me.

"Be nice, Evan," Shaun reprimands. "What's your name?"

"Pisces," I tell him, ignoring Evan's snort when he hears my name.

I finally push myself to stand up, and this time Shaun helps me, gripping my upper arm to steady me.

"Let's at least clean you up before anyone sees you," Evan says, inclining his head at my blood-soaked shirt.

I stare down at my shirt. It's covered in two people's blood now.

"Oh god," I let out, but Evan whispers something and waves his hand and it's like all traces of the blood completely disappear.

"How did you do that?" I breathe out, looking between Shaun and Evan.

Evan holds out his hand. "Evan Lyra, fire elemental," he says by way of introduction.

I uncertainly take his hand. "What's a fire elemental?"

"Elemental fae have ties to all the elements and usually specialize in just one. They can also heal other people. Very powerful and very common," Shaun adds, with a smirk at Evan.

Evan rolls his eyes. "Elemental fae are common, but fire elementals are quite rare. I'm actually a pretty big deal."

The two of them don't seem too concerned that I'm a danger to them, that I just went on a human-eating spree.

Shaun offers me his hand as well, and I shake it. "I'm Shaun Pyxus, wolf shifter," he says, grinning. I see two very pointy canines.

"I'm Pisces Penrose, and apparently I'm a siren?" I say the last part quietly, not wanting to be overheard, even though we're the only ones here.

"So Evan." Shaun looks to his taller friend. "What do you think? Can we keep him?"

"Keep me?" I ask, raising a brow.

"Well, at least for the time being. You probably don't want to be around humans until you get your cravings under control."

"It's normal," Evan says, "especially when you didn't grow up fae."

"Grow up fae?"

"Evan and I are Born fae. So we don't really know what it's like to feed for the first time not knowing what you are. But we have a friend who's Made fae. You'll like him and he can help walk you through the changes."

"You'll make sure I don't ever do that again?" I ask, pointing to the pile of ash that was the man I just mauled. "I don't want to hurt anyone. I don't understand how this could even happen. How did I become this?"

Shaun takes my arm and guides me outside to the back of the bar and we walk alongside the alley towards the pavement. "Most Made fae are turned by other fae. But sirens can't be made by other sirens."

"It was a demon," I say, matter-of-fact. There's no doubt in my mind.

"A song wraith," Shaun corrects.

"If a human survives their attack—which is super rare," Evan explains, "—they turn into a siren. I've only ever read about sirens. I've never met one."

My shoulders sag. And then I come to a halt, ripping my arm free from Shaun's grip. "Why should I trust you?" I had trusted the song wraith, as they called it, and look how that turned out.

Evan and Shaun exchange glances. "We did save that woman from being your first kill," Shaun says quickly. "You don't have to trust us. You don't have to come with us, but tell me, how would you feel if you came to and you'd slaughtered all your family and friends out of hunger?"

I open my mouth to speak, but there's nothing to say. I close it, clenching my jaw.

"Come with us and you don't have to worry about hurting anyone. You can feed off us without killing us. But humans? If you don't learn how to control yourself and keep yourself well fed, you're a danger. And I don't think you want to be."

CHAPTER SEVENTEEN

BLISS

"This place looks good," Dericia says as we stand outside a chill-looking bar and restaurant. "Should we eat here?" She turns from the menu posted out front and looks at the group.

"Sounds good to me," Amelia says. "Tay, you good to eat here? Looks like they've got a real Bloody Mary," she adds with a wink.

"Sure." Taser's voice is monotone, his gaze fixed down the sidewalk on a group walking towards us. "Let's just go inside already."

"I'll go see if there's a wait." Reese bounces inside and chats with the hostess. She pops her head back out. "It's self-seating." She waves us inside, but the group Taser is watching comes to a stop in front of him.

Taser looks like a coiled snake of anger, his fists clenched at his sides.

I look over at the group and immediately recognize them due to my vast social media stalking of them. Three members of the Phantoms—a more classical metal rock band—look us over. I bite my lip as I notice the tallest one, Grim.

Do I have a little crush on him? No, definitely not.

It's a huge crush.

Okay yeah, I'm fan-girling for sure.

There's something about their shows that's so immersive and engaging, probably due to the storytelling element. They also wear masks, but unlike Voracious Maw they're not concerned about their identities being known. I dug deep into the backgrounds of the musicians out of boredom once, so I know them all by sight. It would be so much easier if the wraith wanted me to steal from one of them. At least I'd know where to start.

There's Grim, one of the rhythm guitarists and backup vocalists. Pinkie, their lead guitarist, and Bell, the other rhythm guitarist.

Bell looks up at Taser through thick lashes and smiles softly at him. "It's been a long time, Tay," she says, reaching out and laying her hand on his forearm, her rich copper brown skin contrasting with his slight tan.

Dericia and I exchange looks at her husky voice, edged with a bit of wistfulness.

Taser shoves his hands in his jean pockets and looks away from her. "Yeah. Years."

I honestly am not sure how he could look away from this woman. She's gorgeous. Her hourglass figure is on full display with a see-through lace blouse layered over a low-cut button-up top. Heavy chain necklaces drop just between her breasts, moving as she breathes. Her leather pants are tight and accentuate her curves even more.

"It's good to see you, man," Grim says, offering his hand to Taser. He wears a genuine smile, flashing his full set of white teeth that brings out his golden tan skin even more. He has an easiness about him, his other hand hooked in the pocket of his black jeans. When it's clear Taser won't shake his hand, he sighs and runs his hand through his dark hair instead, scratching himself behind the ear. I definitely don't let my eyes linger on the soft short waves of his hair. "How have you been?" he asks, awkwardly.

Pinkie, the lead guitarist, stands at the back of the group, not looking at Taser. His light brown hair ends just below his shoulders and somewhat hides his face, but I can still make out light skin and deep brown eyes, and the glare that he's currently directing at the sidewalk.

Dericia finally can't take the awkwardness anymore and tugs Taser into the restaurant. The rest of us stand there, unsure of what to make of Taser's reaction. We know he has a past with this band, but I never realized how strained their relationship is.

Amelia smiles softly at the Phantoms. "It's been a long day already," she says, letting just a bit of her succubus charm loose. It's probably unnoticeable to anyone but me.

"Of course, we get it," Grim responds, grinning even wider at us. "You must be Amelia? We've been listening to your EP on repeat for a bit."

"At first we were just stalking Taser, wanting to see what he's been up to, but we've been pretty hooked after hearing 'You Can Always Reach Me,'" Bell adds, her smile warm and inviting. It's so hard to imagine how Taser and them got on such bad terms. Maybe it's Amelia's powers, but I find myself hoping we can all be friends.

"And you are?" Grim asks, turning his attention to me.

"I'm Bliss," I say, shaking his hand, my eyes probably wider than saucers. I stare at my hand after he lets go.

Amelia leans in, adding, "She's our band manager."

He gives a soft chuckle. Bell shakes my hand next. "He has that effect on people."

I laugh, slightly embarrassed. "I'm guessing you also have that effect on people," I add.

She shrugs. "It just comes with the territory of being cool, but you two know all about that. You're succubi, right?"

I nod.

"And your bassist? She's human? It's nice to meet another band that's mixed like that."

Amelia nods. "Kindred human. She grew up with us."

"Awesome," Bell says. "We've got a couple of kindreds with us as well, but otherwise we're mostly fae."

Grim motions behind him to Pinkie, introducing us. Now that Taser is gone, Pinkie is flirty and nice, commending me for taking on the role of band manager. He has the canines and scent of a vampire. I fall into a warm conversation with him and Grim as we all make our way into the restaurant. I find myself hoping this festival will prove to be a chance for Taser and the Phantoms to make up.

"So is this your first Alchemy Festival?" Grim asks me as he and I take seats next to each other at a table near to where Taser and Dericia have sat down. I feel a little bad at not joining them, but Amelia would kill me for not taking this opportunity for networking.

"It's that obvious?" I ask sheepishly.

He grins. "The wide-eyed look does give it away a bit."

"Oh, that's for sure because we ran into you guys. I'm a huge fan."

"Well, good, that means I'll see you at our sets?" He winks at me.

"Oh, trust me, I will be front row screaming my head off during your show."

His deep laugh rumbles in my bones and I want to sigh in contentment from that sound. This man is beautiful.

"How about we just settle for you being backstage and then I can find you more easily afterwards?"

Butterflies soar in my abdomen. "Sure, that works too," I say, putting in quite the effort to sound casual.

Tubbs and Blake have joined Reese and Taser at their table, bringing a round of drinks with them. Amelia excuses herself and goes to sit next to Taser, but not before she stares meaningfully at me, then at Grim. The message is clear. I should eat with them and network. And because it's Amelia there's probably also a message in there that I should flirt my way into Grim's bed.

But I choose to ignore that one.

"So who's your favorite Phantom?" Bell asks, sitting to my right.

I quickly look at Grim, grinning. "Oh, definitely Stormy. She's so much fun to watch during your performances."

Pinkie laughs and Grim shakes his head, chuckling. "The keyboardists always get all the love."

"It's my favorite instrument, actually," I respond.

"Do you play?" Bell asks.

"Not well," I admit. "I've never really prioritized it."

"Something tells me that's not quite true," Grim says. He playfully reaches over and lifts my hand up. "These delicate things look like they could play quite well."

Bell and Pinkie laugh. "Grim is a notorious flirt, just so you know," Bell warns.

Grim smiles at me and shrugs. "It's part of my charm. So tell us more about Goddess' Trance," he says, leaning in closer to me. I can smell just a hint of cologne on him that mixes perfectly with his own natural scent and I breathe in, smiling at him as I launch into our band's origin story.

The conversation with the Phantoms over lunch is amazing. I learn quite a bit about the growth they've been experiencing in the past couple of years. I make a ton of mental notes about that and plan to discuss it all with Amelia and the others later. All three of the Phantoms are hilarious in their own way and have an easiness and chemistry between them. It's obvious they've known each other for a long time, but I don't ever once feel left out of the conversation. I really, really like them, and we make plans to meet up later and hang out again as Grim settles the tab. I offer to pay for my portion but he just shakes his head. "It's on me, gorgeous."

I blush a little and can see Amelia eyeing me from the other table. "Thanks," I say, getting up. Before I can get any ideas about all the possible things I could do with this male, I promise to see him later, and then excuse myself to the restrooms.

I make my way to the back of the restaurant, hoping to hide out in the bathroom until my blush is gone and the Phantoms have left. As I walk, it becomes pretty clear by the smell and the feeling of magic caressing the air that the place is filled with fae and probably fae-owned.

I'm just a couple of booths away from the bathroom when I hear a laugh that makes my blood run cold.

Panic surges through me as flashbacks, mostly emotions and sounds of screeching tires, assault my senses.

I spot him in the booth just before the hallway to the bathrooms and I turn, practically diving into the booth right next to me. My face immediately turns bright fucking red as I realize there is a group already seated there.

All five faces turn towards me with matching quizzical expressions.

Fuck, why can't I have the power to turn invisible or at the very least if I'd fucking listened to Amelia I could use my own magic to make these guys think nothing of me sitting with them. Though I don't think it would ease my own embarrassment. Sometimes I really wish that instead of being able to influence others' emotions that I could just influence my own.

My heart pounding out of my chest and my ears heating, I try my best to give them a carefree smile. "Sorry to intrude," I start to say, but I can hear Jordan's voice getting closer and closer. I rip the ribbon out of my hair quickly, letting my hair fall into my face, and I angle towards the window, keeping my head low.

"I honestly can't believe we aren't opening for the Phantoms," Jordan says, as he and his band make their way to the front of the restaurant.

"Voracious Maw is such a fake act. I don't understand why all these women are drooling over them when they're obviously all gay," Jinx complains.

The rest of them let out barks of laughter and I cringe, able to pick out Jordan's laugh over the others. It skitters across my skin, making me want to curl up in the fetal position. *Just leave already,* I beg.

Finally Dead Hearts leave, the door swinging shut loudly behind them. I find Reese's eyes. She's spotted me and knows I almost just ran into Jordan. She's heading this way, so I get up out of the booth, looking at the guy across from me.

He's got a shaggy haircut, and his wide brown eyes are staring at me. "I'm sorry. Thanks for, uh, letting me crash at your booth for a bit." I hastily scurry away from them, feeling their eyes at my back, and practically run into Reese's arms. She gives me a huge hug and after confirming the coast is clear and Dead Hearts isn't lingering outside the restaurant, we head out as well to where the rest of our band has gathered. Seriously, this place is huge—what are the odds we'd run into Dead Hearts?

"Hey, wait!" a distinctively British voice calls. I turn and see the brown-eyed guy headed our way. We've gathered outside the doors to the restaurant and he comes to a stop just in front of me.

Reese gives him a once over. She turns and explains to Amelia what just happened. They keep their voices hushed.

"Hey, I'm seriously so sorry about that. My ex, he was in the next booth over, and I uh—"

He holds up a hand to stop me from having to explain. "No worries. We figured it was something like that. Glad we could give you cover for a little bit." He smiles warmly at me and I can't help but notice he is entirely too good-looking and probably knows it. He's quite a few inches taller than me, probably about my age, and obviously works out. Tattoos unsurprisingly cover most of his exposed light skin. "I've actually been meaning to track you all down," he says, looking over at the rest of the group then back to me. "You're Goddess' Trance, yeah? Are you the vocalist?"

I shake my head, pointing over my shoulder at my sister. "Nope, that's Amelia over there." I offer my hand to him. "I'm Bliss, the band manager."

"Any relation to you?" he asks, looking between us.

I nod, smiling. "She's my older sister."

"But not by much," Amelia adds, coming over and putting an arm around me.

The guy nods, shaking my hand and then Amelia's. "I'm Simon. I'm the drum tech for Voracious Maw, but I'm filling in for the manager. He couldn't make it out for the festival."

Voracious Maw?

I squash down the excitement that's coming both from the mention of one of my favorite bands and also the nervousness of the real reason I'm here. Simon would be a very good friend to have indeed.

"That sucks. I hope he feels better soon," I say, forcing myself to speak slowly. "It's good to meet you, though. Was that the band in there with you?"

Simon gives a small chuckle and scratches the back of his head. "Uh—erm, no, just some of the crew we travel with."

Amelia and I exchange glances. Simon is *real* bad at lying. Damn, I should have paid more attention to who was in that booth. I try to think back to the moment I sat down, but I was so embarrassed at what I'd done that I wasn't able to meet any of their eyes. What if I'd sat down right next to Wrath? I want to both cry and laugh at the same time.

It's not like I could have pulled off whatever theft the wraith wanted me to do in a restaurant booth. I didn't even know yet what I was supposed to steal. Part of me also wasn't sure I could even go through with it.

But also, what if I had sat down next to Wrath and all he saw was a super embarrassed, red-faced random crazy girl?

I let out a sigh. Is that really what my brain thinks is most important? That I might have embarrassed myself in front of my favorite musician of all time?

Well, actually, when I put it that way, my cheeks start to redden all over again.

"I was hoping we could go over your set list, if possible?" Simon interjects, putting a stop to my spiral. "Just want to know what the vibe of your show will be."

"Does it matter?" I ask.

Simon shrugs. "Not really, just curious at what the crowd will be feeling already when the boys get on stage."

"Probably lust," Dericia chimes in. We all laugh.

Except Simon, who looks around at us, plainly confused.

Amelia puts a hand on her chest. "I'm a succubus, so the crowd will be lusting after me especially by the time I'm done, and then Wrath will get on stage with those pants, you know the ones—" She looks over at me as if I'm not getting it. "Bliss, you know the ones, the flowy ones that show *everything.*"

I put a hand over her mouth to shut her up, as my face threatens to turn red for a third or fourth time—I've lost count. "I'll send over the set list for you, okay?"

Simon looks between us and nods, seeming a bit amused but also still confused. "If you're not busy tomorrow, there's that scavenger hunt for fans to win free stuff and backstage passes and all that. We could use some more volunteers, and it's a great way for you to connect with fans. If you haven't already signed up?"

"We're all signed up for that," I respond.

Amelia groans. "Don't we have to be there super early?" she laments. I just chuckle and pat her on the back.

Simon's eyes roam over Amelia, squinting a bit. "So can succubi seduce anyone?"

Amelia raises her eyebrows. "Not exactly. If someone isn't attracted to us, we can increase their lust, but it would just make them lust after the type of person they like. We can usually coax out the type of feelings someone might experience after a good orgasm —" Simon's cheeks flush to the same shade as mine, "—happiness, contentment, peacefulness—you get the picture."

"So you can't, like, mind-control someone?" he asks.

Amelia lets out a laugh. "We have that same fae compulsion all fae have, and we can use our powers to influence people, but nothing as powerful as mind control. You're safe from us, little human."

"Oh good," Simon says, his shoulders relaxing a bit. "I'm pretty newly registered, so I haven't met a succubus before. And this is my first fae festival." He lowers his voice as he says the last part. Amelia and I both laugh.

"You don't have to worry about non-kindreds hearing you. Fae have a natural compulsion ability that makes it so most humans forget anything weird they see or hear about us, except for kindreds, of course. That's why you get that rune." Amelia points to his wrist, where a rune matching Dericia's glows. His is extra bright, showing how new he is. It takes a few years for the rune's glow to fade.

"Really?" Simon asks, eyes widening. "That's super fucking cool."

Dericia slings her arm around me, frowning at Simon's rune. "Didn't your sponsor go over that with you?"

Simon shakes his head. "My sponsor, well, he's… unique, I'll say." He laughs but seems to really brighten up at seeing Reese. "So you're a fellow kindred?" he asks.

Reese holds out her arm, showing him her rune, which has faded to a pretty unnoticeable scar. But as she concentrates on it, it flares to life, flashing a bright golden white light and fading again. Simon's eyes go so wide they're at risk of falling out. "Teach me how to do that," he breathes out excitedly.

"Sure," she says, giving him a smile. "But then we're really going to need to talk to your sponsor. He should have taught you this."

Simon nods excitedly, and they keep chatting about all things kindred.

Something pricks at the back of my vision and I close my eyes, trying to clear the sensation. When I open my eyes, I find a pair of blue violet eyes watching me.

I excuse myself with a lie about wanting to get a look at one of the stages that's being built on the festival grounds across the street. I leave before anyone can volunteer to go with me, seeing the wraith kick off the wall he was leaning on and walking over to a little grassy area behind one of the stages. Lots of people are already out making the most of the sun and warm temperature.

Dylan—I refuse to believe that's his actual name—sits down at a picnic table, somewhat hidden by a cluster of trees. I stop a few paces away from the table.

"Glad to see you've decided to take me up on my offer," he says without greeting.

"I didn't say I had."

"You are here, are you not?"

"Maybe I'm just here because I want to be," I fire back.

His lips lift a bit in a soft smile. "Let us not waste each other's time."

I huff out a breath of frustration and reluctantly sit across from him. I hate picnic tables. They're so awkward to get in and out of, but somehow the wraith managed to do it gracefully. I, on the other hand, not so much.

I glare at him once I'm settled in. "So get to the point." I avert my eyes after I say it, remembering just who I'm talking to. I did some research after making a deal with the devil, and based on what I know about him, I probably shouldn't poke at him. He's not just any wraith. He's a song wraith, one of the strongest and rarest known to fae kind.

He cocks his head to the side in that preternatural way at my sudden change in demeanor, but he doesn't comment.

"Are you going to tell me what I need to steal?" I ask, forcing a more polite tone.

The corners of his mouth twitch upward. "Tears that strongly flow, released in grief's throe, a stone that only grows, where a seed never sows, blood taken, from the ascended," he recites.

"Excuse me?" From my research, song wraiths are partial to poetry and music or any combination thereof.

"It's what I need you to steal."

"A poem?"

"No, it's a list of ingredients."

"Why not just tell me what the ingredients are?" I demand. "Being cryptic isn't going to help you get what you want any faster." So much for polite.

"Hmm." He shrugs. "I am a patient creature."

I continue to glare, unable to help myself.

"I shall be quick, then, for your sake. The poem is a list of ingredients that I need. I have not yet determined exactly what they all are, except the first. Tears."

"Tears?" I ask when he doesn't elaborate. Quick my ass.

"I need you to collect Wrath's tears," he says as if it's obvious.

"His *tears*?" I ask again. "What for?"

"That part is not any of your concern. But fae with ties to the water element have very strong tears. I need his."

"So is Wrath a water nymph, or a water elemental or something?" That will help narrow down who the guy actually is. "I still haven't agreed to this," I remind him.

He quirks an eyebrow at me but says nothing.

"I'm not going to do anything that will harm anyone. I need to know what you're using the tears for."

"I cannot tell you that. But I will promise that no harm shall come to you or Wrath. And a wraith's promise is binding."

"No harm can come to anyone," I respond, crossing my arms. What if tears from certain fae are extremely dangerous? This is something Liz would probably have lots of information on, but I never studied potions or anything similar.

"I promise I mean no innocents any harm, and I promise no harm shall come to you or Wrath. That is the best I can do."

My gut twists.

"I know you probably won't believe it, but my intentions are honorable," he adds.

I eye him warily, but my gut unclenches with his words. For some reason I believe him. And this is my life we are talking about. If I remain a succubus with no mate, I'm as good as dead. Or I'll have to spend my life hooking up with people I don't want to be hooking up with. And then I might wish I was dead. So really, when it comes down to it, don't I deserve to live? Don't I deserve to be happy?

"Okay, I'm in," I say, reaching out my hand. I don't know if this is strictly necessary to seal our deal, but the wraith extends his hand, gripping mine. Something about his touch is feather light, but we pull away before I can ruminate on it. The bargain is officially struck and now I have to collect Wrath's tears. "Have you figured out who Wrath really is?"

"I trust you will do what you need to accomplish this."

I'm about to respond to that cryptic statement when, out of the corner of my eye, I see Dericia and Amelia coming up the path towards where I'm sitting. When I look back at the wraith, he's no longer there.

"Thanks a lot," I mutter.

How the hell am I supposed to steal tears from someone whose identity I don't even know?

CHAPTER EIGHTEEN

BLISS

ONE OF THE MOST EXCITING THINGS ABOUT THE ALCHEMY FESTIVAL, aside from the luxurious housing and the excitement of all the best metal bands performing back to back across three full days, is the band and crew only masquerade party held the night before the festival actually starts. The party is already in full swing by the time we arrive.

I hand-picked every single mask for us, since I knew the boys would probably wait last minute to get theirs and end up with flimsy plastic ones that would not survive the party.

Amelia wears her signature black lipstick, her eyes smoked out with black, purple, and gray eyeshadow that perfectly matches her black mask with purple rhinestones. Dericia's mask is gold with fake red rubies, so she's chosen a deep rich red lip color and blended a dark warm brown shadow across her lids.

I had more trouble picking out my mask. In order for our plan to work, it needed to be a mask that didn't look like something I would pick out for myself. And it needed to conceal most of my face. I opted for a black mask with a gold metallic paint swirled like marble. Reese and I used her bedazzler to add rhinestones to it. They drip down the bottom edge of the mask. When the light hits it just right, it looks like the bottom half of my mask has been dipped into sparkling water. Reese has recreated her makeup look on me as well but used a bit more black eyeshadow and winged liner to help disguise my eyes. If Jordan lingers too long on my eyes, he'll recognize me all too easily.

That is also the reason I'm wearing a revealing black dress I borrowed from my sister. None of my signature pastels can be worn tonight if I want to firmly rule Jordan out as my mate. I've also added a spritz of Reese's perfume to hopefully cover up my scent.

The party is being held in an old Victorian-style building. Attached on one side is a theater, where some smaller bands will be playing during the festival. On this side is the entrance to a grand ballroom that matches the vibes of the party. Everyone's elaborate masks match the ornate molding and gold trim. The mural painting on the ceiling appears faded and washed out and chandeliers hang every few feet, spaced evenly in a row across the room. The whole place is awash in a golden glow.

We make our way down a set of grand stairs into the ballroom itself, noting several bars set up throughout the venue. Amelia and Blake make a beeline for one, even though we did a round of shots before heading out. The rest of us trail after them.

Music blares from loud speakers and there's a wide area for dancing and mingling.

We acquire our drinks and find a few small circular tables that no one's taken yet. Amelia spots Bill from Moon Blood and waves him over. His masks hangs in his hand. "Billy!" she exclaims, definitely already a bit tipsy at this point. I feel her let loose a wave of appealing magic towards him. "Come hang out with us!"

"I'm surprised I'm not fighting off scouts left and right for the chance to chat," he says, shaking Amelia's hand and then mine. "Good to see you all again. I trust the festival's been fun so far."

"It's been great. Thanks for getting us the hook-up," Amelia says. "This is Blake, by the way, the new guitarist. I don't think you've seen us perform since he joined the band."

Bill and Blake shake hands and settle into a deep conversation about guitars and some other musical things that are a bit beyond me. I scan the crowd for Simon and Grim, excited to see them again and wondering if Voracious Maw will be around.

Taser stiffens beside me, and when I look up, I already know I'm going to see some Phantoms coming our way. Grim is sauntering over to us, flanked by Pinkie and Casper, their bassist. Taser gets up, muttering something about grabbing another drink. Grim comes straight towards me, spinning me around on the barstool I've claimed. I squeal out a laugh.

"Hello, adorable," he says into my ear as he gives me a quick hug. "This is Casper." He motions behind him.

I shake Casper's hand and intercept an approving nod from Bill. He definitely sees it as a good sign that the biggest band at the festival has sought us out. I feel it in my bones. Goddess' Trance is walking out of this festival with a record deal. I fall into a comfortable conversation with the Phantoms and we have a couple more drinks with them. But the whole time I'm scoping out the ballroom for any members of Dead Hearts, both to make sure they don't find me first and so I can figure out which masked guy at the party is Jordan.

I'm betting I'll find him by his panic-inducing laugh first.

Casper and Pinkie are asking me about my role as band manager when I spot the frontman of Voracious Maw headed towards the bar nearest the entrance. He's in full costume, body painted that bluish black color, though I can't make out the scales they somehow glue onto his body.

My thoughts turn to how the hell I'm going to get his tears, but I remind myself I need to cross Jordan off the list of potential mates before I do anything else. Concentrate on one thing at a time, Bliss.

"That mask really suits you," Grim says, grinning. He's taken his mask off. I frown at him.

"You know, this is a masquerade party. You're suppose to keep that on." I point to the mask in his hand.

He chuckles and tucks a piece of hair behind my ear. "I spend so much time in a mask, though. And I can't see very well through this one." He tosses it on the table behind me. "I want to be able to see you better."

A thrill goes through me at his words and the heated way he's looking at me. Both of us have already had a lot to drink. It would be so easy to give into the lust that is starting to pool low in my body. But tonight I have a mission.

I need to be sure that Jordan is not my mate.

I need to ease the panic that threatens me every time I let my mind ponder that possibility.

I scan the crowd again and frown when I see Wrath all the way at the opposite side of the ballroom, standing slightly distant from the rest of the band members, who are all wearing their signature masks. I look back to the bar he was queued in front of just a moment ago, but no one in a similar costume is there. I wonder briefly if he's a vampire and used his vamp speed to get a drink and head back to his band. But that would mean the song wraith was wrong, and he seemed adamant that Wrath is some type of water-related fae.

Dericia catches my eyes and waves me over to her. I smile coyly up at Grim, hopping off my stool and forcing him to take a step back. "You'll have to excuse me."

He grins as he follows my gaze. "Does she have something I don't?" he teases.

I shrug innocently and throw him a wink, heading over to my best friend. Once I reach her she loops her arm through mine and starts walking towards a hallway that must lead to the bathroom. "I have to pee so bad," she says in a rush.

I laugh. "And here I was, thinking you had some tea to spill."

"Nope, just my bladder." We both drunkenly laugh at that and find ourselves in a line out the door for the bathroom. "So, Grim seems pretty into you?" she prods.

I shrug, focusing my gaze on the girl in front of me, who's wearing a green, floor-length, velvet dress. It's beautiful and soft looking, complementing her bright red hair. "He's beautiful, I will say that."

"But no sparks?"

I take a minute to answer, watching the woman in front of me taking out a small piece of paper from her purse. She looks at it for a little bit then slips it back into her bag.

"I mean, there's definitely some chemistry, but no runes. He's obviously not the one for me. What about you? You and Amelia seemed like you were on your own mission this week." I eye her meaningfully and she laughs.

"I mostly just say that stuff to hype Amelia up," she confesses. "Don't get me wrong, I don't mind a sexy escapade here and there, but I will admit something feels like it's missing these days."

I glance up at Reese, noting she's also been studying the dress in front of us. Her eyes are slightly unfocused, probably the same as mine, and she's wearing a slight frown. I don't like seeing that expression on her face and it makes me wonder.

Normally I'd try to bring this up with more tact, but I'm two shots and two drinks in at this point. "Do you ever wish you weren't human?"

Reese glances quickly at me and lets out a laugh, relaxation coming back to her face. "Stars no," she breathes out, patting my arm gently. "No offense or anything. I guess it would be cool to have my own magic, but being kindred and having access to potions and stuff, I feel like I get the best of both worlds, but without the need to recharge my powers." She pauses for a moment and looks meaningfully at me. "Plus, there's the whole 'if I turned fae, I'd be Made fae,' and neither Born fae nor kindreds treat Made fae very well."

I grimace, nodding in agreement. "That's true."

"Not that a lot of Made fae don't deserve it," she says with a shudder, perhaps thinking back to that warlock she encountered on our girls' night.

I sling my arm around her middle and lean my head on her

shoulder. "You're okay, right? After that whole incident at the club?"

Reese laughs, and I can hear it echo through her chest. "Yeah, I'm fine. It definitely wasn't my most favorite outing of all time, but I knew you and Amelia wouldn't let anything happen to me."

"I love you, Reese." I give her a squeeze and she squeezes me back.

"I love you too, Bliss."

We've made it to the front of the line now, the girl in the green dress disappearing into one of the stalls.

Grim kept my barstool warm while I was with Reese. He looks me up and down as I approach and moves so I can take back my spot. I lose track of time as we chat, glancing down at my phone and seeing it's been almost an hour. I'm starting to get worried. What if Jordan thinks he's too cool for something like this? I wouldn't put it past him.

But then I hear it.

The hollow, boisterous, almost fake laugh.

I freeze and Grim glances curiously at me.

"Are you okay?"

I swallow and nod, my eyes darting to the center of the dance floor. I could pick out Jordan even if he was wearing a sport mascot costume in a sea of other mascots.

He's in the center of a group of people all dancing, a beer bottle in his hand. He wears a plain black mask, same with all the other members of Dead Hearts. Jinx with his blue hair is super obvious, and I can make out their drummer and bassist as well.

I force a smile at Grim. "Can you excuse me again for just a few minutes?"

"I suppose I can put up with your absence for a bit, but it'll be very touch and go. Have pity on me and return to me soon, Bliss."

He grins shamelessly and I roll my eyes playfully at his over-the-top words.

I turn and grab Reese's arm, pulling her towards Amelia, who's talking with Taser. I look pointedly at him with raised eyebrows. "Can you give us a second?"

He sighs and leaves without saying a word. My stomach plummets. That was super rude of me. I ignore the look Amelia is giving me, the one that says she thinks I should forgive him already.

"Jordan's over there," I say, angling my head towards the dance floor. Amelia and Reese's eyes follow the motion, and I can see when Amelia picks him out of the crowd, her entire form seeming to tense up.

"How'd you find him?"

"His laugh. Every time I hear it, it makes the hair on my neck stand straight up."

Amelia squeezes my arm in support. "Let's get this over with."

I take a deep breath and nod, squeezing my hands into fists and following Amelia and Dericia to the dance floor. There are enough people dancing now that it should be easy to get close enough to look into his eyes quickly and then leave.

Amelia grabs my forearms, pulling me into a dance with her. I sway my hips to the beat, Reese beside me, but I can't get into it like normal when the three of us are just having fun dancing. My heart pounds in my chest and I can *hear* my pulse beating. I hope Jordan, with his vampiric hearing, doesn't notice it.

Slowly Amelia turns me so that I'm facing towards where they all stand, with her between me and them. She backs up, looking like she's just really getting down to the music, and pulls me along with her. Dericia sticks to my side. I reach out, giving her hand a grateful squeeze.

Jordan is facing me and it takes everything in me not to bolt right then and there. But I still can't see his eyes well enough. I'm not close enough, and even though the ballroom has more than enough light, his face is in a bit of shadow.

"I'm not close enough," I whisper to Amelia, and she nods, a plan forming in her head.

She pulls me a few steps forward and turns me, holding our hands up interlocking until we're almost bumping into the group of Dead Hearts. But in a crowd like this, jostling against someone is normal. So I act natural and I turn, Amelia still holding my hand up in the air as she spins me. I try to get a good look at Jordan's eyes, but my feet get caught up in each other and I fall to the ground.

My knees hit the wooden dance floor with a crack that isn't heard over the music, but I can definitely feel it. I wince in pain and a hand helps me up. I get to my feet, wiping with my free hand at my knee that's now bleeding. I must have scuffed it against the floor.

"Thanks," I say, looking up at the guy who helped me and freezing as I stare right at Jordan. We lock eyes, and I breathe out a sigh of relief when I see they are completely free of any runes.

"You okay?" he asks, reaching out an arm to steady me, taking both of my hands now in his.

I involuntarily take a step back. I nod, not trusting my voice. He'll recognize it immediately. I push away from him and run from the dance floor, deciding last minute that I can't go to where the boys of Goddess' Trance are still talking with the Phantoms and Bill or he'll definitely know it's me. I veer to the side, deciding another drink isn't totally out of the question after almost getting caught.

I get into line at one of the bars and a few moments later someone queues up behind me. I glance back at them and smile.

"Simon!" He's not wearing a mask, but his black hair has been artfully arranged to look as if he just woke up. A bit of it falls into his brown eyes.

He leans in a little and studies my face, and then his cracks into a smile. "Bliss, right? It's good to see you. You look amazing, that mask suits you."

I almost laugh. I specifically picked the mask because I didn't think it suited me. "Thanks," I say and take a few steps forward as the line moves. Simon moves with me and we end up standing side by side. "I'm surprised you recognized me."

He laughs. "I spend too much time with people in masks. Gotten really good at recognizing people just by their eyes."

"Makes sense," I respond, grinning. And that is exactly why I end up reaching into my very limited power source, coaxing a bit of my power out, and letting it flow to Simon. If I could flirt my way into getting an introduction to Wrath, then this whole thing might be easier than I originally thought.

"Let me buy you a drink," Simon offers, as we reach the bar. I smile. It's working.

"Oh that's okay," I start to say, and then arch my brows at him. "It's an open bar."

He grins at me and winks. "I'll get a gin and tonic, please, and whatever she's having," Simon says to the bartender, who looks at me expectantly.

"Make it two gin and tonics."

The bartender nods and gets to work on our drinks, handing them over to us a few moments later.

I take a sip of mine, allowing the herbal burn of the gin to take my mind off coming face to face with Jordan.

"So what's caused you to come running over this way?" Simon asks as we make our way to a table not too far away from where Amelia and Dericia have returned to the rest of the band. He bumps his shoulder into mine, smiling. "Let me guess, you ran into your ex again?"

I wrap my fingers around the cool glass, condensation already coating the outside of it.

"Yeah, I ran into him on the dance floor. Thankfully my mask did what it needed to."

"What it needed to?" Simon asks, cocking his head at me.

"Oh yeah, well..." I hesitate, not sure if I should get into my drama with a human I barely know. But something about him feels comfortable, so I continue. "I had my bond activated recently and I was worried that maybe he would end up being my mate, so I needed to rule him out. Make sure it's not him."

"And did you?" he asks. "Rule him out?"

I let myself smile. "Yes, I did."

"Good." He raises his glass towards me and I mirror him, our glasses clinking together. "You fae and your bonds. I wish humans had that. Having the universe tell you who you're meant to be with, that's fucking cool."

"Yeah, but it takes away your choice," I say back. "And what if you don't get along with them?"

"I thought mates were always, like, madly in love with one another." Simon frowns, confused.

"Not always." I let my hand come to rest on his forearm. "Sometimes fae fall in love with someone who's not their mate. Shouldn't they be able to decide who they love more if that happens?" I can see Simon's throat swallowing, as his gaze falls to my lips. I think he's picking up what I'm insinuating, that if he and I fell in love, we should be able to be together. That's what I want him picturing in his mind.

"Well, yeah, they definitely should," he responds, taking an involuntary step towards me.

I put on my best coy smile and lean in to him. "Simon, did you know I'm a huge Voracious Maw fan?" Whenever I release my power it's all too easy to add a slight purr to my voice that I could never achieve on my own.

A stupidly wide grin appears on his face. "I didn't, but I'm not surprised. They're the best."

I nod, pulling my bottom lip in between my teeth and releasing it. His gaze rests on my lips and I'm so close.

I'm about to ask for my favor when a very tall guy in one of the Voracious Maw masks—unmistakably Eerie, their bassist—approaches and sits down at the table Simon and I are standing at. He unclasps the strap that holds the golden skeleton fingers in place over his eyes and rips the embroidered cloth mask off, breathing in like he's just broken through the surface of water.

My succubus spell is broken almost immediately.

Simon looks at him frantically. "Evan," he hisses, "you're supposed to stay masked."

Evan shakes his hair out, pulls a rainbow scrunchie from his wrist, and puts his long bleached blonde strands up in a bun. "Fuck that. I'm suffocating in this thing. It's one thing to wear it for an hour on stage, but for a whole fucking party? Nah, mate. I'm good."

"He won't be happy you took it off."

Evan opens his mouth to say something then closes it, with a quick glance at me. "Wrath can suck my dick," he finally says, casting a pointed look over at where Wrath stands with the other two band members.

Simon grins at Evan and shrugs as if Wrath might not have a problem with that at all. Evan huffs and looks at me. He motions to Simon for an introduction.

"Ah, this is Bliss," Simon says. "Bliss, this is Evan."

"You can call me Eerie," Evan says with a cruel grin at Simon, who puts his face into his hands with a groan.

I let out an uncertain laugh, as Simon and I take a seat. "I take it the whole anonymity thing wasn't your idea?"

His grin only widens. "Definitely not."

"Bliss!" I hear a deep voice call. I swivel in the barstool and look at Grim as he saunters over. "I thought you were going to come back to me, and here you are surrounded by men who aren't me." He pouts a little and grins, slinging an arm around me and nodding to the other guys. "Evan, nice to see you again. Simon." He nods, tipping his beer bottle at them.

Pinkie, Bell, and Casper have followed Grim over to us and they easily fall into conversation with Simon and Evan.

Grim shifts a bit closer to me, nuzzling me around the neck. "You're quite popular, aren't you?"

I let out a giggle and clamp my hand over my mouth. "I don't know what you're talking about."

"Hmm, seems like young Simon there is quite smitten with you." He winds an arm around my waist, turning me around on the stool so that I'm facing him better. He leans in close with a grin. "I'm not scared of a little competition, just so you know."

"Oh well, that's very good to know, but I think you're mistaken. He's just a nice guy."

"Do nice guys often look at you like they want to fuck you?" Grim asks, his hands moving to my waist. He looks down at his hands, which rest right where my torso naturally dips in.

A blush creeps into my cheeks and a warmth is settling in around my center. His words are definitely rousing the ball of lust inside me that is my succubus power. "He's not looking at me like that." Well, he might be. I did use up the majority of my magic on him. I stifle a groan as I realize just how empty my reserves now feel and that what I used before is now probably going to waste after being interrupted. The lust Simon was feeling will dissipate very quickly, since I'm not very powerful or adept at using my power.

I can't help but glance over at Simon. He eyes flit over to me but then away as soon as he sees Grim's hands on me. "Hasn't he been? Hasn't he been looking at you the same way I'm looking at you?"

My eyes snap to Grim's and I take a shallow breath, like my lungs have forgotten their damn job. He flashes me a toothy grin and takes another step forward, my thighs parting on the stool for him to stand between. He still stands taller than me and angles his head down like he's going to kiss me. I put my hand on his chest, not sure if I want to pull him closer or push him away. He pauses and waits, but before I can make a decision I feel someone watching me. Us.

I peer over Grim's shoulder as best I can manage and stop short. Jordan.

He's taken off his mask and his eyes rake over me. He sneers. "Well, Bliss, I guess I shouldn't be surprised. Always knew you were just a groupie gold digger." My blood chills as I take in his unfortunately still familiar appearance. His dark hair has grown out a bit and he has it pushed back from his face, away from hazel eyes that darken under a prominent brow.

Grim stiffens and turns around. "What the fuck did you just say to her?" I reach out and grab his forearm.

"Don't," I try to say, but it comes out in a whisper no one else but me hears.

Amelia's somehow already coming around to stand beside me, as if she saw Jordan coming this way and intercepted him. Dericia creeps forward, putting herself in between me and Jordan, as Grim takes a step away from the table.

I glance up at Amelia and shake my head. Don't do anything rash, I try to communicate to her.

Jordan holds up a hand, the one he used to help me to my feet earlier. There's blood on it. He brings it to his mouth and licks it clean. "I knew it was you once I got a taste of this. Succubus blood; there's nothing else like it."

Jordan stalks forward, ignoring the warning growl from Taser, who also appeared by my side while I was preoccupied with Jordan's arrival.

"So what's the deal, Bliss? Did you miss me and want to come back? Probably to beg me to fuck you again? You miss this?" he asks, his hand trailing over the obvious bulge in his pants.

Stars, how was I ever into him?

Shame threatens to consume me. I stand up from the stool, my legs wobbly, ripping my mask off so I can breathe better.

I need to get out of here. Nothing good will come from this.

Jordan laughs, the cruel peal of it causing its usual reaction. He looks over at Amelia. "She's gotten her bond activated, hasn't she? Shame I don't see a rune in your eyes, Bliss. Then you'd never be able to get rid of me."

Taser steps forward. "That's enough, back the fuck off." He snarls at Jordan, who just looks at him like he's a piece of disgusting trash, his lip curling up in offense.

"You didn't bond with her either." Jordan laughs. "That's too bad. I always knew you were after her cunt."

"Jordan, I swear to the stars if you don't fucking back off, I'll—" Amelia starts, but Jordan cuts her off.

"You'll what? Sleep with me to death?" The rest of his band-mates snigger behind him.

This is just going to keep going, I think to myself. *Unless...*

"Everyone stop." I push past everyone and head towards the staircase to leave.

"Where are you running away to, Bliss?" Jordan calls after me. I hear a few more people talking back to him, but I just let the music and chatter from the party drown it all out. With me out of there, everyone will eventually cool down. Jordan won't have a reason to keep pushing and my friends won't need to defend me.

I find my way along the mezzanine floor to a set of wide double doors. The glass doors open out onto a stone balcony with carved steps leading down into a beautiful garden. I stomp my way down to it, hoping the beauty and quiet of the space will calm me. Tears prick behind my eyes, threatening to spill. I find a seat along a fountain's edge in the center of the garden. The sound of the water cascading over each tier of the stone bowls of the fountain seems to wash away just a fraction of the agitation and panic that try to root themselves in me.

I take deep breaths, one after another, even as my skin erupts in goose bumps. It's chilly out here. Amelia talked me out of wearing anything over my dress. It might cover my cleavage, she argued. Seems really stupid right about now.

The garden is partially illuminated with patio lighting, washing it in a warm romantic glow. I'm surprised more people aren't out here, stealing quick kisses with their partners. It seems ironic I'm using such a beautiful space to hide from my ex. Maybe I should have headed straight back to the townhome.

That inner part of me that is all primal succubus and zero percent concerned with consequences is pouting that I didn't drag Grim out here with me. We could have made use of some of the shadows here. I mentally shush her.

Leaves rustle, interrupting me from scolding myself yet again. I look to my right, trying to pinpoint where the noise came from. I peer closer, but I can't make out anything. "Hello?" I ask.

It's probably just a bird or something. But I wonder if I did indeed interrupt a couple making use of the space. I would be too embarrassed to come out if I were them. I should leave, go back to the house and get a good night's sleep. Or stay up over-analyzing if coming here was a mistake. If making a deal with *a wraith* was a mistake. *Obviously,* my inner critic sneers.

I'm about to get up and look for a direct way out of this garden to the street when again leaves rustle. But this time, instead of looking and finding nothing, I see a figure emerge from the shadowy corner of the garden to my left.

Not eerily, or creepily. He just walks out into the glow of the lights, and he doesn't slow when he sees me. I can't help but freeze and take in his appearance.

It's Wrath.

His mask is beautiful and even more intricate in person.

But it still slightly creeps me out.

I can't tell where he's looking. Like all of the Voracious Maw masks, it has no eye holes, giving the illusion he can't see out of it.

He seems like he's about to walk right past me, but at the last second he pauses, almost parallel with me, looking over at me. The tilt to his head seems questioning.

"The party sucks, just so you know." I don't know why I say it. He's wearing plain clothes now, a black hoodie and black jeans, instead of his earlier costume. He must have left the party to change.

I glance behind him in the direction that he came, and even though it's not illuminated well, I can now make out a little gate that lets out to the side of the building. I wonder why he's coming in this way. Maybe to avoid large crowds? I don't blame him.

"I met your bassist," I say, again not sure why I'm word-vomiting all over the place. I don't mention that Eerie—Evan—wasn't wearing his mask. A shiver runs up my arms as I wait for him to say something, anything. I rub my hands over my bare arms. It's already much colder now than five minutes ago and I think again how I should stop listening to Amelia when it comes to my cleavage.

Or maybe I can use it to my advantage. Isn't this exactly the opportunity I need to make good on my bargain with the wraith?

I let out the last little remnants of my power. I'm definitely going to need to feed soon, in the next day or so. All the power I got from feeding off Taser is already gone.

Wrath still doesn't say anything. But I watch as he slowly unzips his hoodie, taking it off and wordlessly offering it to me.

He has on a long-sleeved shirt, but his hands are still covered in paint.

I just look at him, and he reaches the hoodie closer to me, urging me to take it. I wrap my hands around it and he lets go. When I don't immediately put it on, he tilts his head again. Is this all my power is able to coax him to do?

He takes the hoodie back. I think he's just going to put it back on, but instead he holds it out for me to step into, like maybe he thinks I didn't understand him.

"Why don't you talk?" I ask, looking between him and the offered hoodie.

No answer.

I sigh again, standing up. "Fine." I slip my arms into the sleeves and allow him to zip me into his hoodie. It smells divine, and thankfully my brain doesn't find a need to comment out loud about that. I also can't place his scent, which isn't crazy. I'm not a vampire or a wolf shifter, so my sense of smell isn't always the best when it comes to fae species.

I think he's about to leave me and go inside, but instead he sits on the fountain's edge. I sit back down next to him.

And your magic is out, my inner voice reminds me. He's literally right here and I can't even use my magic to help me get the tears for the wraith.

I try to think of something to say, fingering the zipper pull of his hoodie while I take a moment to wonder what he looks like underneath that mask, and who he could possibly be.

There are rumors, of course.

Voracious Maw fans have some wild theories about the band members' identities, but the theories all center on other well-known musicians. That never made sense to me, why someone already well known would start a band and grow it from nothing anonymously.

Sure, it could be a gimmick, as Jordan would always say, but I never bought that theory either.

I'm convinced they're just really talented unknown musicians who, for one reason or another, don't want the attention on them.

I can definitely see the appeal of that.

We continue to sit in silence—surprise, surprise—and I realize I'm no longer shivering. I hold up one of my arms, indicating the hoodie. "Thanks. This was really nice of you."

He bobs his masked head in acknowledgement. The lower part of his face, the part uncovered by his mask, is in too much shadow for me to see if he's making any expression with his mouth. I realize I also can't tell what color his hair is. There's a strap that secures his mask, but underneath it is some sort of thin material covering the backside of his head. It probably keeps his hair in place underneath the mask.

I stop myself from sighing this close to him. No tears tonight. I'll have to come up with a much better plan.

The doors on the balcony open, letting a cascade of song, chatter, and bustle out into the empty outside air. I look up and see Amelia, Reese, and the others—including, to my surprise, Grim—descending the steps to the garden. I turn around, as Wrath slinks off into the shadows back the way he came.

"Bliss!" Amelia comes to my side, clutching my hands in hers. "Are you okay? We were looking everywhere for you!"

"I figured you left and went home," Reese adds.

Tubbs and Taser each take turns giving me a hug, but for some reason I can't keep my eyes off the spot Wrath disappeared into. He's met my sister's band before, but I guess maybe he isn't too social?

"I just needed to deescalate that whole situation in there," I say, waving my hand around. I look over to Grim, who's standing to the side, studying me. "Sorry you had to witness that."

He tilts his head. "You have nothing to apologize for. You're okay?"

I nod, giving him a soft smile.

"Good, I'm glad." He smiles back at me, and I'm starting to think maybe I can head back into the party, enjoy myself. Maybe even exist in the same space as Jordan without feeling his overwhelming presence.

Tubbs stiffens, looking around. The way his eyes narrow makes the hair on my neck stand to attention.

"What's wrong?" Taser asks.

I look around in the shadows, wondering if Wrath is still inside them. Maybe Tubbs can sense him? Surrounded by all these trees, plants, and flowers, Tubbs is probably even more connected with his earth magic.

"Something is off," Tubbs says quietly. His eyes lock with Taser's. "Something in the garden is dead."

"Probably a dead plant or something, right?" Reese points out, but she shifts closer to me anyways. I hook an arm through hers. Amelia comes to stand on Reese's other side.

Tubbs shakes his head. "Dead body." His eyes seem to unfocus as he uses his magic. Hearing him describe it before, it almost sounds like sometimes nature can *talk* to him. A dead body? My mind goes to Wrath, but he just left. It's not him.

"What?" Grim asks, looking around.

"I can smell it," Taser confirms. And Blake nods. "Recently deceased."

Grim takes a few steps out from the fountain, scanning the foliage that creates a border around the patio.

Blake and Taser fan out with their vampire speed.

Two seconds later, Blake calls from the far corner of the garden, the one furthest away from the building and opposite the corner Wrath entered and left through. "Over here!"

We descend on his position quickly, Grim taking the lead and throwing his hands out to stop me from getting closer. "You might not want to see."

I look anyways, peeking over his outstretched arm. It's the woman from the bathroom line. Beautiful green, velvet dress, stunning ropes of long red hair.

Except there's blood everywhere.

Her limbs are twisted at odd angles.

Blood drips from nearby foliage.

She was killed here.

Right outside the party.

My stomach threatens to unleash itself on the ground. I put a hand over my mouth, taking several steps back and allowing Amelia to wrap me up in her arms. "Oh my stars…"

Tubbs holds Reese close and Blake puts an arm around my sister. Taser comes to a stop in front of me.

"Grim's calling it in," he says gently, meeting my eyes. I look past him and see Grim with his ear to his phone.

"At the festival, yeah. Get here quickly." The way he's speaking it almost seems like he called someone specific rather than the emergency line for the fae constabulary or the human police. Who would not be much help here.

"Was it warlocks?" I ask no one in particular. Not that I've ever seen a dead body before, but the way she's been fed on—it isn't something I'm familiar with.

"Possibly," Grim says. He slips his phone back into his pocket and turns to address someone over my head. "Probably should get them home. I can stay and wait for the police."

Mumbles of agreement sound around me and I let Taser lead me back home along with the rest of my friends.

Shock has numbed me, but as we walk back to the townhome, exhaustion joins in. I stumble through the front door of the townhouse and up to my room.

It's not until I close the door behind me and catch a glimpse of myself in the mirror that I realize I'm still wearing Wrath's hoodie.

CHAPTER NINETEEN

BLISS

I wake up with a pounding headache. I didn't drink that much last night at the party—not more than usual anyways—but having used up every ounce of my magic on Simon and Wrath, I'm basically hungover. And that's not to mention images of the dead woman in the green dress haunting my nightmares all night long. With a groan, and my eyes barely open, I stumble out of my room and down the stairs to the floor below.

Taser's door is open just a crack and I slip inside, shame, lust, anticipation, the need to escape all swirling around in my stomach. I steel myself by going over my plan again. I need to somehow get Wrath's tears. To do that, I need to get close to him again, which might require using Simon. Either way, I need to use my powers on *someone*. Which means I need to be well fed.

Step one, recharge. Step two, get close to Wrath somehow. I'll figure out the tears later.

Lust stirs inside me, urging me further inside the room.

"Bliss?" Taser's head barely lifts off the pillow as he regards me. I slip forward on soft feet and kneel on the side of the bed. I let the shoulder of my oversized tee slip off. His eyes track the movement and he shifts upwards, leaning his back on the headboard as he wets his lips.

I don't hesitate. I don't want to leave any time to second guess myself. I straddle his lap, and even though the sheets and covers are between us, I can feel him start to harden. "Bliss," he says again, but it's not a question. I lean forward, my lips meeting his in a lust-filled clash.

"I need you," I tell him, lifting his shirt up and over his head.

He nods and gives into me, his hand slipping between us and into the sleep shorts I'm wearing. He meets no further resistance as his fingers slip inside me.

We kiss as I ride his hand, and before long, with my inner fae urging me to feed, I'm already coming apart for him. He groans as my hips buck and my pants come quicker.

He captures my mouth again with his lips and strokes his tongue in rhythm with his fingers as I come back down to myself.

Sex with Taser has never been particularly earth-shattering, but it has always been good.

But right now, as the quick high leaves my body, I find myself not entirely satisfied. Yeah, sex is usually the most satisfying, but usually any orgasm from another fae will replenish my power fairly well.

But this was different. I could feel a bit of power flowing to me, but not nearly enough.

My gaze meets his and I can see the lust in it. My eyes go wide as shame truly hits me. He's still with Stacey. Oh stars.

I jump off him. How could he have let me do that?

How could *I* have just done that?

Am I truly so occupied with myself that I could forget?

I run from the room, even as he calls after me.

Amelia gives me a weird look when I sit down at the picnic table, a latte from a trendy-looking espresso truck in my hands. She has some sort of vegan breakfast scramble in front of her that she's picking at, so I slide it towards me and shovel a few bites into my mouth, groaning a little when I realize it's pretty fucking delicious.

Taser, Dericia, and I all headed out after I'd taken a quick shower, trying to remove all traces of my fucking awful decision to feed off Taser. Reese immediately noticed the weird vibes but didn't say anything. She just took Taser to a different food truck and grabbed some breakfast burritos, probably picking up on my need for space from him.

The festival grounds and surrounding area is pretty lively for early morning, festival and band crews alike getting to work on stage setup and everything else that we have to do. On the way over to the food trucks, I expected to overhear groups talking about the dead woman in the garden. I expected to see the grounds crawling with fae police, but things just seem… normal?

Taser glances over at me and hands me half his burrito. I look at him questioningly. He just shrugs. "You look like you could use this," is all he says. He looks back to his food and eats his half in silence.

I've fucked up so bad, and now things are even weirder between us, but he's still as generous as ever.

"Thanks," I say, even though he's no longer paying attention to me.

"What the hell are you wearing?" Amelia finally asks.

I frown at her and look down at my outfit. It's not the cutest, true. Plain jeans, a pastel pink Goddess' Trance long-sleeved T-shirt that Amelia specially ordered for me, and Wrath's hoodie.

"I'll change into something fancier later," I say, still confused.

"That's not what she means," Reese says, pointing at my sleeve. "It's black."

"Oh!" I let out a soft laugh.

"I didn't think you owned anything black," Tubbs says, reaching over and lifting up the hood so he can see the design on the back. "What band is this?"

I shrug. "I dunno."

"Moonstruck?" Tubbs reads. "Never heard of them."

"You were wearing it last night too," Reese points out. She and Amelia exchange rueful glances. "Where'd you get it?"

"It's a little big for you," Taser adds, picking up on what they're getting at. "Really big for you, actually."

I pull on the strings of the sweatshirt, wishing I could pull the hood up over my head and cinch in the drawstring tight enough to hide my entire face from my friends.

"I don't like it," Grim says from behind me.

I glance up, seeing him standing there looking down at me. I swivel in my seat as much as I can manage on the picnic bench. His grin is making him look even more sexy and handsome than I remember from last night. My stomach does a little flip and I can't help but grin back at him.

"And why not?" I ask, pushing a bit of hair behind my ear.

He sits down on the bench in the space between me and Blake, straddling it so he can face me. He leans in close. "Because it doesn't smell like me, and really if you're wearing men's clothes, they should smell like me."

A blush races up to my face and I duck my head down, playing with the frayed edge of the left sleeve. Grim chuckles and scoots even closer. "I was hoping I might catch you before the shows start. How are you, after last night?" He looks around at the rest of the band. I think the question is directed at all of us.

"Still can't believe it," I say.

"Did you get any details from the police?" Tubbs asks.

Grim shakes his head. "No. They're keeping things under wraps for now."

"No one seems to know anything happened." I grip my latte almost hard enough to dent the cardboard.

"They might be trying to make sure people stay calm until they know more. I have some connections to the investigators.

Don't worry, Bliss. They're good people; they'll get justice for her."

I nod and release my stranglehold on the innocent coffee cup.

"I also wanted to see if maybe we could go grab some food or coffee." He glances at my burrito and latte. "Or we could just explore."

I'm a bit surprised that he seems to be asking me out on a little date. I hear a coughing noise and look over to Reese. She's looking at me and pointedly glancing at Taser, who is now even moodier and looking obviously anywhere but at Grim. I look back at Grim, smiling at him, but my stomach does a bit of a drop as I take in his runeless eyes. I knew it before, of course I did. But what is the point of getting involved with him if he's not my bondmate?

I glance guiltily at the half of burrito Taser shared with me. I'm mad at him and he knows I'm mad at him, and yet he's still been a good friend, even after I just used him. I don't want to do anything that makes him uncomfortable.

I reach out and place my hand gently on Grim's forearm. "Rain check? I forgot how much there is to do before tonight's show." Like the scavenger hunt that's supposed to be starting in about an hour.

Grim looks over at Taser and nods understandingly. "Maybe tomorrow, beautiful. Or we could get drinks tonight after the show?"

I nod back at him and he gets up to leave, catching up with some other members of the Phantoms and throwing a grin over his shoulder at me. I sigh and look at Amelia, who is arching one perfectly waxed eyebrow.

"I know what you're thinking and you're wrong," she says to me.

Taser lets out a huff, staring fixedly at the bunched up wad of foil left over from his half of the burrito.

"What do you mean?" I ask, even though I'm pretty sure I already know the answer.

"You should feed from him, regardless of whether or not there's a rune on his eye."

"What's the point?"

"Super hot dirty sex is the point."

Taser coughs uncomfortably, getting up without further comment and tossing the foil into a nearby trash can, heading back the way we came from the house. I automatically start to get up to go after him, but Reese shakes her head. "I'll go check on him. But later we are discussing what is going on between you two." She pins me with a meaningful look and leaves to catch up to Taser.

Amelia and I exchange glances. "I'd rather discuss what the hell happened with Taser and the Phantoms," I mutter.

"No idea. But Taser hates them."

"Another reason not to sleep with Grim."

"Please. Forget about Taser," she says and frowns. "Okay, I didn't mean it that harshly, but what's going on with them is their business, not yours. Grim seems like a great guy and there's no reason to not pursue things with him just because he might not be *the one*."

I try to let her words sink in, I really do. But there's a resistance to them that won't leave.

CHAPTER TWENTY

BLISS

AMELIA'S WORDS PLAY OVER AND OVER IN MY HEAD WHILE WE TREK towards the outskirts of the festival grounds. A maze erected out of massive bales of hay stands almost two people tall before us. Food vendors galore make a semicircle around the entrance to the maze, and already long lines are forming.

There is absolutely a reason to not explore things with Grim.

I will somehow, someway get Wrath to give me his tears. If I was Amelia, I'd seduce him, make him fall in love with me, and then break his heart. He'd inevitably cry and I would collect the tears and use my succubus powers to make him not think that's a fucking weird thing to do. Problem solved.

I'm not Amelia, though, and all my powers did was get Wrath to be nice to me when I was cold.

I need to befriend Simon. He'll give me another avenue to Wrath and I'll have to figure out where to go from there.

And there Simon is, talking with a few guys, Evan among them.

As we approach, Simon gives us a little wave and shoos Evan and a couple of other guys off to the side.

"Goddess' Trance, my favorite opening band," he says by way of greeting.

Amelia unleashes her sultry smile on him. "Someday you're going to be the one opening for us."

He grins widely. "I have no doubt about that." Dericia lets out a yawn and Simon glances at her, a look of annoyance crossing his face. "Too early for you?"

She quirks an eyebrow at his tone. "What's it to you?" she snaps at him, immediately turning and heading for a coffee truck. What the fuck? Did something happen between those two?

Simon's face morphs back into friendly, and if he was fae I'd wonder if he had a problem with humans. "Sorry, my own band has been giving me a lot of flack for having to do this, as if it's my idea."

I nod. "These guys—" I point to my band, "—didn't want to do it either."

"It is earlier than I normally wake up," Amelia says, echoing Reese's yawn.

Simon looks at his clipboard, his finger skimming down some list. "Okay, well, we do not have much time left before things start. Some of you will be hidden in the maze, handing out prizes to anyone who finds you. And others will be helping anyone who gets lost. If that is your role, you will roam around looking for lost kids or adults. Also, anyone who looks like they're going in there to fornicate, please escort them out." He chuckles a little. "I wouldn't think that would be an issue, but apparently it's happened before."

"Gross," Amelia and I both say at the same time.

"Indeed." Simon points to Taser and Blake. "You both will be using your vampire senses to maneuver around the maze."

Taser and Blake fist bump in a show of vampire superiority and take off in a showy burst of speed into the maze, probably mapping it out real quick.

Simon hands out maps to the rest of us lesser beings.

"Amelia, you and Shaun—" He motions for one of his guys to come over. "You'll be partnered up for this to hand out prizes. Take one of those boxes with you and find your spot on the map."

Simon looks over at Reese, who is still ordering her coffee, makes a little adjustment on his clipboard, and sends Tubbs off with a redheaded woman. He points out a tall brunette fae whose hair is hanging slightly into his eyes. "Bliss, you'll be paired with Pisces. He's one of our guitar techs. You'll also be handing out prizes." He points to a spot on the map marked with a gold star that has "Bliss and Pisces" written on it.

"Pisces?" I say, making a bit of a face.

"You can bond over your parents' questionable baby-naming skills," Simon quips, grinning at me.

Here it is. A potential opportunity to put my plan into action. "I was actually hoping I'd get paired with you." I put just the right amount of flirtiness into my voice and draw on a hint of my power. I don't have much to pull on after my little hookup with Taser, but it should do the trick.

His grin widens. But not in a flirty way. It's almost as if it had no affect on him whatsoever. Odd. It worked last time. I use a bit more of my power, sending it out in a soft wave at him. I rest my fingers lightly on his forearm; physical contact sometimes helps my powers have a better effect. It's a tip I learned from Amelia years ago.

Nothing.

"Unfortunately, I have to be stationed at that booth over there, giving out backstage passes to anyone who finds all the scavenger hunt prizes." Right. Some of which are hidden in the maze somewhere. "You and Pisces are deeper into the maze. Best get going."

I nod, and when I'm out of earshot I sigh. "I can't believe that didn't work." Now my magic is even lower and I can feel my headache from this morning starting to come back.

I watch Simon make his way over to a large booth with a banner that reads "Scavenger Hunt" in a very metal-esque font.

"Bliss?" a quiet but deep voice asks from behind me. The speaker has a British accent very similar to Simon's. I turn around, looking at the guitar tech Simon pointed out. "I think we were paired together for the maze?" Pisces regards me with a careful expression, almost as if I'm some sort of bunny that he might scare off.

I glance back at Simon and turn to face Pisces. "Yeah, I guess so."

He hoists the box of prizes up into his arms and I notice the very end of a tattoo peeking out above the collar of his shirt. "Lead the way," he says, using his chin to point to the map in my hands.

"Oh right," I say, my head spinning with thoughts. When I first talked to Simon outside the restaurant, he said the guys he'd been sitting with in the booth were just some of the band's crew. He was obviously lying, and it makes me wonder if Pisces might be Wrath? He's tall enough and lean enough to be.

I take as inconspicuous a sniff as I can from Wrath's hoodie that I'm wearing and discreetly sniff the air around Pisces by pretending I need to stop and tie my shoe. He walks past me and waits. Since we're outside I can't smell him very well, but I detect enough of a difference to know it's not him. He must really be the guitar tech.

I need to get another chance with Simon, because without him how the hell am I ever going to get enough time with Wrath? Maybe go to their townhouse and pretend I'm there to give the hoodie back, and then catch a glimpse of him?

"Bliss?" Pisces asks, interrupting my planning.

I look up and realize I've walked us straight into a dead end.

"Is this where we're suppose to be?" he asks.

"No, I don't think so. Sorry," I mutter, turning around the way we came. "We need to take a left and then a right, and then another right and—wow, this is more complicated than I thought."

We continue on. I focus on the map this time so I don't lead us straight into a wall of hay.

We're nearly there when Pisces drops the box to the ground and lets out a sneeze. And then another. And then another.

"Sorry," he says, looking around at all the hay.

"There's a reason you brits call it hay fever," I say with a shrug. "Bless you," I add, internally cringing. I should have said that first. I should also ask him about being a guitar tech. I should also ask him some questions about Wrath. Maybe he'll let something slip that'll give me some clues.

"True," he responds as he picks up the box again. "And thanks."

Finally, we find our spot in the maze and settle in. There's a small bench of hay built into the wall of the dead end. I feel like we're lying in wait to scare little kids in a haunted house, but it's not Halloween and I think the draw is getting to meet some of the musicians of the band, not get scared.

"So because Voracious Maw is anonymous, they send out their techs to do all the fan interactions?" I ask, as I take a seat on the bench.

Pisces tests out the strength of the wall and leans carefully on it, crossing his arms. He's wearing jeans and a long-sleeved T-shirt, even though it's already starting to warm up. The sleeves are pulled over his hands so only his fingers are exposed.

He could be a snake shifter. They tend to be cold-blooded and often aren't comfortable except in super hot climates. I inhale again, but I don't smell anything that would give away his species.

I've already looked at his eyes—very beautiful blue ones—but they're runeless.

Guilt coils in my stomach as my eyes wander from his eyes to a slender nose ending in a little point, then to his lips, which he curls inward a bit before relaxing them. If he has a mate, they are a lucky fae indeed. He's the type of guy I wouldn't mind flirting at a bar with—just to get Amelia off my back. Flirting to get information out of him, though? That feels so wrong.

But I have to do it.

"I guess so," Pisces responds slowly. "It's hard to keep the anonymity if the guys are always out and about."

"Like Evan?"

Pisces' eyes narrow at my question, but I wave my hand at him. "It's not my fault. He introduced himself to me completely unmasked. Also the dude is six five and wears that scrunchie everywhere." I grin, but Pisces doesn't match it. My grin falls as an awkwardness settles around us. *Say something flirty, Bliss.* I rack my brain for something and settle on allowing my power to seep out from me.

"I don't know him very well," is all he says.

"Right, guitar tech. I guess you'd interact with Poison the most?" I let my voice take on a sugared quality, taking a small step closer.

All I get is a shrug.

Okay, I get it. I shouldn't be asking him these questions.

Fine, I'll ask about Simon instead.

"Simon seems to be handling the band manager stuff pretty well," I say, trying to goad Pisces into talking about Simon enough to give me some way in there.

Another shrug.

What is up with these men today? Or is my power really that weak?

We fall into an uncomfortable silence. I'm really regretting volunteering for this. As band manager, I have a million other things I could be doing.

I pull out my phone, deciding I might as well answer emails. A few minutes later, I can feel Pisces' eyes sliding over me. I look up, raising a brow at him.

"You know we've met before, right?" he asks.

"Have we?" I ask, mimicking his earlier shrugs. "I think I'd remember someone named Pisces."

His eyes narrow. "Well, it's certainly not as memorable as Bliss."

I pin him with a glare of my own. "What's that supposed to mean?"

He looks like he's about to take another jab at me but stops short, sliding a hand over his face and looking up at the sky. "Never mind," he says.

"No, seriously," I respond, my anger already ignited. "What is your problem?"

He rolls his eyes. "First you try to use your powers on Simon, and then on me. Which of the Voracious Maw boys are you trying to get to?" He smirks and lets out a hollow laugh. "Aren't you dating that one guy? What's his name? Jordan? Just letting him drag you around to listen to music you don't even like. Look at you—" he waves a hand in my direction, "—you look like you were on your way to Coachella and got lost. What is with the fucking ribbons?"

"Why the fuck are you acting like you know anything about me?" I bite out, taking a step towards him. I'm getting ready to push him into the wall and walk away. He can deal with handing out prizes himself. I take a deep breath to steady myself and look away from his heated blue eyes. "I broke up with said asshole anyways. Years ago. Not that it's any of your fucking business. And also fuck you. Just because I'm not wearing all black with neck tattoos doesn't mean I can't listen to metal music. Music is for everyone, so fuck off."

I can feel the tears threatening to spill and my nose is starting to run a bit. I can't fucking believe this guy. He's the guitar tech for a huge band, so what? He thinks he's better than me? I cross my arms and face the entrance to our little dead end spot, because I can hear people coming. I sniffle and wipe my nose with the sleeve of my hoodie. Fuck. Wrath's hoodie. I'll totally wash it before I give it back.

I continue to ignore Pisces the asshole as a couple women in their early twenties spot us and yell out in excitement.

"Yes! Found another one!" one of the girls says as they all come forward. They look a little underwhelmed as they take us in.

"Which bands are you from?" the one in the middle asks. She's got long blonde hair with bright blue streaks running through it and is dressed in black jean shorts, a Voracious Maw crop top, and fishnets. Her two friends are similarly dressed, one with auburn hair, and the other with dyed black hair.

I give them a friendly smile even as I sniffle again. "I'm Bliss. I'm the band manager for Goddess' Trance." I reach into the box and take out a couple of band tees we added into the mix. "They'll be opening for Voracious Maw, so get to that stage early to see them, okay? You'll love their set."

"Awesome," the blonde breathes out as they each take a shirt.

I motion to Pisces, who's back to leaning stiffly against the hay wall. "He's just a guitar tech for Voracious Maw. There's some of their merch in there too. Feel free to take a couple things."

They are the only ones to have found us so far, so I'm not too worried about running out of prizes.

The girls look in the direction of Pisces and giggle, glancing at each other. "Dang, we were hoping Wrath was hiding somewhere in the maze."

I laugh. "Yeah, I wish that too."

The blonde laughs with me. "He's so beautiful. I would die if I met him. Have you run into him yet? I bet you'll see him backstage, huh?"

I don't know if it's the contagious excitement they're exuding, but I can't help myself. "Want to know something really cool?" I ask, and they shuffle forward like we're sharing a secret. "I actually ran into him yesterday."

They all let out squeals at the same time and fire off questions.

"Did you talk to him?"

"What's he like?"

"Is he super hot?"

I let out another laugh. These girls are too adorable and I honestly hope they do get to run into him so they can give him a little love. "He was in his mask, so I don't know what he looks like either. He was very nice but didn't say anything."

"Oh my god," the one with black hair says. "I seriously would die. I can't wait for their performances. We're going to both shows."

"Hell yeah. As you should," I reply. "Have an amazing time, ladies. I hope you win the backstage passes."

"Thanks!" they call out as they clutch their prizes, having taken a Voracious Maw T-shirt and keychain each, as well as the Goddess' Trance shirts I'd handed out.

I smile as they leave, heading out again hopefully towards the end of the maze so they're entered into the running for the back-stage passes. I almost forgot that I'm stuck in here with a fucking dick.

My bad mood comes reeling back and I cross my arms, going to the opposite side of the little alcove we're in and sitting on the little hay bench.

"Just a guitar tech, huh?" Pisces asks softly from where's he's leaning. I don't look at him. "So what? A guy has to be super successful to be worthy of a Born fae like you?"

I straighten up. He's Made? With a side glance over to him, I take in a deep breath and cross one leg over the other.

"Ah, there it is. That's about the reaction I'd expect from a Born fae realizing I'm Made."

"Stop acting like you know anything about me."

"I'd bet if I was Wrath you'd talk to me," he says after a pause. "I'd bet you'd do other things too."

"Seriously, what the fuck is your problem?" I stand up, driven by a fire that's now coursing through me. "Yeah, I would talk to Wrath if he was here, because he's a lot nicer than you are and I haven't even heard him speak." You know what? Fuck this. I kick the box of prizes over to him. We're so far into the maze that only a few groups will probably make it back here. "It's pretty dead out here, I'm gonna go get a coffee. You good to man this station by yourself?" I ask, but I don't wait for a response because he can go fuck himself. I follow the map to get out of the maze and find Reese at the entrance, handing out cute little stickers to any groups with kids.

"I'm on sticker duty," she says, rolling her eyes. "I think Simon hates me."

"Well, Pisces, their guitar tech, definitely hates me. And for literally no reason."

Reese pauses, taking in my sniffly nose and the tears that have leaked down my cheeks. "Oh my stars. What happened?" She reaches out and places her hand on my upper arm, drawing me into a hug.

The whole conversation with Pisces runs through my mind, but I can't bring myself to recount it all to Reese. Tears start flowing more easily and the fire that was there before recedes. "He made fun of my ribbons," I finally sob out as Reese holds me.

I turn the corner and swear.

Another fucking dead end.

I check my map again. I should be able to continue forward and take a left. I twist the map around, thinking maybe I'm somehow looking at it wrong. After I talked with Reese and went back into the maze to talk with Amelia, the two of them convinced me to find Simon and get him to replace me with another volunteer.

"Bliss." Dylan's voice slithers up from behind me.

I whip around. "Fuck, you scared the shit out of me."

"The English language is so lovely, is it not?" The song wraith leans casually against the hay wall, looking at his fingernails.

"I'm sorry, did I offend you?" I throw back. "Maybe you shouldn't sneak up on people." I look behind him, realizing the way I came is now blocked. An uneasiness flows through me. "What did you do?" I demand from him.

"We need to have another conversation, my dear succubus," he drones. "It would seem that you have not grasped the urgency of our bargain."

"Look, I'm trying, but I don't even know who he is. Can't you, I dunno, use your wraith magic to figure out that part?"

"I cannot do this for you."

His eyes aren't the usual blue violet. They're red. I'm coming to realize this means he's in no mood to joke around. He's not bothering to conceal his true identity, nor does he find it worth it to put me at ease.

"I will also remind you that you cannot back out of this deal."

"I know that!" I snap. "I have a plan, okay? I just need to find Simon."

"Simon is not the avenue you want."

"He's my only way to even be in the same room with Wrath."

The song wraith shakes his head, frustration appearing on his face that I haven't seen before. "You have already met Wrath."

I let out a breath of my own frustration. "I know that! But it's not like we exchanged phone numbers."

"His scent is on you, even now."

I look down at my hoodie. "Succubi are not tracking fae. I can't scent him out like a wolf shifter could. My nose isn't even as good as a vampire's."

A vampire.

Taser.

Maybe Taser could.

"I see you have had a moment of inspiration. Good." He turns, waving his hand, and the hay wall that closed us off disappears. "But Bliss?"

He turns back to me and fixes me with those red irises.

"You have until the end of the festival."

His voice fades with him as he somehow evaporates into thin air.

My heart beats quickly, like the ticking of a clock.

I turn and find my way no longer barred, but now I'm not looking for Simon.

No.

Now I need to find Taser.

CHAPTER TWENTY-ONE

PISCES

FIVE YEARS AGO

I PLUCK AT THE STRINGS, CREATING A SOFT MELODIC SOUND THAT drifts through the small venue. Besides the guitar and my voice there's barely any other noise. I waver ever so slightly at that thought, at the knowledge that everyone is watching me.

It's a short song, a simple one. And it marks the end of our show. I finish, the sounds of the guitar fading away through the speakers. I walk back to the edge of the stage and hand off my guitar, and join Mist, Poison, and Eerie at the center of the stage as we thank the crowd.

My ears take in the applause and cheers going around, but through the bright lights I can't make out the people in the crowd very well, especially through the makeshift mask I desperately need to replace.

This was our third gig as Voracious Maw, and I honestly can't believe it, how it all came together.

Eerie claps me on the shoulder as he and the others depart from the stage, leaving me there by myself. I feel so exposed even with the mask, but I push that down, realizing people are still applauding. I bow low to the ground to show my appreciation.

It doesn't feel like enough. I'll never be able to find the words to express this level of gratitude.

I can't believe people are loving our shows so much.

It doesn't seem real.

And it doesn't feel like I deserve it.

Once we're hidden away backstage, I take off the mask, finding Shaun, Benny, and Evan already out of theirs, breathing in large gulps of air.

"Not gonna lie, mate, these things suck." Evan ties up his sweaty hair into a bun. It must have been plastered to the back of his neck the whole show.

I've cut mine shorter so that I won't have to feel it as much underneath the mask.

"Do we really *have* to wear them?" he continues, and I fix him with a glare. We've already been over this.

There's a good reason for it.

Multiple ones.

"I like them," Shaun says, pocketing his drumsticks in the back pocket of his pants. "We look fucking sick."

"They're badass," Benny agrees. "But I am sad all the single ladies can't see how beautiful I am."

I sling an arm around him, pulling him into a sweaty hug. "I'm sure they can still tell."

"I bet we could find some girls with mask kinks." Evan shrugs. "I guess that's worth it."

I shake my head. "We're not hooking up with fans, remember? We're not gonna be that type of band."

Evan lets out a sigh. "Fine. There'll be plenty of hot band and crew members when we go to festivals and on tours and all that."

Shaun and Benny laugh, high-fiving him.

I can't fight the grin on my face, but it's more about Evan's optimism than anything else. I can't really picture us playing at a large festival or getting big enough to warrant a tour. But that stuff isn't important to me. I'm already doing what I need to.

Trying to, in some way, absolve what I've done.

Finding a way to make it about more than just myself.

We opt to head back to the church to celebrate a fun successful gig, instead of going out to the bar. These things don't really pay well, and I'm saving up for a nicer guitar.

All in all, things have become okay. A year ago I would never have thought that. I still blame myself for what happened to Leighton. I'm still learning how to be a *fucking siren*. I've mostly adjusted to the weirdness of literally feeding off flesh, but I still haven't quite managed to control my emotions.

I can feel others' emotions sometimes, but I'm not adept enough to tell when they aren't mine. Just last week, I got angry because Evan was angry at a video game, and I attacked Shaun out of nowhere.

He shifted into a wolf and gave me a much warranted ass-kicking, and all was fine afterwards.

But it took me a few days to look him in the eyes again.

It's also been a year since I've seen my family. They think I'm dead, but that's better than them getting hurt by me.

But I've created a new life. I have good friends, and I have my music.

The four of us end up in the nave of the church, scattered around the pews. We all live here in the renovated section of the building. The rest of the church is still in need of upgrades, the sanctuary of the church probably most of all, but even still, it's turned in to a place where we come to blow off steam or just hang out.

It's a little drafty in here, especially with how cold it's turning outside, so I pull the sleeves of my wool sweater over my fingers to help ward off the chill.

Shaun passes me a beer from a cooler he brought in and hands another to Evan. Benny is walking a pew like it's a balance beam, holding out both arms and putting one foot directly in front of the other. As he passes Shaun and the cooler, Shaun puts out a beer for him to grab and he continues down the aisle.

"We need more artwork in here," he muses, as he reaches the end and turns around in one graceful movement.

In a blink of an eye he uses his vampire speed to race back the way he came and back towards me. He plants himself next to me.

"How are you not exhausted?" Shaun muses.

"Shows always give me the zoomies afterwards," Benny replies, shrugging. He opens the beer and takes one long pull from it.

"I always get the zoomies during the show," I say, opening my beer as well and taking a sip.

"I've noticed." Benny grins.

Evan comes over and nudges Benny's foot. "What about the artwork?"

Benny shrugs. "I dunno. Can't we replace that thing?" He points to the massive cross hanging above the altar.

Evan laughs. "I kind of like it, actually."

"Then let me paint a mural on that wall," Benny pleads, pointing to our left. "I just think this place needs a bit of color."

"You can paint one," Evan finally relents. "But it needs to be something really grand. A masterpiece, okay?"

Benny grins. "All my works are masterpieces." He winks at Evan and zooms off in a blur to grab his supplies.

Shaun and I look at Evan with brows raised. He hasn't even let me change the color of my bedroom walls. He shrugs. "We're gonna be practically tearing this portion down to the studs at some point anyways."

Shaun and I share amused grins. I hear footsteps towards the entrance to the sanctuary and look around, expecting to see Benny hauling in an armful of paint supplies, but instead my heart stammers and I can't breathe.

Evan, Shaun, and I are all on our feet in a matter of seconds.

"Who the fuck are you?" Evan asks, his voice dripping with violence.

The church is completely locked, so he must have had to break in.

I put myself in between my friends and my cousin, who's completely ignoring Shaun and Evan and staring at me like he's seen a ghost.

Which is fair.

"Pisces?" Simon asks, his voice raw. He swallows a few times, trying to get his throat working. "It really is you."

His shock heats into anger.

"You've been here this whole time?"

"Sces, who is this guy?" Shaun asks, gaze traveling between me and my cousin.

I take a step forward and Simon takes one back. "Sces? Is that what you're going by now?" He shakes his head in disgust. "I can't believe this. You're here and you're... fine?"

"I can explain," I say, but Simon shakes his head again, taking another step back.

"Everyone thinks you're dead."

I stop cold, though I don't know why. I know they think that. It was what I intended when I left what basically sounded like a suicide note for my parents to find.

But hearing him say it hits different.

"I— I had to. There's so much you don't know."

"So tell me. Explain this. Explain how you're here. Explain *why* you're here."

Shaun whispers behind me to Evan, "Who is this?"

"I think his cousin," Evan whispers back.

"And he thinks Pisces is dead because...?"

"Because I told him to make his family think he's dead because I figured that would be the safest for them."

"You did *what*?!" Shaun hisses.

"Would you two save this for later?" I ask, my voice lethally quiet. My eyes stay on Simon.

"Right, continue," Shaun says.

"Why would you want his family to think he's dead?" Simon

levels at Evan. "What kind of sick fuck are you? Pisces, why are you hanging out here? Is it drugs?"

"No, it's not drugs," I say, looking helplessly at Shaun. "Can I? Am I allowed to?"

Shaun shakes his head. "Sorry, Sces. You're gonna need to use your compulsion."

Compulsion. All fae have compulsion, but it only works on humans, except kindreds. Though I really don't have much practice. "Evan, can you?"

Evan takes a step forward, but Simon looks pleadingly at me. "Pisces, what the fuck are you talking about? What's going on?"

Before I can answer, Benny comes speeding back into the church, stopping right next to Simon. "Hey, who's this?" he asks, a friendly smile on his face.

Simon yelps, having seen a blur coming straight at him. "What the fuck?"

"Simon, it's okay," I say, going to my cousin's side. "This is Benny, he's a friend of mine."

"He's the fucking Flash," Simon breathes, looking wide-eyed at Benny and then back to me. His face screws up in confusion. "Is it drugs, or are you some sort of superhero?"

"Neither," I respond, looking again at Shaun for help.

He's already seen Benny, but any one of the guys could make Simon forget that pretty easily.

Simon glares at me, and I find I can't help but glare back. "Pisces, seriously, tell me what the fuck is going on."

"I can't!" It takes everything in me not to scream. Fuck, this isn't supposed to be how things went. How did Simon even find me? He's supposed to think I'm dead, so no one will look for me. I need to keep my family safe. I've fucked up again.

"You need to come back with me," Simon says, grabbing my arm and trying to pull me out of the church. "I don't know what these guys got you messed up in, but I'm getting you out."

I dig my feet in. "No." I rip my arm out of his grasp. "I'm here because I want to be."

"You can't mean that. Look at this place. It's a dump!"

"Hey!" Evan quips, then adds under his breath, "The other wing is actually quite nice."

Simon goes to grab my arm again. "We're getting the fuck out of here, Pisces."

It happens before I can stop it. My teeth slide out and my vision completely blurs. All I can focus on is ripping and tearing and the blood that coats my mouth. I feel hands wrap around my upper arms, hauling me backwards away from the flesh I so desperately need.

I'm thrown down onto a pew and Benny is on top of me, yelling, "Sces, stop!" He snaps his fangs in my face and I snap my siren teeth back at him, but he's restrained me enough that I can't even nip him.

"Fuck, he got you good," Evan murmurs a few feet away.

Someone is breathing heavily and I can smell the blood. "Snap out of it, Sces," Shaun says from my right. I realize he's holding my shoulders down on the pew.

I look between him and Benny and take a few calming breaths, and then everything comes back to me.

"Oh god," I whisper. "No, no, no." I push Benny and Shaun aside, my siren teeth back in my gums. I run to my cousin. "Simon!"

Evan is cradling Simon in his arms. There's blood everywhere. "What are you waiting for? Heal him!"

"Sces," Evan says softly. "I already am. Look."

Guilt and terror war inside my stomach as I take a closer look at Simon's injuries. I reach out a hand and grip one of his.

Evan's magic continues to wash over Simon, knitting skin, muscle, and sinew back together.

"He'll be fine," Evan murmurs to me. "Just a little nip really. I forget how easily humans bleed."

I roll my eyes at Evan. The second he's done healing Simon, I pull him into my arms. "Simon." I push his dark hair out of his eyes. "Are you okay?"

His eyes flitter open and he looks up at me, horror sketching across his face briefly. He looks around wildly, pushing himself out of my grasp, his hand going to his throat. He scrambles backwards until his back hits the side of a pew.

"What the fuck are you?" Simon eyes us all with fear. "I— I don't understand."

"I'm sorry, Simon. I'm so sorry." I move towards him, but he tries to move backwards again so I stop. "Fuck. I'm so sorry."

"What are you?" he breathes out.

I don't dare look at Evan or Shaun. I don't want them to stop me. "I'm fae. A siren, specifically."

"You bit me," Simon says, fear still ruling his eyes.

"Yeah, he does that sometimes," Evan says.

I glare at him. "Not helping."

"Your teeth," Simon says, ignoring Evan.

"Yeah, I know, they're scary. God, I'm so sorry, Simon. I—" I look around helplessly. How am I supposed to explain any of this? I got angry at Simon, maybe even because he was angry with me. And then I bit him. I almost killed him, and worse, if Evan hadn't been here, I wouldn't have been able to do anything to save him.

My head slumps forward. I look to Evan. "Make him forget. Send him home. Maybe add in there something about not looking for me again," I say in resignation. Simon can't be around me. He'd be in too much danger.

"What?" Simon asks. "No, I don't want to forget. I just found you."

I turn around, seeing him pushing himself to his feet. Tears are in my eyes, blurring my vision. "You can't be around me. It's too dangerous."

Simon wipes at his throat where I bit him. "I'm fine now. I don't get what's going on, but I can't lose you again." He plants his feet firmly and crosses his arms. "I'm not going anywhere."

"You don't have a choice," I say, shrugging. Before I can think better of it, I cross the remaining distance between us and sweep my cousin up in a hug. "I am glad I got to see you one last time. But it's better if you don't remember me like this anyways."

I release him and nod to Evan, who takes a step forward.

Simon shakes his head. "No."

Evan pauses, looking at me for instruction, but when I turn and see Simon staring Evan and me down defiantly, I find I can't give the order again.

"I just found you. I'm not going anywhere. Tell me what's going on. I can handle it."

"Pisces, we need to wipe his memory," Shaun says. "It's better for him."

I look over to my friend. Maybe he's right, but— "I can't," I tell him. I'm too fucking selfish. "Can't we tell him? Humans become kindreds all the time, right?"

Shaun shrugs. "He'd need a Born sponsor and he'd have to register and take tests. It's a long process and we don't even know he's cut out for it. Plus, it will put him at risk. Fae society is more dangerous than human society. You know this better than anyone."

"I don't care," Simon tells Shaun. He comes to stand in front of me, looking me directly in the eyes. "I'm staying." He turns to Shaun. "What's a kindred?"

Shaun sighs, taking another couple of beers from the cooler and handing one to Simon. "Kindreds are humans who have either grown up in fae families or have become part of fae society. They're protected and need either a fae guardian, or for adults—a sponsor."

Simon looks at me. "Okay, be my sponsor."

I smile softly. "I can't do it. I'm not Born fae."

"What the fuck does that mean?" Simon asks, grinning.

"This is going to be a long night," Benny says with a chuckle.

We settle into the pews, pushing a few around so that we can all face each other, though Benny and Evan sit a little away from us, having their own side conversation about the mural Benny wants to paint.

Shaun explains the concept of Born and Made fae, while I study Simon's face. He seems to be taking everything in stride. In fact, he's actually responding to all this information better than I did.

Though to be fair, I also had to deal with the new craving for blood and flesh. But that's Simon, the text book definition of easygoing.

"Simon, how did you find me?" I ask, before Simon can ask any more questions.

"Oh, right." Simon grins hesitantly. "I followed you back after your show. Took me a while to figure out how to sneak in here, but there's an open window in the basement."

"You were at the show?"

He nods, hesitance turning into excitement. "When I heard about a progressive metal band wearing masks to remain anonymous, it made me think of you. I thought, Pisces would eat that shit up. I've never given up looking for you. I saw the note you left and it definitely seemed like you'd—" He pauses, clearing his throat, not wanting to actually say it. "Everyone thought you'd done it. Driven your car off a cliff somewhere, or I dunno. But I just didn't buy it. You had started writing music again. You'd been doing better and had been making an effort to get your life back, so I didn't want to give up on you.

"And then I listened to some Voracious Maw singles, and I heard your voice, and I knew it was you. I couldn't quite allow myself to believe it, but I still knew it. So I went to a show. I figured, I'll go and I'll see this guy and even in the mask I should be able to rule it out, but then I was sure. Same height, same build, same voice."

"You seem surprised to see he's alive, though?" Shaun asks.

Simon nods. "Well, yeah, I mean I knew it, but still, *seeing* it is something else entirely." He meets my eyes and smiles at me. "I fucking missed you."

"I missed you too," I tell him, putting my arm around him and pulling him in for a hug. Tears streak down both our faces, which makes me smile even more. "So what do you think, mate?" I ask Shaun. "Can we keep him?"

CHAPTER TWENTY-TWO
PISCES

She walked off in *my* hoodie and never came back.

I lean my head back against the hay. Which I regret instantly as it dislodges particles that send me into a sneezing fit again. At least Shaun has some really good quality fae allergy potion. It's saved me a few times before, when hay fever has struck just before a show.

"Sces? You around here?" Evan asks, just as he rounds the corner to my little section of the maze. "Ah, there you are."

"Told you to just follow the sound of sneezing." Benny comes into view a moment later.

"Can I leave?" I ask immediately.

Benny and Evan both look around. "Where is your maze partner? Simon was very clear not to abandon the buddy system. He didn't want you to get lost like the last time you were in a maze."

"I was eight," I say hotly.

Benny shrugs as if he's not sure about that. "Simon says you cried for your mum."

"Careful," I warn, letting my siren teeth slide out. "I'm a little hungry." And the rage from before when I was talking with Bliss hasn't subsided.

Benny just grins, and I can't resist the urge to tackle him into the hay.

I don't bite him, just nip at him a little. But the absurdity of it is exactly what I need to cool off.

"You're not eight now, either of you," Evan says, sighing. Benny and I turn and look up at him. Catching sight of each other, though, we burst out laughing. Benny has hay all over him, stuck in his hat, caught on his jacket. I imagine I look much the same.

"Where is your maze partner?" Evan asks, looking around.

"Left," I say simply, hopping back to my feet and brushing myself off. I reach out a hand to Benny, my teeth sliding back into my gums as I lift him to his feet. I make a show of brushing him off, letting my hands linger and using much too much pressure. He lets out a laugh and Evan shakes his head at us.

"You two realize you don't have to be so touchy-feely off stage?" he asks.

Benny and I grin at each other. "We know," Benny says to Evan with a wink.

"She's wearing your hoodie, mate," Evan says to me, abruptly changing topics, since he knows Benny and I will just be even more touchy-feely to annoy him. Evan doesn't mind physical contact, but he likes to be in control, to dominate. And hugs aren't really like that.

I let out a sharp growl from the base of my throat. "I know," I grit out, a lingering bit of anger rearing its head.

"She showed up with it," Benny prods.

"I know," I repeat and let out an exasperated sigh. I explain to them how last night I saw her in the garden after I came back with a change of clothes. I knew everyone would want to see me in full costume so I obliged, but even though I've filled out quite a bit in the last year, I wanted to cover everything. My lanky arms, my scars. I didn't like being so close to people that they could see them, even through the paint I wore.

So I ran into her. Bliss.

She looked so beautiful with the moonlight illuminating her

soft creamy skin and making her golden-brown hair glow. And her eyes.

They were so fucking mesmerizing, a bluish green that I could get lost in, not to mention the left—

"Pisces?" Evan pulls me out of my thoughts. I didn't realize I stopped talking.

"So she had no idea who you are?" Benny says, prompting me to continue.

"No, she doesn't." I shake the hair out of my eyes. "She had zero interest in me, Pisces, but if Wrath had been here I'm sure then I'd have gotten her attention. Fucking hate people like that. Just trying to climb a social ladder. She also tried using her power on Simon. I overheard her trying to flirt with him."

"Trying to?" Evan asks, curiosity setting his eyes alight. "She's a succubus, right?"

I shrug. "Yeah, but Simon appeared uninterested."

"Uninterested in a succubus?" Evan asks, amused again. "Odd."

"You can say that again," Benny says. "Has anyone else noticed him acting odd?"

They both look at me.

"I thought it was just the stress of taking on the role of band manager?" I muse. "The way he was with Bliss was odd, though."

"Is she not physically his type?" Evan asks.

"I don't think he's super picky about physical appearance for either men or women. It's about their personality," I say, starting to ramble. "She's got a shit personality, so maybe it's not so odd after all." I sit down on the hay bench. "And seriously, what's with the fucking ribbons?"

Benny and Evan let out little chuckles.

But for some reason I don't think they're laughing with me.

I let out a sigh. "I fucked up, though," I admit, my eyes finding Benny's.

"What do you mean?"

"She was trying to flirt with Simon, and then with me. I could feel it. But I could also feel *guilt*. She's up to something, but I have no idea what. It pisses me off that she's messing with Simon. I might have lost it on her."

"You bit her?" Evan asks, his face going paler than normal.

"No, no, nothing like that." I groan. "Honestly, though, that might have been better."

"Stars, what did you say?" Benny asks.

Before I can launch into the full story, a new set of volunteers comes to relieve us from our duties. I leave the prizes to them, heading out with Evan and Benny.

As we walk out, one thing settles clearly in my mind.

I took it too far with Bliss.

CHAPTER TWENTY-THREE

BLISS

BETWEEN THE MILLION AND ONE THINGS I HAVE TO DO AS BAND manager, I finally manage to carve out some time to go check in on everyone at the townhome. I haven't run into Taser yet, and now that my flirting went so poorly with Simon, I've been keeping busy so I don't run into him anywhere. Between Taser, Simon, Grim, and Jordan, I'm seriously starting to develop quite a few boy problems.

I am still fucking furious with Taser—and myself.

Simon I will never be able to hang out with again out of embarrassment.

Grim is gorgeous and flirty but has no rune.

Jordan I need to avoid like the plague.

And now Pisces, who was a complete ass for absolutely no reason.

I come to a stop in the living room, looking around at everyone. Blake and Amelia are playing a card game at the coffee table and Reese is in a heated discussion with Tubbs over Voracious Maw's drummer, Mist.

They're both arguing that he is the best drummer in existence, but they can't seem to agree on why.

"It's the way he'll intentionally lag on a beat that makes their music so interesting," Reese is saying.

Tubbs shakes his head, pointing his set of drumsticks at her. "That part is great, don't get me wrong, but that's easy if you have good timing, which all drummers should. It's the inspiration he takes from all different genres for me."

I stop paying attention to the weird discussion.

"Would you two just get a room with Mist already? Have a threesome!" Taser mutters under his breath as he flips through a magazine. His eyes sweep over to me and I angle my head towards the staircase. I don't check to make sure he follows. I know he will.

We end up in the primary suite. I poke my head out to make sure no one else came upstairs before I close the door. When I turn Taser is taking his shirt off.

"What are you doing?" I yell at him.

He looks at me like a deer in headlights. "What?" He throws his shirt back on. "I thought that's why you wanted me up here. You didn't exactly recharge much this morning. I thought you needed to power up again, my bad."

"You and I are never doing that again," I mutter, crossing my arms.

Taser lifts his brows at me. "Oh, because you have Grim now?"

My eyes whip back to his. "What?"

He takes a step towards me and I take one back. He stops and shakes his head, putting his hands in his pockets. "Sorry, that was uncalled for. You can sleep with whoever you want."

"You're fucking right I can," I say. My voice almost sounds like Amelia's in this moment.

"So what's going on then, Bliss?" Taser asks, eyes boring into mine. "You barely talk to me these days, but then you used me this morning. So why am I here?"

I let out a hollow, hoarse laugh. "Is this a good time to remind you that you cheated on your girlfriend with me?"

His eyes widen. "Shit," he mutters, sitting down on the bed. "Amelia told you?"

"She didn't have to. I overheard you say it."

Taser puts his head into his hands. "If it makes it better, I broke up with her the next day."

"You broke up with her?" That's news to me. Tension I didn't even realize I've been holding in my shoulders melts, and I feel myself relaxing. If they've been broken up since that day, then what I did with Taser this morning was completely fine.

But you didn't know that and you did it anyway, a voice reminds me.

He nods. "Of course I did. She obviously deserves better."

"And what about me? Don't I deserve better?"

He finally looks at me. "I did the best for you that I could. I wasn't just going to let you die. I know I'm one of the few people you'd be comfortable feeding with." He stands up and stops in front of me. "I'm not going to apologize, Bliss. I'd do it again."

I roll my eyes. It's the same thing Amelia said. "You and Amelia both act like the ends justify the means."

"They do." I start to argue, but he shakes his head. "No, Bliss. When the ends are life and death and the means aren't, then the ends do justify the means."

My mouth snaps shut. How the hell do I argue against that?

"So whatever," he continues, "hate me, or don't. But I did what I needed to. And I'll do it again, if you ever need it." He starts to leave, but I reach out and grab his arm. He's completely right.

"Stars, I'm sorry." I search for the right words. "Thanks. For being there for me. You're a good friend. One of my best friends. And I put you in a really tough situation."

Taser wraps me up in a bear hug. I can't stop myself from smiling. "You never need to apologize for just trying to stay alive." We both fall silent, enjoying the comfort we're each getting out of this hug.

After a few moments, I break the silence slowly. "So friends do friends favors, right?" I ask, still being crushed into him.

He breaks the hug, his hands coming to rest on my shoulders. "Sexual favors?" he asks with a grin. I swat at his upper arm.

"No." I shake my head. "I was wondering if you could track a scent for me."

He scrunches up his face at me. "Wrong fae, Blissy."

"Don't call me Blissy. What do you mean wrong fae?"

"I'm not a wolf shifter. Or any animal shifter that would have the ability to sniff things out."

"But you have all those superior senses!"

"Yeah, like, I have a great sense of smell, but I can't track things like a fucking dog."

My shoulders and head slump. "Damn."

"Why?"

"I need to find the owner of this hoodie to give it back to him," I lie.

"It's Wrath's hoodie, isn't it?"

"What the fuck? How did you know that?"

Taser goes over to the bed and sits down on it. He lies back, putting his hands behind his head. "I've seen him wear it. He's a huge fan of Moonstruck. The man's got really good taste."

"You know Wrath? Like his real identity?" I ask.

Taser just grins at me.

"Can you, uh—introduce me?"

Taser sits up and frowns, shaking his head. "Sorry, Bliss. I can't. The guy really likes his privacy, and I'm not gonna mess with that. If he didn't tell you himself, then I'm sorry, I can't help."

I let out a sigh. It's not like I can be mad at Taser for that. And now that we are back to being friends, I don't want to be mad at him at all. "You're right. I'm sorry I even asked."

"I can get the hoodie back to him? If you want?"

I shake my head. "I should really wash it," I hedge. It's not a lie. I do need to wash it, since I got my snot on it this morning. "And I'd like to thank him, even if it's only to his masked face."

Taser laughs. "Alright, well if that's all you wanted from me, I should go back and check on Tubbs. Make sure Reese didn't upset him too much."

I quirk my brows at him.

"She gets mean when she debates music and music theory."

We both laugh at that, making our way back down the stairs.

"What do you even know about it?" Reese is saying to Tubbs, who looks at us for help once we're in the room.

"What do I, a drummer, know about drumming?" Tubbs asks incredulously. Reese is pacing back and forth.

"Reese, let's give the poor guy a break," Taser says, taking Reese's arm and leading her away from Tubbs.

"Not until he admits that 'Darkest Impulses' is played in a four-four!" she says loudly. I stop myself from laughing at how serious she is right now.

Tubbs looks at me for backup, as Taser takes Reese out of the room completely. "It's not a four-four, it's a—" I place my finger on his lips and nod.

"I know, I believe you. Let's grab some snacks, okay?"

Tubbs sighs but nods. "I don't understand how my own bassist can doubt my timing."

"Well, at least she lets you lead during shows," I remind him and he laughs.

"Barely."

CHAPTER TWENTY-FOUR

BLISS

"Alright, listen up. For those of you who don't already know me, I'm Shaun! One of the play line techs for Voracious Maw," a guy with short dirty blonde hair calls. He stands on the top steps of the building the masquerade ball was held in.

I stand shoulder to shoulder with Amelia and Reese, looking around at everyone gathered. Fae and kindreds from most of the bands here stand at the bottom of the steps, waiting for Shaun to explain the game.

He holds up an upside-down baseball cap. "You've all played sardines before?" he asks, and a round of murmurs goes around the crowd. Apparently Voracious Maw started a tradition of playing this game at every festival they played at. "Well, for any of you who haven't, it's like reverse hide and seek. I have all your names in this hat, and whoever's name I pull will be the one that goes and hides. The rest of you seek them out and when you find them, you hide where they're hiding, got it?"

"Yeah, we've all played before, mate, get on with it," Evan heckles from below. He's not easy to miss, heads taller than almost everyone here. I scan the faces of the people he's standing next to, wondering if any of them could be Wrath, but then my eyes land on their rude guitar tech and I avert my gaze.

A vampire with wavy brown hair and bright blue eyes speeds up the stairs and stands next to Shaun. He holds out his hand for the hat. Shaun hands it over and closes his eyes, picking a name out of the hat.

He reads it and searches the crowd. Pointing towards the left side of the crowd, he calls, "Simon! You're the one hiding. Come on up."

I fight the urge to roll my eyes as Pisces pushes Simon forward. Simon saunters up the steps with a bold grin. I envy his attitude a little bit. I know if I'd been chosen to hide, Amelia would have had to physically carry me up those steps. I'd have probably found some reason to bail.

In fact, I don't really want to play this game at all, but Simon invited Goddess' Trance and I knew we couldn't say no. This is a great way for Amelia and the others to network with other bands, which means potentially opening for them, or getting invited to other festivals.

Thankfully, Dead Hearts doesn't seem to be on the guest list, but the Phantoms are. I spot Grim in the crowd and he winks at me. He puts his attention back on Shaun, who is now joined by Simon and Evan.

"In a minute here we'll put an invisibility spell on Simon and then he'll go hide. The whole festival grounds is fair game. Out of bounds are from where the townhomes are—" he points to his left, "—and the shopping district." He points to his right. Then he points out in front of him. "Stages are fair game, but not the parking lot beyond. And behind us—" he motions back beyond the building, "—the greenbelt is also out of bounds. Simon can pick anywhere inside the perimeter to hide. Also, you're not allowed to seek in groups. Everyone has to separate and go alone. No forming teams."

"This'll be easy peasy," Taser says confidently to Blake, who nods. They'll no doubt be using their vampire speed to track Simon down.

"Not so fast," Shaun says, overhearing. "Another rule," he says, motioning for the vampire who held out the hat earlier to start handing something out. "Everyone will be wearing a special wristband. This suppresses your fae abilities so everyone has a fair shot."

"Oh, come on," Blake whines, pretending to pout.

"Nah, otherwise it'd be over in a heartbeat. Any wolf shifter would sniff out Simon in a matter of minutes. Trust me, this makes it more fun. The wristbands are easy to rip off if you need to access your power in an emergency, but it will disqualify you from the game."

Everyone nods in understanding. Shaun continues on. "Simon will have a head start, and he'll be invisible for approximately twenty minutes. So in the meantime, while he hides, we've got drinks." Shaun points to a table. "So grab a refreshment and let's make this a fun tipsy game of sardines!"

A cheer goes around the crowd.

Shaun approaches Simon with the invisibility potion. "Can I have a drink before too? Considering it might be my last one," Simon says, grinning wickedly at Evan. Shaun doesn't look amused and eyes the potion warily. He hands a small dose of it over to the drum tech.

"Say your prayers, mate," Evan says, spreading his hands and shrugging. "Didn't have time to test that properly. Hope it works."

Simon shoots a reassuring smile at Shaun, and without much thought, uncorks the potion and chugs it down in seconds.

Almost as soon as he's done, he disappears from sight, except for the glass vial he's holding. He must hand it off to Shaun as it seems to float into his hands. "Alright, twenty minutes starts now," Shaun says, setting a timer on his watch. "Cheers!"

Once we get our wristbands on, Amelia and Reese tug me over to where someone's set up a table with coolers of beer, hard lemonade, and ciders. I select a blackberry cider, crack it open, and settle off to the side with my friends as we wait for the game to start.

I stare down at my wristband. It's totally unnecessary. I can't think of any advantage my power would have given me. No one will have seen where Simon went, so I can't flirt any information out of anyone, and I can't use my power on Simon from a distance.

I think through my options here. This game is something Voracious Maw always plays at festivals. It's very likely that Wrath is here somewhere. If I can get to Simon earlier on in the game, I might be able to watch some of the Voracious Maw guys interact with their guards down. They could reveal something that'll allow me to piece together who Wrath is.

Grim approaches and sweeps me into a hug. "Kinda wish we were getting to seek you out. I think I'd win."

"And why's that?" I ask, a flirty lilt to my voice.

"I'd be very, very motivated to find you first," he teases. I can't help but let out a laugh.

"I don't think you'd be the only one," Amelia says as she watches another group approach us. Pinkie and some others I haven't met are eyeing us appreciatively, but it's easy to convince myself they're just looking at Amelia and Reese.

"You all excited for this?" Pinkie asks, grinning.

We all raise our cans and cheers, falling into a conversation about how the festival is going so far. The twenty minutes pass too quickly and Shaun shoos everyone apart to start searching for Simon.

Alright, Bliss, I hype myself up. *You can find him, just think about where he'd likely hide.* I can do this. Simon seems like the type to get creative with his hiding place. I send up a prayer to the stars to help me out with my plan. Maybe my intuition will guide me. I stand still, clearing my mind, and wait until a direction pops into my head.

An image of the stages comes into my mind's eye and I decide to follow the whim. Simon, as a drum tech, would definitely know of any good hiding places near the stages. I head that direction, noting I'm not the only one who has had that same thought.

I can see Taser a few paces to my left, heading to the stage that's furthest away from where we started. I find my way to the backstage area of the main stage that's not currently in use. Gear is stacked, ready to be moved. A few roadies mill around, but I don't see Simon. He wouldn't be out in the open like this, though.

I turn down a ramp behind the stage that ends in a sunken concrete area being used to store more stuff. Maybe he's hiding behind some of the gear. I round the corner and let out an exasperated sigh, almost turning around immediately before he can see me. Pisces is sitting on top of some instrument cases that have been stacked, playing an electric guitar, even though it's not plugged into anything. I notice the gear cases all have Voracious Maw stickers on them, some so faded you can barely make out their logo.

"Bliss?" He stops picking the strings.

I turn quickly, heading back the way I came. I can hear him set the guitar back into its case, closing it hastily. "Bliss, wait!"

I don't.

"What do you want?" I ask, as he falls easily into step with me.

"In that big of a hurry to find Simon?" he asks. I look up and see his eyes narrowed at me.

"Well, yeah, that is the point of the game," I snap, slowing to turn and face him down. "You don't seem to understand how the game works." I motion to where he was sitting, obviously not playing despite wearing one of the wristbands.

"I figure I'll let others find him first, then it'll be easier to find everyone."

I raise an eyebrow at him. "You're suppose to try finding him *first*," I explain. "Is this your first time playing?"

He shakes his head. "No, but I don't really feel like playing today."

Why am I even talking to him? I turn and keep walking. Where else would Simon be? I stop again when I hear Pisces following me. "What are you doing?"

He cocks his head at me. "I'm going to try to find Simon, since you've explained this super complicated game to me. I get it now," he says dryly.

I roll my eyes at him again. "Asshole," I mutter, continuing on and trying to ignore that he's definitely following me.

When I head in the direction of the next stage, Pisces speaks again. "Simon wouldn't hide out in the open like this," he drawls. "He's really good at this game."

Taser runs past us just then, following after Reese, who is squealing as they run around the backstage area. It seems Pisces isn't the only one who has lost sight of the game's objective.

"Are you trying to help me find him?" I ask, continuing my search of the backstage. I head out onto one of the stages. It's empty except for a couple of miscellaneous wires taped down to the floor.

"Yeah, cause that's what I want, for you to find my cousin so you can flirt with him."

"So why tell me where he wouldn't hide?"

"Maybe I'm lying," he says, a wicked grin on his face.

Ignore him, I tell myself as I leave the second stage and head back the way I came. Maybe Simon is hiding in one of the buildings closer to where we started.

Pisces lets out a sigh. "He wouldn't pick a *good* hiding place. He'd pick a funny one."

I stop and look at him. "Why are you telling me this?"

He shrugs.

It's not possible for my eyes to roll any harder.

He could still be lying, but at this point my approach to this game is likely moot. "Why don't you lead, then?" I snap.

"Okay," he says simply. He turns to the left, headed to the grassy picnic area where I made my deal with the wraith.

He comes to a stop in the middle of the grassy area and spins around slowly in a circle, scanning for Simon. He laughs. "Figures," he mutters and heads off. I hurry after him, not able to match his long strides.

He pokes his head into the overly long high slide in the playground. The festival hasn't opened yet so the playground is pretty empty. Pisces comes back up and looks over at me, an annoyed expression on his face. He waves to the slide and I poke my head in to see. Towards the bottom the slide straightens out a bit, enough for Simon to lounge there comfortably, hiding. He sees me and smiles. "Bliss! Come on in!"

"You hid in a slide?" I ask, a bemused smile lifting the corners of my mouth.

"I figured it'd be funny to see how many people could hide in here before people start to see us."

"Or until the slide breaks," Pisces says with a soft chuckle. I glance at him and quickly avert my gaze.

"Well, guess we should get in. Watch your head, mate," Pisces tells Simon, as he heads up to the top of the slide. I follow him.

Once I know Pisces is down the slide, hiding just above where Simon is, I ease myself into the slide, thankful I'm in jeans and a long-sleeved shirt. *This is ridiculous*, I think to myself.

I slide down, the static of the plastic tube probably putting my hair into a state I don't want to think about. But I gain a little too much momentum as the long slide drops suddenly and before I can stop myself I slide right in next to Pisces, instead of holding myself in place above him.

He wraps an arm around me before I can collide with Simon's head. "Easy there, little succubus," Pisces mutters, tucking me in next to him. "Don't give our drum tech a concussion."

I'd like to give you a concussion, I mutter internally and Pisces *chuckles*. As if he can hear my thoughts. I glare at him.

"Let me go."

"You'll take out Simon if I do."

"Please don't fall on me, either of you," Simon says from below us.

"This was a very stupid idea," I mutter.

They both laugh.

But it's Pisces' laugh that I can feel rumble in his chest. I start to slip and without meaning to I place my hand on his shoulder, helping to keep myself where I am. Simultaneously he tightens his grip, causing my chest to press into his, and our faces to only be a few breaths apart. Through his shirt, I can feel—

My breath hitches. Are those nipple piercings?

His eyes travel up my face to my hair and I subconsciously run a hand over it, trying to smooth down the staticky frizz. I notice his sticking up a little bit too, and I can't help but laugh.

He uses his free hand to smooth his hair down and runs it over mine as well, tucking a piece behind my ear. He swallows and looks down to Simon. "Any sign of anyone else?" he asks, thankfully giving me enough time to blow out a breath.

I take a deep inhale, which is a mistake because Pisces smells better than anything I've smelled before, including food. His scent is masculine and clean. There's a breeze to it that reminds me of ocean air, but also a warmth to it that I can't place.

I think he can tell that I'm smelling him. I can't figure out what type of fae he is, even this close. It doesn't necessarily mean he's not a type of fae I haven't met before, but it's likely.

"Shh," Simon responds, then in a low whisper, "I think I hear—"

"Boo!" Evan yells as he quickly scrambles up the slide from the bottom. I'm not sure how he manages to get his six-five frame into the space so quickly, but my heart jolts inside my chest. Pisces chuckles again, no doubt being able to hear and feel it.

"A slide? Really, Simon?" the brown-haired vamp from before says, sliding down enough so that he's just above Pisces and I. He blocks out enough of the light from the top of the slide that I can't see much anymore. Another guy gets into the slide after him— Shaun, I think.

"Honestly, I'm surprised I didn't look here sooner. This is exactly the type of thing Simon would do," Evan muses. "Hey, is that Bliss up there?"

"Hey, Evan," I reply, not really able to see him anymore. I can just barely make out Pisces' face, and that's only because I'm still way too close to him.

"Well, this sure is cozy in here," Evan responds. I can somewhat make out him crawling up the slide a little bit more, getting into Simon's space.

"Watch it, mate," Simon says, trying to move up the slide a little bit, but he only hits his head on Pisces' shoes. "Fuck," he mutters, rubbing a hand over his head.

"No complaining, mate, you did this to yourself," Pisces says.

Shaun shushes us. He crouches in the entrance of the tunnel. "I can hear more people," he whispers.

We all fall quiet. And then a bark of laughter that I know is Tubbs comes from the bottom of the slide, and more laughter towards the top. "I can see Evan's boots sticking out," Tubbs says to someone who's at the top of the slide. Taser pokes his head in at the top.

"Any more room down there?" he asks, laughing.

With Taser at the top, and Tubbs at the bottom, it takes only a few more minutes for everyone else to find Simon's hiding place. The entire group breaks out laughing as one by one we ease ourselves out of the slide.

When Simon and Evan are clear, Pisces releases me without a word, even so much as going to give me a slight push, and I go sliding forward, almost falling to the ground. Tubbs sweeps me up and sets me on my feet.

Pisces emerges next, a smirk on his face, and he completely ignores me, going to stand with Evan.

What a fucking asshole.

Shaun and the other guy, who I assume is either a band member or a tech, come sliding down next. Both are too short to be Wrath.

Pisces and Evan are the only ones tall enough that I've seen so far, but it's not either of them. Pisces, I thankfully ruled out yesterday, and Evan is clearly the bassist, Eerie. No one else in the group playing sardines seems to have the correct build to be Wrath. Maybe he just isn't playing.

The group reconvenes at the stairs of the building we started at. I fall into standing next to Amelia and Reese, who are unfortunately on the topic of having sex in tight spaces, the slide having sparked their imaginations.

I'm super thankful when Simon stands up at the top step, giving a little whistle to get everyone's attention. "Alright, time for round two! As per the rules, the one to find me first gets to hide next! So, Pisces, come on up!"

Evan cheers, giving a couple whoops of encouragement as Pisces heaves out a sigh and heads up the steps. Shaun measures out another dose of the invisibility potion and Pisces smirks at Evan, drinking it down without comment.

"Twenty minutes, Sces!" Simon calls to a now invisible Pisces.

I grab another drink with my band as we wait. Grim and some of the other Phantoms come over to chat again, and I fall into a nice conversation with Grim.

"You did really good in that last round."

"I cheated," I say with a smile.

Grim grins.

"That's very, very naughty, Bliss," Tubbs says, standing next to me. I elbow him in the stomach, and he groans, putting his hands up.

I notice Taser has stepped aside, gone over to chat with Evan and Simon.

"Bliss cheating?" Amelia asks, feigning shock. "She's too much of a goody-two-shoes to do that."

"I followed their guitar tech."

"That isn't necessarily against the rules," Tubbs says.

I laugh. I guess not.

Amelia and the others keep talking, but Grim and I tune out of the conversation as we watch Pinkie head slowly over to where Taser is. The Phantom's lead guitarist plants his feet right in front of Taser and the rest of our group falls silent. Taser looks at Pinkie, a snarl ripping from his throat. Pinkie lowers his head. I have to strain to hear what he says over the other people in the crowd.

"Could we talk?" Pinkie's voice is low, but I'm able to pick up those words.

I can't hear Taser's reply, but I don't need to as I watch him immediately turn and leave. He heads away towards the town-houses, ripping off his wristband and throwing it in a trash can as he passes it.

I want to go after him, but I know he'll want alone time. *You're defeating the purpose of storming off,* he'd likely say. I can hear it so clearly.

The twenty minutes are now up anyways, and it's time for the next round to start.

I definitely do not want to be the first one to find Pisces, so I've already decided once we're allowed to start seeking, I'll be sticking around here, giving everyone else a head start.

I linger on the steps, making it look like I'm thinking about which way to go, as I scan my surroundings. My head is starting to hurt a bit as the alcohol amplifies my waning power. I try not to focus on it, instead thinking about if I were Pisces—an arrogant prick—where would I hide?

Probably somewhere showy and hard to get to. Like in a tree or something.

I decide I might as well search the building behind me. It's got a ton of places Pisces could hide in, and while I'm pretty sure he went far away from here, it'll take me a while to search the whole building, so I might as well.

Ideally I'll be able to find him earlier on, but not too early. That way if Wrath *is* participating, I can maybe try to figure out who he is. Just as long as I'm not the first one there.

I steel myself and enter the building. There are the stairs that lead down to the ballroom, and off to both sides of the lobby are hallways that must lead to bathrooms and probably a kitchen. I decide to check the lower levels first and make my way up. I'll definitely be staying far away from the garden. I suppress a shudder as images of two nights ago flash through my mind.

The ballroom itself is completely empty, but there are doorways leading to more bathrooms, and also outside. I check each space pretty thoroughly but doubt anyone would want to hide in a bathroom. There's a doorway that's slightly ajar and behind it, a stairway.

I pause at the top, wondering if this is one of those moments where in a TV show everyone is yelling at the dumb girl not to go down the steps. But I decide to anyways, figuring I might as well rule it out. I do want to get to the hiding spot so I can observe how people are acting. Maybe someone will slip up in the fun and games of it all and call someone Wrath and I'll be able to figure out his identity.

One step closer to the life I want.

I get to the bottom of the stairs and turn, finding a long corridor with a few rooms. I check them out one by one and when I enter the last one, I feel a little warmth settle in my belly, as if this room is kept at a higher temperature than the others.

But then the door slams shut behind me and I wheel around, letting out a yelp. Pisces stands there, like he was hiding behind the door. He's slammed it shut, I realize.

"What the fuck?" I mutter, going to the door. I yank it open and try to take a step out, but find I physically can't.

Pisces smirks. "We're stuck here. It's part of the wristband magic. Prevents you from finding my hiding spot and leaving to tell the others."

"You guys take this game way too seriously."

He shrugs. "Sure, but it's more fun this way." Says the guy that didn't seem interested in playing before.

"Why'd you close the door?" I ask suspiciously.

His smirk turns into a grimace. "I wasn't sure who you were at first. Kinda was hoping to freak one of the guys out."

I roll my eyes at him and go lean against the opposite wall.

How the stars did I find him so easily? And quickly? I wasn't even trying.

Silence settles over us, and only the occasional noise from outside permeates the space. Neither of us seem to want to break it, which is just fine by me. I'd rather not talk to him. I spend the next several minutes looking from the window to the open door, anything to keep my eyes off Pisces.

I keep expecting someone else to show up. It's not like this hiding place is all that hard to find.

I check my phone. I don't have any service down here. Well, that's not great.

No email or games to pass the time.

A few more minutes tick by. Pisces clears his throat, and I glance at him, but he drops his gaze immediately. Was he about to say something?

I stop myself from sighing. At least conversation would be less boring.

And if we're talking, maybe anyone looking for us will hear us and find our hiding spot that much sooner.

"I figured you would have hidden somewhere else," I say, finally breaking the silence. It's the only thing I can think to say.

He lifts a brow. "Why?"

"This is so close to where we started. Just seems like it'd be too obvious."

He shrugs. Stars, I *hate* that. "Sometimes right under people's noses is the best hiding spot. Why were you searching here if you didn't think you'd find me?"

I mimic his shrug and don't respond. There's a small window in the room. I stare out of it, seeing a few shrubs and occasionally people's feet as they walk past the building. Definitely in the basement, then.

"Ah," Pisces says knowingly. "You didn't want to find me. Why?"

"Why do you think? The first time I was stuck with you wasn't really that fun." I rub my temples and cross my arms, deciding to sit on the floor. It looks clean enough. From this angle, I can see out the open door, so hopefully if anyone comes this way they won't miss me and they can hide with us. I desperately need a buffer.

"No, I guess it wasn't," he agrees after a pause.

I huff out a laugh. "You guess? Just so we're clear, you owe me an apology." What he said to me was so out of line.

He watches me from the wall he's leaning on and hangs his head. He breathes out a long stream of air and comes to sit next to me. I arch my brows at him, narrowing my eyes.

He slides down the wall till he's sitting with his legs spread out straight in front of him. He looks at me sideways, and then straight ahead. "I'm sorry for implying you're slutty and I'm sorry for implying that you're just arm candy."

I roll my eyes, not really sure if he's being genuine.

"I'm also sorry for making fun of your name."

"Yeah, about that—who are you to talk?" I ask now, glaring at him. I almost forgot about that part of it.

He smiles sheepishly at me and a traitorous part of my mind can't help but find his smile endearing and charming. *Just because he's a cute guy doesn't mean he can get away with being a jerk,* I remind myself.

He bends his knees and rests his elbows on them, his hands hanging in between his legs. He fiddles with his fingers. "You ever think maybe our mothers had something against us? Like their labor was so hard they had to get back at us in some way?"

I let out a laugh. "If that's the case, I would have thought Amelia would have gotten the weird name. Apparently they put my mom on more drugs during my delivery, so it should have been easier."

Pisces chuckles and the sound does something to me. It's deep and rough. I look over at him and he meets my gaze, growing somber. "I am really sorry, about before. I was already feeling angry about something else. I took it out on you and I shouldn't have."

I guess I can't really blame him. And I was only talking to him to try to get details on the band. That wasn't super nice of me. "Apology accepted."

He smiles softly at me and leans his head back against the wall. His dark brown hair falls into his eyes and he sweeps a hand across his forehead.

"Just so we're clear, I don't know how to braid hair, so we'll have to skip that part of our new friendship," he jokes.

I reach up and touch the ribbon that's tying up my hair into a ponytail. But I match his smile.

"Can I ask you a question about your job?" I ask, hoping he won't think I'm just trying to get information about him.

He looks at his hands. "I guess so."

"How'd you get started as a guitar tech? I'm thinking if Goddess' Trance does another big gig like this—which hopefully we will—I should try to hire some techs."

Pisces and I look towards the door, hearing a muffled sound, but it seems too far away to be anyone coming down here. Turning back to me he says, "I honestly just got it because I was already friends with some of the guys. You could probably ask around, see if any musicians you know want to make a little extra money. Though there are a lot of technical things they'd have to be familiar with. It's not as easy as just playing the instrument."

I nod. I'll task my musicians with asking around.

"Can I ask you a question?" Pisces asks.

"Sure," I say, a little scared of what he'll ask.

"You said you broke up with that guy? Goddess' Trance's old guitarist?"

"My question was way easier," I reply, mostly to stall and gather myself. I was not expecting him to bring up Jordan.

He laughs, the sound echoing around the empty concrete room. "You don't have to answer if you don't want to."

"Yeah, we broke up. I finally saw how terrible he was treating me. It was like I had a blindfold on the entire time we were dating. I actually realized it after a Voracious Maw show. Something about Wrath's lyrics helped the blindfold come off, I guess."

"Seriously? Which lyrics?"

"In 'Owe,' when Wrath sings 'You don't get to decide when my fate ends' and then screams 'It's not up to you!'" I pause, smiling. "There are a ton more I could list, but when I heard those lines for the first time it was eye opening."

Pisces doesn't say anything, his eyes roaming my face.

"And he crashed his car while driving me home that night. I almost died," I continue.

A guttural sound comes from his throat and I can see he's no longer looking at me but at the wall opposite us. His jaw clenches and his fists tighten into balls.

"Are you okay?" I ask.

He breathes in and out slowly through his nose a few times and nods. "Yeah. I'm sorry, it's just—I'm sorry you had to go through that."

I place my hand on his forearm. I wonder if he can somehow relate to what I've told him. His reaction seems to indicate as much. But I don't want to pry.

The cords of muscle along his arm seem to relax as he allows his fingers to uncurl. I remove my hand and let out a sigh. "I can't help but wonder what Wrath has been through in his life, for his lyrics to be that powerful. That life changing, ya know?"

Pisces doesn't respond. I look up and find his eyes have narrowed again. *Fuck.* I forgot how mad he was when I was asking him questions before about the band.

"I didn't mean—I'm just talking about the lyrics. Not asking you to spill any details."

Pisces stands up. "Yeah, but I can't help but feel like you're only talking to me because I know him."

"You think I'm trying to use you?"

Pisces stares down at me, his hands curled into fists again. "Aren't you? You're trying to flirt with Simon and now you're telling me a sob story."

"It's not like that at all."

"But you want to get to Wrath, you want to meet him."

"I mean, yeah, I do, but I swear I'm—I'm not trying to—" I fall silent, because isn't that exactly what I'm trying to do? I hang my head in shame. Maybe Pisces is right. *But I'm not shallow,* I want to tell him. It's not like that. But it still isn't right, is it?

Pisces nods in frustration, like he's caught me admitting it. "I was right about you."

I scramble to my feet, coming to stand in front of him. "What does that mean?"

"You're all about status and appearances. You're interested in getting closer to Wrath because he's successful and you think he's probably hot under the mask, right?"

"That's not at all—" I try to say, but he interrupts, shaking his head.

"Save it, Bliss." He seems like he's about to launch into a tirade, but his phone buzzes. He takes it out of his pocket and concern sketches across his face. "Fuck, Simon's called me about ten times." He answers the phone. "Hello—? Simon? Hold on, slow down, mate. I'm fine. The service is bloody awful down here." His gaze flicks to mine. "Yeah, she's with me. She's fine."

He yanks the phone away from his ear, and I can hear my sister's voice yelling through the phone. He holds it out to me and I take it. "Amelia?"

"Bliss, thank the stars. Where are you? No one has been able to find Pisces and it's been a while and Jordan and his friends crashed the game. We realized you were the only one we couldn't find and… oh stars. I thought—I thought…" She trails off and I hear the phone being passed around.

"She thought Jordan might have gotten to you," Reese finishes for her. "Amelia's really worried. We all were, obviously. Plus, after the masquerade party…" She doesn't have to finish the sentence.

"Is Amelia okay?" It sounded like she was having a panic attack.

"Yeah, she'll be alright. Where are you two?"

I look out the window of the basement as I respond, wondering if I'll be able to see any of them. "We're in the basement of the building the party was in. We're not really hidden, so I'm not sure why no one has found us yet."

"Okay, well why don't you come out now? The game is over."

"Alright, we'll be up in a minute."

I disconnect the call and hand Pisces' phone back to him. "Game's over. I guess I win. Lucky me," I mutter.

I roll my eyes and rip the wristband off, effectively erasing the magic keeping us in here. I hear another rip as Pisces follows suit.

He's on my heels as we head out of the basement towards the stairs.

"Bliss," he calls, as I'm about to start up the stairs.

I whirl around at him. "Save it. I don't get what your deal is.

Yeah, I want to meet Wrath. He's an amazingly talented musician. Who wouldn't want to meet him? But maybe I also wanted to get to know you too." With that, I turn and stomp up the steps, thankful that he keeps silent as he follows me.

I reach the door and try to turn the handle. I pause.

It's locked.

"Um, that's not good."

I try it a couple more times, more forcefully just to make sure.

Pisces shuffles in beside me and tries to open the door, putting his weight into it, but it doesn't give.

"Fuck," he swears, pulling out his phone. I'm standing close enough to hear Simon pick up on the second ring. Pisces is standing so close to me, my nose is almost brushing against his torso. The little stairwell isn't really meant for two people to stand side by side.

Pisces puts his arm out on the wall next to my head, looking down and meeting my gaze in the dim light. "Yeah, the door's locked."

"Can you unlock it?"

"Unlock it? Why didn't I think of that?" Pisces rolls his eyes. "It locks from the other side."

Pisces breathes in and out deeply, maybe trying to keep a bit of calm.

After a couple minutes we hear pounding on the other side of the door. "Pisces?" another voice calls. It sounds like Evan.

"Ev? Can you get us out of here?"

"Yeah, just stay back, and don't touch the handle."

It takes a few seconds, but suddenly the door handle turns bright red. Pisces urges me back down a few steps, putting himself in between me and the door.

I hear Evan kick the door handle and it crashes to the ground, still glowing red. "Come on," Pisces says, helping me step over the molten handle as Evan swings the door open.

"Well, that was fun." Evan grins. He turns around and leads us over to where Simon, Reese, Taser, and a few others are waiting.

Reese comes over and brushes some wisps out of my face. "Are you okay?"

I look at her, confused. "Yeah, I'm fine. We didn't even realize we were locked in. Guess that explains why no one ever found us."

"The door must have gotten locked after you went down there," Simon says. "Huh, weird. Well, I guess you win."

"What's my prize?" I ask, putting a little sultriness in my voice just to spite Pisces. Fuck what he thinks.

Simon laughs nervously.

"Well, you did get to hang out with Pisces one on one for a little," Evan says cheerily. "Isn't that a pretty great prize?"

I arch my brows at Evan but turn my attention back to Simon. "I think I'd rather have been trapped in there with you, actually."

I can hear Pisces let out a breath, and out of the corner of my eye I see him walk off without a word.

Simon, however, is beaming at me with a pleased but also bewildered expression that's actually extremely endearing. "I mean, if you want, we could hang out some time—?" Evan swings his arm around Simon and pulls him away from me, and Simon turns bright red.

I can't help but laugh. "So where's Amelia?" I ask Reese.

"Blake took her back to the house. She needed some space to calm down. I've never seen her that terrified."

My face falls and I nod. "Okay, let's get back, then. I wanna check on her."

CHAPTER TWENTY-FIVE

BLISS

Apparently it really pays to be a headliner at a music festival—especially a fae one.

The Phantoms have been spared not a single luxury; their lodging for the week is a much nicer house that stands alone at the end of a row of townhomes. There's a pool, a huge yard, and room after room.

And the Phantoms themselves have spared no expense with the party. Drinks are flowing. There are at least three different rooms playing music. It's a little overstimulating, if I'm being honest.

I already know Amelia and Reese will want to spend a ton of time here dancing. And I know they'll also be wanting to find some fun companions for tonight.

"Bliss! Amelia!" A familiar voice calls, and I immediately want to melt into a puddle on the floor and drain through it into the ground, where I will seep deeper and deeper and never be seen again.

Oh, is that dramatic?

Simon saunters over to us, clearly a drink or two already into the night, and slings an arm around me. "Bliss! You made it! I was worried the Phantoms didn't invite you all."

Amelia huffs and throws her hair over her shoulder. "Succubi are always invited to the party, little human," she says, putting her finger under his chin and tipping his head up. She's not taller than Simon, but somehow she looks it.

I duck my head out from under Simon's arm, my cheeks bright pink. Amelia notices and gives me a questioning look, but I just shake my head and point at Simon's drink. "Where'd you get that?" If he's here, I definitely need a drink.

He gets very excited, as a drunk person naturally does at the prospect of others drinking. "Right this way, my sexy succubi friends!" He turns around, suddenly very serious. "Is that okay to call you?"

"No, I'm extremely offended that you would think we're sexy," Amelia drawls.

But drunk Simon apparently doesn't understand sarcasm. "Oh my god, I'm so sorry," he splutters.

"She's messing with you," the brown-haired vamp that was on the slide with us earlier says, clapping a hand on Simon's back. He looks at Amelia. "Right?"

Amelia just grins, winking at the both of them. She heads off to seek out drinks.

"I'm Benny, by the way," the vamp says, holding out his hand to me. I shake it.

"He's another of our techs," Simon says with a cheesy smile that I've come to realize is a tell. I take in Benny's blue eyes and his height. He looks around six foot—definitely the right height to be Poison, but I won't push.

"Nice to meet you," I say. "I should go find my sister," I add, seeing that she and Reese have already made it to a kitchen island stocked with booze.

I head over there and unfortunately for me, Simon is at my heel. "So, Bliss, long time no see," he says.

I turn around and make a face at him, my pathetic attempt at flirting momentarily forgotten. "We saw each other earlier today."

"Oh right, well, I just mean…" He stumbles over his words again. "I just mean that we didn't get to hang out much."

Amelia pours us drinks, even filling up Simon's cup some more. I feel into my power reserves. There's not much there, but there's a tiny bit. I reach for it, my voice growing a bit huskier. "You seemed so busy, especially at the scavenger hunt yesterday," I say with the barest hint of a pout. Amelia—being able to sense exactly what I'm doing—sniggers and makes some excuse to be somewhere else. Thankfully.

"Yeah, about that, I'm really sorry. If I could have spent some time with you yesterday, I would definitely have. Being band manager is a lot more work than a drum tech, and honestly I miss that."

"Well, it seems to me like you're doing a good job," I say, taking a step closer and letting my hand rest on Simon's upper arm.

He blushes and a super goofy grin spreads across his face. Obviously my powers work a little easier on fae and humans when they're drunk, but it's odd that they're working today when they didn't work yesterday.

Maybe he was just super stressed yesterday and my powers just couldn't pull out his lust?

"Thanks, Bliss, that actually really means a lot. I don't want to let him down."

"Let who down?" I ask softly, smiling at him encouragingly and letting a bit more of my power seep from me.

"Wrath," Simon lets out. "He's my oldest friend and I— I just don't want to ever let him down. He's been through so much, ya know?"

"I don't know," I say, stepping into his space more. Stars, this is so unethical. But if I can pull this off, I'll be free. "Simon, would you do me the biggest of favors?" Sugar coats my voice so thickly I almost laugh. I don't sound like myself at all.

"Anything, Bliss." His eyes are on my lips.

I'm a horrible fae.

"Would you introduce me to him?" I tug on my bottom lip with my upper teeth and let it go. My eyes wander between his eyes and his lips.

"Yes, absolutely," Simon agrees. He leans in. "He'd be so lucky to meet you." Simon is so close to kissing me and I'm about to let him because my powers are now almost completely zapped.

But before we can, Simon is thrown through the air, hitting the wall and crumpling to a heap. I scream, looking around for his attacker, and my eyes land on Jordan.

Out of the corner of my eye, I see Simon not moving.

Oh stars, oh stars.

Is he dead?

Reese and Amelia go straight to him, and when I look back at Jordan, Taser, Tubbs, and Blake are in between me and him.

They don't even have to do anything, though. The music stops completely. The lights all come on at once. "What the fuck is going on?" Pinkie yells, standing up on the DJ's booth.

I push my way in between Taser and Blake. Taser puts his arm out in front of me to stop me from going any further. "Don't even think about it," he tells me, a little snarl lacing his words. "He's not getting close to you."

Grim makes his way over to Jordan, arms crossed. "Dead Hearts, get the fuck out."

I hear Jinx whine like a little bitch at that.

But they're outmatched. So they go, but not without Jordan leering at me. "Can't fuck your little human if he's dead," Jordan says with a smirk.

"We need to report him," Taser says.

Grim nods. "We'll take care of it, don't worry."

Jordan and his band leave. I turn and run to Simon.

"Is he?" I pause, looking at Amelia, because I'm too scared to look at Simon's crumpled form. I can't bring myself to say dead.

"He's alive," Amelia says, just as Simon's head snaps back up and he opens his eyes.

He looks around at everyone and locks eyes with Benny, who crouches down. "Mate? You okay? What hurts?"

"I'm fine." Simon shifts so he can sit upright. A few seconds later he stands up and rolls his shoulders. "I think I just got the wind knocked out of me."

There's a dent in the wall behind him.

"Are you sure?" Benny asks, noticing the wall as well. "You hit hard."

My eyes go to Simon's lips as his grin widens. The ones I almost kissed.

This is all my fault.

"Fuck." Simon looks at the wall. "Shitty craftsmanship?" he jokes, but when he looks at me I can tell he's a bit terrified.

Of what I got him involved in.

"I'm so sorry, Simon," I say, taking a step back from him. I need to stay far, far away from him.

"Why?" Simon follows me, reaching out to take my hand.

"That was my ex. He only did that because of me."

Grim shakes his head. "I don't think it was just you, Bliss. Dead Hearts and Voracious Maw do not get along."

Simon nods.

"It's true," Benny affirms. "They have big beef with Wrath. There's some bad blood from a festival a couple years ago."

"Oh," I say, my shoulders sagging with a bit of relief.

"I should get him home, though," Benny says, taking Simon by the shoulders. "See you all later."

"Bye, Bliss," Simon calls over his shoulder as Benny leads him outside. "See you tomorrow!"

I can feel Grim coming to stand behind me. "He sure seems smitten with you."

I don't say anything because even though Simon's okay now, that could have gone so horribly wrong. I could have gotten him killed.

"Bliss?" Grim asks, trailing a finger up my arm. "Any reason you're trying to seduce the human when I'm here and more than willing?"

I shudder but not from revulsion. My inner succubus slut is

stirring and wants to be unleashed. Goose bumps flair up along my skin and Grim takes notice.

"Want to get out of here?" he asks, his breath tickling at my ear.

I whip around and put some distance between us. "Sorry," I say, forcing a smile. "I— I just can't right now."

Grim swallows and looks at the wall and then back to me. "Of course. No worries."

I leave him standing there with no other explanation. Amelia and Reese have found themselves back on the dance floor, the center of attention, of course. Males of all types are gathered around them. Amelia raises her solo cup in the air. As she brings it down to take a sip, I grab it and down the whole thing in one go.

"Fuck, Bliss," Amelia says, but I don't listen to her. I grab Reese's cup and drink that too. Then I dance with them. At some point some male comes up behind me to dance and I let him, the feeling of his hands on my hips stirring my inner fae, but even as drunk as I am, I don't let her out to play.

The party passes in a whirl of dancing and drinking and then at some point I'm in my bed and Amelia and Reese are each tugging off one of my boots, laughing their asses off.

I giggle along with them, but only for a moment before the drunken stupor whisks me off to sleep.

CHAPTER TWENTY-SIX

PISCES

"You're late," the song wraith tells me as I come to a stop in an alleyway behind a coffee shop and some trendy restaurant.

I put a sleeve-covered hand over my mouth to try to quell the smell coming off the dumpsters nearby. "You're surprised I didn't rush to meet with you in a trash-filled back alley?"

The song wraith looks around, unamused. "I forgot you fae sometimes have overactive senses."

"Can you not smell it?" I ask, genuinely curious. I don't know much about wraiths and don't have access to the kind of books that would educate me on them. And it's not like I can ask my friends more. They might not think it's odd for me to learn about the being that turned me, but I'm not a great liar. Shaun would know something's up. It's like he can smell a lie as easily as I can smell the rotten fruit discarded to my left.

"These upcoming shows are very important." The wraith ignores my question. "You need to make sure to feed beforehand. And you should use your lure."

"Lure?" I ask, even though I know what he means. Sirens can lure prey out to them. I've never done it before because I've never needed to. But apparently I can lure an unsuspecting fae out and feed off them. It honestly sounds a bit unethical.

There's another reason I haven't done it before.

"I don't know how."

The song wraith glares at me. "Figure it out."

He takes a menacing step forward. But I'm past being scared of him. He can't do much worse than he already has.

"Pisces, in order for our deal to work, I need you at your strongest. The lure will increase your ability to connect to your fans tenfold."

"I get it, but I've never figured out *how* to. I'm not saying I won't. I'm saying I can't."

The wraith shakes his head at me, annoyance flickering across his face. "It's instinct. You don't need to know—" he taps his head, "—you need to feel." He taps his heart. Or where his heart would be. I'm not sure if wraiths have hearts. "You've done it before, you just don't realize what you did."

I'm about to ask what he means, but the wraith dissolves into nothingness. Fucking prick.

I've been sitting at the edge of an artfully human-made pond, trying to figure out how to use my lure. All that I've managed so far is luring a duck over to me, but I'm pretty sure that's just because it thought I had bread. It left as soon as it realized I had nothing to offer.

I ponder what the wraith meant when he said I've done it before.

In all my time being a siren, I've never consciously used my lure. I've talked at length to my friends about it, but seeing as I'm quite possibly the only siren in existence, they had no idea how it worked. Evan and Shaun went to the fae council, searching in its vast libraries for any information on sirens, but since sirens are so closely tied with wraiths, a lot of the information was restricted. And what they were able to find, well, we questioned the validity of it. All of the books they could find had been written by Born fae, and not the open-minded kind.

When had I done something to get someone to appear—

The wraith. I'd lured the wraith, hadn't I?

When I went out and sang the song he used to turn me.

I focused on him and he appeared.

Meaning my lure could not only bring me a fae, but one that I focused on.

Did it work on humans? Could it work on the dead?

Leighton's face jumps into my mind, and I don't stop to think if it would be a good idea or not. I start singing, letting all of my anguish into my song, letting my heart ache for what I used to have. Except that the ache is noticeably weaker. My mind wanders to a unique set of eyes that I can't seem to erase from my mind. The blue-green eyes that caught my breath when I first saw them. Wondering what happened that changed them.

I finish my song, pondering if it worked.

Minutes tick by and nothing. No one shows up.

The grassy area by the pond is as quiet as a gravesite.

It didn't work.

I get up, throwing a stone into the pond at an angle, watching as it skips across the surface. If the wraith needs me stronger, then he's going to have to fucking help me. So whatever, I give up.

I head back to the house, my thoughts running rampant. What type of realm is Leighton stuck in? If time moves differently there, is she even herself anymore? Will she remember her time there when the wraith brings her back?

Will she still hate me?

I still hate her. The pain she inflicted on me was almost worse than I could inflict on myself. But it's my fault she's gone. I have to atone for that.

And a sick part of me wants her back in a romantic sense. The part of me that would rather leave this world than have to keep walking around in it alone.

But I'm not alone, I remind myself. The faces of my friends filter in and out of my mind's eye. A shuddering sob escapes me quickly as gratitude for my friends hits me in waves. I'm not alone.

I turn down the street the row of townhomes is on, stopping short when I see a small figure walking slowly towards me.

It's Bliss.

And she's wearing a thin set of silky pajamas, her legs and arms bare in the tank top and shorts.

"Bliss?" I call. She doesn't answer me, but she does come to a stop right in front of me.

Something is wrong. Her usually bright and gorgeous eyes are almost glazed over. She looks at me like she's looking through me. Her teeth chatter and she's shaking from the cold, her nipples pebbling beneath her top.

Fuck.

My lure did work. I was just too far away and she was asleep.

Fuck, fuck, fuck.

What the hell do I do now?

"Bliss, can you hear me?" I take off my hoodie, but it's not a zipper one, so I try getting it over her head. She pushes me off.

"Bliss, it's freezing. Wake up." I give up on trying to get it over her head and instead wrap the arms around her shoulders and tie them together at the front. "I'm so sorry."

She doesn't respond, just sort of tilts her head to the side and lets out a yawn.

"Where the fuck are you even staying?" Think, Pisces. Where is Goddess' Trance's lodging?

I don't know. I haven't interacted with any of them during this festival. I haven't really been interacting with anyone, too consumed with my plan to get the wraith enough power so he can get Leighton back.

I scan the townhomes, as if one might have a blaring neon sign with her band's name on it.

And now Bliss, who yeah, isn't really my favorite person, is gonna freeze to death.

I don't like her. She's rude and conceited. And self-centered.

But even with them glazed over I can't stop myself from staring at her perfectly imperfect eyes.

So I take her hand and lead her back to my townhouse. At least she'll be warm, and maybe Simon has her sister's number or something.

It turns out I don't even need to hold her hand. She seems to just want to stay by my side. I lead her to the couch and wrap a blanket around her while I search for Simon, but after not finding anyone in the kitchen, I turn and almost run into her. Bliss reaches out sleepily and takes my shirt in her hands. My hoodie has fallen off on the couch and she's shivering again.

"Bliss, sit on the couch, okay? I'll be right back."

Nothing. She just steps closer to me, wrapping her arms around me and snuggling her face into my chest.

My heart leaps at the contact. I run my hands along her bare arms, trying to create enough friction to warm her.

"Well, this is new," Evan says from the staircase. Shaun and Benny are behind him. They finish descending and gather around Bliss and I in the living room. I meet their gazes over her head.

"She's sleepwalking," I explain. They just respond with quizzical expressions, so I continue. "I used my lure, I think."

"You think?" Shaun eyes the two of us with disappointment.

"I didn't mean to," I half lie. I didn't mean to ensnare Bliss, that's for sure. "Where's Simon? I was gonna see if he could contact her sister."

"Simon's sleeping off all the alcohol."

Right, the party. "Too much fun?"

Benny points at Bliss. "Her crazy ex-boyfriend launched Simon into the wall. I swear I thought he was dead at first."

I jolt, almost knocking Bliss over. I try to go to the stairs to go find Simon, but she's still clutching onto me. "Is he alright?" I settle for just asking, instead of checking on him myself. "Is he injured?"

"He's completely fine besides having a wicked hangover tomorrow probably," Benny explains. "Not sure how, but not even a bruise."

My relief surges through me, and I find myself wrapping my arms around Bliss again, the contact bringing me even more relief. "What happened to her ex?"

Evan lets out a low growl. "Nothing yet."

"Grim and Pinkie kicked his whole band out," Shaun explains.

I look to Evan. "They need to know not to keep messing with us."

"Agreed."

Benny shakes his head. "Nothing good will come of that."

"We have other problems right now," Shaun agrees, pointing to Bliss. "You need to feed off her to break the lure."

I shake my head. "No, I don't think I need to. My siren teeth, they're not bursting to come out."

"I read that the lure has to be completed with feeding," Shaun reiterates.

But something inside me knows I'm right. I slide my hands over her arms again, feeling the smooth skin. I let my power reach for her, gently prodding. The wraith was right. It's all instinct. I somehow connect to a wave of hopelessness, of desperation that almost knocks me over, but I can *feel* it colliding with my power, growing, surging. The lights flicker as I feed, one lightbulb in a nearby lamp fizzling out altogether.

"Fuck," Shaun whispers. "I've never seen anything like that."

I grab onto her desperation and suck it dry, then I take a step back from her. She lets go of me and slumps forward, since the lure is no longer holding her in a trance. I'm able to catch her before she falls to the floor.

I hoist her up into my arms and head for the stairs. "I'm gonna put her in bed, but we should figure out where Goddess' Trance is staying."

Someone murmurs their agreement, and so I take each step carefully up the stairs so I don't drop her. I lay her in my bed and tuck her in. She curls onto her side, exhausted, but seemingly peaceful. There's a contentment on her face that eases my worry that I took too much of something.

"Bliss?" I don't know why I call her name. I guess to make sure she's asleep. She just burrows more into the bed, letting out a soft sigh that parts her lips.

CHAPTER TWENTY-SEVEN

BLISS

I WAKE UP IN A BED THAT SMELLS BOTH FAMILIAR AND FOREIGN.

But then I realize the walls of this room are a mellow olive green, and not the dusty pink that I've grown accustomed to in the past two nights.

I jolt awake, sitting upright in a bed that is not my own.

I immediately check myself, thinking the worst, but my pajamas are still on and don't seem to be mussed more so than what would happen with a fitful night of sleep. I feel between my legs, noting the dryness and no odd sensation. I pick a fluffy blanket off the bed and wrap it around my shoulders, freezing when I notice someone is sitting in a chair in the corner of the room.

Not someone.

Pisces.

The hood of a plain black zippered hoodie is pulled up around his face, and besides that only his fingers are visible. His lips are closed, but just barely, almost as if he's on the verge of saying something.

No, not saying something.

He's asleep.

Before I can think better of it, I whip a pillow at his stupid face.

The pillow hits him square in the jaw. He startles out of the chair with a grunt, clutching the pillow to his chest like it'll protect him from an onslaught of more plush projectiles.

"What the fuck, dude?" I yell at him. "Did you fucking kidnap me?"

He cocks his head to the side and shakes it fervently, pushing his hood off. "Bliss," he starts to say, but I'm not listening.

I scramble across the bed, almost knocking over a guitar propped up on the wall next to the door as I wrench it open. Pisces doesn't move, just watches me. I look down at my not super modest pajamas and stop myself from fleeing down the stairs.

He may or may not have kidnapped me, but something stops me from running. Is Wrath staying here as well? This could be the closest I've gotten to him since the garden. And there are only two days left until the festival ends.

Two days to get close to him.

I reach for my power, only to find it completely gone. Fuck. Did I totally use it up trying to flirt with Simon?

I turn back to Pisces, placing my hand on my hip. "How did I get here?"

His lips purse as he seems to search for what to say. "You were sleepwalking."

"I don't sleepwalk. I have never sleepwalked."

He shrugs.

"When a woman wakes up in a stranger's bed, the least he can do is explain why!" I yell at him. I pick up the other pillow on the bed and sling it at his face.

I'm out the door before I can see if it hit him, but another grunt confirms my aim.

I march down the stairs into the foyer and open living space, realizing again that I'm in my pajamas still. Five heads turn to look at me, a very hungover Simon being one of them.

"Bliss?" he asks in a confused groan. He jumps up, startled. "Did you?" His eyes go to Pisces, who's come down the stairs behind me. "Did you and Pisces...?" He doesn't finish his sentence, just looks between the two of us in a confused way but—is that hope on his face?

"We better have fucking not," I snap, throwing an icy look over my shoulder at Pisces. I cross my arms to ward off the chill of the AC in the room. "Can someone get me something to put on over this, please?" I add.

A light-skinned, redheaded human woman dressed in tight jeans and a black crop top comes in from the kitchen. "What the fuck is going on?" Her accent is British but a bit different than the others. Essex, I think they call it.

I point at Pisces. "He kidnapped me somehow last night and I would just like some clothes so I can get the fuck out of here."

Once I get my power back I am going to… Well, I don't know. But I'll do something, like seduce Pisces until I have him wrapped around my finger. Then I'll encourage him to do something super embarrassing.

I let out an enraged huff.

The redhead's eyes widen and she shoots Pisces a withering look. "Kidnapping?"

Pisces shakes his head. "I did not kidnap her. I found her sleep-walking outside and brought her here."

She looks between me and him, her gaze softening as she takes me in.

"I've never sleepwalked in my entire life," I tell her. "I went to sleep in my own bed and woke up in his." I throw daggers at Pisces as he shakes his head, but the glare that the redhead turns on him makes mine pale in comparison.

"What did you do?" she accuses, starting to pummel her fists into his chest. He doesn't try to stop her or ward off her attacks. But Shaun and Evan have appeared at her sides, each taking an arm and carrying her away from Pisces, who just looks exhausted. He slumps into the wall, letting it hold his weight.

"Lily!" she yells. Two other women—fae by their scents—have already poked their heads into the living room to see what the commotion is. Their amused expressions are quickly schooled into seriousness at the redhead's tone. "Get her a change of clothes." The redhead points her chin at me, since Shaun and Evan are still holding her back.

Lily, a lithe tall blonde, rushes up the stairs. The other fae glares at the men in the room. "Get your hands off Gwen, or I will bite your dicks off," she informs them in a soft but lethal voice. Her canines are sharper than most fae's, but not as sharp as a vampire's. Probably a wolf shifter. She's not much taller than me, wearing black leather pants, black boots, and a gold sparkly top that brings out the warmth of her brown skin. Her hazel eyes fix a withering look on Shaun, who seems to be unsure of whether to release Gwen.

The shifter growls. "Go easy on them, Niamh," Gwen says. Niamh's pupils contract a bit. She turns and heads back into the other room.

Shaun releases Gwen, who smacks him in the face. "Touch me again without permission and we're going to have a problem."

"Didn't you just say to take it easy on us?" Shaun mutters with a hand pressed to his face. "Fuck, that hurt."

"Sorry. Should I have used a rolled up newspaper instead?" Gwen smirks. He glowers at her and goes and takes a seat at the table. Her comment helps me place his species as well. Another wolf shifter.

I meet Simon's gaze as he takes in everything that's happening.

Lily comes racing back down the stairs with some clothes, which I hurriedly put on over my own.

I make sure to thank her and turn to thank Gwen, but she's busy staring angrily at Pisces.

His head turns my way and he frowns, his bottom lip curling inwards as if he's biting back his words. Something about the expression is familiar, but I can't put my finger on why.

I take one last look at Simon, remembering what Jordan did to him yesterday and how close it seemed he came to death. "I'm glad you're okay."

I leave, running down a few houses to the one I'm staying in.

I burst open through the front door and fold over, panting. Stars, I'm so fucking out of shape.

Amelia runs down the stairs, having heard the front door open. "BLISS, WHAT THE FUCK? Where have you been?!"

The rest of the morning passes in a flurry of nerves and excitement as we all prepare for Goddess' Trance's first set of the festival. As I stare out onto the stage where everything from the drums to the lighting has been set up, I smile to myself. Not only is this a huge day for my sister and the rest of the band, but for me. I wasn't quite sure I'd be up to snuff to carry out such a large show—the biggest in Goddess' Trance history, but I was.

"You're killing it," Simon says at my right, coming to stand and admire the stage with me.

"Let's wait to see how the show goes before we celebrate," I respond, a smile coming to my lips easily. Despite my very odd and awkward night and morning, I feel surprisingly full of joy today. I actually feel like I'm on top of the world and nothing—not even a kidnapping—can bring me down.

"Nah, I'm taking notes, seriously," Simon says warmly. "It looks like I'll be band managing a little bit longer. It's not really what I'm best at, but you seem almost at peace in your role."

He's not wrong. I do feel peace.

I love doing this job. I've missed it.

"About last night," Simon starts but falls short.

I stay silent, prodding him to continue.

"Pisces didn't kidnap you," he says. "He swears he found you sleepwalking out on the street."

I'm about to repeat that I've never been a sleepwalker, but I just sigh instead. "You believe him?"

"I do." Simon gives me a soft smile. "All I know is what he told me, but I know him, Bliss. He would never hurt anyone if he could help it. Please believe me. He says you were cold and shivering and he obviously wanted to get you back to your sister, but he didn't know where you guys were staying. So he brought you back to his bed to sleep and get warm."

"Why did I wake up with him in the room just sitting there like a creep?"

Simon lets out an awkward laugh. "He couldn't wake you up and was worried so he stayed up all night watching over you. He must have fallen asleep."

I nod, but I still don't understand how I was sleepwalking. "Did he have anything to do with me sleepwalking?" Or is this somehow the wraith's doing?

"How could he have? Is that something fae can do?" Simon asks, seemingly a little frightened at the thought.

"I have no idea. It's impossible for all fae powers to be catalogued due to how differently they can manifest in each individual." I know because I checked when I was twenty. I was hoping there was some secret succubus power that would allow me to feed differently.

"Pisces is a really good guy. I think you'd actually really like him if you got to know him. Oh, also, Wrath wants to meet you." Simon's smile grows wider, almost mischievously.

He does?

Yes.

Yes.

Yes!

When?

I hide my excitement. "Really? Why?" I try to put some doubt into my voice, like I don't believe him.

Simon nods enthusiastically. "We told him about last night, and I think he wants to help Pisces smooth things over."

"I do owe him his hoodie back," I say slowly, as if I'm coming around to the idea of meeting him. I scrunch my face in thought for a couple seconds and nod. "Yeah, okay."

"Great, you'll really like him. He's one of my best friends." It almost sounds like Simon wants me to date the guy. Wrath should thank him for trying to be a good wingman.

But I doubt he and I would have a future together. There's no way he's my mate. He saw my eyes that one night, even though I couldn't see his. He would have said something. Not even a guy who barely talks would stay silent if he met his mate.

Simon and I continue chatting until it's time for Goddess' Trance to go out on stage. I give each of the band members a huge hug, gripping Taser even more tightly than the rest. "Give 'em hell, Tay," I say. He kisses me on the cheek quickly and heads out with guitar in hand to a pretty enthusiastic welcome, which is very, very exciting. Most of the crowd here probably aren't familiar with us, since we're a late addition to the line-up, but I see enough people wearing some of our merch that I know there'll be a good amount of people singing along with Amelia.

As Amelia opens up with a few notes of "Venomous," I smile wide.

This—this is what I love.

I think back to Liz and I sitting on the steps of the fae council building.

You don't wait around, Bliss. You live. You follow your joy.

Was this what she was talking about?

CHAPTER TWENTY-EIGHT

BLISS

Goddess' Trance finishes up their set and I'm bouncing back and forth on my heels as Amelia walks off the stage to huge cheering from the crowd. I'm beaming at her as we collide in a tightly squeezing hug. "You killed it, Amelia! I'm so fucking proud of you."

"Thanks, Bliss," my sister says, tears welling up in her eyes. "This was fucking incredible."

"You were amazing," Simon says from behind me. We spent the show listening together, often looking over and grinning at each other over how well the crowd received Amelia and the others. My sister shines her winning smile on Simon and he grins at both of us.

"Well, I need to chug down some tea and water," Amelia says, giving me a knowing look and leaving me to talk more with Simon. Already the band techs working this stage are breaking down Goddess' Trance's set and bringing in Voracious Maw's instruments and switching out the backdrop.

Simon's phone rings and he gives me a sheepish smile. "I gotta take this. It's the label."

He takes a few steps away from where a group is loading up Tubbs' drum set. Simon's dark hair hangs into his eyes a bit and he gives his head a little shake to get the hair out of his line of sight. His eyes drift over to mine and we smile at each other. I can hear him excitedly talking to the person on the other end and he's nodding enthusiastically, even though that person can't see him.

Eventually the conversation wraps up and he races over to me, a huge grin on his face. "We've just secured our largest tour in the states," he tells me.

"Seriously?" I grasp his forearms and give him a little shake. "That's amazing! When does it start and when will you be in Seattle? Because I'm planning to be right at the barricade for that show."

Simon throws an arm around me. "It starts in the fall. I don't have the exact dates yet, but I'll do you one better than the barricade. The label was asking about an opener to tour with us. Guess who's name I threw in?"

"Who?" I ask, my breathing becoming quicker. Is he about to say Goddess' Trance?

His eyes twinkle a bit mischievously. "Goddess' Trance."

I give him a light push on the shoulder. "You did not," I breathe out, stopping myself from hopping up and down.

"I did." His grin doubles in size, if that's even possible. "The label seemed super into it. Thought it was a great idea."

I squeal like a little girl and throw my arms around him, giving him a quick kiss on the cheek. "You are the best, Simon. Seriously. Amelia and the band are going to flip."

He gives me a tight squeeze and we make promises to chat later about the details once the label officially signs off on it. I don't foresee Amelia or anyone else having an issue with it. A legit tour is exactly what Goddess' Trance needs to keep growing. This could be life changing for us. Simon has some work to do before Voracious Maw goes on in a half-hour, so we say our goodbyes. I turn around to look for Amelia but I think she's already headed back to a little trailer set up by the stage to shower and change. I stick around, figuring the rest of the band will come back to watch Voracious Maw play. I've been waiting to see them live again for forever.

I actually kind of forgot about the fact that I'd be getting to see them perform after all the drama this morning, and everything that's happened already this week.

And then I almost slap my hand against my forehead. I should have brought his sweatshirt. I didn't even think about it, even though I saw it lying on a chair in my room when I got back home. He's gonna think I'm never going to give it back.

But I guess I can give it back to him when we officially meet like Simon promised.

I turn this way and that, trying to see any of the band members, but they haven't appeared yet. With nothing much else to do, I double check with the venue staff that all our gear has been loaded up and sent back to our trailer. Everything is looking good and Simon's crew is now doing mic checks. I look out in the crowd and already see a huge amount of people. Some have been camped out in front of this stage since the first band went on before Goddess' Trance, but the amount of people has almost doubled now.

I hear a bit of a commotion and turn around. The four band members in their costumes are headed my way, surrounded by some people from venue staff to keep excited fans back a little ways. The guys head up the steps to the platform the stage is on. Simon greets them and gives Wrath a hug, which I find incredibly endearing. They chat a bit. Simon motions towards me. I blush as Wrath's masked face turns in my direction.

He inclines his head towards me and I nod back at him. Simon is going to get me my in with Wrath. And then I'll make good on my bargain with the wraith.

I take in Wrath's mask and outfit. I've seen it before, but he's still a work of art. I peruse the patches of dark blue and black iridescent scales that start at his collarbone and run the length of his exposed torso. Through the lacy robe he wears, I can see they've even glued some to his back as well.

Seeing him up close in his full costume takes the breath of out me. He looks ethereal but also frightening.

But also super hot.

He says something to Simon that I can't make out. The other

band members have moved closer to the stage to peer out at the crowd, which brings them closer to me. Eerie has his usual rainbow scrunchie around his wrist, but aside from that he's dressed similarly to Poison and Mist, all in black. They banter between themselves as Wrath and Simon make their way over towards us.

Wrath looks my way as he passes, and I smile nervously. When is Simon going to introduce us? Hopefully after the show?

The other band members ask him yes or no questions only, so he can just shake or nod his head. I wish desperately someone would ask him something he actually has to respond to, so I can hear his beautiful voice. I know what it sounds like when he's singing, but to hear him converse normally—it would just be so cool.

Amelia calls out my name. I turn and see her watching from the platform a little way back, angled so you can see the stage from the front, but still restricted to backstage people only. I say bye to Simon and head over to my friends. I don't say anything yet about the tour. I want to double check with Simon again before I do, because Wrath also has to sign off on it, doesn't he?

What if he says no because he thinks I'm a hoodie thief and will steal all his hoodies on the tour? Or what if he thinks I'm insane for assuming his guitar tech kidnapped me? Although to be fair, I went to sleep in my own bed and then woke up in Pisces'. He'd have thought he'd been kidnapped too if the roles were reversed.

Once Simon introduces us, I'll just have to use my succubus charm to smooth things over.

Though I'll really need to feed if I'm going to pull that off. Not to mention committing my little theft.

I settle myself in beside Amelia on some bleachers and we all hang out there as we wait for the show to start. Taser seems to be in a much better mood. I lean back against Dericia's knees as she braids my hair to pass the time. She does two French braids that stop at the nape of my neck and ties ribbons around them. I usually bring extras with me. I never know when some jerk will pull one off.

Eventually the entire crowd quiets down as a soft atmospheric melody begins to play. The sun has already set and the stage is still dark, but I can see Wrath's figure walk slowly out on to the stage towards the microphone stand. Just before he begins to sing, the lights flare on brightly, pointed on him, and the entire crowd cheers. But the cheers from the women in the crowd are for a whole different reason.

He's wearing the pants. The ones Amelia teased me about. They're loose-fitting pants that cling to him in a way that makes something very apparent.

And the way the lights hit him seems intentional.

Reese draws in a breath. "The lights and those pants are really doing the stars' work," she says with a laugh. "Damn."

"Damn is right," Amelia agrees.

"Weird," Taser says. "I thought I was straight, but…" He trails off and we all laugh, but quiet down quickly as Wrath begins singing a song that I've had on repeat for quite some time.

Amelia and I are moving side to side and screaming out like teenage fan girls as Eerie, the bassist, turns his back to the crowd, falling slowly to his knees in front of Wrath. Eerie slides down to the ground, until his legs are spread straight out in front of him, and his head falls back over the edge of the stage. We aren't the only women screaming. Wrath, continuing to sing the chorus, straddles Eerie, resting one of his hands around Eerie's neck, and slowly drags his hand down Eerie's torso, interrupted by the bass that Eerie is somehow continuing to play.

During a break in the lyrics, Wrath bends down and slowly shifts Eerie's mask up so that just his lips are uncovered and leans in, giving him a full long kiss before he jumps up off his bandmate and goes right into the next verse. Eerie slowly gets back up, using one hand to pull his mask back down, the other reaching out to Wrath as if he's lusting after him still.

The crowd is a puddle of screaming women and men. Taser and Tubbs exchange glances. Tubbs give a slight cough and they break eye contact. Amelia and I chuckle. We can pick up on everyone's arousal pretty easily.

After Voracious Maw's fairly explicit performance, I'm practically buzzing out of my skin. I haven't fully fed in so fucking long and my powers are completely gone. Amelia keeps looking at me.

"There are about forty-five minutes before the Phantoms go on. Go find Grim and feed yourself, please." She gives me a meaningful look. "I can practically feel your lust coming off you in waves."

I shake my head, but I don't respond. She's right. I need to power myself up and Grim is obviously extremely willing. He'll probably be pretty comfortable to be with. He makes me laugh.

But he's not my bond.

But what if I never find my bond?

What if despite everyone's reassurances, my bond doesn't actually exist?

What if I can't complete the deal with the wraith?

I think about staying here with my friends, but then I remember that Simon is going to introduce me to Wrath and I don't know when. I might only get the one chance to befriend him and I might need my powers to convince him that Simon's idea to bring us on as openers for them is a good idea, especially after I get his tears.

So I say bye to my friends and make my way backstage, hoping to catch a glimpse of Grim. To my disappointment I don't see him yet. The band is probably still somewhere getting into their costumes. None of the Voracious Maw guys are around except for Simon, who's in the middle of a phone call and looks like he's simultaneously directing where the roadies should move their gear.

A little ways off I see a familiar face that sends my stomach twisting. Jinx, Jordan's best friend and bandmate, is standing a bit behind Simon and he's spotted me, a smirk already fixed on his face. He's walking my way, so I turn and quickly move the other direction, weaving through several venue staffers, hoping Jinx will lose me in the crowd.

I decide to go behind the stage in an area that's off limits to anyone without backstage passes, but it also seems to be an area that no one is using. I cut through to the other side and end up close to the grassy picnic area with the maze from the scavenger hunt on the other side.

I spare one second to glance behind me.

Jinx is standing still, looking around. I see it when he spots me. A slow grin spreads over his face, and he starts moving, heading right towards me.

I try to blend in with the crowd that's milling about waiting for whatever show they're going to next. The maze is roped off currently, but I figure if I can slip in there, I still have the map, so I could pop out on the other side and circle back around to make my way back to Amelia, to safety.

What is Jinx playing at?

I duck under the tape that's closing up the entrance to the maze and make the first few turns from memory, taking out my map from yesterday. As I'm trying to orient myself I walk past a section I know is a dead end.

A hand snakes around my waist and pulls me back into a muscular, too hard chest. "Hey there, Bliss," Jordan all but hisses in my ear, his breath hot and sticky on my neck. I wrench out of his grip and he puts on a confused look. "What's wrong, beautiful?"

"Don't touch me."

What the fuck is he doing here?

My eyes grow wide as I realize it. He used Jinx to herd me into the maze.

He laughs. "Why not? You're all turned on. I don't even have to be able to smell you to know that you are. I know what a slut you are for that stupid band."

He tilts his head to the side. "Is that what I need to do? Put on a mask? Is that what finally gets you hot?"

I want to gag at his words. They're disgusting. He's disgusting.

But he's not at all wrong about how I reacted to Voracious Maw's show.

"Come on, Bliss," he says, stepping closer. "You know you want it."

Before I can say anything to that he lunges forward, grabbing the back of my neck. His teeth rip into me, tearing my throat apart. He's more savage about it than he's ever been before. He rears his head back like a rabid animal and pulls my wrist up to his hand, biting into it hard, slurping at my blood and taking way too much.

He pushes me into the wall of hay and grinds into me. I scream out as much as I can, but his bite has gone too deep. My scream barely makes any noise.

Jordan smiles down at me, my blood dripping from his lips as he pushes me down forcefully onto the dirty straw-strewn ground. My head bangs against asphalt, my vision beginning to darken as Jordan squats down so his face is in mine.

"You're so fucking sexy when your blood is all over the place like that," he says, smiling at me, a crazed look in his eyes. "Soon you'll be begging me to take this sweet cunt and when you do, I'll be littering your skin with bites."

He saunters off, wiping my blood off with his sleeve. I feel my body starting to shut down.

I try to call out after him, for what I'm not sure. But I don't think he realizes how low I am. A tear slides down my nose as my head falls to the side, and just as I close my eyes, I see two pairs of feet stop just short of me. One set is wearing black platform shoes, the other black combat boots. For some reason that makes me smile as I give in to my body's decline.

CHAPTER TWENTY-NINE

PISCES

"Do something," I say to Evan as we look down at Bliss sprawled out on my bed. She's bloodied and unconscious, her hair splayed about her, tangled and mussed. I clutch the white ribbons that tied her braids. I found them on the ground next to her, stained, ruined.

Evan healed her wounds when we found her, but she didn't wake up. Her heart beat continues to grow faint, stuttering. She's too low on her powers. She's dying.

We rushed her here, Benny using his vampire speed and Evan and I running after her. I've never run faster in my life.

Benny had already left, going in search of any of the Goddess' Trance members. Or even Simon, who was nowhere to be found after the show.

"I've done all I can. She needs to recharge her powers." Evan is pissed. I can tell. It's wafting off him and is fueling my anger even more. I'm gripping onto the door frame so hard my fingers are turning white. Evan and Jordan have history. Bad history. Evan is convinced he's Bliss' attacker. I'm inclined to agree.

"How does she charge them?"

"She's a succubus, mate," Evan says, turning to me, and with a sigh he puts a hand on my shoulder. "She's needs to... you know..."

She needs an orgasm. "Okay, so, how do we help her do that?"

Evan lifts a brow. "Do I need to have the birds and the bees talk with you?"

"That's not what I meant. She's unconscious, so you can't just, you know..." I trail off, but Evan understands what I'm saying.

"Try to wake her up," he says, his hand still on my shoulder. "You'll need to take care of this. I can't do it."

"Why not? Are you okay? Are you low on power too?"

He looks over at her sleeping form. "Her wounds were deeper than they looked. I'm spent." He looks me directly in the eye. "Take care of her, Sces, and whatever you do, do *not* feed on her, not in this state."

Right.

No pressure.

I fed earlier on Benny, I remind myself.

"Okay, so you reckon I should start with cuddling or something?"

Evan shakes his head at me, a bemused half-grin sketching across his face, but it's gone in an instant. "I'm not sure that's going to be enough."

With that, he slides the door closed behind him and I sigh. I'm still in costume so I make sure not to trip on my shroud as I lower myself onto the bed beside her, freezing as I sit there. I can't just start. She's unconscious. But she's also dying right before me. I can feel it, a small thread of pulsing power, growing fainter with each passing second. I lower my head towards her. "Please wake up," I murmur. My gaze travels to her mouth. Her lips are lightly parted, her breathing shallow. It feels too intimate to kiss her there so I lower my mouth to her neck, feeling the urge of my siren teeth wanting to slide out.

I rein in that impulse, pressing a faint kiss to her throat, on the side where she's not been bitten. The other side almost looked like what I do to Benny when I feed on him, but even though it's healed now, I want to avoid it in case she still aches there. I remind myself that Jordan isn't as big of a threat as I am, so I need to be careful. I nuzzle her a little bit. "Please wake up," I say again, my voice pleading.

What will she think if she wakes up? That I kidnapped her again? The image of her throwing those pillows so forcefully at me brings a fresh wave of anger. But not at her. I still think she's a bit stuck up, but she's got a fire that I wish I had. And her prick of an ex tried to take that away from her.

I trail kisses up her throat and plant one on her jaw. It's not working. She's still fading.

I place my hand on the curve of her waist, running my hand up and down slowly, as I try to think of what to do next. My hand follows the curve as it swings outward towards her hips. I trail my hand across her stomach, my fingers lightly catching on the waistband of her jeans. She lets out a low murmur and I flick my gaze to her eyes, still closed. I go back to kiss her neck and slide my hand towards her chest, my hand going up under her shirt. I realize too late that I'm leaving black paint streaks across her skin and clothes. "Bliss," I whisper, remembering how she played with the frayed edges of my hoodie. "Bliss, please wake up."

She lets out a soft moan as my hand trails underneath her bra just lightly. I kiss her neck again. "Wake up so I can heal you properly," I whisper. I haven't done anything with a woman since that night at the club so many years ago. I've kissed Evan, Shaun, and Benny. But it's not the same, because it's usually just for a performance. I run my hand down towards the top of her jeans. "I'll do whatever you need me to, just please wake up."

She's not waking up.

I can't wait any longer or else I risk her dying. I slowly unbutton her jeans and move my hand inside, dragging my fingers against her lacy panties as I stroke her slowly across her center. She lets out a gasp. I look back up at her and see her eyes opened in shock. She watches me, startled.

Her lips part like she's going to say something, but she can't seem to get the words out.

I also open my mouth to speak but freeze. I'm still in Wrath's costume. If I talk to her, she'll know I'm that asshole from before who was rude to her. Then she might refuse to let me help her. I don't want to risk it, so I cock my head to the side, waiting for her to say something, to put together what's happening.

She slowly nods as if it's painful for her. "Please," she finally gets out. And with that, I return to stroking her. I feel her body respond, wetness beginning to pool and coating my fingers even through the thin fabric of her underwear. I get up from the bed and slowly peel her jeans off, exposing her pale smooth thighs first, then the rest of her legs. Bliss lets out an impatient moan, more alert, so I don't hesitate anymore.

I allow her beauty to sink in finally. The weirdness of the situation has kept me from getting hard, but as I yank her thong off her and toss it on top of her jeans, I feel my blood start to pulse as it redirects towards my cock.

Grabbing under her knees, I pull her towards the edge of the bed so I can worship her properly. I meet her gaze as much as I can through my mask. She's watching me closely, her breathing still too shallow for my liking.

I run my thumb along her center and her breathing hitches. She lets her head fall back and seems to relax even more, so I continue, pressing a kiss to her inner thigh, gripping my hands around both her thighs, feeling how soft and thick they are. I know they rub together when she walks and I've always found that one of the hottest things about women.

Spurred on by the scent of her, I dart my tongue out and swipe along her core, lingering on her clit, and sucking just a little bit. Bliss moans again and so I settle in, right there between her thighs, knowing there's not really anywhere else I'd want to be right now.

I drive my tongue into her before replacing it with two fingers, opening her up so I can get more of a taste. The urge to bite into her thighs is so strong, I'm practically salivating. I keep my focus on her, though, on how she's responding to me. I can feel her sitting up, wanting to reach out and grab onto something, and I internally curse my mask and hood for preventing her from threading her fingers through my hair. So I reach up with my other hand, gripping her hand in mine and locking it down across her stomach to prevent her from squirming too much as I drive her towards her climax.

She begins to buck and thrash as I continue my attention on her. I remove my fingers so I can grip her thigh and hook it over my shoulder, driving my tongue into her from a slightly different angle. As I chase the most divine taste I've ever had, something *odd* happens. My tongue lengthens and thickens and suddenly I'm deeper in her, flicking my tongue against *that* spot inside her. She lets out a moan that's half a scream as I repeatedly stroke my tongue inside her. There's a burst on my tongue as I feel her coming on it. I moan into her and she falls back against the mattress, completely sated.

I withdraw from her, my tongue returning to its normal size. I run my fingers across the tip of it as if it'll grow in size again, but it doesn't.

I look up at Bliss, relieved to see that her skin has a glow to it I haven't seen yet. She's propped up on her elbows, looking at me with a mix of contentment and confusion. And I feel as though I got a release too. There's a pleasantness that courses through me in waves, making me feel a warmth everywhere in my body. Is this the high one gets from succubus sex?

"What happened?" she asks.

I open my mouth to explain, but I stop short, cursing my mask.

She raises her brows at me and nods. "Right, you're all anonymous and everything. Don't worry, I won't pry."

Bliss gets up on her knees, looking down at me, where I still kneel on the floor. She reaches out, gently brushing her pointer finger across my lips. I resist the urge to nip at it. Or bite it off completely.

I should really get away from her.

I stand up awkwardly, towering over her now. I hand her clothes to her wordlessly and she changes into them, taking a look around at the room.

"I don't suppose I could borrow another hoodie?" She looks over at me with a soft smile. "I promise I will give both of them back."

I reach into a duffle bag I threw haphazardly onto the floor and grab another black hoodie, this one with the Voracious Maw logo on it. Thankfully it's one I've worn while also wearing my Wrath cologne, so she shouldn't smell my actual scent on it. Bliss beams up at me and throws the hoodie on. It dwarfs her immediately, way too big on her. She pushes up the sleeves, but they just slide back down.

"Thank you," she says, coming up on her tiptoes, drawing my head down towards her so she can plant a quick kiss onto the cheek of my mask. I thank the mask and the black paint that hides my blush.

She moves towards the door, but I reach out and grip her forearm, stopping her. I pull the ribbons out of my pocket and hand them back to her, not sure she'll even want them. Bliss reaches out and takes the bloodied white ribbons but hands them back to me. "Can you just throw them away, please?"

I nod, and she leaves.

I fall backwards onto the mattress, tired, confused, and most of all, hard as a rock.

CHAPTER THIRTY

BLISS

It occurs to me as I'm leaving the room that it's the same one I woke up in this morning. I head down the stairs, pondering whether or not Pisces and Wrath are sharing that room. And if so, where did Wrath sleep last night if I was taking his bed?

My feet hit the last step and I hear Taser's voice coming from the living room. He comes into view as I round the corner. His arms are crossed and he's glaring at the rest of the guys. "You should have waited for me," he grits out, leveling a look at Evan.

"They weren't going to let her fade off while they were waiting for me to track one of you down," Benny replies, coming to stand next to Taser, placing a soothing hand on his shoulder. "Everyone here is looking out for her, okay?"

"We're her friends too," Simon says from his seat at the table.

I scan the room, seeing Shaun leaning against the wall and Niamh next to him. "Don't worry, Taser. I'd never have let them try anything," Niamh says.

"Try anything? He's up there with her doing exactly that."

"He healed me," I say, coming up and touching Taser on the elbow. He lets out the breath he was holding and wraps me up in his arms.

"Thank the stars, Bliss. I was so fucking worried. Benny tracked me down and I tried to get here as fast as I could, but Wrath was already healing you. I'm so sorry I didn't get here in time. Are you okay?"

I think back to Wrath's tongue.

I'm more than okay. I pull on Taser's arm. "I'm fine."

A creak on the steps makes my head swivel in that direction as Wrath walks down the stairs, coming to a halt in front of Taser and me.

Taser levels him with the same glare he's been giving everyone else. "You should have waited for me."

Wrath's lips pull in towards his teeth. It seems like he's trying to keep himself from saying anything. His head is angled my way, but because of his mask I can't tell where he's looking.

"Why?" Evan asks, getting up from his seat and coming to stand next to Wrath. In his black platform boots he stands just an inch or so taller than Wrath. "Seems like he did a great job of healing Bliss."

He nods my way, and I know I'm giving off a little bit of a glow from recently feeding. I turn scarlet at the attention and lower my gaze to the floor. When I look back up, Wrath's white teeth are flashing against his skin in one of the sexiest smirks I've ever seen.

Fuck, that should not be a turn-on.

It should be making me mad.

My sexual encounters shouldn't be the discussion topic right now.

But my stars, does my body want to take Wrath back upstairs.

I need to get out of here.

I tug on Taser's arms. "We should go. I need to check on Amelia and Reese. They'll be worried."

"They're already on their way over. I texted them when you were upstairs."

That's just going to make this whole situation even more embarrassing. I look between Wrath and Simon, wishing I could talk to both of them more, but I need to intercept my friends before they get here. "Well, we should um, go," I say lamely. I wave at

Simon and look at Wrath, my mouth opening and closing. "Bye," I finally manage to say.

"Feel free to come back anytime. I think when you've woken up here twice in one day you can think of it as home," Evan says with a wicked grin. Niamh slaps him on the back of the head and I shoot my own grin at her, ushering Taser out of the house.

Once we're down the steps and headed to where we see Amelia and the others coming towards us, he puts out an arm and stops me. "Are you really okay?" he asks, looking me over as if he's expecting to find scars.

But I feel great. Better even than the last time I fed off Taser fully, in the shower. I'm not sure how, but my power well feels completely recharged. "I'm great, don't worry about me," I tell him again. "I appreciate you always helping me out."

His gaze jumps back and forth between my eyes then drops to the ground. "I was so fucking worried, Bliss. When Benny found me and told me what happened. I—"

I interlace his hands in mine. "I know. And I need you to know if our roles were reversed, I'd be doing the same for you." I breath out a shaky exhale as he gathers me up in his arms. We stay like that until Amelia, Reese, Blake, and Tubbs reach us.

"Bliss! Are you okay?" Amelia asks, practically ripping me out of Taser's arms. Giving him an apologetic look over my head, she wraps me up in a hug too. "Did you find Grim?"

Reese snuggles in from the other side and I squeeze both my sisters tightly. "It's kind of a long story. But I'm okay. Promise."

Blake and Tubbs take turns giving me hugs as well. As we make our way over to the main stage for the Phantoms' show, I fill in the entire group on what just happened, all the while playing with the drawstrings of Wrath's hoodie, wondering just who in the world I let go down on me.

"So what's our plan to kill Jordan?" Tubbs asks the others. I roll my eyes and punch him softly in the shoulder.

"We cannot retaliate," I tell him.

"Oh, I think we absolutely can and should," Taser says with a growl.

I come to a halt on the sidewalk and all their eyes turn to me. "We can't. He almost killed Simon. And then he attacked me. We need to lay low."

"I think you've just stated exactly why we need to do something," Blake responds, throwing an arm around Amelia. "Don't worry, though. Taser, Tubbs, and I got this."

Amelia and Reese exchange looks. "We already called the fae constabulary," Reese says. "We need to let them take care of it."

The guys mutter under their breath, but I don't pay much attention to them. I'm still glowing with a really good buzz and I can't stop thinking about Wrath's tongue. My slutty fae mind is definitely in the gutter.

"Let's change the subject, please," I tell my friends. I don't really want to think about the attack right now, especially when I'm feeling the best I have in a very long time.

I can feel Amelia staring at me, probably at the glow emanating from my skin. "This is actually amazing," Amelia says, motioning to me and my glow. "Also, Wrath does look like he'd be really, really hot," she muses.

Dericia murmurs her agreement, letting out a sigh. "They all look like they're super hot under those masks."

Jordan's voice echoes in my mind. *They're probably all really fucking ugly. Why else hide?* But I just know he's wrong, or I guess I don't care. I think if I saw Wrath without his mask, I'd find him beautiful.

"Haven't you both seen them without masks? Years back when you opened for them?" I ask, suddenly wondering if I should have been asking my sister for help on getting closer to Wrath.

Amelia hums in thought as Dericia's face scrunches in confusion.

"No. Not Wrath at least," my sister says. She looks to Reese and Taser. "Remember, there was that whole thing after the show? Someone died outside the venue and there were cops everywhere."

"Someone died?" I ask, stunned. "How am I just now hearing about this?"

"Well, you almost died that night too. I guess I never realized I hadn't filled you in," my sister continues. "But yeah, I think some of the Voracious Maw guys found a dead guy in the back alley of the venue and had to stay to talk to the human police. So they never came out afterwards."

"So what happened?"

"An overdose, maybe?" Reese says, thinking back.

"I never got the details," Taser says. "Their bassist and guitarist came out with us, but they didn't know much about it."

"That's crazy," I say.

"But Taser, you met Wrath before the show, right?" Amelia asks. The lack of a segue back to the original topic throws me for just a minute, but we're all pretty used to how quickly my sister can switch gears and moods. "Is he hot?"

Taser runs a hand over his face. "I feel I shouldn't answer this on principle."

I laugh and link arms with him. "I don't need to know what he looks like."

Amelia looks at me as if I'm crazy, but I'm content in the knowledge that I'm not *that* shallow.

"Will you still hook up with Grim?" Dericia asks. I wish someone would change the subject to something far away from my sex life—and dead bodies. I could do without dead bodies for a while. The night of the garden threatens to flash through my mind, but I shut that down quickly.

As I try to get my thoughts in order, Amelia answers for me. "You really still should. He definitely is super hot. And if you're into masks, well, he also has one, so really..." She trails off, her thoughts going so deep into the gutter I definitely do not want to follow.

We make our way back to the platform seating where we watched the Voracious Maw show earlier and sit down, chatting idly as more and more people fill in around us. Simon, Shaun, Benny, and—unfortunately—Pisces, have taken seats behind us.

Simon waves at me and whisper yells a greeting to us just as the stage lights flare on and the crowd starts cheering.

I take one last look around me, noticing Wrath isn't there.

At least not in his costume. The lights around the stands get darker and the stage gets brighter. I can't make out the people sitting around us enough to determine whether one of them is the one who healed me.

As the Phantoms conclude their show with a huge finish, lights flashing on stage, and all the fans screaming for an encore, Amelia, Reese, and I stand up, starting to make our way off the platform. If the Phantoms do another song, we'll catch it from the backstage area, but I want to be ready to greet Grim when he comes off stage.

I'm not at all aware that Pisces and the other Voracious Maw crew members plus Evan have followed us, chatting with Taser, Tubbs, and Blake. I certainly don't check over my shoulder multiple times to see Pisces lingering apart from the group, not really interacting much with anyone.

We all collectively listen in as the Phantoms play one last song to their adoring fans. I bounce back and forth on the balls of my feet, continuing to feel the urge to look around for Pisces.

Why do my eyes keep searching him out? It has to be a stress response or something. If I can avoid him, he can't be mean to me. And I can't avoid him if I don't know where he is. That's all it is. Survival instinct.

"Bliss," comes Pisces' deep voice from behind me. It has a softer quality this time, almost a question.

I turn around and find him standing at my right shoulder, looking down at me with his head cocked to the side.

"Can we talk?" he asks, his deep gorgeous blue eyes boring into mine.

Nope.

I want to turn around and ignore him.

He is such a dick.

And yet I can't help but feel like I should at least hear him out.

Things were going okay between us while we were hiding during the game. Until I brought up Wrath. Maybe that's a sore spot for him. How many fans have probably attempted to hit on him, flirt with him—date him even—just to get a glimpse of one of the Voracious Maw boys?

And I'm not much better. Though I have my reasons.

I let out a sigh. "Fine."

He leads me out from the backstage area and heads out into the throng of people, making sure to stay by my side, probably knowing my strides could never match his.

He towers over me as we walk, his height and lean muscular build causing the crowd to part for us.

A particularly rowdy group of drunk men comes barreling towards us and he switches to my left side, shielding me from them as they're forced at the last minute to go around him.

We wander through the festival grounds until we're close to the maze. My eyes zero in on the entrance.

Pisces tugs on my sleeve. "We could sit over there?" he asks, pointing to a picnic table. When I don't respond, he must follow my gaze, spotting the maze.

"Shit, Bliss, I'm sorry. I didn't mean to bring you back here." That snags my attention and I stare at him. The question must be plain on my face because he frowns. "Simon told me what happened. How Wrath and Eerie found you."

"Right," I say, but I find myself looking to the maze again. The entrance of the maze, roped off with a single strip of caution tape and a small sign saying the maze is closed, almost dares me to face it.

I take a few steps towards it and feel Pisces at my back.

"Bliss, where are you going?"

"I need to see it, where I was attacked."

Pisces overtakes me and puts his hands on my shoulders, stopping me in my tracks. "Maybe you should wait. Give it a few days," he says softly, in that deep voice of his. His hands drop to his sides.

I shake my head, darting around him, and duck inside the entrance, going under the tape. I come to a stop where the path splits in opposite directions.

"What did you want to talk about?" I ask, my arms starting to get cold as the night air cools another degree or two. There's enough light from the streetlamps and the patio lighting they used inside the maze to see where I'm going.

"Are you sure you're okay to be here?" he asks. He sneezes, just like the day we were partnered to give out prizes. After a moment, he continues, "I get wanting to face your trauma, but there's no rush."

I nod, but I don't agree. I drove the very next day to the place where Jordan crashed the car, almost killing me. I knew if I didn't I would never drive on that road again. It's a Band-Aid you have to rip off.

I turn around and face him. "I need to do this now. Before they take the maze down. I want to go look at the spot where I was attacked."

He motions for me to lead the way and I do. I'm not sure how my brain remembers it, but I know the exact path I took trying to get away from Jinx, and I know even before I turn the corner that I'm going to find my blood.

And there it is.

It's dried, but it's coated the hay-covered asphalt floor of the maze. I notice splatters on the walls as well.

"Fuck," Pisces breathes out. "Do you know who attacked you?"

"My ex, Jordan. He's a vampire."

Pisces growls and the sound reverberates through my body. I turn and look at him, finding him staring stonily at the blood splatters.

My heartbeat starts to pick up its pace and I find I'm having a hard time taking a full breath.

I turn and break into a sprint away from the scene of my attack.

"Oh stars," I say, coming to a stop and placing my hands on the hay wall in front of me. Pisces is behind me seconds later.

"Bliss, are you alright?" He places a gentle hand on my shoulder, slowly turning me around. I cave and bury my face into his chest. He strokes my back soothingly as tears streak down my face. "I'm so sorry, Bliss. God, I'm so sorry."

Pisces pulls me into him even tighter and I let him scoop me up as he carries me to one of the little benches made out of hay. I curl into him, letting my nose rest against his collarbone.

"I shouldn't have brought you anywhere near here. Fuck, I keep making everything worse," he whispers hoarsely, but I don't think he meant to say it out loud.

I clutch his shirt and finally pull my head up. We meet each other's gazes, and for some reason the sight of his runeless eyes makes me sob even harder.

I'm only here at the festival because I'm trying to get a mate. I was only attacked because my mate bond is broken.

That's not entirely true, a voice in my head reminds me. Amelia asked me to be here. Even if it weren't for the wraith's deal, wouldn't I have eventually caved and come with my sister to support her?

I got attacked because Jordan attacked me.

It was on him and nothing else.

I hastily wipe at my cheeks, trying to dry them, and sniff to clear my nose.

I am not going to keep crying over anything related to Jordan. I've wasted enough tears on him.

I am done crying.

The only tears I want to see now are Wrath's. I'm going to get my mate and become a water nymph.

I straighten up in Pisces' hold. "I'm okay now. Sorry for running and crying all over you."

He smiles softly at me, dipping his head. "It's fine. Least I could do."

He lets me get up and I turn and face him, wiping again at the stray tears that have leaked down my face. "What did you want to talk about?"

"I wanted to apologize—" He's cut off mid-sentence by a scream that feels like it reaches into my soul and slashes it to ribbons. Sheer panic courses through me at the fear in that scream.

"Stay here," Pisces says, starting to take a step, but then he stops. "Never mind, I'm not leaving you alone." He firmly grips my hand in his and we run towards where we thought we heard the scream.

But no other sounds follow it.

We hit a T in the maze. "Which way?" I ask.

Pisces looks down both ways and pulls me to the left. The path cuts to the right a few yards afterwards and we're led into a little dead end, where—

Oh stars.

I recognize her instantly.

Her blue-streaked blonde hair is splayed out around her head, almost like a halo, and her limbs are limp next to her, covered in blood. I try not to focus on how deep her wounds are. At how many of them there are.

She's wearing the Voracious Maw shirt we handed out to her a couple days ago.

Pisces draws me close into his body, looking over my head behind me, probably searching for whoever did this.

I pull out of his grasp and go check her pulse. There's nothing. Her artery is still beneath my fingers.

Pisces keeps his eyes on the entrance to the maze. I wonder if the sight of blood does anything to him. I still don't know what type of fae he is, and he doesn't smell like a vampire, but maybe I'm wrong.

He pulls out his phone, dialing something quickly, and speaks quietly to the person on the other end. While he still has his phone to his ear, he reaches for me. "Come on, Bliss, we need to get out of here."

He pulls me after him, while continuing to talk on the phone. I gather quickly that he's talking to an emergency dispatcher. We come out the entrance in front of the maze. Police lights are already making their way towards us as cop cars drive carefully onto the grassy lawn surrounding the maze.

Pisces tells one of the officers where we found the body and then his arms close around me again, as he leads me to a picnic table. We sit with our legs on the outside of the bench, and Pisces runs his hand up and down my arm to keep me warm as I settle into his side.

I can't seem to get the images of the girl out of my head.

"We met her."

"I know," he responds quietly, lowering his cheek to rest on the top of my head. "I know."

"Do you think it was a warlock?" I finally ask after a long pause. My mind can't help but compare the blonde girl with the woman in the green dress. The similarities are too much. We watch the rest of the police close down the scene with tape and police gates. The swirling blue and red lights take over my vision until it's the only thing I can see.

"I'm not sure," is all he says.

But something doesn't seem right. The attacks I heard about on the news were more public and random. This felt more purposeful.

Like maybe she was lured here.

Or herded, my mind points out.

A silhouette approaches us, but I can't make out who it is until he's only a few feet in front of us, the streetlamp nearby shedding its glow on his face.

"Bliss, you were the one who found the body?" Grim asks, looking from Pisces to me.

"Yeah, we both did." Pisces gets up, as members from Voracious Maw, Goddess' Trance and the Phantoms all converge on us.

"We heard a scream and found her. It— It looks like the other attack," I tell Grim, as he comes and sits down next to me.

Grim glances at Pisces. "Can you give us a minute?"

Pisces looks between us, an unreadable expression crossing his face, but he nods and heads off to his friends, giving me one last look over his shoulder.

"Do you know who she was?" Grim asks.

I shake my head. "No, not really. Pisces and I met her during the scavenger hunt. She was here with her friends to see Voracious Maw. She couldn't have been more than twenty. I can't believe this." Tears start falling again and I wipe furiously at them. I said no more tears, but this feels like the only thing I can do in this moment.

Grim puts his arm around me. "I'm so sorry you were the one to find her."

"I think—" I start to say, but stars, I can't get the words out. I start sobbing harder. Amelia and Reese are there in seconds, and I try to meet their gaze through my tears, but my vision is too blurry. "Stars, it's all my fault," I sob out. "I don't know much about the warlock attacks, but I don't think this is the same. I think it was Jordan who attacked her. Maybe the woman in the garden too." Would I have ended up just like them if Eerie and Wrath hadn't found me?

Grim stiffens beside me. "I'm not sure these were vampire attacks, but I'll talk to the investigators. They'll want to talk to you again at some point." He squeezes my shoulder. "I'm gonna go see if I can help out," he says, more so to Amelia and Reese. "Call me if Bliss needs anything."

Reese replaces Grim to my left and Amelia sits down next to me on the right. I'm not sure how long I'm there for, but I rest my head on Reese's shoulders. At some point a fae officer makes her way over, asking me a series of questions. The next hour or so passes in flashes, both quickly and slowly. I don't remember how I get home, but at some point I realize I'm all tucked into bed, with Reese next to me.

I turn so I can see her and curl up closer to her. I beg sleep to take me.

CHAPTER THIRTY-ONE

BLISS

Amelia and Blake have been holed up in Blake's room since we got back last night. Since Jordan or possibly another homicidal fae was out there somewhere, it wasn't safe for Amelia or I to be hooking up with random fae we didn't know, and Blake volunteered to "feed" her immediately.

Taser, Dericia, Tubbs, and I sit around the living room of the rental. Dericia is napping on the couch, her feet in Tubbs' lap as he plays a game on his phone.

Taser is halfway through a bag of chips, sitting at the dining room table next to us. I'm trying to read, but my current romance novel is not holding my attention. It's not a bad book, I just can't get all the events of the previous days out of my head. The memory of Jordan ripping into me comes ramming into my head at random times, as do the images of the two dead women—Carly and Stephanie.

Grim stopped by earlier this morning. I asked for details on the attacks, on whether they'd figured out if Jordan was involved. I also asked if he knew who they were. Their names, their life stories. He told me as much as he knew from his police contacts.

My breathing turns more rapid, and one look at Taser tells me he can hear my increased heartbeat.

"Want a chip?" he asks, somehow knowing I don't want to talk about it. I nod, throwing down my book and joining him at the table, where he hands over the chip bag. I take one out, dipping it into the salsa and crunching into it, letting the taste bring me back to the present moment.

"So Amelia and Blake are currently using the buddy system," Taser says slowly. I look over at him as I dip another chip into salsa. "If you also need a buddy, um…" He coughs awkwardly. "Let me know. I know you probably feel okay with Grim or even Wrath, and I know things with us haven't been easy lately, but I'm not sure you should trust anyone right now."

"You really think either of those guys is going around killing people?"

"No," he responds slowly. "Look, I just mean, for your safety, I'm here if you need to feed."

I smile, an immeasurable surge of gratitude flooding me. I reach out and grip his hand in mine, giving him a light squeeze. "I'm so lucky to have you as my friend, but we shouldn't—we can't do that anymore."

Taser's eyes fall to the floor. "Why not?"

"Because someday, probably very soon, you're going to find your mate, and when you do, this friends with benefits thing can't fuck that up like it did with you and Stacey."

"You really don't need to worry about that," Taser says, still not looking at me. He takes a chip out of the bag and cracks it into teeny tiny pieces, the chip dust falling to the table. He watches it intently, like it's the most interesting thing in the world.

"I do, Taser. I really care about you and I want you to be happy."

He looks over at me and gives me a soft smile. "Bliss, you're one of my best friends. And I spend most of my time getting to play music that I love with my best friends. I don't need any more in life."

"Yeah, but—"

He cuts me off with a light squeeze to my arm. "Bliss, don't worry about me, just know I'm here if you need, and seriously, I don't mind."

"Okay, but when you find your mate, there will be no more of this."

He smiles again and nods at me. "You talk as if you don't have a mate yourself."

"I might not. You know about that spell, how my bond is incased in some sort of unwieldy magic."

"Yeah, but it's there."

His words stop me in my tracks, preventing me from taking that oh-so-addictive downward spiral into hopelessness. It's like a bucket of cold water was thrown on me, and I get goose bumps.

Taser stands up and places his finger underneath my chin, lifting my gaze to his. "He's out there, okay? And until you find him, I'm here for you."

I stand up and throw my arms around his torso, hugging him tight. I'm not entirely sure how I deserve a friend like him. I've been so focused on myself and what happened with me that I completely ditched my closest friends. I put the rift between us, and as Taser wraps his arms around me and presses a light kiss to the top of my head, I vow that I will do whatever it takes to mend that rift, to make it as if it was never there in the first place.

The doorbell to our rental rings, interrupting our heart to heart. I jump out of Taser's embrace and go to answer the door, but Taser's already there, using his vampire speed to reach the door first. He rolls his eyes at me. "What are you not getting about there being a homicidal fae somewhere out there?"

"What? You think whoever it was is going to politely ring the doorbell before coming in to murder us?"

"Well, yeah, if it's what gets them into the house." Taser shakes his head at me and motions for me to get back. I take one very small step back as the doorbell rings again.

"Anyone home?" Simon's very muffled but distinctive British accent sounds on the other side of the door.

I roll my eyes at Taser and push him aside, throwing open the door and grinning at Simon, noting that he's flanked by two very tall guys, both of whom I've met before. I ignore the one to my left. "Hey, Simon," I say, motioning for them to come in. Simon wraps me in a quick hug as he comes inside, then turns and greets Taser, shaking his hand.

Pisces and Evan, both easily over six four, tower above us as they prowl in behind Simon. Evan dips his head in greeting to me and Taser.

"Good to see you again, mate," Evan says to Taser, a hesitant smile on his face. Pisces ignores us, his eyes skimming over the living room and then to the dining room table where our chips and salsa are still out. He eyes Taser uncertainly.

"To what do we owe this honor?" Taser asks, his expression matching Evan's. I know Taser likes these guys well enough, but after their last meeting things are a little awkward.

And after the events of last night, I'm not sure what to feel about Pisces. So the awkwardness builds. He was so nice, letting me sob all over him. But now in the daylight, I'm having trouble reconciling last night with my previous dealings with him.

"Well, we wanted to come and officially offer you the spot as our opener on our next tour," Simon explains excitedly. Pisces looks over at Simon, something like annoyance on his face, as if maybe he's not super happy about this, though I don't understand why. I'm not even sure why he's here. It's not like a guitar tech would have a say in which band opens for the one he works for. And it's not like our paths would have to cross all that much during the tour. He'd be working strictly on Voracious Maw's guitars, and I would be solely dealing with my band.

His gaze finds mine and I'm caught staring at him. I quickly look away, turning to Simon. "I'll go grab the others!"

Within minutes Amelia and the rest of the band are gathered

round. Amelia and Blake are a little annoyed at their no doubt multiple rounds of sex being interrupted, but as my sister takes in my beaming smile, her face softens and she grips my hand in hers, smiling at me.

"Bliss, do you want to do the honors?" Simon asks, practically bouncing up and down on the balls of his feet.

I nod excitedly and grip my sister around the shoulders. "Goddess' Trance is going to be the opener for Voracious Maw's next US tour!" I'm practically shouting at her by the end of my sentence. Amelia's eyes go wide in a combination of what looks to be excitement and disbelief.

"Are you fucking serious?" she asks, her voice coming out breathy.

"I'm super fucking serious!" I reply, looking over at Simon.

He lays out the logistics to the rest of the band, the dates, the travel, all that. As I listen, my eyes wander off to Pisces again. He's leaning against the wall looking completely bored. He looks up at me, a smirk appearing on his face.

I scowl and look away, returning my attention to Simon as he's exchanging numbers with everyone so we can chat more. There are contracts to sign and hotels and tour buses to figure out. We won't always be able to make use of portals to travel. With the amount of people, and all the gear, we'll definitely have parts of the tour where we'll have to drive the whole way between locations.

Dericia comes over to me and slings her arms around my shoulders, giving me a huge hug. "This is so fucking amazing. Bliss, you are the best manager we could have ever asked for."

My returning smile is genuine.

Amelia is beaming and looking so radiant. I'm just happy she's finally getting the recognition she deserves. Everything else is a fucking bonus.

Simon motions to Evan, who's been standing quietly behind him, a friendly smile on his face.

"Amelia, this is Evan, pretty obviously our bassist," Simon says by way of introduction.

"Of course," Amelia replies, extending her hand to Evan. "It's great to meet—" She stops short as her eyes meet Evan's and the two of them fall completely still. A look of awe crosses both their faces, but in an instant both of them recoil. Amelia rips her hand away from Evan's, appearing horrified. Evan's eyes narrow on her, looking like she's just kicked his puppy.

Without a word, Amelia backs out of the room, running up the stairs faster than I've ever seen her run.

In a second long glance with Dericia, we somehow communicate that she'll go after my sister while I try to smooth over whatever the fuck just happened.

Dericia rushes up the stairs after Amelia while I turn to Evan and Simon. "I'm so sorry, I'm not sure what all that was about. Amelia's always been a bit quirky," I say with a laugh. "She's one of those flighty artist types, probably just thought of some new lyrics…" I trail off as Pisces comes to stand by Evan, who still looks pissed off.

Simon looks between the two of them and back at me. "It's alright, Bliss. We totally understand," he says, though by his tone I can tell he's extremely confused, just like everyone else.

"I didn't think you really knew Amelia," Taser says to Evan, the only one apparently willing to broach what actually just happened.

"I don't," comes his clipped reply. He turns and walks out of the house, the door falling shut behind him so fast a picture hanging on the wall next to it shudders.

"Well, I guess we should go," Simon says uncertainly. "Bliss, I'll stop by later and we can hash out more details?" I nod and Simon motions for Pisces to follow him as he goes after Evan.

Taser, Tubbs, and Blake all retreat to the living room, talking quietly about Amelia's reaction.

Pisces is about to close the door behind him. He turns back and pins me with his dark blue eyes. His gaze rakes down my body, coming back and settling on my face. Smirking, he comes and stands before me, reaching out and taking one of the strings of the hoodie I'm wearing between his fingers. The one that belongs to

Wrath. The one that I keep nervously fiddling with and can't seem to stop wearing.

He cocks his head to the side as he plays with the string. His eyes flip back to mine as he leans in close and whispers in my ear, "When do I get my hoodies back?"

CHAPTER THIRTY-TWO

PISCES

"Well, that was all sorts of fucking weird," Simon says. We all sit around the living room of our rental. It's almost exactly the same as the one Goddess' Trance is in, just mirrored.

Evan sits on an overly plush green sofa, his back straight, his whole body stiff. His anger is wafting off him in waves and he looks pale and drained, like he's seen a ghost.

Simon looks between Evan, Shaun, and me. Benny must be upstairs.

"Someone want to explain what just happened?" Simon prods. He looks at me and I shrug.

He turns to Shaun, who gives him an incredulous look. "I wasn't even there. How would I know?"

"What would have Evan this pissed off?" I ask Shaun. Even if Shaun wasn't there, he has insight into Evan that the rest of us don't. He thinks for a moment, eyes wandering from Evan to mine.

"His family, for starters," Shaun supplies. Evan glances at him but still doesn't speak.

Shaun considers something for a few moments longer. Suddenly his eyes go wide. "No…" is all he says.

"No what?" Benny asks, coming to sit next to me, snuggling

closely, a yawn escaping him. I wrap an arm around him and he curls into me more. I can feel my jaw aching, my siren teeth wanting to push through my gums and bite into him, but I focus harder on Evan as he shifts uncomfortably.

After a long pause, Shaun finally says, "He's found his mate."

Benny jumps up in surprise, letting out a little whimper.

"Isn't that a good thing?" Simon asks.

A pang of jealousy surges through me. What I wouldn't do for a true mate bond. And here Evan is furious that he's found her. I understand his reasons. His family wants him to be bonded so he can take over as heir, but everything Evan chooses to do is the opposite of what his family wants. Amelia looked furious as well. Weird that both of them would reject something that I so ache to have.

"No," Shaun says simply in answer to Simon's question.

"I don't get it. Amelia's beautiful and talented," Simon presses. "I thought Born fae mates are supposed to fall madly in love with each other."

"It's not that," Shaun says as Evan gets up off the couch, mumbling about how he needs to be alone. I can't help but glare at his back, as his tall form slowly disappears up the stairs. I wish I was in his position. I wouldn't waste it.

"It's his family," Benny supplies when Shaun doesn't continue. He explains in detail to Simon why Evan has never, ever wanted a mate.

As Benny goes into the story again, the one I've already heard, I find my anger dissipating. It's not Evan's fault that I can't have what I want. And it's not like if he wasn't mated to Amelia that I would have been. And I wouldn't even want to be mated to her specifically, not that there's anything wrong with her. I just wish I was worthy of being mated to someone.

"How did they find out they were mates?" Simon asks, but just as Benny is about to start explaining, Simon's phone rings. I consider asking Benny to explain it to me instead. How do Born fae know? Is it a smell? Is it an aura? Something they just sense?

I've never asked before, because my jealousy has always been too much.

I realize it doesn't matter, because however Born fae figure it out, it's not like if I know, suddenly it'll make it so that Made fae can get mates too.

Benny and Shaun head into the kitchen to grab some snacks. I know Evan wants to be alone, but my feet take me to his room of their own accord. I hesitate and knock softly on his door.

"Yeah?" he mutters.

I push open the door, pausing in the doorway and looking at him sprawled out on his bed, shoes still on. They hang over the edge of the bed. He just watches me as I stand there trying to figure out what to even say to him.

"I'm jealous of you," I finally say, staring guiltily at my feet. "I was mad at you for a few minutes there."

He huffs. "I never wanted to have a mate. She'll just end up being another pawn for my parents to control."

"She didn't look happy to find you either, so can't you just not bond?" I remember Shaun saying something once about how the bond isn't official until a couple has sex.

"We can try," Evan says. "But it's hard. If we resist, the stars will just keep throwing us together till we finally give in."

"If anyone can tell the stars to get fucked, it's you," I say, waving a hand at him.

He barks out a laugh, but it's hollow.

We fall silent.

After a moment, Evan sits up on the bed and beckons me closer with his pointer finger. I finally step fully into the room and go to stand in front of him.

"Sces, can you take my mind off this?" He reaches out and grips my hand. "I need to feel pain. Something to ground me besides this anger."

I tilt my head to the side. "I don't think I should do that." I lift a finger to his chin and bring his gaze to mine. I hold out my arm, covered in thin little scars. "Trust me, it doesn't help."

His gaze is hard as he unbuttons his shirt and slips it off, revealing his pale smooth torso beneath. "I don't care right now. Feed on me," he says, pulling me forward so I'm forced to kneel between his legs on the mattress. He leans back and I hover over him, my siren teeth pushing through my gums despite my reluctance.

But I'm starving since denying myself a bite of Bliss the night before.

Evan grins at me, running his hand down the center of my chest, fingers playing over my shirt. I pull it off to save it from getting blood on it, since Evan won't be able to clean it right away with his magic after I feed from him. I push myself on top of him as he settles back into the pillows.

Pillows that are about to be splattered with his blood.

I tear into his shoulder first, the smoky scent of him filling my nose, while the spicy copper of his blood floods my mouth. I rip pieces of him out and he groans in pain, his face a grimace, his teeth clenching together. I have enough control that I can pepper kisses on his flesh as I continue to maul him, trying to soothe the sting and pain a little, but I know it doesn't help much. He cradles the back of my head, encouraging me to keep going.

"Take everything you need," he hisses out between bites.

So I do. I eat until I feel completely full. In my post-feasting haze, I curl up next to Evan, licking a bit of blood off his chest as I snuggle into him. I can still hear his heart beating nice and strong, so I fall asleep next to him, completely content.

"Well, I'm not gonna lie, I'm a little jealous," Benny says from the doorway of the bedroom. I ease my eyes open and stare at him, noting Evan's scent enveloping me. "You sure did a number on him, Sces."

I grimace and look over at Evan. He's started to heal, but he needs warmth to help recharge his powers. The bed is covered in his blood and it's dried around my mouth.

"You clean yourself up. I'll make sure he gets warm enough to heal."

I crawl out from Evan's side, pressing a kiss to the top of his head. He smiles faintly, like he's somewhere nice in his dreams, but he continues to sleep peacefully. I get it now. My feeding off him put him to sleep, where he can escape his real world problems.

"Sces, use me next time, okay?" Benny says as I pass him in the doorway. "I don't like seeing him like this."

"I don't like seeing any of you like this," I mutter. I try to leave, but Benny grabs my arm.

"You know we don't judge you for this. It's your nature. It's who you are, and we love you."

"Even if I'm a Made monster?" I try to say the words jokingly, but it falls flat, serious.

"If you're a monster, then so am I," Benny says with a shrug.

"Doesn't it bother you that we don't get to have mates? Why did the stars do that to us? Are we really that bad?" The questions pour out, even though I don't mean to voice them.

Benny forces a smile. "Just because we don't have a magical mate bonding ceremony, doesn't mean we can't fall in love. And hey, I have you all, and for now that's enough for me. Now go shower. You're making me hungry." He eyes the blood and I turn and look at Evan again.

"Will you be okay with him like that?"

Benny nods but swallows thickly.

"Feed from me?" I hold out my arm.

He eyes me like I'm the most delicious snack and nods. "Later, though. I want to make sure he's good."

With that, Benny heads through the door, closing it behind him as I walk a bit unsteadily into the hallway. I almost feel drunk off the power Evan has given me.

Shaun and Simon are downstairs still after I've cleaned myself up. I pull the hoodie hanging off the back of the couch as I pass it.

It's my last one. If Bliss needs any more, I'll have to go buy another one.

I smile to myself as I recall her face after I whispered those words to her. She turned bright pink to match the new pink ribbon in her hair. Her mouth opened in a small gasp and I couldn't help but think of how she'd come undone for me the day before.

I groan internally as I realize that will never happen again. For one, I've been such a prick to her, and two, she'll probably find her mate soon, if she hasn't already.

My sour mood turns even worse. I decide to go walk around the festival. Shows won't start for a few more hours yet, but I want to grab a snack and just get out of the house for a bit.

Most of the festival goers are in all black from head to toe. Each flash of colorful clothing immediately catches my attention, and each time it's not a curvy petite woman with a ribbon in her caramel-brown hair, I feel both relieved and disappointed.

But it's not like I won't see her again.

Goddess' Trance is coming on tour with us in a few months. And she *is* their band manager. I try to quash the excitement that springs up in my chest, because even though she's been wearing two of my hoodies, she's not mine and she never will be.

Do I even want her to be?

Maybe I'm just obsessing over her because she's a gorgeous succubus.

I turn down into the grassy little area near the maze. It's pretty quiet, not too many people around.

I pause, because there, under the shade of a large tree, sitting on a picnic blanket, are Grim and Bliss.

And he's kissing her.

CHAPTER THIRTY-THREE

BLISS

AMELIA SHIFTS HER HEAD FROM SIDE TO SIDE, EXAMINING HER HAIR IN the mirror. Dericia and I have her sitting on a chair in front of the floor-length mirror in our bedroom. She's perched there impatiently. "Do we really need any more sparkle?"

Dericia snorts in amusement, grabbing another thread of the silvery hair tinsel, as I section out another thin piece of hair to attach it to. "We're almost halfway done," I assure her, but she just groans.

"I'm so bored," she complains.

"Well then, let's talk," I say.

Her eyes light up. "Do you have some tea to spill? Any more random sexual encounters?"

Dericia hands me another piece of tinsel.

"No, I haven't had any more sexual encounters, but I do have some tea." I point at my sister's reflection in the mirror. "I'll spill on one condition."

She arches her eyebrow in question.

"I'll tell you my tea, if you tell me what the fuck that was with Evan earlier?"

Amelia looks down to the side, avoiding eye contact and

fiddling with her rings. Dericia went after her yesterday, but Amelia refused to say much.

"What do you want to know?" she responds evasively.

"Well, for starters, I know you met him a while back, briefly, but you said you didn't really hang out with him."

"I don't know him at all," she responds slowly.

"Then why did you react like that?" Dericia asks, looking for another spot in Amelia's hair to add more tinsel.

Amelia makes a non-committal noise and stares fixedly at her hands.

"I guess I'll just have to save all this tea for myself." I drop Amelia's hair and start walking to the door.

"Fine!" Amelia rushes out.

I stop and come back to her side.

"I've never really talked to him. Like, I mean, I've seen him around and stuff. I was introduced to him after we opened for them, after the show, at the bar." She goes silent for a moment. "My bond was activated two years ago, so I wouldn't have seen it then, when I met him before."

Dericia and I both draw in a breath. "He's your mate?" Reese asks.

Amelia just nods. Dericia's hands are still in her hair, as if she's totally forgotten the task at hand.

"So remind me why that's a bad thing?" I finally manage to ask. I know she wants to focus on her music right now, but I never thought Amelia wanted to stay un-bonded forever.

"It just, it wasn't supposed to happen like this. My music is finally taking off. And I'm happy. I don't want to be tied down to someone. I'm free right now and I don't want anything to change." She meets my gaze in the mirror. "And I *like* sleeping with different guys. It's fun. I don't want to give that up."

Reese goes back to adding more tinsel. And I stand there kind of speechless. Is it some cosmic joke that my sister who loves casual sex found her one true love and me who hates it and needs a partner hasn't?

"Sorry, Bliss," Amelia says.

"Why are you sorry?" I meet her gaze in the mirror, frowning.

"I know you want your bondmate, but I just don't want this. To be honest, I don't think I ever have."

Dericia snorts a laugh and we both look at her, confused. "Sorry," she says, her hand going to cover her mouth. "It's just, I don't think it would matter, even if you did want to be mated to Evan. Based on his reaction, he definitely didn't like this little plot twist either."

Amelia grunts, crossing her arms. "I don't get what his deal is anyway. He should be feeling fucking lucky. I'm a catch. Like, what does he have to complain about?"

Dericia and I both grin, rolling our eyes at one another. "Why do you care about his reaction when you claim not to want the bond?"

"Whatever," Amelia says, waving her hand dismissively. "Spill your tea now, Bliss, or I'm never telling you anything ever again."

I only smile wider at her empty threat. But spill I do, telling them how I found out that the other guy who'd come over with Simon was Wrath himself and he's the one that went down on me. I don't feel guilty telling them this since we'll all be stuck on tour together for six weeks. I also share how conflicted I am over how he's been acting. They already know about how he made fun of me when we were volunteering in the maze together, but I fill them in on all the rest—well, except for the part where I still need to steal his tears.

And now that I know *who* he is, I'm that much closer to getting them, aren't I? A thrill goes through me at that realization. I still feel conflicted about stealing from him, and manipulating him and Simon. Pisces started out being rude and mean, but he held me last night. Let me cry all over him. He might have been about to tell me who he was before the maze—I specifically think "the maze," and not "the body"—but obviously he hadn't gotten the chance.

"I still don't like him," Amelia says. "Maybe this tour is a bad fucking idea."

I raise my pointer finger at her. "We're not backing out of this tour. I don't care if Taser ends up mating with their drummer and Mist ends up rejecting him, we're not backing out of this tour. It's the big break Goddess' Trance has been waiting for."

"But we'll have to deal with them for six whole weeks." Amelia groans. "I'll have to resist having sex with Evan for six weeks so that we don't complete the bond, and uh—" she motions to herself, "—look at me. He won't be able to resist and so I'll have to do all the work."

Reese and I laugh. "We'll run interference," I say. "It'll give me a reason to stay away from Pisces." Especially after I get his tears. Hopefully, I'll be able to use my powers to make him think nothing of it. It's too much to hope that I could make him totally forget. I'm not that powerful, even if I was fully recharged right before.

"I know how you can stay away from Pisces. You can spend your time keeping Simon away from me," Reese says. "Talk about a douche."

"What?" I ask, suddenly unsure of where this conversation is going. "Did I miss something? I know he was a little rude at the maze, but did something else happen?"

Reese rolls her eyes. "He's the textbook definition of hot and cold. He's either super nice to me, wanting to know all about growing up a kindred, or he's acting like I'm dog shit he stepped in. I swear I was about to slap him the last time I saw him."

"I'll slap him for you," Amelia says, grinning wickedly. "I hate men like that. Seriously the worst."

My mind is reeling with this new information. I go over all my interactions with Simon. True, there was that time where my succubus flirting did *not* work. But that was just embarrassing, and not at all his fault. Then I go over every time I've seen him interact with Reese, which is very limited.

"Sorry, Bliss. I know you're friends with him." Reese pats my shoulder.

"Well, not for long if he's been acting like that towards you," I respond immediately. "You fully have my support in slapping him, but let me talk to him first?" Maybe there's some sort of explanation for his behavior.

Dericia smiles at me with a bemused expression, like she thinks it's a waste of time, but she'll allow it. "I love how you always want to see the best in people, Bliss. Don't ever change."

Amelia makes a gagging noise. "Ugh, grab a yearbook why don't you?"

Dericia and I laugh and hug each other. We throw our arms around Amelia too, planting kisses all over her. "Yuck, gross. Get off me," she mumbles, even as she hugs us both back.

"I'm hungry," Amelia announces as we finally release her, immediately standing up. "I cannot sit in this chair anymore."

Dericia shrugs. "We can take a break."

Amelia nods and looks at me through the mirror. "Plus, Bliss, you need to get ready for your date." She grins.

A blush creeps into my face at the mention of it.

After Grim shared a little about the investigations and checked that I was okay, he asked if I wanted to meet him for a late lunch. Nothing fancy, just grabbing something from one of the food trucks and finding a little place in the grass to sit and eat. A little festival picnic.

"I'm pretty much ready, just need to change," I say. I couldn't help but put on Wrath's—no, Pisces'—hoodie earlier. It was too cold and his overly large hoodies are the comfiest things ever. A thought occurs to me, and I sniff his hoodie. Amelia and Reese both look at me like I'm insane, but I take another sniff. The hoodie doesn't smell like Pisces. Don't get me wrong, it smells good, but not as good as Pisces' scent. I laugh.

"I think the Voracious Maw boys disguise themselves with cologne," I explain to Reese and Amelia, holding out my sleeve for them to smell.

"That's actually genius," Amelia says, laughing.

We gossip a bit more as my sisters help me pick out an outfit.

About fifteen minutes later, I'm headed out the door, Dericia swatting me on the butt like she's a coach and I'm a football player.

"Go get him," she says excitedly. I know she and Amelia want me to hook up with Grim.

Even though I fed off Wrath two days ago, I still feel relatively good. I know my powers will start to droop and I'll need to do something soon, but do I do it with Grim?

I'm certainly not going to feed off Pisces again.

Even though I can't help but recall how he felt, what his tongue was capable of.

I mentally shut out that memory and attempt to lock it down and forget about it. We are so not going there again.

Grim's waiting for me by a food truck selling chocolate-covered strawberries with all sorts of toppings. He grins as he sees me, and I let him wrap me up in a tight hug.

He laughs into my hair as I tighten my arms around him.

He steps back and looks me up and down. "You look gorgeous, Bliss." He gives my ribbon a slight tug. I found another white ribbon in my suitcase. Even though the last time I wore a white one I was attacked, I have higher hopes today.

"Thank you," I say, allowing myself to look him up and down as well. I can't lie to myself. I definitely like what I see, but butterflies swirl in my stomach, and even though all the movies and romance books make it seem like butterflies are good, I know they're just a bit of anxiety.

But they settle down the more we walk around and talk about what food to get. By the time we order from a mediterranean style food truck, I feel much more comfortable.

We find a quiet section of the festival grounds with a grassy area, shaded by nearby trees. Grim's brought a blanket. He unfolds it, whipping it out in the air so it settles gracefully across the grass. We each give it a few tugs at the corners to smooth it out and sit down with our food.

"So, Bliss is your given name?" Grim asks as he spears a bit of meat with his fork.

"Yeah," I reply, a smile coming easily to my face. "I think my mom was a bit high on drugs when she delivered me. Thought she was being funny."

"So your parents knew you'd be a succubus?"

I stop myself from laughing, remembering that sometimes Made fae don't always know the ways of Born fae. "It's part of the prenatal care. Fae parents have a test performed to see what type of fae they'll be giving birth to."

Grim nods thoughtfully and laughs. "That actually makes a lot of sense. Same as finding out the sex, I suppose."

"Um, so what are you?" I blurt out then hide my mouth behind my hand. "Sorry, I just haven't been able to place your scent, and Taser won't talk much about you."

Grim smiles at me, a mischievous look in his eyes. "Promise you won't freak out?"

I raise my brows at him. "I'll try my best."

"I'm a hellhound." I breathe in sharply but remain quiet as he continues. Hellhounds are created by lesser wraiths, considerably less powerful than a song wraith or a dream wraith, but still nasty things. "Stormy, Casper, and I were all turned together. We went hiking and got lost. A mountain wraith got to us."

"Wow, no wonder I couldn't figure you out." I've never met a hellhound. I've not met a lot of Made fae, I realize. And I'm also realizing a lot of what Born fae learn about them isn't right.

"There's something else I should tell you too," Grim says, turning a bit more serious. "At one point the fae council approached us, wanted us to hunt down wraiths for them. Hellhounds are sometimes able to track their magical signatures."

I nod. I don't know much about his species, but I do know that. "So what? You hunt wraiths and in your off time you play in a band?"

"Sort of. The band is actually kind of a cover for us."

"Us?"

He nods, laughing. "Not everyone of the Phantoms is a hellhound, but we all are contracted with the fae council. We got into the metal scene because we love the music, don't get me wrong, but fae flock to this community. Haven't you ever marveled at just how many metal bands are actually fae? And where fae go, so do wraiths." He winks at me. I've no doubt he can see the gears turning in my head as I process this.

"How many wraiths have you—?" I struggle to remember the right word. Caught? Defeated? Killed?

"Three," he says proudly. "It might not seem like much, but it takes a while to find them, then some really complicated magic to banish them."

"How do you banish them?"

"It's different for different wraiths. And it depends on how strong a foothold they have here in this realm."

I nod along as he tells a story about how the Phantoms defeated a river wraith they encountered playing in Brazil.

"We were able to track it by finding the fae that summoned the thing. A water elemental that wanted to try use it to become more powerful. Anyways, we should have been able to banish it without too much trouble since it had only been summoned to this realm once." I nod, recalling some of the random facts I learned in school a while back and also my more recent research. A wraith can only come to this realm first if they've been summoned, then they can come and go as they please, but depending on how they've been summoned they're usually controlled by the one who summoned them. "But this one was possessing someone, so that was tricky. Hard to banish a wraith while it's inside a fae's body."

"Why would a wraith need to possess someone?" I can't help but ask. I didn't even realize that's a possibility.

"Each time a wraith is summoned back to this realm, they gain more of a foothold, right? Well, until they have a really good foothold here, they aren't fully corporeal. So when a wraith can't physically interact much they're known to possess fae."

I think back to shaking hands with the song wraith. He certainly seemed corporeal. So how many times has he been banished and brought back, then?

Grim continues with his story, explaining how they basically exorcised the wraith from that poor fae. I sip on my lemonade, completely enthralled. He reaches over and takes my hand in his. "Any other questions?" he asks.

I think for a moment and smile. "Does everyone call you Grim?"

He laughs and presses a kiss to my hand. "Not everyone. Some people do call me Hayden. Though I'll admit, it's unusual."

I laugh too. "Dericia would probably end up calling you Hay Hay."

"She calls Taser Tay Tay, right?"

I nod.

"I'm surprised he lets her."

"There really isn't a *let her* when it comes to Reese," I explain.

Grim grins widely at that. "I can totally see that."

"What happened with you and Taser?" I ask, the smile falling from both our faces.

Grim sits up straighter, letting my hand go. His mood seems to darken a bit and I mentally kick myself for having brought it up.

He looks out at the crowd that's formed around the food trucks as everyone tries to grab food before the first bands of the day start their sets. It's the last official day of the festival, and usually the busiest from what I've heard. More of the bigger headliners are playing today, including the Phantoms.

"Taser used to be our rhythm guitarist. Pinkie and him were best friends. I'm not sure how they met, but they were practically joined at the hip. They started this band. And Taser and Bell, they fell for each other, and fell hard—" he looks at me before continuing, "—and then everything fell apart when Bell's bond was activated. She's an air elemental. Anyways, her and Taser swore they wouldn't let the bond get in between them. They were in love." As he tells the story, I picture Taser with Bell, the two of them gazing longingly into each other's eyes. It's heartbreaking.

"But then she met her bondmate, right?" I prompt.

He lets out a sigh. "Yup. She fell in love with her mate, and even though she loved Taser, it wasn't anything compared to that bond. We tried everything to make sure Taser felt like he could stay with us, but he left the band. Pinkie never really forgave him for leaving *him*, you know? There was some other stuff too. A couple of the guys wanted to use a fae as bait for a wraith, and Taser didn't agree. I didn't either, for the record. But anyways, it all got a bit fucked after that. Things were just never the same."

I lay my hand on his forearm. "That sounds really hard to go through. We had a similar issue with Goddess' Trance, minus the wraith-hunting part," I add.

He nods knowingly. "That old lead guitarist you guys had. Your ex. I never really liked him."

I laugh. "How come?"

He pushes a strand of hair behind my ear. "I read an interview with him and your sister—when I was stalking Taser online to see how he was doing—and I dunno, his answers just seemed really narcissistic."

"I'm not at all surprised," I reply.

"I asked around about you, after that scene he made." He gently strokes a finger along my jaw. "I'm sorry you had to go through that. And I know you have a true bond waiting out there for you, but that doesn't mean we can't have something special just for a little while, if that's what you want," he adds at the end.

I let out a breath. I don't know what to say to that. Mostly because I don't actually know what I want. I want to feel powerful. I don't want to keep walking through life starving, but I look at his runeless eyes and can't help but think what's the point?

But just because it won't last forever, doesn't mean it's not worth it. And I like him. He's nice, caring, but also fun and sexy. "I think, maybe, that doesn't sound so bad," I say with a tentative smile.

He returns it, leaning in closer and running his thumb along my lower lip. I make no move to stop him and he leans closer still, his lips brushing against mine. My fingers find his forearm and trail along his arm to his chest, where I plant them. Grim moves his hand to the side of my face, angling me so he can deepen the kiss.

Warmth spreads through me and I kiss him back, winding my fingers into his shirt.

Awareness that we're in public comes flooding through me and I break the kiss, a little breathless. Pink colors my cheeks. I look down at the picnic blanket, catching my breath.

"If you want to take this somewhere a bit more private, I definitely won't mind," Grim says, chuckling as he smooths down my hair.

I glance out at the grassy area we're sitting at. It's still relatively quiet here, most of the festival goers down by the stages and food.

But my gaze lands on a tall figure, dressed all in black from head to toe.

Pisces.

He's looking at Grim and I, but before I can even really register it, he's turned and walking away.

I almost get to my feet, some weird tug in my stomach pushing me to go after him. But to do what? Say hi?

Thank him for the hoodies?

Slap him in the face for being an ass when we first met?

Slap him so hard he cries and I can steal his tears and run off?

"Do you know him well?" Grim asks, his gaze traveling over to me.

"Not really, but he's kind of an ass."

"You could say that," Grim responds, darkly.

"Why don't you like him?" I ask, swiveling to face Grim again.

Grim's eyes follow Pisces as he disappears into the crowd.

"He was with you when you found the body? And earlier when you met the girl during the scavenger hunt?"

"Yeah." He was also in the garden that first night. But he showed up after I'd sat down. There's no way he killed Carly—the redheaded woman. Her dress flashes in my mind. *Unless he was coming back to clean up the evidence?* I shake my head to clear the thought. There's no way.

He nods, his eyes dark again. "It's not the first time a fan of theirs has turned up dead."

"Seriously?" I ask, brows sky high. He nods. *No way, huh?*

He turns his gaze to me, his eyes narrowing. "That's another thing I wanted to tell you. Sometimes the fae council tasks us to investigate fae-related crimes."

"And you think what? That one of the Voracious Maw boys is killing fans?"

He doesn't say anything, his gaze going back to where Pisces has long since disappeared.

"You think Pisces Penrose is killing fans?" I ask incredulously.

"I didn't say that. But there are definitely reasons for you to stay away from him."

"Like what?"

He grimaces and stands up, helping me to my feet. "There are things I can't tell you, but please just be careful around them, alright?"

My thoughts don't stop racing the whole walk back to the townhome. It's pretty clear that Grim suspects someone tied to Voracious Maw in the death of Stephanie—the blonde girl with the blue streaks. He hasn't outright accused them, but warning me to stay away from Pisces seems to indicate he thinks Pisces might be involved. I'm already having enough trouble trying to match Pisces, the sometimes asshole, to the guy who can write and sing such beautiful lyrics. What would Grim say if I told him about meeting Wrath in the garden the first night of the festival?

I turn and walk down the row of townhomes. Just a few porches before mine, I see a group of guys sitting on the steps. "Bliss!" one calls, and I see Simon get up and head down the steps to greet me.

"Hey," I say, as he comes to a stop in front of me and gives me a quick hug. Pisces and Evan sit on opposite sides of the porch, their long legs stretched out in front of them. Benny sits a step below Evan, leaning his head back on Evan's thigh. Evan idly runs his hand through Benny's brown waves and the vampire seems to vibrate with joy.

"All the paperwork for the tour should be sent over," Simon says, looking at me hopefully. "We're still on, right? No one changed their minds?"

"Nope, we're still all set." I look over at Evan, who watches me carefully. I pitch my voice a bit lower, knowing the rest of the guys can still probably overhear me, but that's okay. "I think Amelia was just a bit caught off guard."

Simon nods understandably. "Same for Evan," he says, but a snort from Evan makes me think Simon's just being polite.

Maybe this tour is a huge mistake, but we actually already signed the contracts this morning before we could second guess it.

"Anyways, I should probably go. Got to get ready for the shows tonight," I say, trying to hurry away from them. I see Pisces shift in my periphery.

"Hey wait," he says, his voice so much deeper than I keep thinking it will be. It slides over me in a gentle but firm caress that makes my insides turn to mush. Now that I know he's Wrath, his voice sounds so familiar, exactly how I'd expect Wrath's speaking voice to sound. He walks slowly down the steps and comes and stands next to me. Simon gives us some room, going to chat with the others.

"Yeah?" I ask, wanting to turn and flee, a little bit from awkwardness and also a little bit from Grim's warning, even though I can't get myself to believe it.

He pulls something out of his pocket and hands it to me, unable to look me in the eye. White ribbons fall into my hand. Two completely spotless white ribbons.

"Where did you get these?" I can't help but smile up at him.

"They're the ones you were wearing before. I, uh, cleaned them."

"They're spotless," I say, trying to look him in the eye, but he keeps staring down at his shoes.

"I've a lot of experience in magically cleaning blood out of things."

"Oh right," I say. "Aren't you a vampire?" I almost laugh, but then the memory of his tongue makes me pause. Taser certainly has never used that *neat* trick on me.

Pisces cocks his head to the side. "Erm, no."

"Oh, sorry, I just assumed. You said blood and…" I trail off, feeling stupid. He doesn't have the sharp canines all vamps have, but I also could have sworn I saw him as Wrath use his vampire speed at that masquerade party. Maybe I'd just had too much to drink already by that point.

I inhale, trying to pick up his scent, and I feel even more dumb for thinking he's a vampire. It's not the same slightly metallic, slightly earthy scent. It's something softer. Sea salt and something musky and warm but not overpowering.

"Are you smelling me?" he asks, the corner of his mouth lifting in a smirk.

A blush creeps into my cheeks, and now I'm the one looking at my shoes. "Yes, sorry, I was trying to place your scent, and I realize I've never met anyone like you."

"I'm a siren. Very rare, I'm told," he responds, grimacing.

"I've never met a siren," I say, forgetting about my embarrassment long enough to start to study him anew.

"Well, you strike me as someone who doesn't hang out with Made fae very often."

My gaze hardens at that. Didn't he just say sirens are rare? So why would that indicate I don't hang out with Made fae? "Why do you keep acting like you know anything about me?" My eyes threaten to start unleashing droplets. And those aren't the tears I need. I start to turn, but he reaches out and tugs on my sleeve, getting me to turn back to him.

"Sorry, I shouldn't have said that. It's just Goddess' Trance isn't a mixed band, so I just kind of assumed there's a reason for that."

I shrug. "It's not on purpose," I explain. "We just all grew up together, except for Taser and Blake."

He nods in understanding. "I guess I was just thinking about your old guitarist. He hates Made fae."

My hand goes to my neck at the mention of Jordan. Pisces' eyes track the movement and his throat bobs. "Yeah, well, that's one of the reasons he's not in our band anymore."

"What are the other reasons?" Pisces asks, his voice soft and gentle. His gaze travels back to mine.

I let out a hollow laugh. "You got a few hours? It's a long story." I look down to the ribbons in my hand and let out a sigh. "Thanks for cleaning these," I say. It actually was very thoughtful of him. I could always get more, but these ones are special. Liz and Amelia got them for me one year for my birthday.

"Sure," is all he says. He continues to stand there, towering over me.

I smack my hand to my forehead. "Your hoodies! I keep forgetting to get them back to you!" I turn towards the townhouse but pause and look over my shoulder. "Come on, I'll go grab them."

"Erm, okay." He follows me at a little bit of a distance, as if he's too good to walk next to me. I roll my eyes, even though he can't see it.

We enter the townhouse a few doors down from where Voracious Maw is staying and I groan as I see all the band members gathered around the living room. "Hey, Bliss," Dericia calls cheerily. "How was your date with the super sexy Grim? Oh, did you bring him back to recharge—" She breaks off as Pisces, not Grim, follows in after me.

"Well, I wasn't expecting that," Taser says with a chuckle, patting Dericia on the forearm.

Amelia just arches her brows at me in question and I ignore all of them. "Wait here," I call to Pisces as I race up the stairs. I grab both his hoodies and race back down, coming to a stop before him in the entryway. I hand over the black hoodies, a little sad to see them go.

He doesn't take them immediately. I wave the bundle towards him, trying to get his attention. He shakes his head as if he just mentally went somewhere else and focuses on what I'm offering him.

"I guess you can't wear another man's clothing if you're dating Grim now," he says quietly.

"I'm not," I say quickly, too quickly. He looks at me, his head tilting in that perpetual question. He knows that I know that he saw me kissing Grim earlier. "I mean, well, we went on one date, that's all."

"Hmm." He takes the hoodies, tucking them under his arm and turning to the rest of the band. "Have a good show tonight," he says and heads out the door. I go out after him, but I don't have anything to say so I just watch as he heads down the steps, throwing one last glance my way as he strides back to his townhome.

"Mystery solved." Blake quietly sniggers to Tubbs, who tries to keep in a laugh but blurts it out.

"You were hooking up with Pisces Penrose?" An incredulous look passes over Tubbs' face. "I'm a bit impressed, actually."

"Please, why be impressed? He's the one who won the lottery hooking up with Bliss, not the other way around," Amelia says, swiping up a magazine from the coffee table and swatting Tubbs on the head with it.

"What? He's sexy, and incredibly talented, and even I can appreciate the abs— What?" he yelps as Amelia continues to swat him.

"Bliss is sexy and incredibly talented and she has amazing tits and an amazing ass so that lanky, nerdy, too tall douche should be throwing himself at her feet."

"Amelia, please," I say, going to take the magazine away from her. "You might accidentally hit him in the eye and then he won't be able to play the show…"

I trail off as Tubbs breaks down in a fit of coughing. At first I think he's just laughing too hard.

Blake claps him on the back. "You okay, man?"

Taser gets up, going over to Tubbs, but he jumps back as Tubbs starts vomiting blood all over the floor.

"Okay, I swear I did not hit him that hard," Amelia says jokingly, but her eyes reveal concern as she takes in all the blood.

Tubbs looks around the room, eyes growing wider as blood starts to drip from his mouth onto the floor. He continues to cough and can't seem to stop.

"Shit, we need a healer fast," Taser says, looking from me to Amelia. None of us are healers. But I think I know who is.

"What the fuck is happening?" Amelia goes to stand behind Tubbs, supporting a bit of his weight as he slumps in his seat.

"Did he catch something?" I ask, but an illness coming on this suddenly in fae isn't something I've ever seen before. To Tubbs I ask, "When was the last time you recharged your powers?"

He doesn't respond, eyes closing in pain as he coughs up more blood.

"He recharged this morning," Taser answers for him. "We definitely need a healer."

"There's a first aid booth down at the festival," Blake says, but we so don't have time for that.

"I'll be right back." I race off to the nearest healer we have.

CHAPTER THIRTY-FOUR

BLISS

I HAMMER MY FIST ON THE DOOR, THREE TOWNHOMES OVER. IT TAKES a while for anyone to answer, but finally Simon comes to the door, a scared, wild look in his eyes. "Bliss?" Surprise coats his voice.

I push my way in. "I need to speak with Evan, please. We need a healer, fast."

"About that," Simon says, turning to look into the living room.

I follow his gaze and gasp in shock. Evan is sitting on the floor, slumped against the couch, sweat coating his skin, and blood dripping down his chin, just like Tubbs.

Lily—the blonde fae that grabbed me some clothes the other day—kneels next to him, and I can feel the hum of magic as she heals him.

Except that it's not working.

He doesn't seem to be getting any better.

My wide eyes meet Pisces' as he looks over at me.

He mirrors Simon's scared expression.

"What the hell is happening?" I ask.

"No idea. One minute he was fine, the next, blood everywhere," Simon informs me.

"Tubbs, our drummer, he's—" I motion at Evan, "—he's in the

same condition." I swallow, trying to calm myself. "Are you going to be able to heal him?" I ask Lily.

She looks just as scared and concerned as everyone else. "I'm not sure, he's not responding to my magic."

I hear a groan and notice Niamh sitting upright on the other couch, also coughing up blood. Shaun is trying to get her to lie down, but she's fighting him. "I'm fine," she growls out in between spitting up more blood.

"Two of them?" I ask. Fuck.

Pisces comes over and stands next to me. "What type of fae is Tubbs?"

"An earth nymph," I say, and Pisces frowns.

"What?" I ask. I can see his thoughts swirling.

Shaun comes over to us as well, his hand rubbing at his temples. "This is something beyond just an illness."

"I'm completely useless here," Lily announces, standing up. She goes to Gwen, murmuring something soft into her hair. Gwen curls inward on herself, eyes traveling back and forth between Evan and Niamh.

"I think they've been hexed." Shaun rubs a hand over his face. His hair looks like he's run his hands through it multiple times. "They don't have much time. We need to figure out some sort of anti-spell."

Aunt Liz.

She could help us. I fish out my phone and call her. She answers immediately.

"Bliss! How are you? It's actually funny you just called—"

"Liz, I need your help," I say, interrupting her.

"What's going on?" Immediately her tone is serious.

"Tubbs, and a couple other friends, it's like they've been hexed. They're coughing up blood and we've tried healing them, but it's not working."

"They haven't improved at all?"

"No, in fact, they seem worse." I look back to Evan and Niamh. "Can you tell us about a spell, or—"

She cuts me off. "I'll be there in about five minutes."

"What?"

"I came to the festival! I wasn't gonna miss all of Amelia's shows, especially not your first gig back as their band manager. I just got here."

My mind spins with the synchronicity. Maybe the stars are looking out for us after all. I give Liz directions to the townhomes, instructing her to come here.

"My aunt, she's good with this type of thing. She's already on her way." I look at Pisces. "Can you go get the others? Have them bring Tubbs here? Better to move him than both of them." Evan and Niamh are coughing up even more blood now, barely any breaks between fits. Benny crouches down between them with damp towels, trying to comfort them as much as possible.

Pisces nods and without a word he's gone, racing down the street to the others. I told them I'd be right back, but I wasn't expecting to stumble in on this.

Aunt Liz arrives first. I let her in, sweeping the door wide open, and glance down the street to see Pisces and Taser helping Tubbs walk. He stumbles and they switch to carrying him between them.

Amelia, Reese, and the rest of the band is behind them.

Liz has immediately gone to her patients. "Bliss!" she calls. "Get my bag."

I take her duffle bag she's brought with her. She takes out a leather case and sets it down on the coffee table, unrolling the straps that bind it closed. "Thank the stars I didn't leave this at home." She glances at me and then at all the other faces watching her. "Give them all some room, everyone, okay?"

She takes Evan's wrist, checking his pulse, doing the same for Niamh. "Bliss, mix me up some bloodroot." I immediately sit down to do as asked.

"What's bloodroot?" Simon asks, curiously watching, though remaining a good distance away as per Liz's orders.

"It'll slow whatever it is that's attacking them. Help replenish the blood they've lost."

I run to the kitchen, mix the ground bloodroot powder with water, and separate it out into two glasses. Liz gives one to Evan. I give one to Niamh.

Finally, Pisces and Taser get Tubbs into one of the armchairs, though they have to support him so he doesn't topple forward. I go back and mix up one other glass of the tonic for Tubbs. I catch Amelia's eyes. They've gone straight to Evan. She looks terrified.

"He'll be alright. Liz is helping them. They'll all be okay," I tell Amelia, giving her arm a squeeze. I go to Tubbs, helping him drink the bloodroot.

Liz straightens up. "Okay, so now we need to figure out exactly what this hex is. How the hell did someone get all three of them?"

"Could it be something they ate?" Simon asks. "Like food poisoning?"

Liz shakes her head. "No, this was deliberate, and targeted." Her eyes zero in on the inside of the jacket Evan is wearing. Shaun helps Evan out of the bloodstained jacket.

Liz holds it inside out and points to something smudged on the inside. On closer inspection it looks like some sort of wax seal with a pentagram and some other symbol etched into it. "This is the culprit. It's a blood-clotting hex."

"How do we stop it?" I ask.

Liz sets about mixing up some powders and casts an enchantment over it. The powder shifts as if moved by an invisible wind. She sprinkles it over Evan and the little wax hex seal. The seal breaks apart upon contact. She turns to Niamh. "We need to find that wax seal. It'll have been placed on her person."

Simon and Gwen start to inspect her clothes. "Got it!" Gwen says, pointing to the collar of Niamh's button-up shirt. Liz shakes the powder over her too, making sure to get some of the wax seal. Getting the picture, Taser and Pisces start inspecting Tubbs, getting more and more frantic as they can't find it.

"It's not here!" Taser yells, looking widely at Liz. "What do we do?"

"Remain calm. It has to be on his person. It wouldn't have fallen off once attached."

They continue to look but neither can seem to find it. Liz and Amelia take over, pushing the boys out of the way. They search Tubbs' pockets, and Blake and Taser even lift Tubbs out of the chair so we can make sure it's not stuck to his back somewhere, but we see nothing.

"Wait," I say, my gaze landing on his shoes. "Hold up his feet!"

And sure enough, there on the bottom of his shoe is the wax seal. Liz sprinkles the concoction on it and over the rest of Tubbs.

We all look expectantly at her. "They'll be fine now, but they're going to have to sleep a lot. This hex takes a lot out of a fae."

"How do you know so much about this?" Shaun asks, arching a brow at her.

She grins at him. "I used to work for the council. Specialized in hunting down fae who put hexes on people."

Simon watches Liz with wide eyes. "Fuck, that's cool."

"Badass," Benny agrees.

Shaun hauls Evan onto the couch and Amelia quietly moves Evan's feet onto it. She brings a blanket up over him and gazes down at his peaceful but still blood-covered face. "We should probably get them cleaned up— Oh stars!" she exclaims. She whirls around and faces everyone. "The shows! We're both fucked," she says, looking at Pisces.

He frowns, glancing at all three of the hexed musicians, his hand running along his jaw. I might notice how it's freshly shaven. "We're out a bassist and a backup vocalist."

"And we're out a fucking drummer," Amelia laments, coming to me and throwing herself around me. "We're gonna have to back out of tonight's show. We can't play without a drummer."

I look over at Tubbs. Taser is cleaning off his face with a warm wash cloth. "I'll let the festival know," I say, my shoulders slouching. I start to look up the number for our contact at the festival on my phone.

"Hold on," Pisces murmurs, taking my phone out of my hands.

"You're down a drummer; we have a drummer," Pisces continues, holding my phone out of reach as I stand on my tiptoes, trying to grab it back.

"Thanks for rubbing that in," I huff out, rolling my eyes.

He stares at me, and even though his hair falls a bit into his eyes, I can see an arched brow. "We're down a backup vocalist and a bassist, you have a singer and a bassist." He looks pointedly at the group gathered around listening. "Let's trade. Dericia fills in for Evan, Amelia fills in for Niamh, and Shaun will drum for Goddess' Trance."

Everyone looks at him, and I swear all our mouths have dropped. "Are you insane?" Shaun finally says, laughing. "It would take me days to learn just a few of their songs, not to mention a whole set list."

"Yeah, and like, I could definitely learn your whole set list in a day, because your bass lines aren't super complicated—" Dericia says.

"Gee, thanks," Pisces quips.

"—but no way will I have them down in the two hours we have left," Dericia finishes.

"It was a good suggestion, Sces, but not everyone is as musically gifted as you that they can pick things up that quickly," Benny says, swinging an arm around Pisces' torso, not being tall enough to go around his shoulders.

Pisces looks down at the guitarist. "Remember that super dumb, ridiculous test that the fae council makes all adult kindreds take in order to register with them?"

"Yeah," Benny says, eyebrows knitting together.

"Remember how Evan was supposed to tutor Simon, but Simon wasn't really getting any of it?"

"Yeah..."

"And remember how Evan just ended up giving him that learning potion?"

Liz snaps her fingers. "Learning potion! That's just a bit of waterberry, lemon zest, and worm root."

"Do you have any in that pouch of yours?" Pisces asks.

Shaun raises his brows at Simon. "You cheated on your registration test?"

Simon smirks at him. "It wasn't my idea. Blame Evan. I didn't even know it was an option until he brought it up."

Shaun considers his friend for a minute. "That explains why you got such a good score."

Simon just shrugs, a full grin touching his lips.

"I've got all the necessary ingredients. I just need a bowl and something to mix it up with," Liz says, rocking back on her heels in front of the coffee table.

A few minutes later three different glasses containing the learning potion sit on the coffee table.

"How does this work?" Reese asks, lifting up one of the glasses and giving it a sniff, instantly making a face at it. "How badly do you need a bassist, because I do *not* want to drink this."

Liz rolls her eyes at her. "Here's a chaser," she says, handing Dericia a juice bottle. "You'll drink the potion and place your hand on Evan's temple. Set your intention to learn the songs on the set list and then it'll be done."

"We'll have to wake them up. It works better with consent, correct?" Pisces asks, looking at Liz for confirmation. "And it doesn't last more than a few hours," he reminds us.

Liz nods and claps her hands together. "Alright. Reese, Amelia, Shaun, get your potions ready and stand next to your buddy."

"Hold on," Amelia says. "I can't do this."

"Really, Amelia, the taste isn't that ba—"

"No, I mean I can't do this." Amelia motions to her throat. "I can't sing two shows." She looks at Pisces for backup. "It would be hell on my voice. Do you really need a backup singer?"

"Niamh really elevates the sound, and we don't have her vocals pre-recorded," Gwen says.

Amelia nods. "Then use Bliss. She's got an amazing voice too."

"Amelia!" I squeak out. I shake my head. "I can't do that. On stage? In front of people? No, absolutely not."

"You'll be masked," Pisces says softly from behind me, finally handing back my phone. I continue to shake my head.

"I—"

"Bliss, just do it," Amelia says, rolling her eyes. "It'll be fun and, I dunno, Liz can make you some sort of confidence potion or something, right?"

Liz laughs a bit. "Bliss, you don't need one. You've got a beautiful voice."

I fidget with my phone in my hands, wishing I had on one of Pisces' hoodies with the frayed drawstrings to play with.

"It's okay," Pisces says, nudging my arm to draw my gaze to him. "We'll just go without a backup vocalist. It's not a big deal." He looks to Gwen, who nods but frowns, as if she doesn't agree.

I open my mouth to thank him but close it. I'll be wearing a mask. No one will know who I am. No one will see how pink my cheeks will no doubt turn.

"Fine," I say, squaring my shoulders. "I'll do it."

Pisces studies me, a soft smile on his face, but it's not him that I look at. I look at Amelia as she hands me the potion. "You'll do amazing, Bliss." She smiles at me. "Okay, team," she says after I take the potion from her, clapping her hands together like a cheerleader. "Let's fucking go!"

Liz and Amelia rouse the three hexed fae just enough for them to consent to letting us learn from them. Dericia, Shaun, and I down our potions. I shudder as the sludge goes down my throat. It tastes like mud and ash, or at least what I assume those would taste like since I don't make a habit of eating those things. I place my hand on Niamh's temple, thinking of the songs on Voracious Maw's set list. Ones I already know fairly well, since I listen to them on repeat so often. The intricacies of how Pisces wants the backup vocals to sound comes flowing to me. I can *hear* the notes Niamh hits, feel the emotion Pisces wants each song to evoke.

All of a sudden the connection is broken. I know the movements Niamh makes while she's doing her sultry dances up on the platform. I know what to do between segments of the show. I know how often Niamh usually drinks water to keep her vocal cords lubricated, but not too much so that she has to pee before the show is over. I know her vocal warm-up routine.

I look over to Dericia and Shaun and can see a similar look of awe on their faces.

"This is so fucking dope," Dericia says, grinning widely. She high-fives Shaun and looks around at the other guys, pointing to Benny. "Am I expected to make out with Benny? Evan showed me the usual shenanigans they do during 'You Want Me.'" She arches a brow at Benny and Pisces.

Benny shrugs. "I have no problem with that," he says, grinning so wide his vampire canines are on full display.

"Well, of course you wouldn't." Dericia shrugs, flipping her braids over her shoulder.

Shaun snorts and shakes his head. He extends his hand to Reese. "Welcome aboard, substitute Eerie."

CHAPTER THIRTY-FIVE

PISCES

I watch from backstage as Goddess' Trance does their sound check. As per usual they sound amazing. When Simon suggested them as our opener for the tour, I immediately said yes. There isn't another band I'd have picked over them. But in the days after, I wondered if I'd made a huge mistake. Not only is there the issue with Evan and Amelia, but Bliss is a constant irritation to me.

My mind—without my permission—continually wanders back to that day I helped heal her. My eyes—again without my permission—seek her out, loving the dip of her hourglass figure, the softness of her abdomen, and her thick thighs that I keep thinking about being in between.

She is sure to be a distraction during the tour.

But not in the way my cock wants.

Because she's standing with Grim, his arm around her.

Shaun glances over at me and I motion to our front-of-house engineer, Marcus, to follow me over to the drums. I pass Grim and Bliss as they stand there watching the sound check.

"Did you report the hexes?" he asks her.

"My aunt did. She still has some contacts in the fae council. She's going to send them what's left of the wax seals."

My arm brushes Bliss' as I pass. She stares at me and I inhale sharply and grit my teeth.

I keep going without saying anything, feeling her eyes on my back. Shaun gets up from the drum kit and nods his head in approval.

"It'll work," he says, coming to stand next to me and Marcus.

They discuss inputs and other things with Taser, but I'm not listening. I keep looking over my shoulder at Bliss and Grim. They seem to be arguing about something, but I can't hear from here.

Fifteen minutes later, Goddess' Trance's set starts. Amelia strides out onto the stage, the crowd spotting her immediately. There are appreciative whistles, lots of cheering, and more than one sign out in the crowd asking if she'll marry them.

I can't help but grin. This band is going to go far. I can feel it.

Amelia takes the microphone. Dericia, Taser, and Blake head out with their instruments, urging the crowd on.

"We've got a special treat for you all tonight," Amelia yells into the mic, hyping up the crowd. "Our drummer came down with food poisoning, but we're grateful to have a very special guest fill in for him this evening! Give it up for Mist!"

Mist strides out, masked up and hands painted with our trademark blue-black body paint. He holds his arms up, each holding a drumstick, and the fans lose their shit. Cheering mixes with full-on feral screams as Mist's fanbase, who came out early to see Goddess' Trance, gets the best surprise they could have ever hoped for.

Mist takes his seat at Tubbs' kit and counts down for the first song, seamlessly merging his own skill with the knowledge Tubbs was able to pass to him through the learning potion.

CHAPTER THIRTY-SIX

BLISS

Thankfully, I'm able to watch Goddess' Trance's full set before I need to do my vocal warm-ups and start getting ready. As if I've done this countless times, I find my way over to the trailer backstage.

As I enter, Simon waves me over. "Bliss, you're up for makeup."

"Makeup?" I ask.

He nods. "You need to be painted just like the boys."

"Let her get dressed first," Gwen says, motioning me over to a changing room.

I change into Niamh's ensemble—a gorgeous black lacy dress that almost perfectly matches Wrath's shroud. It hugs my curves, flowing down to brush the floor. Lacy sleeves run down to my wrists. My hair is up in a half ponytail, the white ribbon Pisces gave back to me holding it in place. When I exit the changing room, Gwen hands me Niamh's mask. It's similar to the ones Eerie, Poison, and Mist wear, except it only covers my eyes and the bridge of my nose, allowing me to sing. The multiple straps look too complicated for me to attempt to put on myself without ruining my hair, so I clutch it, afraid to drop it.

Gwen flitters off somewhere else—a ton of stage manager tasks to take care of—and Benny is currently painting Pisces' chest, something I should not be watching because my eyes can't seem to break from where Benny's hand is applying paint over Pisces' pecs.

I swallow thickly, my eddying power reserve begging me to find release from Pisces again.

My gaze drifts down his chest, to where his pants are slung low on his hips. Benny has already painted there. But up close I can see the slight V that urges my eyes lower. The way his pants cling to him, it's clear he's *big*. And the obvious thought that follows that is how much bigger he'd be if I ran my tongue over—

"My mask is up here, darling."

My eyes snap to the eye holes in Wrath's mask, as a blush creeps over my skin.

He's smirking at me and lifts his pointer finger, wagging it at me. Benny grins widely, looking between us.

"Well, that about does it," Benny says, getting the last patches of skin on Wrath's neck and collarbone, moving the pendant he always wears aside to paint underneath it. "I'll do the scales later." He excuses himself and goes to change into his outfit for the show, leaving Wrath and I there staring at each other.

"Do you need help with yours?" Wrath asks me, his voice growing deeper.

I nod. Wrath brings the paint over. "It's better to do the paint first, then the mask."

He covers two fingers with paint and lifts them to my cheek. It's a bit cool to the touch, but if he notices my shudder, he doesn't react. He swipes it along one cheek and then the other, and expertly blends the paint out over my face. His fingers run along my jawline, the touch sending warmth down my body. I can feel the callouses on his fingers that guitar strings have given him over the years.

He taps my bottom lip once. "Niamh usually wears a dark red lip color." I nod. I'll add some after.

He moves the paint down my neck, lifting the collar of my dress to make sure the paint doesn't have a gap.

"Hands," he orders softly. I place one in his and he paints it up to my wrist. He does the same to the other.

And all too soon, he's done.

He releases my hands and steps back, looking me over.

I catch my breath. "Well, will I pass as Niamh?" I ask shakily. Stars, his hands felt good.

He smiles and shakes his head. "She's a bit taller than you. I'm sure some of our more serious fans will spot the difference." He strokes his jaw in thought for a moment and tugs my ribbon free, letting my hair cascade in waves down my back. "Hold out your arm," he commands, and I obey. He wraps the white ribbon around my wrist.

Wrath takes my fingers in his hand as if he's about to plant a kiss on my knuckles. But he just holds my hand. I can't tell where he's looking.

"Are you nervous?" he asks.

I half smile. "Not anymore. With the learning potion it almost feels as if I've done this before."

"Good." He smiles at me and drops my hand. "Is Grim going to watch?"

"Yeah, he's hanging out backstage still," I say. "We're not together," I add for some reason. Not that it's any of his business.

"Does he know that?"

"Of course. He knows that, um— Well, maybe eventually I'll find my bondmate, so..."

Wrath's mouth ticks to the side, almost a frown. "Right."

I hate that he's upset about that. I reach out, gripping the front of his black robe. The material is soft and light. I want to say something but words escape me. I can hear his breath grow heavier.

He steps closer, pushing me against the counter.

I look up into his mask, trying to see through the gaps in the skeleton fingers, even though the material underneath is too opaque. My gaze travels south, to his lips. They're painted with the same blue-black paint, but I can still see how he pulls in his bottom lip, as if he's trying not to say anything.

He fails. "Bliss." It's a murmur, barely audible, but I step forward, coming up on to my tiptoes.

I'm too short to close the distance, but he doesn't lean forward. I can tell from the set of his mouth he's fighting to keep what little distance between us that we have left.

"Hey, Wrath," Reese calls from the doorway. "I can't fit my braids into the mask."

Wrath quickly takes two steps back and I can feel a blush creeping in. Reese looks between the two of us, grinning from ear to ear. "Sorry to interrupt." She pauses and Wrath coughs uncomfortably. "No one is gonna mistake me for a six five British bassist, though, anyways."

Reese holds up a black silky material that the boys usually wear underneath their masks to cover their hair. I noticed in recent shows that Eerie had ditched it, allowing his hair to flow freely.

Wrath nods. "Leave your braids out, then. I'd like people to know who you are."

She grins at him. "Awesome," she replies. "I'm so fucking pumped for this!"

Reese skips out of the room. I reach for my mask. "I guess it's time to go," I say, holding the mask out for Pisces to help put on. He secures it swiftly, making sure the straps are tight but not too tight. He places his thumb on my bottom lip, and I think he's going to kiss me. He leans in closer.

"Red lips, remember?"

Then he's gone from the room and I let out a sigh, feeling the pulsing between my legs and wishing Reese hadn't interrupted.

But it's a good thing.

Because he's not my mate.

I've always loved Voracious Maw's performances. But it is so much better being onstage with them during one. For once in my life I can understand why people enjoy being the center of attention. There's a thrill to it. Though without the mask I wear, I'd feel way too exposed to be under the spotlight. The show begins the usual way, always with a song that starts off a bit slow so that Wrath can prowl out onto the stage, towering over the crowd. He walks up to the microphone stand, plucking the mic off it and coming to stand in front of the crowd as he starts to sing.

The bass line starts in and Dericia walks in from the other side of the stage, flipping her braids around, drawing audible gasps and cheers from the crowd as they realize she's filling in for Eerie, and that Eerie must have gotten food poisoning too.

The guitar starts in as Poison enters stage left. Again a round of cheers erupts, almost drowning out Wrath's vocals. Mist appears behind the drum kit up on a platform behind Poison, and the crowd loses their minds again. I follow Gwen's direction as she motions for me to ascend the platform behind where Eerie normally plays. I take my place at the mic stand, just before my part begins.

A thrill goes through me as the crowd cheers at seeing me up there as well.

I begin harmonizing with Wrath's voice and he startles a bit, his voice faltering almost imperceptibly as he turns around and looks up at me on the platform. I wonder if I've messed up, but then I spot his grin, his white teeth flashing against the dark body paint that covers his lips.

The song ends with a flourish, my arms matching the sultry movements I learned from Niamh. Simon walks out onto the stage as the cheering starts to subside, causing another round to start up again. Wrath hands the microphone to Simon, who waves to the crowd.

"How's everyone doing?" he says, greeting the crowd. "Listen, we've obviously got a little bit of a change up here." He motions to Reese. "Our bassist is noticeably more attractive than usual." He grins. The crowd cheers in agreement, and I can't help but think Simon is so going to pay for that comment once Evan hears.

"All jokes aside," Simon continues, "our bassist, Eerie, and our usual backup vocalist are sleeping off a nasty bout of food poisoning. They'll be fine, but we're honored to have some pretty spectacular fills in from Goddess' Trance's band and crew with us tonight. Give them a warm welcome!"

The crowd does as told. I give a little wave and Dericia whips her braids around, mimicking how Eerie usually head bangs. Simon hands the microphone back to Wrath and the stage lights dim, even though the sky still holds onto the sun.

An atmospheric backing track to one of Voracious Maw's heaviest songs begins playing and Wrath's screams fill the stage, an offering of fury to the stars.

By the time we're halfway through the set, I realize I'm quite enjoying this. My arms ache a bit from all the slow sultry dancing I'm doing up on the platform, but I'm having a hard time keeping the smile from taking over my face.

When Wrath starts singing my favorite song, I stop trying. I realize I'm not the only one having a blast. Reese spins around, braids twirling around, as she imitates Eerie. I bet she's smiling ear to ear under the mask.

I catch sight of Amelia and Liz backstage. They wave at me and I shoot my smile their way. As Poison starts in on a beautiful guitar solo, Wrath prowls my way, hoisting himself up onto the platform; quite the feat, considering how far off the ground it is.

I think he's just going to sit and chill with me for a little bit, but instead he gets to his feet, coming and standing behind me, which makes my breath hitch. Good thing I'm just dancing during this part of the song. I falter a bit but continue swaying my arms and hips even as Wrath slides his arm around my front, placing his hand at the column of my throat. His other hand goes to my hip as he pulls me back into him. I angle my head up and look at him. He lowers his mouth to my neck, giving me a quick kiss, the edges of his mask biting into my skin just briefly.

"You sound divine," he murmurs, a faint smile touching his lips.

With that he's gone, lowering his hand to the edge of the platform and jumping off it. He lands a bit unsteadily on his feet but runs back to the microphone and pulls it off its stand, nearly missing the start of the next verse.

I breathe out a sigh of relief and begin another round of harmonies. I can still feel where his long fingers gripped me. Did he come up here just to tell me I'm doing a good job? Gratitude swells in my chest at how kind the gesture is.

The rest of the show passes too quickly. Before I know it, I'm wedged in between Poison and Reese as we all bow. The crowd throws flowers and gifts and other presents up to the stage—I'm pretty sure I see men's boxer briefs thrown towards Reese's side. Reese and I make our way off stage, leaving the boys to continue to bask in the crowd's admiration.

Wrath bows low to the crowd, expressing his gratitude to them. Poison and Mist throw things out to the crowd. I can make out drumsticks and guitar picks being tossed through the air, and hands all grasping for the chance to catch one. Poison even lowers himself, reaching out to a fan and clasping their hands, thanking them for their support.

Everyone is so loving here, I can't help the beaming smile on my face as I make my way to Amelia and throw my arms around my sister. "Thank you for encouraging me to do that. I loved it!"

"She's caught the bug now," Amelia says to Liz, grinning as well as she pulls me into a firm hug. "I've always thought you were wasting your voice not getting into performing."

I shrug. "I don't think it'll ever be serious with me and singing, but maybe I can fill in every once and while."

Amelia squeezes me. "Actually, I was thinking maybe Goddess' Trance needs a backup singer."

I laugh. "Nah, I don't think so. Without me as a band manager you guys would be hopeless," I tease.

Arms reach around my middle as I'm swept upwards in a strong pair of arms. I struggle a bit until I hear Grim's reassuring laugh. "Hey, babe," he says in my ear. "You were incredible up there. I had no idea you could sing."

He puts me down on my unsteady feet and spins me around to face him. I clutch his forearms to steady myself and see the white ribbon still fixed to my wrist. My stomach drops as I look at Grim. Part of me is realizing I don't want to be celebrating with him. My eyes wander off to my right, where I see Wrath giving Reese a quick hug. He turns to Mist and practically picks him up in celebration.

I can't help but wonder what it would feel like for him to come over and wrap me up in his arms, not to comfort me like he did that night in the maze, but in celebration.

Grim follows my gaze and reaches out, gripping my chin gently between his thumb and forefinger. "Bliss," he says softly. "Remember what I told you."

I return his serious look and nod. Except I can't exactly stay away from Pisces Penrose. Not since we'll be going on tour with him.

A phone rings. Liz pulls out her phone and heads further backstage to get away from the noise.

I disentangle myself from Grim, wanting to find Wrath, and stars—I don't know. Even if nothing can come of this, I think, I think I want to see where it could lead. I think he feels the same way. I think he wants to find out what's between us.

And I know the wraith is up to something. I know this is what I am *supposed* to be doing, but now I want it for myself, not for whatever his plan is.

I search for him. I'll pull him aside. I'll kiss him, even if our masks get in the way. And I'll see if he kisses me back.

Maybe.

As I look around for him, I can feel doubt and insecurity starting to creep in. What if he doesn't kiss me back?

I don't think I could survive the rejection.

A moment later, a scream makes my blood run cold. I tense as we all look towards the spot behind the stage. Before I can even think about it, I take off running, still in my costume, mask and all.

Amelia and Grim call out after me and multiple sets of shoes pound on the concrete. Whether they're running after me, or running to where the scream came from, I don't know.

I make it there first.

Gwen stands there with her hands over her mouth, frozen in place, eyes locked on a body that's crumpled a few feet away from her.

I come to a halt next to her, reaching out and grasping her arm. "Gwen, what happened?"

Wrath reaches us next, coming to stand in front of Gwen and I, shielding us from the body. It's so much worse than I could have imagined. Stars, it's horrible. I'm not an expert, but it looks like the woman fell from the stage's scaffolding. I look up at the metal beams constructed high above us and immediately wish I hadn't. It's a very long way down.

"Bliss," Wrath says softly, bringing my gaze to his mask. I can't see his eyes, so mine end up resting on his lips again. "Take Gwen over there." He motions to where there's a ledge in the large stairwell we're in. I do, steering the other girl over so she can lean against the wall. She stares at her feet now.

"What happened?" I ask again.

She shakes her head. "I came down here because I heard a noise. I thought maybe I saw Simon. But when I got here…" She trails off, waving her hand towards the body, where Grim and a few other Phantoms have now gathered. Simon, Poison, and Amelia have also made their way down, along with my aunt.

Liz is still on the phone, exchanging words with someone.

Heated shouts erupt as Grim roughly shoves Wrath backwards. Poison and Simon come to his aid just in time, preventing him from tripping over himself. "What the fuck?" Simon spits out.

"Get him the fuck out of here!" Grim snarls. "This is a crime scene."

"What are you? A cop?" Simon quips, annoyed.

"Kind of," Grim replies, with a savage smile. "And I'm pretty sure he did this." He lifts a finger and points it at Wrath.

Pinkie comes to stand next to Grim, a pair of iron shackles

materializing in his hands. "Take him into custody," Grim instructs Pinkie.

"Wait!" I shout, running over and wedging myself between Wrath and Grim. "How do you know he did this? You told me yourself you don't have any evidence."

"You knew this fucker was investigating me?" Wrath seethes. I glare at him, trying to tell him to shut the fuck up before he gets himself dug into an even deeper hole.

"By the looks of it, this human was killed before Voracious Maw went on stage. And once again they're a Voracious Maw fan," Stormy says from where she's kneeling down beside the body.

I shake my head. "None of that proves anything."

"He had access, and this is the fourth body tied to the band that's been discovered. Who knows how many more there are?" Pinkie says, again as if any of that is evidence.

"Fourth body?" Simon asks.

Grim lists out each of the murders. The garden. The maze. And now here.

"What's the fourth?" I ask, afraid to hear the answer.

"Years ago. After a Voracious Maw concert in Seattle."

"That was natural causes," Taser responds.

"That's what the fae constabulary wanted people to think."

"Can you tell time of death?" I ask Stormy, ignoring Grim and Taser as they argue about the murders being tied together.

She nods at me, holding her hands out and performing some sort of magic incantation to get the time of death. I've watched enough fae detective shows in my life that I know it's possible.

She glances back up at Grim. "Six forty-five."

"That's fifteen minutes before our set started," I point out.

"So?" Pinkie asks.

"Wrath couldn't have done this."

"How do you know, Bliss?" Grim asks.

I shift uncomfortably on my feet, but I steel myself and pull my chin up. "Because he was with me. In the trailer. He was helping me to finish getting ready."

"Is that all?" Grim asks, his brows rounding.

"Anything else isn't your business," I say simply, shrugging.

Wrath lets out a low rumble from behind me as if in agreement.

Grim takes a few steps away to clear his head, or shake off whatever emotions he's feeling.

"And afterwards?" Stormy asks.

"Then we were all together, waiting to go on stage." A chorus of murmured agreement goes through my friends.

Grim frowns, looking back to the body.

"Besides," Wrath hisses out from behind me. "I'm a fucking siren, that's not how I feed. Maybe you should get your facts straight before you accuse a fae of murder."

"There's one more thing," Stormy says. Grim gives her a warning to stop, but she ignores him. She pulls out a piece of paper from the human's pocket. "We've found a similar note on all of the bodies."

She unfolds the note with her gloved hands and holds it up so Wrath and I can both read it. Everyone else gathers closer, trying to see what it says.

Come meet me by the tour bus before the show
   –Wrath

"What the fuck?" Wrath says, shaking his head. "I didn't write that."

"Someone is impersonating you, then," Stormy says, eyeing Grim as he lets out a sigh.

"A Frath?" Simon asks, eyes wide. He slaps a hand over his mouth with a groan. "Pretend I didn't say that."

"It wouldn't be the first time," Wrath responds.

"What do you mean?" Pinkie asks.

"People like to imitate our costumes," Poison supplies. "There was one time where a fake Wrath—a Frath, as you called it—" he looks at Simon, "—almost got backstage because everyone just assumed it was the real guy."

"You think someone is dressing up as Wrath to lure women in and kill them?" Amelia asks. Liz has finally gotten off the phone. She comes and stands next to my sister.

"Well, we aren't sure about the dressing up part, but—" Pinkie starts to explain.

"Wait," I say, looking to Grim, but he doesn't look at me, so I address Pinkie instead. "At the party the first night. I saw Wrath standing in line for drinks at the masquerade ball and then like five seconds later he was standing next to Eerie across the room. I thought he was a vampire so I didn't think much of it at the time, but what if there were two of them?"

"Someone's been impersonating me?" Wrath mutters. Poison comes and wraps his arm around his friend.

"I think I might know who," Liz says, holding up her cell.

"Who?" Simon asks, looking from Wrath to Liz, concern forming lines on his forehead. "We gotta find them and make sure this doesn't happen again." He looks over at the body and I swear his skin turns green. He makes a noise that sounds like a precursor to vomiting and takes a step away.

Liz ignores him and looks at Grim. "I just got off the phone with Urvine. You know him?"

Grim nods. "He's our liaison with the council. Gives us jobs sometimes."

"I had him trace that hex seal. Its magical signature and style matches someone they have on record exactly."

"Who?"

"Jinx Belcross."

Jinx?

Wait, could Jordan be involved in this too? Are the hexes and the murders connected?

"You guys getting hexed and these murders aren't necessarily connected."

"They could be, especially with the right motive," Liz counters.

"Jordan Yarrow is Bliss' ex, and he has had it out for her and Goddess' Trance ever since they kicked him out of the band. If he thought Voracious Maw and Goddess' Trance were getting close, he could very well have decided to get pay back."

"But what about the murder from three years ago?"

"He's always hated Voracious Maw, even before he was kicked out. I think he always felt insecure about them. He didn't like that I liked their shows," I point out.

Amelia nods. "He was always super outspoken about not liking their gimmick—sorry," she adds hastily to Wrath, who only cocks his head at her. "He hated their masks, and hated how they'd really gotten the female gaze down. Probably because he never could have done something like that himself."

"Dead Hearts isn't doing super great," Taser explains. "I've been asking around ever since the masquerade party. I heard their label is pretty close to dropping them."

"So what?" Poison asks. "He's trying to sabotage us and frame Wrath for murder?"

Grim sighs, nodding. "It's worth looking into."

"Glad you think so," Liz says. "Urvine's assigning the hex case to you guys."

CHAPTER THIRTY-SEVEN

PISCES

THE BARTENDER SETS A GLASS DOWN IN FRONT OF ME, THE FOAMY beer sloshing a bit onto the wooden bar top. I bring the glass to my lips, letting the cold hoppy beer glide down my throat with a few swallows.

I head back over to the table the others are at and slide in next to Benny. I'm starting to notice my siren's hunger eddying in the depths of my stomach. I take another drink of my beer, hoping it'll somehow curb that appetite, even though I know it won't help. But for now, a warmth settles into my bones and that's good enough.

Benny side-eyes me as he listens to Shaun and Simon bicker about whether we should switch over to some new microphone inputs for the drum kit. "You okay?" he asks me.

I have the urge to lay my head on his shoulder. But I just wrap my hands around the glass. "No, I'm not. Someone out there is using me to target women. And it feels like there's nothing I can do."

"We posted on our socials to be wary of anyone pretending to be us, both online and off," Benny points out. It was the first thing Simon did after Grim and his gang of undercover fae cops finally took the body and stopped accusing me of murder. My mind is reeling from both the murders *and* that the Phantoms are under-cover investigators that have been keeping tabs on *me*.

I really don't like that guy.

"It doesn't feel like it's enough."

My gaze snaps up to the door of the pub, where Bliss, her aunt, and the members of Goddess' Trance—minus their drummer—file in, taking a table across the room from us.

Her eyes meet mine as she takes the end seat in the booth, but she doesn't stay there long. She looks to the group, muttering something, then walks over to me—to us, I correct myself.

"How are you doing?" she asks, stopping in front of our booth. I slide over and motion for her to sit. To my surprise, and pleasure, she does.

Her smell wafts over me, and I glance at the white ribbon in her hair, tying up half of it into a ponytail, a few wisps framing her face.

My eyes drop to her glossy lips.

"Okay, I guess," I say, throwing Benny a look to stop him from correcting me.

Shaun and Simon stop their bickering and greet Bliss, sliding the basket of chips her way in offering.

She takes one, biting into it, and I can't help myself watch as she chews.

"You alright?" Simon asks. "It's been a really weird day."

"I'm okay," she replies with a small smile. "I can't believe every-thing that's happened."

"Well, on a positive note, you killed it. We told Niamh about your performance. She was stoked," Simon informs her. "Then she promptly fell back asleep. Evan, on the other hand, is up and playing video games instead of resting, because he's an idiot. How's Tubbs doing?"

She grins. "Tubbs is good. Also playing video games. He even tried to come out to the bar with us, but Taser and Blake finally talked him out of it."

"Bliss!" Grim calls as he strides into the bar. I mentally curse the man. He's probably a good guy. But I still don't like him.

"What's wrong?" she asks. I can see Amelia and the others tense in their booth as they watch.

"We went to the flat Dead Hearts was staying at. Looks like Jordan cleared out, but the rest of the band was still there."

Grim pulls up a chair, making himself at home. He spreads his legs wide—which I roll my eyes at—and his knee knocks against Bliss'. It's not his job to comfort her. *It's not yours either,* a snide voice in my head shoots back.

Grim eats a couple chips.

It's getting really hard to keep my siren teeth beneath my gums. A tiny part of me wants to eat this guy. Okay, maybe a big part.

"How are you going to track him down?" I ask, my voice accusatory, as if it's Grim's fault that Jordan got away.

"Well, he's probably gone into hiding if he's smart." Bliss lets out a snort at that. Grim continues, "But we think we have a shot at getting a lead on him."

"Sounds promising," Shaun drawls.

"How?" Bliss asks, ignoring Shaun's quip, her eyes wide with apprehension. She definitely doesn't want her possible murderer ex-boyfriend on the loose. I don't either. If he so much as dares to attack her again, he is going to be getting very, very intimate with my siren teeth.

"Jinx Belcross is still here. We have enough evidence to arrest him for the hexes. We could potentially strike a deal. A reduced sentence if he gives up his friend."

"He won't," Bliss says, her shoulders slumping. "They're too loyal to each other, like brothers."

"Okay," Grim says slowly, ignoring the rest of us to focus solely on Bliss. "Plan B, then. You use your powers on him to get him to give up Jordan."

"Fuck that," I say immediately. "He helped almost kill her."

Bliss' gaze cuts to mine, a look of annoyance crossing her face. "It's not up to you," she says, though her voice doesn't have the bite I think she intended.

"We'll be there with you. You'll be perfectly safe." Grim says all this to Bliss, but he looks at me at the last part.

"No," I say again, though Bliss is right. It's not up to me.

Bliss stands up and I groan.

"I'll do it. I don't want him or Jordan to hurt anyone else."

By this point all of Bliss' friends and family surround our booth. They overheard, and Amelia is now berating Grim for even suggesting Bliss be in harm's way. I agree wholeheartedly with her.

Taser, though, cuts a path to Bliss. "If you're going to do this, you need to top off."

I stand and push my way in between them, about to snarl at Taser. I rein in the impulse just barely and turn to Bliss. "You can use me."

Bliss takes a deep breath and blows it out through her nose. Slowly she says, "Would everyone just take a step back and stop trying to tell me what to do?"

No, I want to say, but I stop myself. What do I even care? Sure, I don't want Bliss harmed because she's a good, decent fae. The same way I don't want to see Jordan hurt any more humans. But why am I going so far to make sure she's safe? We aren't even really friends, are we?

I don't even like her, I remind myself. She's self-absorbed and only seems to want to get closer to Wrath, not the guy under the mask.

Is that true? Fuck, my mind is really not on my side right now. But I realize that inner voice is right. She's not conceited like I originally thought. She's caring and strong and beautiful. *And completely out of your league.*

She looks to Taser. "Stop back seat feeding me. And you—" she points to me and I stiffen, lowering my head in shame, "—stop pissing all over the place and marking territory that isn't yours to mark." She sets her sights on Grim. "Honestly, the best person to get Jinx to talk would be Amelia. She's stronger than me. But I'm going with her."

Amelia starts to nod but stops at the last part. "No, you aren't. In fact, I think Liz should take you and Reese back home."

"You too?" Bliss asks, looking a little hurt. "Why is everyone acting like I'm five?"

Reese comes to stand next to her, hooking her arm through Bliss'. "Everyone knows you're not a child, but Bliss, you haven't been feeding regularly. I think everyone's just worried."

I want to tell her to feed from me. I want to see her with that glow again.

Bliss shakes her head at her friend. "No, I'm going with Amelia. I'm part of the reason that Jordan is doing whatever it is he's doing. I need to help."

Amelia makes to argue, but Liz steps in. "Let her make her own choices."

Grim clears his throat, bringing everyone's attention back to him. "You'll both be safe. We'll be there with you and he will be restrained."

I grind my teeth in frustration and catch Amelia's gaze. She looks at me with a brow raised, as if to ask what the fuck I'm going to do about it.

I step in front of Bliss so Grim gets my full attention. "I'm going with, and if that fucker touches one single strand of her hair, I'm going to rip. Him. Apart." I enunciate each word so he understands it's not an empty threat, and I have the teeth to back it up.

Grim swallows, looking up at me. I tower over him by a few inches, and I'm in his face. He takes a step back and nods. "Fine," is all he says.

We waited at the bar until Grim had given us the all clear. His team arrested Jinx and detained the rest of Dead Hearts to interrogate and see if they knew anything about Jordan's attacks or Jinx's hexing. Maybe they were even involved, but that's for them to figure out.

Plan A didn't work, as Bliss predicted, so it's time to try it the succubus way. I'm focusing on making sure Bliss stays out of harm's way, and to a degree, Amelia as well. Even though Evan wouldn't admit it, he wouldn't want any harm coming to his bondmate.

Bliss and Amelia stride in through the front door to Dead Hearts' flat. Shaun, Benny, Taser, and I flank them.

Taser and I are both here for Bliss. And once again I'm aching for her to cut these other men loose. I'm starting to wonder if I'm just getting addicted to her because she's a succubus. Maybe the more I'm around her, the more I'm going to crave her. That has to be it, right?

Grim's already there, organizing with his team. He already explained earlier that it would take too long to take Jinx to a fae facility to be interrogated, and time is of the essence. We don't know Jordan's motive for sure, so it's likely he could keep killing.

Bliss and Amelia eye where Jinx is seated at the dining room table, hands stretched out on the table, handcuffed with power-suppressing shackles. The same ones Grim wanted to strap on me. The girls keep a wide berth between themselves and the table, inspecting the room.

I move to follow and Grim shoots an arm out to stop me. I don't say anything, just arch a brow at him, snarling.

"You know you two are doomed, right?" Grim asks, his voice hard.

"Right, and you aren't?" I shoot back mockingly.

"There's a Born fae out there that she's going to fall madly in love with. So whatever it is between you two isn't going to last."

"There isn't anything between us. She's a succubus. I let her feed off me, that's it." I give him a sidelong glance. "Seems like maybe there's something between you, though. Or at least on one side." I smirk. I can't help it. And he started it.

Grim sighs, choosing his next words carefully. "Look, I'm just realizing how frustrated I am that she and I will never be anything more. I don't want you to get hurt when one minute she's with you and the next she sees a Born fae with a rune in his eye and falls madly in lo—"

"What?" I push his arm away from me. "A rune? In his eye?"

Grim looks at me as if I'm an idiot. "Yeah, that's how Born fae identify their mates. They each have a rune in their eye that only the other can see. It's behind the iris, in the white of the eyes."

My stomach bottoms out.

In all my limited time of being a Made fae, I've never found out that's how it all works.

"Only their mate can see it?" I ask, my thoughts whizzing around in my head. How have I never known this part? I knew there was a ceremony that activated the bond, but never how it was identified. "So when Evan and Amelia looked at each other the other day and realized they were mates, it was because they both saw a rune in the other's eye?"

"They're mates?" Grim asks, momentarily surprised, but his expression turns exasperated quickly. "Yes, then they would have seen runes," Grim says in a rush. "What about this are you not getting?"

"Just to be clear, both fae see it?"

"Yes. By the stars, man, what is the problem?" Pinkie interjects, having been listening in the whole time.

I fall out of step with them, and they both turn and look at me as if I'm insane. But I just roll my shoulders and firmly continue on. Because now I'm fucking pissed.

CHAPTER THIRTY-EIGHT

BLISS

Stepping foot into this house, my hair stands on end. I can smell Jordan's scent, clear as day. Amelia makes a face. "Stars, it reeks in here. And not just smelly boy gross, there's something else."

I don't want to, but I take another sniff. I can smell what she's talking about. There's a rotten smell underneath everything else, something pungent once I notice it.

"Hexes," Bell supplies, motioning to the table where Jinx sits, smirking.

That's what the smell is. I've never made a hex, but I know sulfur is a common ingredient.

Interrogation equipment is still being set up, a camera and microphone so they can record what Jinx might say, so Amelia and I take a look around the place.

The flat is much smaller than the townhome we are staying in. The festival organizers threw the smaller bands into two-bedroom flats, and if Goddess' Trance hadn't filled in for one of the bigger spots, we likely would have been in one of these flats as well.

The other members of Dead Hearts aren't here, whether

because the Phantoms have cleared them out already, or because they also took off after Jordan left.

I'm guessing the former, however, noting the half-packed duffel bags and articles of clothing strewn about the floor. There are also empty beer bottles on the countertops still. Amelia passes by the couch, and I notice her pick something up. It's a small leather-bound journal that's been shoved in between couch cushions. She puts it under her shirt, sticking it in her bra band, and looks around, completely nonchalant. I arch my brows at her and she winks. I'm not sure why she took it—my sister isn't a klepto.

But I guess I'll have to ask her later. If I say anything now, the Phantoms might overhear and I doubt they'll approve of her removing things from…

Well, I guess it's not like this is a crime scene, but still.

Bell waves us over to where she's double-checking Jinx's handcuffs. "We're ready to begin."

Amelia and I take seats across from Jinx, both of us leaving a bit of room between our chairs and the table. Neither my sister nor I want to get too close to Jinx, even if his magic is contained.

His smirk deepens and he leans back in his chair, his shackles clanking. "Well, well, if it isn't the slutty Rassard sisters."

Amelia grins like she's in on the joke. "That's a good one. Never heard it before."

Jinx fixes her with a glare, his lips sealing into a thin line.

"Go ahead," Stormy says to Amelia. "Let's get this over with." She seems to want to get out of here as much as we do.

I can feel as my sister reaches into her power well beside me, drawing on her persuasion and coaxing it out until it spreads towards Jinx. She focuses it on him, leaning forward in her chair and adopting a sultry smile. "Jinx," she murmurs in her husky voice, her fingers dancing across the table towards him but not getting too close. "Where's Jordan?"

Jinx barks out a laugh. "Keep your lust away from me, whore."

Amelia blinks, a bit thrown off. She pushes more of her power into it. "Try an easier question, maybe?" Bell suggests.

Jinx laughs again, a bit hysterical. "It won't work. I'm immune."

Amelia tries again. "Why did you hex Tubbs and the others?"

Jinx gnashes his teeth together, leaning forward in his chair and pinning Amelia with a wild-eyed look. "It. Won't. Work. I have zero desire for you or your slutty sister. I have standards."

Amelia looks as if a bucket of cold water was dumped on her. She looks at me and then to Bell and Stormy, getting up out of the chair.

I follow her, seeing Pisces out of the corner of my eye. I expected him to be right at my side with the way he was acting earlier, but now he just looks pissed, standing behind Grim, arms crossed, Benny standing close beside him. His jaw ticks as he glares at me. I wonder what changed in the last ten minutes.

"He's right, this won't work. He has absolutely no desire for me, or Bliss, so we can't use that as leverage here."

Grim comes over to our little circle. "What's the issue?"

Amelia explains, shrugging. "I'm sorry, I don't think there's anything left here for us to do." She looks to me with pity on her face. "I'm so sorry, Bliss."

"There has to be a way to break him," Grim murmurs.

I turn and look at Jinx again, studying him. He's looking around, probably searching for a way to escape. But there's no way for him to get past all of us without his magic. I think about how Jinx has always been at Jordan's side. I don't think it's love. I don't think either of the fae are capable of such a complex emotion. But there's something there, some tie.

It's always seemed like Jinx would do anything for Jordan.

Even go to jail for him.

How desperate, I think.

And there it is.

I sit back down across from Jinx. "Bliss," my sister and Grim warn at the same time.

I ignore them. I pull up my own powers and muster a sense of something I'm utterly familiar with.

Desperation.

I'm not at all sure it'll work. Succubi powers draw out good feelings. Lust, love, relief, ecstasy. Things people feel during and after sex. I've never heard of a succubus being able to make someone feel shameful, desperate, or hopeless, but is it really so crazy? Isn't that how I often feel afterwards?

I let it leak out of me, trying my best to center it on Jinx, but I can tell it's flowing out all around me. I try to rein it in, channeling it directly towards Jinx. I can tell I have him when his face contorts into a pain that is not at all physical, only emotional and spiritual.

"You want to help Jordan, don't you? That's always what you've wanted?"

Jinx nods, tears starting to leak down his cheek. "Yes."

"You're trying to help him now, aren't you? You want to make sure he's safe, right?" My voice is soft and kind.

He nods again and doesn't stop. Tears continue to fall freely as he rocks in his chair. "I'm protecting him."

"You're afraid of what could happen to him?"

"Yes, yes, I want to make sure he's safe."

"I can help you with that," I say, reaching out across the table. "Let me help you."

Jinx clasps my hand in his awkwardly due to the shackles, but the contact helps me focus my powers on him. "What was Jordan's plan?"

"To take you and Voracious Maw down, so that Dead Hearts would have a better shot."

"And how was he doing this?"

"By framing Voracious Maw for murder."

Grim motions for me to keep going. "Anything else?" I ask, my eyes going back to Jinx.

"The hexes. We were hoping you'd both pull out of the festival. And it would make you look guilty for leaving after the dead body showed up. But then you didn't, so he killed again."

"Jinx, we want to help Jordan. We want to bring him in safely and get him some help. Where is he?"

Jinx shakes his head, full-on sobbing now. "I don't know. He left me. He left me here. I don't know—I can't help him anymore."

"Yes, yes, you can, you can still help." I squeeze his hand. "Is there anything you can think of that would help us find him?" I push what I have left into him, letting him stand on the edge before falling too far into a desperate oblivion where his mind will be useless. I don't know how I know, but if he goes over that edge, there's no coming back.

Carefully, ever so carefully, I push a little sprig of hope towards him.

It's enough. His eyes snap to mine, and he nods, a soft smile breaking across his face. "You can track him." Jinx looks around at Grim's team. "He summoned a wraith to do some of his dirty work. You can track the magical signature."

"Great job, Bliss," Grim says, giving my shoulder a squeeze. "Let him go now."

I withdraw my persuasion and unclasp his hand. Jinx blinks a few times like he's sobering up. His face scrunches in pain. He'll have a hell of an emotional hangover now.

"Oh stars," he swears, slumping into his seat. "What have I done?"

"Take him now," Grim orders to someone behind me. I'm almost completely spent. Amelia helps me out of the chair and into an armchair in the living room, as Pinkie and Bell start escorting Jinx out, probably taking him to some sort of holding facility in the fae realm.

I try to meet Pisces' eyes, but he's staring at the floor. I wouldn't mind seeing if he'll help me feed later, but he won't look at me.

A yelp sounds out as Bell is pushed into a wall and Jinx rips his way out of Pinkie's hold. He heads straight at me, using his cuffed hands to grip me by the collar. "What the fuck did you make me do, you whore?" he yells at me, slamming me up against a wall.

"Bliss!" Grim yells out. I look up and see him running my way. Jinx is ripped off me before Grim can get to me, Pisces throwing him to the ground. I can't seem to take my eyes off the two of them as Pisces rips into Jinx, the sounds he's making threatening to make me sick.

"Stop, Pisces!" Pinkie yells, trying to get Pisces off Jinx, but he doesn't stop.

Oh my stars.

He's eating him. Literally eating him.

I stumble forward on unsteady feet, trying to push Pisces off Jinx, even though he definitely deserves it. Pisces snarls at me, whipping his head around to look at me, his siren teeth gnashing together, and his eyes so dark they almost look black. I stop myself from recoiling. I put my hand on him.

"Pisces," I say, trying to get his attention, but he goes back to eating. Jinx's arm is in his mouth and he's practically chewed it off at the elbow.

"Pi!" I scream. He stiffens, letting Jinx's bloodied arm thump to the ground. It looks still attached. Mostly.

I reach out and pull Pisces up, and he seems to come back to his senses. He looks down at the kitsune, who's screaming in agony, and then at me. Jinx's blood is covering his face and the front of his shirt.

His eyes meet mine and they narrow. He scowls at me and shrugs. "I said if he touched a hair on your head, I'd rip him apart. And I did."

He levels his gaze next on Grim, who's got Jinx firmly in hand, as Bell tends to his wounds, using her healing magic to basically regrow his arm.

Jinx is lucky the air elemental is here, otherwise he'd have quite the scar, since the shackles mute his powers to heal himself.

Part of me wishes Bell wasn't here to heal him.

He deserved it.

Well, maybe. I'm not quite sure anyone deserves being eaten alive.

My eyes find Pisces again and he's scowling at me.

"What is your problem?" I snap at him.

"Nothing," he grinds out, his teeth completely back to normal.

Now that I've seen his siren teeth, I can't believe I let him anywhere near my sensitive areas.

He starts to walk out the door but turns and glares at me again. "How could you not fucking tell me?" He points at himself. "I didn't know what the rune meant. You did. How could you not fucking tell me?"

Ice.

That's what it feels like. Someone must have pushed me into the icy Pacific Ocean.

Something tugs on me, but no one is touching me. I look at Pisces, I stare at his eyes, looking from one to the other. But there's nothing. No rune.

"There isn't anything there," I say, my voice barely above a whisper.

And yet, something inside me feels like it's cracking, like pieces of dried mud flaking off with each breath.

"Are you really going to pretend you don't see it?" Pisces asks in a threateningly low whisper. "I've wanted something like this my entire life, and you're going to deny me it?" Tears gather in his runeless eyes, my own eyes threatening to unleash as well. I reach out a hand to him, but he smacks it away.

"Fuck you, Bliss," he says, but before he can storm off, a form materializes before him. In one instant Pisces is standing there alone, the next the song wraith has him pushed against a wall, hand to Pisces' throat.

Tears are streaming down his face, which now sports a confused look.

"What the fuck?" Pisces manages to get out, despite his airway being cut off.

Tears.

Oh my stars.

"Leave him alone!" I shout, trying to tug the wraith's hand from Pisces.

"My dear, dear Bliss. I've come to gather what you owe me," the wraith replies, looking at me out of the corner of his eye as he places a small glass vial next to Pisces' face. "I just needed you to unlock them."

Something clicks into place. He never needed me to steal them. He needed me to cause them.

Oh stars. Fuck. Fuck. Fuck.

Pisces tries violently to throw the wraith off him. "You bastard," he says, snarling. "You fucking played me."

What?

The wraith smiles, finishes collecting the tears, and pats Pisces on the cheek like he's been a good boy. "Thank you both for playing your roles perfectly. I'll be in touch for next steps."

He lets Pisces go and the siren falls to the ground, almost like the song wraith leeched the energy out of him. When the wraith turns around he's met by guns in his face. Grim, Pinkie, Bell, and Stormy all have their guns aimed at his head.

The wraith clicks his tongue. "Those won't do any good, I'm afraid."

"These aren't just any guns," Pinkie spits.

The wraith makes a noncommittal noise and lifts one shoulder, then lets it drop. "Either way. Let me leave and I will cause no harm to any of you. Get in my way and you won't like what will happen."

Grim cocks his gun, readying to shoot. "I think there's no way we let you just walk out of here."

"So be it, then."

Before any of them can get a shot off, they all simultaneously drop their guns in pain, as if the metal is scorching hot. With a wave of the wraith's hand, they all go slamming backwards into the walls of the house and the wraith simply dematerializes back into the nothingness out of which he came.

I don't know who to run to, Grim or Pisces. Amelia makes the decision for me, running to Grim and checking him out first. I go to Pisces and try to help him up, but he pushes me away.

"We're gonna need another healer," I hear Amelia say as she helps Bell to her feet, a large gash in her head.

Grim nods but not to Amelia. He nods at Pinkie, and they both step forward.

"Bliss Rassard, Pisces Penrose, you're both under arrest by the authority of the fae council and elders."

The shackles are slapped on before Amelia can finish her string of curses.

"What for?" she yells at Grim. "They were both attacked! Are you stupid?"

"They've both been working with a wraith. That's a felony, Amelia."

I lock eyes with Pisces, mine wide and afraid. We've both been working with a wraith, the same wraith, and had no idea? What was he playing at?

Pisces' eyes aren't shocked, though, they aren't afraid. He's pissed and glaring at me.

"Pisces—" I try to say, wanting to explain, but he cuts me off.

"You knew we were mates and didn't tell me. I want nothing to do with you, Bliss. Ever. Don't fucking talk to me again."

CHAPTER THIRTY-NINE

BLISS

The interrogation room isn't like the human ones on TV. It's not cold and sterile, like a doctor's office, but ornate and plush, exactly what I'd expect from the fae council.

"Why was the wraith collecting Pisces Penrose's tears?" Grim asks, seated in the matching plush armchair, opposite me. There's a fire in the hearth, and the room has a nice warm glow from the flames.

I'm in shackles, of course. Unable to use my powers, which isn't really different for me. At most, the iron metal is cold, hard, and a bit uncomfortable. I need to itch my nose, but the shackles are heavy, and the last time I tried to scratch an itch on my face, I almost hit myself with the chains.

"I already told you, I don't know." That's what I've told Grim for most questions he's asked. It's not totally that I'm trying to be obstinate. I can't stop going over Pisces' words in the my head, replaying them in a never-ending loop.

He saw a rune in my eye?

How is that even possible?

And regardless of that...

Why, then, did I not see one in his?

It's hard to focus on what Grim is asking, when I can't even process the last twenty-four hours.

Grim lets out a sigh, shaking his head. "Bliss, you've got to give me something."

I try to push Pisces from my mind, which turns out to be impossible, but at least I'm able to force myself to focus. Maybe Grim is right. Maybe if I come clean, tell them what I know, things will work out. Maybe they'll let me go since I cooperated.

As Grim was leading me out of the Dead Hearts townhome, handcuffed, Amelia stopped us, throwing her arms around me, despite Grim's warning to keep her distance. She whispered into my ear, "Don't say anything. I'll get Liz. She'll know what to do. Don't say anything."

Except, Liz hasn't been allowed in to see me. In fact, the only person I've seen in the past several days is Grim and the fae that delivered my meals.

I was either in this interrogation room or in a locked room that served as a cell.

Today, apparently, will be different, though.

Someone knocks on the interrogation room door, a thick wooden door spelled to keep me inside, unless escorted back to my room. Grim gets up, opening the door for an older fae male, who walks in like he owns the place. Giving the room a once-over, the male settles into the chair Grim just vacated, wearing an expression that suggests he finds the room lacking.

It's Yves Lyra, the head of the fae council and the man who nearly caught me with the song wraith in the hallway of his own estate.

"Sir," Grim says, having closed the door and taken up a position standing next to Lyra.

"She still hasn't said anything?" he asks, like he's not looking directly at me from across the room.

"Nothing useful, no. But I'm sure with more time—"

"No, no more time." Lyra fixes me with a stern glare. "Tell us what we want to know, succubus. Tell us about this song wraith."

Grim gives me a pleading look over Lyra's head.

"I don't know anything."

Grim's eyes fall, like I'm now past his help.

"We know you were working with the thing. And really, you should be more mindful. You're already proving to the fae world that succubi aren't up to the same moral standards as most Born fae. In fact, you're acting like a Made fae."

I glare at Lyra but say nothing. He can slander my character all he wants.

He watches me silently for a few moments and waves his hand dismissively. His legs are crossed and he's reclined like he's totally at ease here.

"What about this supposed bond?"

My glare changes subjects, moving to Grim. He should have kept his mouth fucking shut about that.

"I don't know what you mean."

Lyra lets out a frustrated breath. "Come now, this bond that the siren mongrel thinks he has with you."

I force myself to scoff, drawing a wide-eyed look from Grim. "A bond between me and a Made fae? It's not possible, you know that."

"You deny it?" Lyra presses.

"Of course I do. Made fae can't bond. I see no rune in his eye. He's probably lying. Like you said, Made fae and their lesser morals." I hate myself as I say the words. My insides twist with guilt and shame. I don't know what is between Pisces and I, but if it is a bond, Yves Lyra can never know about it. Alarm bells blare in my mind at the thought. Best case scenario, they'll treat Pisces and me like a science experiment trying to figure this out. Worst case scenario... I won't let my mind go there.

Grim's mouth presses into a thin line, like he's rethinking how he views me. It's a twist of the knife in my stomach, but I press on.

"You might not have a high opinion of succubi, but I'm still Born fae. Born fae and Made fae are not meant to fall in love or bond. If we were, the stars would create bonds between our species."

Lyra nods in agreement. "So you think he's lying?"

"He has to be." Stars, I'm going somewhere horrible in the afterlife for sure.

Lyra nods again, unfolding his legs and getting up out of the chair. "Well, that's good news. See her back to her room. Perhaps she'll feel like talking more about the wraith tomorrow."

"Sir, I can assure you, I had no prior contact with such an abhorrent creature." I'm laying it on thick, but maybe, just maybe, if he thinks my allegiance lies with him, he'll let me go. Then I'll find a way to free Pisces, somehow.

Lyra smiles. The effect it has on his face is disconcerting, like his mouth has no business being in that shape. "Hayden, take her back to her room." He says nothing more, exiting the room.

I ready myself for bed, showering and changing into a set of plain but comfortable pajamas. There's a selection of books in the room, a hearty fire roaring, and a plush velvet armchair and ottoman that's honestly perfect for curling up on. I'm settling in for another long evening of reading when a knock sounds at the door.

I jump up, wondering if I'm about to be set free, when the door swings open. Pinkie leads a grungy and—I sniff—smelly Pisces into the room. He hasn't shaved in days and he's wearing the same blood-covered clothes as the day we interrogated Jinx. His under eyes are hollow, his cheeks gaunt.

"Stars, what have you done to him?" I ask, running over to Pisces and helping him into the chair I was just about to curl up in.

"You've met Lyra. You think he'd waste a room like this on a Made fae?" Pinkie says, throwing some PJs onto the bed. "Grim pulled some strings." Pinkie heads to the door, about to lock us back up in the room together.

"Wait! He hasn't fed in days!" I call after him, but Pinkie just shrugs and closes the door anyways.

Pisces groans, drawing my attention back to him.

"Pisces, are you alright? What can I do?"

He mutters something, but I can't hear. I lean in closer, aching to reach out and feel him. I place my hand on his cheek. "What did you say?"

He opens his eyes, looking up at me with those beautiful but still runeless blue eyes. "I said," he says louder, "get the fuck away from me." He knocks my hand aside and closes his eyes.

"Pisces, please, let me help. At least let me explain."

"What's there to explain?" he snaps, eyes opening again. There's hate in them as he takes me in. "I'm just a liar, right? Just a mongrel siren with lesser morals?"

"I—" I'm about to say that I didn't say that. But I did; not the mongrel part, but everything else. They must have played Pisces a video of my interrogation. Damn Grim. He didn't pull strings, he set us up. "Please, let me explain."

"No. Leave me alone, Bliss." I can hear the exhaustion in his voice.

"Okay, fine, I'll leave you alone, but you have to feed first." I put my arm out in front of his face, closing my eyes in apprehension. His teeth look like they'll *hurt*. Badly.

"I said get the fuck away from me."

I open my eyes and roll them. He's recoiled from me as much as he can in the armchair. "What, you don't like the taste of succubus?"

His eyes flicker to mine, and a blush colors his cheeks faintly. He turns away from me completely. "Stay away from me," he repeats, but his words are a bit muffled, as if he doesn't want to open his mouth too wide. *His teeth,* I think. His siren teeth must be coming out and he doesn't want me to see them.

"Well, either you hate me and should have no problem ripping into my flesh, or you don't hate me and don't want to harm me, so best to feed while you're still in control."

He pins me with a withering look. "I'm not going to feed from you at all."

"Because I disgust you?"

He growls deep in his chest. "I won't feed from you because I'm not going to subject you to that kind of pain."

I think back to the time I sleepwalked to him. "Is there another way you feed?"

He shrugs, looking away from me. "I need to shower," he mumbles, taking the collar of his shirt and smelling it. I swallow what I'm about to say and nod, going to sit on the bed with my book and give him some space.

Only when he's inside the bathroom and the shower starts, do I realize the pajamas Pinkie left for him are sitting on the foot of the bed, still neatly folded. The door to the bathroom doesn't lock—I checked, wondering if I could lock myself inside to avoid Grim's interrogations—so I could quickly chuck the clothes in, but I don't want to invade his privacy. And the shower has a glass wall, so I'd likely get an eyeful, which in a different situation would be totally welcome on my end.

I barely make it a few pages in my book before my thoughts drift to Pisces' eyes. I put the book down and put my face in my hands. I need to explain to him. I need him to understand that if I saw a rune in his eyes, I would have said something. I would have done something. Cried in relief? Ran up to him and hugged him? I'm not sure, but I wouldn't have ignored it.

The shower stops running. A few moments later, Pisces steps back into the room, a towel wrapped around his waist, allowing my eyes to roam over his chest. My eyes keep trailing over his piercings. He has silver, straight barbells running through each nipple. I think my brain short-circuits for a minute. My eyes trail down his abdomen, following the V that's visible just above the towel.

My power is definitely waning if even the seriousness of our situation can't stop me from lusting over a guy I thought was an asshole until recently and who currently hates my guts. He picks up the folded pajamas, taking the bottoms into the bathroom and leaving the shirt on the bed.

Part of me hopes he never intends on putting that shirt on.

He comes back out in the pajama bottoms, his bare feet padding on the carpet over to the armchair. Droplets drip from his hair still and the image of him in the shower, with me joining him, jolts me, goose bumps erupting over my arms.

I force myself to look at his face, instead of his abs. Seeing again how sallow his skin looks helps shake off my lust. He needs to feed. And soon.

"Pisces, I—" I don't know how to start. I try again. "If I saw a rune in your eye, I would have told you."

He doesn't so much as look at me.

"I know how the mating bond works, Bliss. If I see a rune in your eye, you see one in mine. That's how it works."

"I don't know what's going on, but I promise you, I don't see one. But we can try to figure it out."

"Just stop."

I shut my mouth, preventing more words from spilling out. Instead, I take a deep breath and nod. He needs time to cool off. Fine. It's not like we won't have plenty of time to talk later.

But there is a more pressing matter. So I switch gears.

"Pisces, if you don't feed and you get too low on power, you're going to attack me and it will be painful." I get up off the bed, going to stand in front of him. I'm not going to take no for an answer this time.

"I can go a while without that," he mumbles, not looking at me. I step closer into his space.

"But you don't need to suffer." I kneel down in front of him, trying to get him to look me in the eyes.

"I'll wait," he says, looking at me for a few seconds. He has to squeeze his eyes shut, as if looking at me is painful for him.

"We aren't getting out of here anytime soon, Pi."

Pisces snaps up out of the chair, and suddenly I find myself lifted off the ground, back slamming against the wall, his hands caging my head in. "Don't call me that, ever."

I can't breathe for a minute. He's towering over me, a wall of muscle and height and anger. Swallowing thickly, I nod. "Okay," I whisper, eyes falling to the floor.

He stiffens and sighs, arms falling away.

"There's this other way to feed, a lure."

"What's that?"

"I focus on someone and sing, and they come to me. I didn't kidnap you, okay? But it was my fault that you sleepwalked. I wasn't trying to," he adds hastily. "I was trying to lure someone else, but it didn't work."

He was trying to lure someone else? Another woman, maybe?

For some reason, that stings.

He lowers his head, almost touching his forehead to mine. His damp hair brushes my skin, he's that close. If I move just a little, it would be so easy to close the distance and kiss him. Why do I even want that? Suddenly, I'm no longer afraid of being caged in by him, but it's like he reads the change in my energy and backs away, going to sit on the edge of the bed.

I stay leaning against the wall.

He looks up at me, his bottom lip curled inward the way it does when he's upset. "Can I try the lure on you again? I'll feed off your emotions instead of your flesh."

Shakily, I nod. I don't want to lose control like that, but it's probably better than having those insane teeth shred my skin to pieces.

He closes his eyes and he's silent for a little bit. He opens his eyes and they find mine, and he starts to sing. It's not a song I've ever heard before, but the lyrics cause goose bumps to erupt all over my arms. Suddenly I'm striding forward, pulled to him by some invisible force. I come right up to him, standing in between his legs.

He reaches out and grips me by the hips. "I think physical contact is part of it," he says, more to himself. But I barely register it. I'm too focused on his lips, on the way he always breathes through his nose. Strong breaths, because he has strong lungs. I place my hand on his chest, wanting to feel his heartbeat, wanting to feel his skin. I wonder what emotion he'll feed off, because in this moment I only feel the closeness between us, the desire to touch him.

I only know he's done feeding when it feels like I'm waking up from a half-sleep. My vision becomes sharper, and more awareness floods into me.

"Was that it?" I ask, a bit awed. It seems too easy.

He nods, a bit more color in his cheeks and a soft glow to his skin. Skin that I still want to touch.

He stands, pushing me back, gently this time, but his hands still grip my waist. I keep my hands on his chest. I don't want to move. At least, I don't want to move farther apart. Pisces inhales deeply, and I wonder if my scent does the same to him as his does to me. I close the distance he put between us, catching his gaze in mine. I wonder what my rune looks like to him.

If he fed off my feelings of lust, is he feeling it too? And if he took some of my lust away, what does it say about me that I still have some to spare?

I run a hand up over his chest, to the side of his neck, tracing his tattoo. I've never seen it fully like this. Water lilies wrap from his left collarbone around his neck, ending below his right ear. There are other details threaded through the tattoo that I can't make out right now, too focused on how his skin feels. My fingers just barely brush the ends of his hair. I want to run my fingers through it. I want to bring his face down to mine and capture his lips.

I want to know what he tastes like.

Our breathing grows more labored and Pisces' hands start running up and down the curve of my waist. He brings his fingers towards the waistband of the sweats I'm wearing, hooking into the band and beginning to pull it down.

Stars, how I want his fingers to find my core. I want him to push me back onto the bed and take these clothes off me. I want to strip him down to nothing and run my fingers up and down his length. I take a step closer, so our bodies are flush. And I can feel him. I can feel how hard he is.

Pisces groans as I lower his head to mine. He rests his forehead on mine. "Bliss," he whispers, as his fingers dip into my pants, finding their way blocked by my underwear.

He runs his fingers along the outside of my underwear, brushing nowhere near close enough to that spot.

And then all too suddenly I see something flash in his eyes, some sort of change in energy. He pushes me away, his hands going into his pockets. Pisces glares at me and turns his back on me. "Bliss, I can't feed you. I…" He trails off for a minute. "I don't want to."

He takes a blanket from the bed and pushes the armchair so it's by the window, facing away from the bed, settling into it.

A pit forms in my stomach, gnawing into the lining and sinking its teeth in. I sit down on the bed, the little bit of warmth I was feeling while he fed off me gone and my mind whirling.

CHAPTER FORTY

BLISS

THE NEXT MORNING IS SILENT. I FINALLY DRIFTED OFF TO SLEEP after silently crying for what felt like hours. Pisces—despite there being plenty of room in the bed for both of us—slept on the floor.

When I wake up, eyes dry and crusty, he's already awake, sitting in the armchair and staring off out the window. He barely looks at me as I go through my little routine of getting ready. I put my ribbons back in my hair and dress in the bathroom.

I don't know what to do with myself. I clear my throat to say something to him, but he glares at me, and any words I might have said die in my throat.

So I just sit with a book on the bed, reading, until finally Grim comes to gather me for another interrogation. It's crazy that I'm relieved to be going into the interrogation room again.

But as Grim leads me down the hall, he goes the opposite way. "Where are we going?" I ask as I follow him.

"Your aunt has been causing quite the commotion for the council. She has enough support that the others finally forced Lyra's hand. You're being released."

"What?" I reach out and stop Grim, my hand gripping his forearm. "That's amazing."

But Grim doesn't seem pleased. "You broke the law, Bliss. Just because I can't prove it, doesn't mean I'm happy to be letting you go."

My brows shoot up to my hairline. "You want to throw me in jail?"

Grim shakes his head, blowing out a breath. "You were working with a wraith. People got killed. And I don't know who's responsible for that. Maybe Jordan is just a scapegoat and you and Pisces are behind this whole thing."

"You really think that?" I can't believe what I'm hearing.

"I don't know what to think because you won't talk to me, Bliss."

"We're friends. How can you believe that I would be responsible for anyone's death?"

"We *were* friends, Bliss. Now I'm not so sure." He motions with his chin to keep going, so I shake my head and in my best Amelia impersonation I throw my hair over my shoulder. This hallway leads out into a foyer where Liz and Amelia stand, waiting to take me home. I ignore Grim's presence at my back and throw my arms around my family.

"Stars, I'm so glad to see you," I say into my sister's hair.

"Same here," she murmurs back, hugging me tight. "Let's get the fuck out of here."

I turn back to Grim. He's waiting, hands behind his back in the doorway. "What's going to happen to Pisces?" I ask. "Why is no one here to pick him up?"

"You said so yourself, Bliss. He's Made, you're Born." Without any more of an explanation Grim turns and heads back into the estate.

Amelia tugs my hand. "Come on, sis, let's go."

I shake my head. "I can't just leave him here."

"You can and you will," Liz says firmly. "It's not like you can stage a prison break."

I take one last look behind me, as if I could see all the way into the room to catch a glimpse of him. Of the siren that might be my bondmate.

Maybe I can't stage a prison break, but I am going to get him released somehow.

I convince Amelia and Liz to stick around London for a few more days. I need to get into contact with someone from Voracious Maw. Evan or Shaun, they'll know what to do to get Pisces released. Liz had the foresight to pack some clothes for me just in case, and when we get to the hotel, I shoot a quick text to Simon and change.

Amelia's tying a new ribbon into my hair as my phone beeps. Simon's texted an address to me. Amelia insists on going with me, and I'm grateful for the company, honestly. I know it's a big step for her. She hasn't seen Evan since he was sick.

We find our way to an old church just outside London and make our way up the crumbling steps.

The property is creepy looking, and it doesn't help that there seems to be a thick layer of fog encompassing the grounds. Amelia uses the ornate metal door knocker to announce our arrival. It takes a few minutes for the door to open and Simon greets us with a somber expression. "Hey, succubus sisters, come on in," he tries to joke. Amelia passes him, squeezing his shoulder lightly. I stop and give him a quick hug.

"The others are this way," Simon says, leading us down a hallway, then through another hallway. The place is like a maze. "Here we are."

We come to a stop in a large open living room where the entirety of Voracious Maw—excluding Pisces—is seated, wearing matching worried expressions.

Evan and Amelia exchange a quick look but say nothing. Whatever might be going on between them, or not going on, is put on hold for now.

Shaun gets up, shaking both our hands. "What brings you here?"

"It's obvious, isn't it?" I say, taking a seat that Shaun motions to. "The fae council has Pisces and we need to get him out."

"We know," Evan says flatly.

"You *know*?" Amelia repeats. We exchange glances.

"Yes, we know." Evan unfolds his crossed legs and gets up, the movement oddly familiar. It takes the same amount of time for him to cross over to one of the windows as it does for me to put two and two together.

"Evan Lyra, right?" I ask. Evan's shoulders tense.

"Right," he replies, turning back around and looking at us. "It's my father that's keeping Pisces."

"So what? You're not going to do anything about it?"

The fire in the hearth blazes for a beat, as if Evan is thinking about calling it to him. "Of course not. But we can't just stalk in there and grab him and leave."

Shaun gets up, going and standing next to Evan. "If that's why you came here, then it's best for you to go. We've got this under control. We'll get him out. He's our friend, not yours, not after what you did."

"What I did?" I exclaim, looking between the two.

"Maybe we should all take a minute," Benny says softly from his seated position on the couch. "Arguing isn't going to help."

I ignore him, narrowing my eyes on Shaun. "What did I do?"

Shaun laughs hollowly. "You're Born fae. You know what a rune means, and yet, you didn't tell him you were mates. All the times you've seen him, you said nothing."

"There was no rune!" I yell. Amelia puts her hand on my forearm. I take a few breaths. "His eyes are runeless. And supposedly he sees a rune in my eye. What am I supposed to do with that?"

Evan shakes his head like he thinks I'm lying. "We don't want or need your help. What are you going to do anyways, sleep your way into the fae estate and lead Pisces out the front door?"

"Watch yourself, bondmate," Amelia threatens. "I'd love a reason to kick your fucking ass."

"Like you could," he shouts at her.

"Enough!" Simon yells, slapping the coffee table hard with his fist. He's glaring at us all. "Fighting isn't going to help Pisces. We need to work together."

"*We* are," Shaun says, motioning to them but not to Amelia and I. "They don't need to be part of it. They got him arrested in the first place, and she—" he points at me, "—was working with a wraith of all things to steal Pisces' tears." He turns and levels his gaze at me again. "So no, sorry, I don't trust you to help us get him out."

"It's not what you think," I say, looking worriedly at Amelia. I still haven't explained it to her, but for some reason she hasn't asked.

"I don't give a shit." Shaun steps closer to me. "We're getting our friend back and we don't need or want your help."

Bliss, I can't feed you. I... I don't want to.

I don't want to.

Tears threaten to run down my face, so I look down at my feet, nodding. I don't say anything, just turn and leave, Amelia and Simon coming after me.

I can hear Amelia tell Simon to leave us alone. Once we're outside, Amelia takes me back to Liz and the hotel and from there we find the nearest portal, taking it back to Seattle.

CHAPTER FORTY-ONE

BLISS

THE NEXT DAY, I'M BACK IN MY APARTMENT AND I DON'T WAKE UP until three in the afternoon. Or should I say, I don't get out of bed. I busy myself with random tasks until The Wild Mare opens. I need to go meet with Amber and talk about coming back to work early. I took off time originally for my starmoon, and Amber was insistent that I leave it somewhat open-ended. She understood how much I needed to find my mate. But I don't think either of us expected me to want to come back to work so quickly.

A few days ago I was thinking this conversation would be about me quitting to be Goddess' Trance's full-time band manager. But now I don't know if that's a good idea.

Even if Pisces does get released, I can't go on tour with them, can I? It will be too awkward. Too painful.

I arrive just before opening, Lowell letting me in and allowing me to mix myself a drink while I wait for Amber to get off the phone. Apparently she's in a meeting that's been going on for hours. I finish my free drink and ask Lowell if there's anything I can do to help him out.

"There are some trash bags from the kitchen that need to be taken out," he says sheepishly. "I was waiting for the rain to stop."

I smile in return and nod. "I'll get them."

I take the trash out to the alley. There's a light drizzle, but it's not pouring like it was before. I heft the bags into the dumpster, feeling a bit sorry for myself. For a while there I thought my life was improving. I thought things were finally looking up. When I turn around, I startle, almost jumping backwards.

The song wraith is standing there, looking at me, face unreadable.

"What do you want? Trying to get me arrested again?" I look around, making sure we're alone. Though as much as that eases my worry about being caught dealing with a wraith, it terrifies me, despite the knowledge that the wraith promised not to harm me.

He cocks his head at me. "Is that anyway to greet a friend?"

"Right…" I hedge, trying to brush past him. I need to get back inside. He catches my arm and spins me around.

"I wasn't under the impression you wanted out of the deal, but if that's true… Well then, I suppose I'll just keep what I owe you to myself."

"I didn't deliver," I say, confused.

"Oh, but you did. I had to step in at the end there, but I got what I needed."

"Okay then, so where's my bondmate and when are you going to un-succubus me?"

The wraith smiles almost fondly at me. "Bliss, you already have your bondmate."

Pisces' face flashes in my mind. "But he can't be." Even though I can't deny that I wouldn't mind if it was true.

"Why not?"

"Because he's Made. So we can't have a bond. They don't work like that."

The wraith raises a brow at me. "And who says? Are you saying fae tell the stars what to do?"

"No, of course not, but it can't be true. I don't see a rune in his eye. So he can't be my mate."

The wraith nods knowingly. "Because Made fae don't have

runes. The rune is a result of the activation ceremony. Pisces has not undergone one, so he has no rune."

"So what? He needs to have a ceremony?"

"No, a ceremony would do nothing for him. You'll see in time."

"So why does my bond feel so weird?"

The wraith pretends to pick lint off his immaculate suit. "The magic interfering with your bond was why you had the odd reaction with the stone. And why your bond ties feel different."

"Okay, so fix it."

"It is already fixed. The bond is strengthening the more you're around him. It'll heal on its own and break the magic surrounding it. So that just leaves one last thing I owe you. What will it be, then? Water nymph? Wolf shifter? I think you'd make an exquisite earth elemental."

I lower my eyes. Is it really that simple? I just tell him what I want to be and he makes the change?

Can I really turn my back on my essence, my core? Using my power on Jinx showed me there is so much else to be discovered about my powers. And if Pisces has another way to feed, then maybe so do I.

I lift my face back up and meet the wraith's eyes. "No, I'm not going to change who I am."

"Are you sure? Your entire existence seems quite exhausting."

I ignore the slightly insulting statement and square my shoulders. "I'm sure. I'm just going to have to find out the right way for me to be a succubus. The way that works for me."

The wraith smiles almost kindly, reaching out his hand. I clasp it, shaking his hand in goodbye. "It's been a pleasure, Bliss Rassard."

"Wait," I reply, earning a wider smile. "Why did you need his tears? What are you doing with them?"

"They're an ingredient for a spell."

I already knew that. "What spell? It must be a pretty important one if you're going to all this trouble? What are you planning?"

"Bliss, I have already told you, I mean no harm. That is all I can tell you. But don't worry, this isn't a final goodbye. You will be seeing me again."

"Coming from you, that sounds like a threat."

He smiles again, but this time it's more of a grimace. And then he's gone, leaving me in the alleyway. The rain has started to pick up again and I realize I'm soaked through. Turning, I make my way back inside The Wild Mare. But instead of returning to work early, I will be giving Amber my notice.

I'm going to get my bondmate back. Even if he hates me.

I have to believe that what's between us is strong enough to overcome everything.

CHAPTER FORTY-TWO

PISCES

TWO YEARS AGO

THE TOO-WARM GLOW FROM THE STREETLIGHT AT THE CORNER barely reaches where I sit staring at the lake across from me. It's become part of my little ritual whenever my emotions start to get the better of me.

I sit on the bench and stare at the water, forcing myself to take deep breaths. Letting the sounds of the crash play in my head while grounding myself. I focus on the damp grain of the wooden bench beneath me. Let my fingers feel the cool metal of the bolts holding the planks together.

I can see the car going over the bridge, like some sort of out-of-body experience. I hear the loud splash, if you can even call it that, as the car hits the water.

I can see her face, eyes open, unseeing, blood dripping, head slumped against the dashboard. At least she hadn't drowned.

I told myself that over and over and over again after I woke up in the hospital.

Because I thought I had drowned.

I almost did.

Everything had almost winked out for me as I struggled to get out of the car. As water filled it at a rate that sent me into a panic.

I force air out through my lips and breathe in fully through my nose.

I'm here. I'm alive.

Even if the guilt eats at me. It's better to feel that than nothing at all, I remind myself.

The chilly night air absorbs some of my spiraling, forcing an alertness into my body. It's why I come out here at night. It's hard to get angry or frustrated or upset when it's so damn cold out.

The cold air demands a clear head.

I'm about to leave when I notice him, standing a few paces away, staring at me.

I recognize the wraith instantly.

No surprise there. His face haunts me almost as often as hers does.

"You." It's all I can say. I mean it in a threatening way, but the word comes out pathetically. I've started charging at him before I can even stop myself or think that maybe it's not the best idea to attack the demon that turned me.

A song wraith.

Shaun brought me a few books on song wraiths—the few he was able to get hold of—but seeing as they were supposedly all banished centuries ago, I gave up ever trying to find a solution to what I've become.

Instead of colliding with him, I go *through* him, crashing to the ground.

I twist myself around and look at him, my siren teeth escaping my gums without my permission. "Undo it!"

The wraith, quicker than I can even react, hauls me back up. He has me by the shirt collar and holds me off the ground, which is quite the feat considering he's an inch or two shorter than me.

But obviously so much stronger.

"Do not attempt to bite me, siren. I will rip every one of your teeth from your mouth if you do."

I clamp my mouth shut as he throws me to the ground. I scramble backwards across the paved walkway, the rough concrete scraping at my skin. "Why are you back? What more can you take from me?"

"I have no plans to *take* from you. I would like to give instead."

"What does that mean?"

He crouches in front of me, and I can't help but think his pristine slacks and button-down shirt won't have a single wrinkle when he stands back up.

"I will admit, I did not expect you to survive. You had so much pain in you that night." The alley. He tricked me into feeding him. After Evan and Shaun explained the basics of how Made far are, well, *made*, I understood it was a miracle I'd survived. It's the reason I've never met another siren in the last four years. I wouldn't be surprised if I am the only one in existence. The wraith continues on, either oblivious to my current train of thought or un-remorseful. "But to my surprise and delight, you've survived."

"Why would you care?"

"I am sure you think I relish in dealing out death, but I don't." He stands back up, holding out a hand to me. I ignore it and push myself to my feet. "I wish I could feed without harming innocents, but it can't always be avoided."

I arch my brow at him. I don't really care what he's going on about. I want him to undo what he did to me. "Change me back," I say, voice hardening. "Fix me!"

The wraith gives me a condescendingly soft smile. "That I cannot do. The change you have gone through is permanent, I'm afraid."

"At least try! There has to be some way!"

"The only way to unmake what you are would be death. Is that what you want?"

No of course not, should be the words that come out, but I find I cannot speak them. I hate what I've been turned into. If death is the only way to not be a monster, I can't deny the appeal.

Too slowly, too late, I reply, "No."

The wraith looks unconvinced, his head cocked to the side. "I thought you had found meaning in life again," he muses, starting to walk around me in a circle, until he's behind me. I stay where I am. If he's going to kill me, so be it. I don't think I could stop him even if I wanted to fight. "Your music, it has helped people. I thought that's what you do now. You help people through your music, or through your group of misfits taking in little Made orphans."

I bristle at his word choice. Maybe I will fight after all. "Leave them out of it."

"What if I could offer you another way to absolve your sins?"

He's right behind me. His words too close to my ears. I whip around and he's gone.

"Remember that night in the alley?" His voice comes from behind me. I turn again and he's standing with his hands in his pockets, head still cocked to the side. "I told you that you could save her."

"Not falling for that again, *mate*," I say, snarling at him.

He smirks at me and lifts a shoulder casually. "I'm not asking you to. I want to give you something, like I said. In exchange, you would be helping people."

"So there's a catch."

"Not really," he replies. Something in his form almost seems to ripple. He can tell I've noticed. "I don't have much time. I want to make a deal with you."

"What's the deal?" I'm wary of anything this wraith has to offer. I know I can't trust him. But I do know wraiths are bound by their deals.

"You can feel emotions of those around you. Tell me, does it get more intense when you're performing?"

I blanche. How does he know that? Without meaning to, I nod. Nothing in the books Shaun has given me has really explained that. I pick up on emotions, but when I'm singing, when I'm performing, I can feel myself take on the emotions of the crowd. The bigger the shows, the worse it's been getting.

The wraith takes out a small pendant, attached to a thin gold chain. The pendant itself is the size of my pinkie and the color of a dark blue sky just after sunset.

"This allows the emotions you take on from the crowd to pass to me. It will be easier on you as well. The rate you're going, you will burn out."

His words strike a chord in me. I thought I just wasn't feeding regularly enough. But maybe this is a different downside of being a siren that I haven't considered. There really isn't much information out there on fae like me.

"This is what you're giving me?" I ask, eyeing the pendant as it swings innocuously from his hand.

"No, this is what I get in return. The power this pendant absorbs will flow to me. It'll allow me to feed without harming others."

I don't really know what to say to that. Perhaps that's enough reason to accept what he's offering.

"If you wear this at each of your performances and you develop a following, a truly loyal following," he continues, "I will deliver you an offering."

"And what is that offering?"

"I will bring your love to you."

My *love?* Leighton's face appears before me. "You can do that?"

"Yes," he says simply, spreading his hands as if to say why not?

"You can bring someone back from the dead, but you can't undo what you've done to me?"

The wraith narrows his eyes at me. "Siren, I am growing tired of this conversation. I cannot change the type of fae someone is, nor can I unmake a Made fae. Moving people between realms is difficult but not impossible." He swings the pendant closer to me. "Will you do as I asked? And in return I will bring her to you."

I owe Leighton this.

In spite of everything we put each other through, I owe her a second chance.

I reach out and take the pendant from his outstretched fingers. "Yes."

CHAPTER FORTY-THREE

BLISS

"THIS PLACE GIVES ME THE CREEPS," REESE SAYS, STARING OVER AT the small cemetery to the right of the church. I didn't notice it the first time we came here, but today the tombstones stand out in the brighter sunlight.

Amelia, Liz, and I all look at Reese, giving my best friend a once-over. She's dressed all in black, a lacy black dress, black tights, black boots, and a black leather jacket. Her lips are painted a dark blood red, and she's smoked out her shadow and liner. Amelia, who is dressed similarly, smirks at Reese. "Really? I think we fit in very nicely here. These two—" she motions to my aunt and I, "—are the sore thumbs."

Liz scoffs. "As the only one here who's actually dealt with ghosts, I take offense."

"What?" Reese breathes out. "Ghosts aren't real."

Liz raises her brows at my friend and smiles, shaking her head softly like she's amused at our disbelief. "If that's what you need to tell yourself."

"Why is this the first time I'm hearing about you dealing with ghosts?" Amelia squeaks. "I love ghost stories!"

I give both my family members a short glare then reach out and knock on the door, using the old and very ornate knocker that has a gargoyle face on the base.

I don't really love the idea of coming back here. I'm not sure if a couple days will have been enough for the guys to cool down, but I'm hoping. I have a plan to get Pisces back. Well, half a plan. And I need them to help with the rest of it.

A couple moments pass and no one answers the door.

I knock again, but again nothing.

I turn to Amelia. "What should we do?" I ask, though I don't really expect anyone to answer. "I guess we can try again later?"

"That's a good idea. We can grab some breakfast and come back," Liz offers.

"Breakfast?" Reese asks, squinting at the sun's downward arch through the sky. It's around sixty-thirty here in London, but in our time it was almost ten-thirty in the morning. I should feel rested enough, but I didn't sleep at all last night, too anxious to try to get part of my plan in motion. Liz nods and amends her statement. "Okay, we'll go have dinner, then try again."

As we start to descend the stairs, the door creaks open behind us. I whip around and see Niamh standing there. "Hello?" she asks, her voice sounding a bit distrustful. I can see in her eyes when she recognizes us. "What are you doing here?" The accusation in her voice hurts. Not that we'd really become friends exactly, but she is definitely a girl's girl and I appreciated the support she showed me during the festival.

I take a deep breath and head back up the stairs until I'm standing on the opposite side of the threshold from her. "I need to speak with the guys. About Pisces." Maybe that last part is obvious, but I'm not sure how much Niamh knows about him being my mate.

She looks over her shoulder. Simon comes to the door. Niamh throws me a look, something between pity and anger, as she leaves me to Simon.

His hair is wet, and I assume he's just gotten out of the shower. It makes me think of how Pisces hadn't showered or shaved in the few days they were keeping him stars knew where. I wonder if Grim or Lyra have moved him back to wherever they'd originally been keeping him, now that I'm not there, or if he now has that room to himself. I hope it's the latter.

"Hey, Simon," I say, but he doesn't look pleased to see me.

"Hey." He dips his head in greeting and thankfully steps aside, motioning for us to come in. I walk through the front door, Reese, Amelia, and Liz following me.

"Any update on Pisces?" I ask. I already know from Liz that she hasn't heard anything about him being released or transferred, but Evan has more connections than she does, so maybe they have more up-to-date information.

Simon shakes his head. "No, and we could have told you that over the phone," he replies, letting loose a frustrated sigh. "Sorry. I —" He runs fingers through his wet strands. "I know it's not your fault. This whole situation is just fucked."

I nod. "It's okay. I know I'm the guys' least favorite person right now. But I wanted to try again, to help. I think I have a plan. If Shaun and Evan could just listen for a little bit, I think we can get Pisces out."

"They aren't here."

Amelia groans. "When are they getting back?"

"Excited to see your mate?" Simon's lips quirk upwards into an amused smile.

"Yeah, super," my sister replies, rolling her eyes and plopping herself down on the nearest chair. Simon clocks her movement and nods his head in the direction of the living room we were in last time we were here.

"We can wait in there until the guys are back. They shouldn't be out too much later."

"Where are they?" Reese asks tentatively, and I'm reminded of some of their previous interactions.

He looks over his shoulder at her with a smile. "They heard about a freshly turned warlock and went to go find him. That's kind of what we do sometimes. Well, not me, they won't let me go with them, but they go out and find orphaned Made fae, bring them in, give them a place to live while they adjust to the change."

My heart seems to grow in size. "Pisces helps with that?" I ask.

Simon nods. "Yeah. That's originally how the guys found him."

There's still way too much I don't know about Pisces. So many things I wish I could have the chance to find out about him. And I will, just once we get him free.

"When was he turned?" I ask curiously.

"A little over six years ago now, I think," Simon says. He pulls a couple more armchairs over so we can all sit together. Reese and Amelia take a seat on a little couch and the rest of us take an armchair.

"So he's not one of the Made fae that have been alive for hundreds of years?" Reese muses.

"Nah, he's still a baby, I guess," Simon replies with a laugh. He gets up, going to a wall with a few smaller framed pictures, plucking one off the wall and handing it to me. "This was taken a couple weeks after I found him again."

"Found him again?" I ask, taking the framed photo and poring over every detail. Simon stands in the middle next to Pisces and the two are surrounded by Benny, Shaun, and Evan. All five of them wear the biggest smiles. I don't think I've yet seen Pisces look this genuinely happy. What I would give to be the source of a smile like this on his face.

"Pisces and I kinda lost contact after he turned. He just up and left afterwards. We didn't know what happened to him, until I finally tracked him down. And I've stayed here with them since."

I nod. "You all look so young here," I say, tears starting to well in my eyes.

Simon smiles softly at me, squeezing my shoulder. I hand the photo back to him and he replaces it on the wall. He comes back and sits across from me. "Shaun and Evan have been trying to get Pisces released. It's not been going well. Evan hasn't been able to convince his dad."

"Yves Lyra can't afford to look weak against wraiths," Liz

explains. "They'll have a hard time convincing him that Pisces is innocent with the evidence against him."

Simon nods, his earlier softness replaced by ire. "But they let Bliss out." He looks to me, panic in his eyes. "Not that I'm not glad for that. It's just—"

"I know. It's unjust, the double standard."

Simon lets his head fall forwards. "I wish there was more I could do."

There's sound and motion towards the opening in the living room. I look and see Shaun letting a backpack drop onto the floor. He looks exhausted and his eyes narrow as they find mine. "What are the succubi doing here?" he mutters as he trudges further into the room. Evan follows him, going to the fire to warm his hands.

Benny smiles at us. "Hey, good to see you all again."

"Bliss wants to talk about helping Pisces," Simon explains, but Shaun cuts him off.

"We've already talked about it, and as we've already stated, we don't need her help." Shaun straightens a bit when he sees my aunt there, looking at him with an arched brow. He lets out a sigh and mutters something, turning back to the window he's placed himself at.

Evan sits on the floor in front of the fire and leans back, letting it practically toast his neck. He looks to Amelia once before finding the ceiling much more interesting.

I look around at the three of them. They didn't seem to bring anyone back with them.

"Did you not find the warlock?" I ask.

"What?" Shaun replies, looking to Simon.

"I explained where you all were."

I notice blood on Shaun's shirt then. And more on Benny's and Evan's. My eyes go wide.

Benny sits down next to Evan, pulling his knees into his chest. "We were too late."

"What do you mean?" Reese splutters, taking in the blood as well.

"He'd attacked a fae family, and the fae constabulary had already gotten to him. We tried to help heal him, but he was already gone, and a couple of the family members that were attacked also died."

"Stars," Reese mutters at the same time Amelia says, "Fuck."

Evan glances at Amelia and back to the rest of us. "Look, I can admit we might have been a bit harsh last time." He throws a glance to Shaun. "But we can't trust you."

I'm about to argue against that when Benny speaks up. "Bliss, you were working with the wraith to steal Pisces' tears. You have to understand why we'd be hesitant to trust you." He looks at Evan and Shaun, pointedly. "But, I'm willing to hear you out."

Shaun starts to argue, but Benny shakes his head. "Pisces was working with the wraith too. And we'd let him explain if we could get in to see him. So—" he looks back to me, "—start from the beginning."

So I do.

I tell them everything.

It's not the first time I've told Amelia and the others what happened, but I go through the story again for the guys. About how my bond was messed up. About how awful it's been not being able to feed properly. About how the wraith promised Pisces wouldn't get hurt.

I tell them again how I never saw a rune on Pisces' eye. And I tell them what the wraith told me. That Made fae wouldn't have a rune.

And then as I finish telling them everything, I turn to Benny. "I have to get him free. Not just because I want the chance to fight for us, but because he doesn't deserve to be locked up. And I think it's my fault he even got caught..." I trail off. I can't help but feel like Jordan fixated on hating Voracious Maw so much simply because I liked them.

Benny nods. I can't bring myself to look at Evan and Shaun just yet. Simon reaches over and clasps my hands. "It's not your fault, Bliss. You didn't get him arrested, and you didn't force him to also make a deal with the wraith."

Shaun huffs out a hollow laugh. "Pisces really fucked up. You both did. A fucking wraith?" He shakes his head and takes a deep breath. "I apologize for being too hard on you before. Honestly, part of all this is that I'm pissed at Pisces for not telling us what he'd done."

"You aren't alone in that," Evan mutters. He stands up, perhaps having recharged his powers enough. He looks around the room, eyes skipping over Amelia this time. "Simon mentioned you had a plan?"

I nod. "Half of one, anyways. I was hoping you'd all help."

Shaun comes and stands before me, extending his hand to shake. "Anything you need."

Benny unlocks a door for me and leads me into the bedroom. Pisces' scent hits me immediately and I breathe it in deeply. "Are you sure it's okay for me to sleep here?"

I feel I'm invading his personal space. He was so angry with me before. I don't think he'd want me here. I tell Benny this, but he just slings an arm around me. "Look, I know him really well and I know you'll both find a way past this. Pisces has always been hurt that Made fae don't have mates. And now here you are. He might be a little angry with you about the misunderstanding, but he'll get over it. He's been wishing he had someone like you for so long." A longing look comes over Benny's features and I wonder if Pisces isn't the only one wishing Made fae had mates too.

I put an arm around Benny and hug him back. "If Pisces has a mate, then maybe you do too," I say softly. Benny smiles at me and nods, but he doesn't say anything more on the subject.

"I changed the sheets on his bed so they'd be fresh when he got back. You can rest here, and I'll find rooms for the others."

I smile at him. "Thanks." He turns to leave. "Maybe make sure Amelia is far away from Evan's room."

He grins at me. "Already way ahead of you." With that he's gone.

I close the door behind him and turn around to take in the room in more detail. The walls are beige, covered in framed posters and a couple art pieces that upon closer inspection I realize were painted by Benny, his loping signature legible in the bottom right corners.

The closet is pretty neat, lots of black—no surprise there, but there's also a couple sweaters in varying colors of blue, brown, and beige. One dark green one that looks well worn.

I try not to touch anything—I don't want to pry into his life too much. I want him to invite me in instead—but I fail.

I run my fingers along the strings of his acoustic guitar that's snuggled neatly into its stand. As I turn to go sit on the bed I accidentally knock over a notebook. It falls open as it hits the floor, and a loose piece of paper falls out. Picking it up, I realize it looks more like a journal and the loose paper is actually a photo.

I snap the journal shut, not wanting to invade his privacy by reading what's written inside, but the photo I can't seem to look away from. It's Pisces and a woman I've never seen before.

She has long black hair, lots of piercings, a round face. He has his arm around her, but she looks almost permanently angry, like she wishes she could be anywhere else. And Pisces...

There are bags under his eyes, and his deep blue eyes look tired and dull. He's much thinner in this photo. And a lot younger. Even in his sweater that he's wearing with the sleeves pulled almost over his fingers, I can see how skinny he is.

He looks miserable.

A knock at the door makes me drop the picture. I catch myself hoping it's him at the door, even though I know it can't be. Simon walks in instead. *Pisces wouldn't need to knock on his own door*, I remind myself.

Simon eyes the photo and I sheepishly hand it to him. "I knocked over this journal and it fell out. I promise I wasn't trying to snoop."

He nods and hands the photo back to me. "That's Leighton."

"Is she…" I find I don't want to voice my question. "Are they dating?" The picture is obviously old. And this room, while nice and definitely several steps up from looking and smelling like a boy's room, doesn't have the feminine touch I would assume a girl-friend would bring. There are no women's clothes in the closet, no evidence a girlfriend ever stays here with him. It's dumb of me to assume he's single, though. How many times has a bond inter-rupted a couple already together?

Simon shakes his head. "No, she died."

I almost drop the photo, but I don't. Instead, I reverently put the picture back into the notebook as carefully as I can. "Stars, I'm so sorry."

Simon nods, going to sit on the bed. "It was a while ago. Before Pisces was turned. They'd been dating for a few years. But God, they were horrible for each other. And to each other. You ever know that one couple that just brings out the worst in each other? That was them."

My stomach drops at hearing that. It's not exactly what I experi-enced with Jordan, but I could relate to the toxicity.

"And she died? While they were together?" I pick up on what he's not saying and he nods.

"Pisces should probably tell you the rest. But it fucked him up. And just as he was starting to put himself back together, that song wraith showed up. Turned him but also left him to die."

I think I've heard that from somewhere. That's why there aren't many sirens. They usually die when turned and also song wraiths aren't common as it is.

"Fuck." It's all I can say.

I go and sit next to Simon, throwing an arm around him. "We're gonna get him back," I say. I sound so sure. But my stomach is a knot.

We sit like that for a little while until Simon leaves and I decide I should try to get some sleep despite the jet lag. I know they prob-ably have a potion somewhere around here and Liz brought her own, but since I haven't been sleeping much I probably won't even need it.

There's a hoodie hanging on the back of the desk chair, and I can't help myself. I take it and cuddle up in Pisces' bed with his hoodie, breathing in the scent of him and trying to imagine what it would be like if he was here.

I can feel the bond purring but also tugging at me. It wants me to go to him. I could probably follow it to the fae council, where they have him locked up still. But for now I'm content to breathe him in. I just wish he was in the bed with me, with his arms around me.

The longing feeling brings tears to my eyes and I let them fall.

I cry and cry even as the bed dips and I feel Reese and Amelia slide in on either side of me, holding me closely as I finally drift off to sleep.

CHAPTER FORTY-FOUR

BLISS

With Liz at the helm, planning it out, it didn't take long to gather everyone. After a few reluctant meetings at the Voracious Maw church with Grim, we formed a plan. A pretty good one at that. And with a bit of luck, perhaps a little bit of persuasion on my part—though I didn't have much to spare—we were able to get Grim to agree to release Pisces in order to lure Jordan out.

In the weeks since Pisces and I were arrested, Grim's team managed to narrow down where Jordan was hiding. It seemed he'd fled to Barcelona, Spain. And so that's where we meet up, gathering in a hotel room.

"We'll set up our trap in Ciutadella Park. There are tiny fae sectors within the park but no portals, so as long as we have it surrounded, he won't be able to escape once he's there." Grim points out the sectors on a map that's spread out on the coffee table. Sectors are just smaller versions of districts and often don't have names of their own. I've already seen the map, so I don't crowd around the table like everyone else.

When Grim arrived with Pisces, I'd hoped that we would have some time to talk, for me to explain, but he ignored me every time I tried. So I'm left to study his features as he looks over the map in concentration, perhaps trying to memorize where all the sectors are located. I can feel my bond growing excited to be so close to him again. Thoughts of touching him and kissing him and *more* keep interrupting my mind and I have to force myself to focus on the mission at hand. I remind myself constantly how inappropriate it would be to try to seduce him when he's still mad at me, and we are here to catch a literal murderer.

That seems to take the wind out of my inner succubus' sails, but only just barely.

I still let my eyes drift over the lines of his face, the straight long nose that ends in a soft point. His ears that peek out from underneath his hair that's grown out since I first met him. The way his mouth is always betraying his emotions in the way it's set. My mate.

He's my mate.

When I look at him, it all makes sense. Of course he's mine. He couldn't be anyone else's. And I find I want to belong to him. I want him to want me and call me his.

The ache in my chest swells. And I let it. Because it's a reminder of everything that's happened.

Grim continues to lay out the plan. In a matter of minutes we are packed up and headed out to the park. Dusk fell quite some time ago and a warm breeze blows about, caressing and calming.

The park is closed, of course. It's late, almost midnight. But Benny gets the gates open quickly and we all slip inside. He closes the gate almost shut, leaving an unnoticeable gap so that when Jordan makes his way here, he won't get stuck outside the park.

We spread out into groups around the fountain of the Cascada Monumental. Evan and Grim come with Dericia and I as we take up positions out of sight behind a large gazebo.

Simon, Amelia, Shaun, and Pinkie are across the way from us, also getting into their hiding spot, covered by a grouping of trees and bushes. Bell, Stormy, Benny, and Taser are roving, ready to use our comms to tell us when Jordan's arrived.

"I still don't get how we're even certain Jordan will show up," Reese mutters from our crouched positions.

"You'll see," I tell her, though my eyes are on Grim. He's also not totally convinced this will work. Pisces may be two for two when it comes to his lure, but as Grim pointed out when I laid out the plan to him, maybe it only worked because I'm his mate.

Pisces stands out in front of the fountain, watching the many sprays of water jet out of the pond.

"We're right here," I say into our comms. He looks to his left, towards where he knows we're just out of sight. He gives a single nod but says nothing.

He takes a seat on the ground, sitting cross-legged before the fountain, eyes closing in concentration. His face lifts up towards the stars almost in silent prayer, and his bottom lip curls inward for a moment.

It takes several minutes, the hum of his lure magic building subtly. And then Pisces' eyes snap open.

"I've got him," Pisces says into his mic.

"We've got the entrances covered," Benny says. He and Taser will use their vampire speed to pick up on wherever Jordan enters the park, Benny having unlocked the rest of the gates just in case.

Minutes tick by and I wonder if Jordan will be sleepwalking like I was the first time Pisces lured me. If that's the case, it could be a while before he shows. Reese shifts beside me, letting out a yawn.

"You know you didn't have to come right?" I ask, reaching out and clasping my best friend's hand.

"Proving Jordan is behind those murders and capturing him was the only way to free your mate. Of course I'm gonna be here."

I hug her tightly, feeling that earlier ache soothed by her. "I'm so grateful for you. I know lately it's been so weird, but—"

She stops me. "Don't even worry about it. If best friends can't handle one little hardship, then they have no business calling themselves best friends."

"I love you," I say, grinning.

"Love you too."

"You two about done?" Taser says into the comms. I hadn't realized ours were picking up the conversation.

"We're done." Reese laughs.

"Good, but just for the record, I love you all too," Taser says. "Since we're being sappy and all."

"Oh, it's sappy time?" Simon asks. "Well, in that case—"

"Save it, mate," Benny interjects. "We've got one psychotic vampire entering the park. Heads up, he's not sleepwalking, and he looks pissed—confused but pissed."

It becomes evident why it's taken this long for Jordan to arrive, as he makes his way down one set of the monument's steps. His movements are jerky, obviously against his will, as the lure deposits him in front of Pisces. To Jordan's knowledge it's just the two of them.

"Who—?" he starts to ask but stops when Pisces turns around. Jordan's confusion and anger melt into amusement and he laughs, the sound making my skin crawl, but the usual fear that accompanies it is noticeably absent. "A siren lure, interesting. I thought that was just a rumor."

Pisces doesn't respond. It's a ploy to get Jordan to keep talking, enough to incriminate himself.

"So what? You were feeling a bit hungry and decided you want a bite of vampire? Or—" he pauses, cocking his head to the side, "—is this supposed to be pay back for feeding off Bliss?"

Again Pisces doesn't respond.

"You know you and her will never work, right? A Born fae with a Made? Keep dreaming, siren boy." How does Jordan even know about Pisces and I? I file that question away for later, but the thought that maybe Jordan has been keeping tabs on me really creeps me the fuck out.

"Seems to me like you're projecting," Pisces says, a smirk appearing on his face. "You know what I think? I think it eats you up at night that she's not your mate."

Jordan's amusement falls away. "Succubi are bottom of the food chain anyways. Someone like me needs a higher class of fae for a mate."

"Right," Pisces responds, looking off to the horizon as if he's bored.

Jordan huffs out a breath of frustration as he tries to move away from Pisces. "Fine, let's just get this weird siren feeding shit out of the way so I can go."

Pisces' smirk widens into a feral grin. "What makes you think after I feed there will be anything left?"

"Siren lures are meant to feed off emotion, aren't they? That's what I've heard."

Pisces shrugs. "I don't think there's a hard and fast rule."

Fear finally finds its way into Jordan's eyes. He thrashes against whatever magical hold Pisces has on him.

"Why did you do it?" Pisces asks, taking a threatening step towards his prey. Jordan is almost a full head shorter than Pisces and the way my mate stalks forward towards him does something to me. Each step is powerful, deliberate.

Pisces circles Jordan, waiting for an answer.

"Do what?" Jordan asks, licking his lips.

"Try to frame me for murder?"

He swallows. "I didn't. I don't know what you're talking about."

"You viciously murdered at least three women."

"No, that wasn't me. It was Jinx."

"Your weasel shifting friend has an alibi for all three."

"Bring it home," Grim mutters besides me.

I wait with baited breath for Pisces to draw out a confession. They're circling it like water down a drain.

"It's just you and me," Pisces says, coming to stand behind Jordan. He leans down to whisper in his ear. "Why don't you just confess? Who knows, maybe it'll make your time in the afterlife not so bad if you own up to what you've done before you die."

Jordan stills and slowly looks around, a smile curling his lips. He laughs again. "Does she get off on watching you feed? Did you enjoy the taste of her sweet cunt?" I startle at the question and Reese squeezes my hand. There's no way Jordan could know Pisces healed me if he hasn't been keeping close tabs on me. Or is he just assuming and taking a stab in the dark?

Pisces comes to a halt before Jordan, standing in between the vampire and the fountain.

"Time's up, *mate*," Jordan says. He lunges forward, pushing Pisces into the fountain, biting into his throat. Jordan gets up, cackling. He toes Pisces' limp body in the water and spits on him. "I'm going to have so much fun tracking down Bliss. She's going to be mine. And I'm going to march on over to the fae council and tell them how you admitted to murdering those humans and how you told me all this before you tried to kill me."

Jordan picks up Pisces by the scalp, wrenching his head up out of the water. He leans down close to Pisces, whispering, "It won't take any convincing. You're a crazed siren, after all."

All reasoning leaves me as Jordan takes Pisces' head in between his hands, snapping his neck with his vampire strength in less than a second.

A second.

A second for me to lose everything.

"No!" I scream.

I run out from our hiding place, Grim at my side. I slam into Jordan, knocking him down into the shallow water and punching his face and chest with as much strength as I can muster. "How could you?! How dare you?!"

I'm just a collection of anger and fury, blood spraying as strong hands grip me and pull me off the vampire.

"It's done, Bliss, it's done. We got him," Taser murmurs softly, folding me into his chest. "Shh, it's done."

No, no, it can't be. This can't be happening.

My mate.

My mate.

"No!" I shriek, running back into the pond, gathering up Pisces in my arms. I smooth his hair back from his face, tears raining down on his face from my eyes. I find Evan in the semicircle of bodies that has come to stand there around the fountain. "Fix him!" I yell at Evan. "Heal him! Why are you just standing there?"

Evan's face is as tear-streaked as mine. He wades into the fountain, coming to a stop next to Pisces' other side. "I'm so sorry," he says, to me or to Pisces, I don't know.

"Heal him," I whimper. "Please, this can't… This can't happen."

Evan puts a hand to Pisces' cheek, gently caressing it once. He looks into my eyes. "I can't bring back the dead." He almost chokes on the last word.

I'm vaguely aware of Pinkie and Stormy cuffing Jordan. I pick Amelia out among the crowd of our friends. She's staring at us in the fountain, tears welling up in her eyes, Reese turned around in her arms, hiding her sobs.

Something moves in the water beside me, and before I can register it, Pisces hurls himself upwards, coughing up water and cracking his neck back into place.

"Pisces?" I yelp, grabbing at his shirt and helping him to sit up. "Pisces?!"

He finishes hurling up water and looks wide-eyed at everyone. "What happened? Did I black out?"

I fling myself at him, pushing him back into the water and sobbing into his chest. He just holds me as Evan fills him in. "We thought you died." Evan turns to Benny. "If we broke your neck, would you die?"

Benny exhales in relief. "No, but let's not test that theory. Made fae are generally not that fragile, but we're all different, so I didn't know… He wasn't moving…" Benny thought Pisces had died like the rest of us.

"I'm fine," Pisces murmurs into my hair. "My neck's a little sore, but I'm fine."

My sobs subside as the ache in my chest evaporates. My mate. He's alive and fine.

Taser and Evan help us out of the fountain and over to where Grim and Simon are standing by Jordan.

"So now we have you on three counts of murder, and one attempted. You're really going for worst fae of the year, aren't you?" Grim asks.

Simon, however, is just looking at Jordan, expressionless. He cocks his head this way and that and takes a step back. "Simon, it's okay, we got him," Shaun says, reaching out a hand to pull Simon away from the psychotic vamp.

But before he can, Simon's hand wraps around a sword that appears out of nowhere, and in one smooth motion he slides it into Jordan's heart.

Chaos erupts for a second time. Grim scrambles to get Jordan away from Simon, but Jordan is dead, definitely dead, a pool of blood growing beneath his lifeless body. Taser puts himself between Pisces and me, and Simon. Evan and Benny do the same for Amelia and Reese. Stormy and Bell stand at the ready, watching Simon warily.

"Oh come now," Simon says, turning in a circle to address us all. "The world will not mourn him."

"Simon?" Shaun asks. "You sound…" *Different.*

Simon turns to face our direction and I gasp. His eyes flash red and fade back to Simon's usual brown. He smiles at me the same way the song wraith did in the alley.

"My dear Bliss, I'm glad you've found your mate again." He dips his head to acknowledge Pisces.

"I don't understand," Pisces says. "What's happened to Simon?"

The wraith waves a hand at his body—at Simon's body. "He is here. I am just borrowing his vessel for a moment."

"Why?" Grim asks.

"Fae sometimes don't pay much attention to humans. You like them well enough, but you rarely keep much attention on them, powerless as they are. Using Simon allowed me access and the ability to get close enough to pull your strings, but also to do what you would not." He points to Jordan's body. "Carrying out justice, for example."

"That's not justice," Grim counters. His hands are curled into fists. "What do you want?"

"I have what I want." The Simon wraith looks at Pisces and I, and back to Grim. Us? He wants us? I don't understand. Pisces moves to shield me and I have to scoot over to peek around him at the scene unfolding. "Do not worry, I mean none of you any harm."

"Tell that to Simon," Shaun growls, pacing back and forth. I wonder if he's going to shift.

"Careful, wolf. If you attack me, you hurt Simon."

"Let him go." Pisces takes a step forward.

"As you wish," the wraith says, the last part of his sentence growing faint as Simon seems to lose consciousness, falling to his knees. Behind him stands the wraith in his own form, looking at us with his red eyes. He takes a step away from us and breathes in deeply. His form seems to ripple slightly and then comes into a clarity I hadn't realized was missing before. "The air here is divine."

"You've been to this realm before," I say, confused.

"I have, but not as I truly am. Not fully corporeal, until now. I could interact physically, but it took a considerable amount of effort. Now I am at full power." The wraith kneels down and presses a hand to Simon's head. "He shall sleep and heal. Borrowing his form was necessary, to kill the one who summoned and bound me."

All eyes fall to Jordan's body and back to the wraith. "What do you mean?"

"The vampire summoned me, allowing me back into this realm. And then he tried to bend me to his will, but I was smarter. I made him think I was helping him, but really I've been helping you two all along."

"You killed someone."

"I've killed many, and it likely won't be the last time," the wraith says simply, as if it's just an average day. "I will be in touch. There is still much left to do, but for now, spend time with your mate. Live your life." He bows his head in a goodbye and vanishes once again.

He told me he'd be back, but I didn't realize it would lead to this.

And as much as I hope we never have to deal with the wraith again, it's becoming very clear Pisces and I have stepped into a very complicated web.

CHAPTER FORTY-FIVE

BLISS

"I think I could sleep for a week," Reese says, digging into the slice of coffee cake she's having for breakfast.

"Make it two weeks," Amelia says, stretching out her long legs on the couch of the hotel room we gathered in last night. She grabs a spare fork and snags a piece of Reese's cake.

The wraith vanished right before Grim's tactical team arrived. They cleaned up Jordan's body and the rest of the scene before the sun broke over the horizon. And after a rather short debriefing in one of the fae sectors of the park, we were allowed to leave, but despite what my sisters are saying, no one went straight to bed.

We're all crammed in the room, some sitting on one of the two beds, Amelia taking up the couch. Evan stands at the window with his back to us. Shaun hovers over Simon—the only one sleeping—on the other bed, constantly checking his temperature, or fussing with his blankets.

Pisces is the only one not here.

After we got back to the hotel, I wanted to pull him aside. Kiss him. Talk to him. Let him feed off me, if he needed. I just wanted to be near him, our bond fully perking up as if waking from a long slumber.

But he made excuses to be alone for a bit and wandered off.

The door swings open and my head instantly swivels, my heart leaping up in my chest.

But it's just Grim and Pinkie, looking haggard after such a long night.

"You're still here?" Grim asks, coming in and collecting the map and other supplies from our planning session.

"He needs rest before we move him," Shaun mutters, once again moving hair back from Simon's forehead. Grim doesn't respond, just nods, but I don't think Shaun sees.

"Pisces is back at the park," Grim says to me instead.

"He is?" I ask, suddenly on my feet, moving to the door. I look at Amelia, who gives me an encouraging smile. Benny leaves his spot leaning against the wall by the door.

"What are you waiting for?" he asks, giving my hand a light squeeze. "May the stars belong to you."

I beam at my friends, and I'm off.

I make my way back to the park, wondering where he might be.

I find him at the top of the Cascada Monumental. Under the covering of the monument, he stands, overlooking the fountain from the opposite side than last night.

"Pisces?" I ask tentatively, stopping next to him. He looks down at me on his left, a small smile tugging at his lips.

"It's beautiful," he says, looking back at the fountain. "I've been here before, with my family, years ago. This was my favorite spot."

"I can see why," I respond. I've found my favorite spot. Next to him, even if we're not touching. I want to tell him this, but I don't know how.

"Bliss, we should probably talk." He shifts his body so he's fully facing me.

"Yes, I've been wanting to talk. I need to explain…" I trail off as he hangs his head. If my happiness about finding my mate is the sun shining and birds singing, then he is moonlight in the rain.

"Pisces?"

"I'm not sure what it's like for Born fae when they find their bondmate. Evan's been trying to keep his distance from your sister, so it's not completely without self-control, but he thinks of her all the time, almost constantly. He feels the love that he could so easily pick up if he wanted."

I nod. I feel that love now. It's inside me, a living, breathing thing.

"But for Made fae, it's not like that. I look at you and I just see another fae. Just one with a rune in her eye. There's no big feeling the way you feel it. I'm not overcome with lust, or desire, or want. Or need." He locks eyes with me, and his are dull, disappointed. "I was hoping to feel that with you. I was. But there's nothing there. I'm sorry. I don't want to hurt you, so I'm just going to say it. I don't want to be with you."

His words feel like an anvil coming down on my soul.

I can't breathe.

He reaches out, tucking a lock of hair behind my ear, sliding his fingers down it, letting it fall to my chest where he's just ripped out my heart.

Pisces hangs his head, leaving me standing there at the top of the fountain, halved in two. I watch my other half walk away without looking back.

LOOKING FOR BOOK TWO?

Hopefully you don't hate me too much after that ending, but don't worry! I'm hard at work on book two and can't wait to get it into your hands! In the meantime, check out my socials and website to stay up to date on book two news!

And if you could do me a huge favor, please consider leaving a review somewhere like Goodreads, Amazon or Storygraph! Reviews from readers like you really help out indie authors like me!

Thank you so much for reading!

ABOUT THE AUTHOR

Saoirse Brey is a fantasy romance writer living in the Pacific Northwest with her family and her dog. This is her first published book. When she's not writing, she's probably knitting. Check out her socials and website for more info and writing updates.

https://www.saoirsebrey.com/

instagram.com/saoirsebreywrites
youtube.com/@saoirsewrites

ACKNOWLEDGMENTS

We might be here awhile! There are so many people to thank and despite having written a whole book, I'm not sure I have adequate words to express how grateful I am for everyone I'm about to list.

First I have to start by thanking my parents. I started writing this book in 2023, and boy was that a wild year. After some big life changes, I decided to seriously pursue this book and my parents are one big reason why I was able to get this book finished. Their support means the world to me and I love them so much.

I also want to thank my friend Sara for being such a great support in this creative journey. Our chit chats, brunch dates, and thrifting adventures have seen me through so many doubts and have really helped strengthen my trust in the universe. You are such an inspiration to me as you continue on your own journey and I'm really proud of us!

Next up I want to thank my critique partner and friend, AJ! I would not have made it through this book without you! Your love for these characters and the world really showed me that I had something special here that could be special to other people as well. And you reminded me what was most important with this book: that *I* liked it. Thank you for being so amazing and for all our writing chats! It never felt like I was going alone on this journey because of our weekly check ins!

Thank you to my amazing friend Tia, for always being around to chat whether it was about writing or about life. You've also seen me through some of the rougher writing days, but have also been there to celebrate all the writing wins. It feels like I've known you for years but it was actually me having a plot problem with this book that allowed me to meet you! I'll forever be grateful for that!

I also gotta thank my wonderful friend Ash! You read at least three different drafts of this book and approached each one with excitement (even though the ending never changed and your desire to punch Pisces never wavered). I'm honestly surprised you aren't bored of these characters yet! You really know how to make people feel special and give them the right kind of encouragement they need. Thank you so much for being my friend and always hyping me up so much!

Next up is Stew! Thank you for always being down to chat writing and whatever else comes up! You always have the best little writing nuggets to share! And thank you for encouraging me to actually come up with some lyrics to put in the book. I didn't think I had it in me, so I'm grateful for the push! There are so many ways where you just *get* me and I'm so lucky to have you as a friend!

Next is a big thank you to Margot for always being such a great sounding board. Thank you for all your help as I tweaked things in the story and sent you scenes I reworked. You're always at the ready with the perfect meme and I will forever cherish the mood board you made for this book!

It's hard to believe that I've been able to make such great writing friends without ever meeting them in person (yet! Writing retreat let's goooo!), but I've found a whole community that is so welcoming and supportive! It would be impossible to name you all but you know who you are! Our discord chats have been some of my favorite things this past year and I love that there's always someone around to do writing sprints with! I don't think I would have gotten as much writing done without this community!

A huge thank you to my beta readers, Rebeca, Ash, Sara, Lindsay, Addy, Margot, Shelley, Beth and Stew! Without these lovely people I would continue to be stuck on draft three of this book.

Thank you to Lucy, my copy editor, for getting this story into a much more readable condition! I've learned a ton from you and I'm excited to put that knowledge to good use in my next project.

Thank you to Samantha, my cover designer, for the amazing cover! It's so perfect for Bliss and Pisces!

Thank you to my lovely ARC readers!

Thank you to my dog Lena! (I know she won't read this—cause you know—she's a dog, but puppy snuggles are a necessary part of my writing routine.)

And thank YOU, the reader, for coming along this journey with Bliss and Pisces! I hope you're excited for book two :)

www.ingramcontent.com/pod-product-compliance
Lightning Source LLC
Chambersburg PA
CBHW021405310726
48971CB00005B/1202